FOREWORD

'During the war, of the 9,000 people employed by Stewarts and Lloyds 56.6 per cent were women. The work done by women deserves special mention. Most of them had never been inside a factory before, yet they stood up to long and arduous hours on night and day shift. It is not often realised that women on some operations were handling one and a quarter tons of shell per hour, and in many special cases this physical effort was exceeded not only in shell manufacture but also in our steel and tube plants. This work was accomplished under blackout conditions, often during "alerts" and with all the irritations and afflictions which total war brings . . .'

Stewarts and Lloyds

ALL WOMEN
not doing work of National importance are asked to volunteer now for WRNS, ATS, WAAF

Many thousands of women are needed now in the WRNS, the ATS and the WAAF, to release men for the offensive.

Every woman who believes she can be spared from her present occupation is asked to volunteer for one of these Services. The nearest Recruiting Centre or Employment Exchange will know, or will quickly find out, whether your present work is even more important. If you were born between January 1918 and July 1922, you may now be accepted for the ATS and WAAF, but not for the WRNS unless you have special qualifications; you should go to the Employment Exchange in the first instance.

You can join the Service you prefer and do the work you choose, except that, for certain types of work, special qualifications are needed. As a rule, practical experience is not essential; training is given.

Volunteers are wanted in the largest numbers for the following:—

WRNS	ATS	WAAF
Many kinds of clerical work	Anti-Aircraft	Cooks
Stewarding	Signals	Motor drivers
Cooking	Driving	Balloon operators
Maintenance	* Special operations	Aircrafthands
* Driving	* Radio mechanics	Clerks
* Radio mechanics	Cooking	Flight mechanics
	Orderly work	Mess stewards and waitresses
	* Camouflage	Radio operators

* Those starred need special qualifications.

There are some vacancies in many other types of work. Pay depends on the type of work done, length of service, and rank. The lowest is 2/- a day and all found. Wives of Servicemen are granted their leave to coincide with their husbands' leave whenever possible.

If you cannot go at once to a Recruiting Centre or Employment Exchange, write to 297 Oxford Street, London, W.1, giving your name (including Mrs. or Miss), address (including county), and date of birth. State which Service you are most interested in, or, if you have no preference ask for information about all three.

AUTHOR'S NOTE

Being a young child during the era in which this story is set I cannot claim to have had personal knowledge of factory procedures at that time. However the title 'Shadow Factory' as once applied to 'New Crown Forgings', a Wednesbury property of 'Stewarts and Lloyds', is still widely recognised in the town and living memory has supported my description of the removal of armaments under cover of darkness and then subsequent transportation via canal. Addressing the question of hours worked and wages paid information was supplied by family and friends employed in similar industries.

Wartime wage was low for the long hours worked but as related from my own experience they had not altered a great deal by 1949 when I earned twenty two shillings and sixpence for a forty four hour week and then in 1964 the convenience of working part time paid a wage of twenty two shillings and elevenpence for a twenty seven and a half hour week.

Meg Hutchinson

ACKNOWLEDGEMENTS

'Black Country at War' – ALTON DOUGLAS
'Stewarts and Lloyds' – Loaned courtesy of Samuel Longmore

Wednesbury Public Library for their never failing assistance.

PROLOGUE

They would be sorry!

The promise made to herself so long ago surged fresh and bright as a beacon in Katrin Hawley's mind.

They would all be sorry!

Hazel eyes, glittering with the ice of vengeance, stared back from the mirror of a small dressing table.

Yes, they would be sorry, every last one of them, and she would laugh. 'He who laughs last . . .'

They had turned their backs on her! They had sent her away, ignored her as they would a pile of rubbish. Discarded her as they would throw away a broken glass!

But broken glass was dangerous . . . !

Those hazel eyes watching from the mirror spewed darts of glacial venom.

It could cut deeply!

Silent, moving with the sinuous threat of a cobra, she smiled.

It could prove lethal!

And it would!

But first it must cut, slash and tear at their lives, stab and thrust, rip each life to shreds as her own had been ripped eight years ago.

★ ★ ★

It had happened at school.

The afternoon break, the fifteen minutes of freedom from the classroom was, whenever weather allowed, spent playing hopscotch in the school yard. The four of them, friends from the first tearful day at Infant School, were intent on the game, Katrin bending to slide her piece of broken floor tile across the chalk-drawn pattern of interspersed squares. The others had objected to her pitch, it was 'more slidey' than their pieces of shattered brick or stones found on the slag heaps of metal foundries; they said it was unfair. But she had stood her ground; hopscotch had no rule saying a piece of tile was not allowed.

Among the shadows a golden-haired head turned sharply to darker-haired companions.

'That's cheating.'

Becky Turner's indignant cry rang again in Katrin's mind.

'. . . It were on the line . . . I seen it, your pitch were on the line!'

'No it wasn't!' Her denial, equally loud, had followed the quick snatch of the tile into her hand.

The golden head tossed again. 'Yes it were, we all seen it. You seen it d'aint you Alice? And you Freda, you seen it as well d'aint you?'

Two dark heads nodded clearly in the eye of Katrin's mind.

'Told you! We all seen it, your pitch landed on the line . . .'

'It didn't! It didn't land on the line! You are telling lies, you are jealous because I always win!'

'And we knows how you win, it be cos you cheats, you be a cheat and a liar Katy Hawley, no wonder your folks d'aint want you . . . ! Well we don't want you neither, do we girls? We don't play with cheats!'

Beneath the sheets Katrin's fingers curled as they had curled about that piece of tile. Eight years had not dulled those words nor the determination which later understanding of them had given rise to.

Explanation!

Rejection swelled hard in her chest. What good had that proved? It had been meant to console, to dim the hurt of the barb thrown by an angry child, but it had merely cast a veil. Consolation had not been elimination; it had soothed the smart but not removed the sting! That had remained buried inside, remained to fester with every passing day becoming a longing, a longing time had cultivated, had nurtured, feeding it with anger until it had grown beyond a childhood need to punish three friends whose words had stung. It had become more than desire for revenge, it was an all consuming passion, a lust no words could eradicate.

Caught in the grip of indignation at being called a cheat, an emotion not helped by being ignored for the rest of the afternoon, by being left to walk home by herself she had asked her mother, 'Why, why would Becky Turner say I was not wanted?'

'It be no more than a spat on their part . . .'

Her mother's reply had been quick, so quick it could have been rehearsed, and that was what time had revealed it to be: a carefully stage managed response.

But the response had held more. The words had been accompanied by a swift flash of alarm in her mother's eyes, a strange expression on her face, a look which only years later had Katrin understood as being a closed 'Ask no question.'

'. . . *no more than words!*'

Her mother had gone to stand at the kitchen sink, her attention given to the vegetables she was preparing for the evening meal, but though her face was turned away, she could not conceal the tightness of her voice.

'. . . *that's all it is, words . . .*'

Potatoes scraped clean of skins had rained like blows into a saucepan set on the draining board.

'. . . *words you should take no notice of! It is just a bit of bad temper on losing the game, nothing more than that; things'll be back to normal tomorrow you'll see, you'll all be friends again.*'

Yet 'tomorrow' had never come. Katrin Hawley's life had never again been normal.

I

He was gone. The man she loved was gone from her life. Miriam Carson watched the spill of cartridge cases drop into a large metal container. They were so pretty, like droplets of light filled water, a gleaming glittering cascade of gold. But that was where the beauty ended, for these small, shining brass objects would become bringers of death. Filled with gunpowder, a bullet at its heart, each one could take the life of a man, shatter the happiness of a family, break a woman's heart as hers was broken.

'We regret to inform you . . .'

The words had spun in her mind, whirled in her brain, danced like black confetti blinding her eyes!

'We regret to inform you . . .'

Dark symbols, strokes and dots, marks made with a machine – but those on that small piece of buff coloured paper had been much more. Like the bullets she helped make, those lines and marks had been lethal, each letter, every word dealing a death blow to her heart.

'. . . killed in action.'

Killed! The finality of it had not registered at the time; how could Tom, her Tom, be dead? It was absurd! He was coming home on leave, hadn't he said so in his letter? It had been a mistake, whoever had sent that telegram had got names mixed up, her Tom was not dead, she knew he was not dead.

She had lived on that belief, fed on the hope, but hope could only nourish for so long before its strength began to wane. That had been almost as devastating as the telegram; losing hope was to lose faith and in that she would be failing Tom. But he had not come home, and in the end hope had withered.

Love had supported her in those long dark months. Not the breath-catching, blood flaring emotion she had felt when in Tom's arms, not his quiet whispered words. It had been the strength of another had carried her, his gentle arms comforted when tears could not be held back, that love which had been hers from birth: the love of a father.

The last of the cartridge cases had trickled into the container, the whole lying like a golden lake, yet Miriam saw only a beach, a stretch of sand stained with blood, littered with men injured and dead. So many had died on those beaches of Dunkirk, so many lives had been swallowed by the demons of war, so many hearts broken. She had tried to think of others like herself, wives, mothers and sweethearts, tried in the loneliness of night to tell herself she was not alone in her grief, that thousands of other women were feeling the same pain, yet that brought no solace; drowning in an ocean of despair, she could think only of Tom. Her father had saved her. He had sat with her those dreadful hours when sleep had been a stranger, had listened to her cry her grief, understood when those cries had become ones of anger against a world which had deprived her of a husband; her father had understood, for he had lived through the grief of losing loved ones, the emptiness of life without the wife he had cherished, the life she must now lead.

'C'mon Miriam wench . . .'

At her side, the gnarled fingers of Simeon Cartwright closed on the container.

'. . . Can't afford to slack. If we be a' goin' to put that 'Itler in 'is place, then our lads will be a' needin' o' every bullet we can mek an' they don't get med if 'ands be still.'

His eyes deep with sympathy, he continued quietly.

'It be 'ard wench, God only knows 'ow 'ard, but we all 'as to go on. A wanderin' mind be a luxury we can't indulge. Daydreams be precious but like so many other things right now, Miriam wench, they 'as to be rationed, kept along of moments afore sleep, for dreams don't win no war.'

Too old for the armed services, long past retirement, Simeon Cartwright had returned – as had many who thought their days in the workplace to be long past – to take the place of sons and grandsons conscripted into the armed forces, engineered into a war begun by one man's fanatical dream of world domination. We must all do our bit was their dogma, but with Tom as with thousands of men that 'bit' had been their life.

Watching the elderly figure half bent from the effort of pushing the container, she heard Simeon's words echo in her mind.

'. . . dreams don't win no wars.'

Her throat tight with tears, Miriam turned back to the making of bullet cartridges. No, dreams did not win wars . . . neither did they return the lives war demanded.

She must not know. She must not ever know!

Watching the slender figure shrug into a smart camel-coloured gabardine trench coat, Violet Hawley felt the sharp prick of conscience. That coat had accounted for more money than Jacob earned in a fortnight. 'It won't have the partin' wi' any clothing coupons; and as for style, you don't get that outside of London nor will it be available there for very much longer . . . things of quality such as that coat are getting harder and harder to come by.'

Harder to come by meaning less easy to steal? That was a question she had no need to ask. Jim Slater had a reputation for 'coming by' things, things often 'lost' during transport or, as seemed likely with this coat, taken from premises during or immediately following an air raid. It was a risky business. Black marketing was frowned upon but looting, stealing from blitzed property, was a crime which carried a heavy prison sentence. She had said as much the time she'd been offered a pound of butter. It was so strictly rationed . . . how come he had this? The question had been brusquely overcome.

Asking no questions resulted in hearing no lies. If she didn't want what was offered there was many another who did. So she had taken the butter, and Jim Slater had taken the money. That had been the first of what had become regular visits, each one having an offering of 'a bit o' summat picked up, a bit on the QT'. A bit on the quiet! At first she had felt a sense of guilt but stretching meagre rations of food, of almost everything which had once made life comfortable, the constant stress of queuing hours at a stretch only to be told what she had stood in all weathers for was 'sold out, there was nothing 'til next week', had pushed guilt aside. Like the one who had brought this coat, she would take while she had the chance, take for Jacob and for their daughter, take anything which would return a little of that comfort to their life.

'I will try not to be late home.' Katrin touched a hand to her hair before turning to look at her mother. 'But I can't promise, air raids have work stopped so often it is piling up, chances are I might be asked to stay on for an hour or two and I really don't feel I ought to refuse.' She shrugged, 'It has to be done.'

'. . . it 'as to be done . . .'

They had been Ella's words, her sister's words! Violet's nerves twanged at the memory. Ella had been right of course but what they had done . . . was it right? Ought they to have waited a while?

'And then what?' Ella had demanded, her thin mouth tightening. '*Wait a bit, an' then a bit more after that, what good'll come o' that? You knows an' I knows this be best all round.*'

It had been best for Ella, her life had not been turned upside down, but what of that other life? What of Isaac?

'Others will also stay on if need arises, there will be someone for me to travel back with so you don't have to worry.'

'I know.' Violet met her daughter's smile. 'But you be sure not to come home by y'self, the blackout has the streets dark as pitch.'

'I will, I promise.'

'See you keep it, and should the sirens blow, you get to the shelter.'

'The sirens will not sound today, I have personally arranged it. There is not going to be any air raid for a whole week.'

Violet watched the smile curve her daughter's mouth.

'. . . So what will you do with the week of amnesty? Would you like me to arrange a trip . . . Rome? Or perhaps Madame would prefer Paris, she has only to say the word.'

'You have heaven's ear do you?' Violet met the laughing eyes. 'Then you might ask they put an end to all this rationing, that would be far more welcome than a jaunt to the Continent.'

'Consider it done! You can go to the town this morning and buy as much as you wish.'

Reaching the packet of sandwiches she had made using the last scraping of butter, the cheese sliced finer than a moth's wing in order to make the weekly one ounce ration serve father and daughter, Violet Hawley searched for her own smile, which every day proved harder to find. The young could make light of everything, laugh problems away; but they did not know the bought not from Fosbrooks, Bishop and Marston nor even Rose Woolf, but from the more exclusive shops of Wolverhampton and Birmingham, none of that had been for Katrin's benefit. Truth a scald in her brain, Violet acknowledged the truth. It had all been done – was being done – for Violet Hawley. Lavishing every penny on her daughter was a safeguard, it was buying loyalty, buying security, buying protection against the truth. Violet leaned against the closed door. Yes, it was buying that as well!

hardship of holding life together, of trying to keep things the way they had always been.

Violet ran a glance over the trim figure drawing the belt of the stylish coat. 'Black market!' The prick of conscience bringing a tinge of colour to her cheeks, she turned toward a table on which gas masks were kept. That coat had not been essential, so why had she bought it? Why spend money which could have paid for butter or bacon, could even have bought precious petrol coupons enabling Jacob to drive to work rather than travel on buses wedged among people dressed in clothes stinking of factories. She had tried to get Jacob to move but work was work, Jacob had said, fresh air was good for the lungs and green fields were pretty to the eye but neither could be eaten. So they had stayed in Wednesbury and Jacob had continued in that factory, gradually working his way up to production manager.

Production manager! Violet's fingers grasped a box holding a gas mask. He should have been a partner, after all it was his brains behind many of the improvements that had seen the firm prosper; but Jacob was satisfied, in his estimation he had done well to get where he was. But there must be more for Katrin, she must not spend the rest of her life submerged beneath a welter of factories, each belching smoke and soot.

'Oh, better take that I suppose. I don't want a ticking off from a police constable or the ARP for being without it.'

Violet turned to the departing figure. The expense of a grammar school education, the cost of clothing

2

'Said it would serve as a lesson to others, have folk think twice before indulgin' in black marketeerin'.'

The conversation between Alice Butler and Becky Turner was listened to by all within earshot on the bus carrying them to work.

'Think twice!' Alice Butler's voice was scathing, 'Puttin' her away for five years won't 'ave effect on nobody but herself and her family, they'll never live it down.'

'Must say I didn't think the penalty would be so harsh.' Becky's reply brought nods of agreement from several women.

'Harsh? It be bloody brutal!' Hair tucked beneath a paisley scarf tied turban fashion, Alice's head swung emphatically. 'Them there magistrates wouldn't have come down near so hard were it a man had stood afore that Bench.'

Becky took a ticket from the conductor, flashing a smile before tucking the small slip of white paper into her bag and answering, 'I think you most likely be right.'

'Most likely!' Alice's derision hooted along the body of the bus. 'It's a cold hard certainty! Had it been a bloke had up for handlin' stolen goods he'd have been let off with a caution . . . "needed more in a factory or a mine" would have been the verdict. Justice . . . hah! Ain't no justice where a woman be concerned, her can join up alongside men, do her bit along of them in every occupation 'cept coalmining, yet catch her doing what a lot of men be doing right under the noses of the bobbies and see what happens; a woman gets put inside.'

'My mother was sayin' it won't end when that five years ends, the real hardship will come once Freda comes out of jail, says folk round here won't want no truck with a wench convicted of dealin' on the black market, mother says they'll see it as takin' food out of the mouths of kids.'

From the front of the bus the conductor called the next stop then yanked on the cord, setting the bell to sound. Rising from her seat, Alice wormed past passengers standing shoulder to shoulder in the aisle, her righteous anger turned on the conductor whose double pull was the signal for the driver to continue the journey.

' 'Old on! This war has taught everybody a lot these past couple of years but it ain't yet taught me how to walk through bodies as though they wasn't there.'

'We 'ave a schedule to keep an' it don't allow waitin' of wenches too busy talkin' to watch for their stop.'

The man's terse reply brought murmurs of approval from some of the passengers and Alice's irritation flared to anger. Who did this smart arsed bugger think he was talking to! Clearing the last of the people blocking the aisle, she halted on the minute platform where the conductor stood.

'We all 'ave schedules!' Brown eyes blazing fire played on the man's face. 'My own bein' a half past seven start in that munitions factory; now should it be I get quartered, that I lose fifteen minutes pay along of clockin' on after that time cos you was in so much of a monkey's wrassle to be away you didn't give time for me to get off the bus, then you're goin' to 'ave a sight more to worry over than gettin' to the depot canteen in time for a cuppa.'

The conductor sniffed. 'Oh ar, you goin' to report me to the bosses for wantin' to mek sure the rest of these folk gets to work on time? Fat lot of notice they'll tek of that!'

'No, I won't do any reporting. Unlike the specimen standin' afore me I don't need no bosses to fight my battles, I can do that very well for myself.'

The conductor laughed in open mockery. 'You says the war has taught a lot of things, has it also taught you to box?'

Resisting Becky's push urging her to climb down from the bus, ignoring the murmurs attesting to several more concerns of 'being quartered', Alice's icy reply did not cool the fire of her glare.

'It had no need to, but it could be called upon to teach you how to wear a truss, for you see it won't be your face will feel the blow. Though I guarantee you'll remember the sting of it every time you wish you could use that which won't never function the same way again. Like dough without yeast, it won't rise.'

Exclamations and tuts of disapproval at hearing such words from a young woman followed after the pair as they skipped onto the footpath.

'That put the snotty nosed sod in his place!' Alice glared defiantly after the receding vehicle. 'He'll think twice afore soundin' that bell next time.'

'He ought to have more sense than to have rung as quick as he did, he could see the aisle was blocked solid.' Becky added her own condemnation as they walked along a street busy with people hurrying to various factories and steel foundries with which the town of Wednesbury was filled.

'That bell will be the only thing he'll be quick with should I tell our Rob he fingered my bum as I waited to get off the bus.'

'But he didn't!'

'I know that and the conductor knows that,' Alice answered airily, 'but our Rob will know only what I tell him and I'll tell him that man touched my bum.'

'You wouldn't!'

'Wouldn't I!' Alice tossed her turbaned head. 'One more smart arsed remark out of that one and it could be he won't be able to talk for a month. In fact . . .' She smiled, a wicked glint in her brown eyes, 'if he's on our bus goin' home tonight I might just tell him my brother is wantin' a word with him.'

Passing through wide gates painted with splashes and streaks of green and brown, the whole camouflaged to resemble stretches of open heath, the two sprinted for the workshop as the gateman pulled a watch from the top pocket of a jacket as ancient as himself and mouthed the word 'TIME'.

Breathless from the dash across the wide yard, Alice snatched her card from a rack attached to the wall then slotted it into the large dialled time clock, breathing relief at seeing the resulting time stamped black and clear on the buff coloured card: seven twenty nine. One more minute and her pay would have been docked. In fact, it didn't allow a minute, one second past seven thirty and a quarter of an hour would have been taken from her pay, and that would mean less pocket money given back from the wage packet which must be handed unopened to her mother every Friday teatime. Less! Alice's irritation at the exchange of words with the bus conductor became sudden mutiny. Any less and her mother might as well keep the lot! With so many men pulled from the workplace and drafted into the forces, women had been put into the jobs left vacant; they did the job of a man but they did not receive the same wage. So much for government gratitude! 'You are doing well to be earning as much as you do, many girls of twenty one and older earned nowhere near that sum.' That had been the management reply when she had voiced dissatisfaction at a wage of seventeen shillings and ninepence in return for slogging her heart out sixty-one hours a week. Seventeen shillings and ninepence! And all she was handed out of it was half a crown. Two shillings and sixpence, her mother keeping the rest!

A measly two and six! Alice's thoughts were acid. How far did that go when it had to provide every article of clothing, every item of make-up? Lord, a lipstick, supposing you could get one, cost three bob on the black market, and stockings – the 'spivs' selling them asked no less than six. Six shillings for stockings which had cost three and elevenpence before the war.

'When you finally gets to wakin' up yoh might shift y'self an' let a body get to that time clock!'

A shove making her stumble a few paces, Alice turned a furious glare to a stockily built woman, steel curlers jutting from beneath a turban lying like a line of silver caterpillars on her brow.

'Who d'ya think you're pushin'!' Alice's demand sizzled like fat on a hot stove.

'I don't 'ave to think.' The woman slotted her own card into the clock, slamming the lever down with a vicious thump. 'I knows who yoh be, an' I also knows yoh be a cheeky young bugger.'

'You knows that does you? Then you must know this, but I'll tell you again just to refresh your memory. A cheeky *young* bugger be a sight better than bein' a miserable *old* bugger with a face ugly enough to stop that time clock should you look straight at it; but then you can't look straight at anythin', not with them cock eyes you can't.'

The woman's one turned eye seemed to turn even more inward to touch her nose as she aimed a blow which Alice adroitly dodged.

'Yoh waits 'til I sees your mother, see 'ow free y'be wi' that tongue o' your'n when 'er be finished!'

The woman stomped away, threats rapidly lost among the slap of leather drive belts and the din of machinery.

'Eeh Alice, you'll be for it when your mum gets to hear of what you just said, and her will, Lizzie Baker isn't one to lose the opportunity of makin' trouble.'

'Then somebody should tell Lizzie Baker the trouble that'll bring on 'er. Her'll find two can play the tittle-tattle game and who'll come off best. Ain't only Lizzie Baker knows of her rentin' out that back bedroom to any who can pay five bob for a bit of hows-your-father.'

Fastening the heavy duty green twill overall she preferred to the boiler suit type worn by most of the women, Becky cast a glance at the flushed face of her friend.

'I can't get over the difference in you,' she said, the last button secured, 'at school you wouldn't say boo to a goose yet now you're ready to have a go at anybody. Talk of a turnabout, yours isn't so much a change as a transformation.'

'I don't know about transformations,' the voice of the foreman boomed, 'but I does know about transfers an' that be what you pair will be gettin' should it be I tells the management you don't be pullin' your weight, you'll be gettin' your callin' up papers in next week's post an' the government don't allow no pickin' and choosin' o' jobs, you goes where they say, an' seeing the shortage o' farm workers I'll be placin' no bet on you both not gettin' sent to one; see 'ow you likes workin' sixty an' seventy hours a week ankle deep in pig muck!'

Wouldn't prove much of a change, she already worked sixty hours a week! Head at a defiant tilt, Alice walked to her place then, as she touched the button which brought life to the as yet silent machine, called to Becky.

'You know what his trouble is?'

'Trouble?' Becky's film star copied eyebrows rose in a questioning arch.

A sideways glance telling they were both still being observed by the foreman, Alice pulled sharply on a lever securing the machine's heavy jaws about a rounded bar of metal before setting it to rotate.

'Ar.' She turned the turret of the Ward 3A Capstan, bringing into position the sharp cutting tool then watching it bite into the bar and slice away steel in fine silver ribbons. 'He's like a hoss left too long in the field . . . he ain't gettin' his oats.'

Her brain a minefield of irritation, Alice let her dissatisfaction ride. Sixty hours slaving in this place week after week with the foreman watching every move, Lord you couldn't go to the lav for what he didn't count the time it took. The work was tiring, twisting that turret every couple of minutes, heaving long rods of steel, feeding them into the machine had her longing for the clock to reach six. But that labour, hard as it was, she didn't mind, it was her way of fighting this war, and she should really look for no reward other than the knowing of that. But there ought to be more! Certainly more than a half crown a week.

'Your Country Needs You.'

The slogan on the posters pasted onto the walls of almost every building flashed its picture into Alice's mind. It needed every man and woman . . . but not necessarily working in a 'munitions factory.

'. . . You'll be gettin' your callin' up papers . . . the government don't allow no pickin' an' choosin' . . .'

No it didn't. Alice swung the turret, excitement adding strength. Not if you waited for conscription, the government order for every able bodied woman under forty years of age to take employment of her choice or be compelled to accept that ordained by them, refusal resulting in imprisonment. That would not be the case should she volunteer for the forces; if she did that she would be able to choose which service to join.

'. . . See ow' you likes workin' sixty an' seventy hours a week ankle deep in pig muck . . .'

But she would not be ankle deep in pig muck, nor in any kind of muck. Messing about with animals or grubbing in fields was not for Alice Butler; but the WRNS, the Women's Royal Naval Service – the uniform alone was worth anything the job called for. Or maybe the WAAF, the Women's Auxiliary Air Force – that uniform was equally sexy.

Pique vanishing beneath a mental aura of glamour, Alice gave herself to the romance building in her mind.

Another of those letters. Violet Hawley stared at the white envelope on the hall carpet.

She had known it would come. Fingers woven tight together she felt the blood chill in her veins. She had known it would come, and now it had.

What would it say? What demand would it make this time? For that was what that letter was, a demand. She did not need to open it to see that, she had seen it twice before. And twice before had refused to acknowledge it.

This would be no different, whatever it dictated she would not do it, they could not force her!

She must act exactly the same way as those other times: she must burn the letter, destroy it, pretend it had not been received. That was the logical thing to do, the sensible thing; if it had not been received then there was no demand to answer.

Slowly, a step at a time as though approaching some living threat, Violet walked to where the letter lay. Nobody would know it had been delivered, nobody could hold her word in question. Sustained by the thought she snatched up the envelope and carried it quickly into the kitchen.

She turned to the dresser and took from a shelf the box of matches kept along with a supply of candles for use in the Anderson shelter Jacob and some of his fellow members of the Home Guard had erected in the garden. Shelter! Violet shuddered. A few pieces of corrugated sheeting bolted together and covered with soil, what protection could that afford against a bomb? And being inside it, spending hours in near total darkness lying on those narrow framed bunk beds covered by rough grey war issue blankets, the dank smell of earth filling the nostrils, fear leaving you almost unable to breathe as the whistle of a falling bomb came ever nearer . . . It was like being buried alive, alive to the horror of waiting, listening, praying the next bomb to rock the earth would not land on your little bit of it. A living nightmare. She had tried to make it more comfortable. Every day she aired the blankets and every day sprinkled 'Aunty Sally' over the metal strips of those beds, splashed it on the walls and the packed earth floor but disinfectant did not eliminate the sour odour of damp nor did it deter spiders and beetles. Like the prayers she whispered night and day asking this war be ended, her efforts were ignored.

Ignored! She turned again to the unopened envelope. That was what she must do. She must ignore this letter, what was not read could not be worried over. But what if someone came to the house, if the demand written be made in person?

Dread snatched breath into her throat. They would knock . . .

Anyone coming here would have to knock, have to announce their arrival and thus warned she would refuse to answer.

Solution arrived at, she struck a match and held the flame to one corner of the envelope, watching the gleam of orange gold lick across the paper, leaving in its wake a blackened curl. The flame almost touching her fingers, she carried the charred remnants to the sink a smile on her lips as the last vestige burned to a crisp. Should anyone call to enquire after that letter? She turned on the tap and flushed away every shred of evidence. She would simply not be at home.

'Might be a long time before you buy any more of them.' A trace of envy in her voice, Becky Turner spoke to the young woman who was twisting about to check the seams of her stockings were straight.

Damn! Katrin swore silently. She had hoped to be gone from the washroom before any of the factory girls came to wash their hands prior to eating their packed lunch. There really should be a separate washroom for office personnel; she could most definitely do without the smell of slurry oil wafting from grimy overalls onto her clothes. She ran both hands along each leg in turn before replying. 'Why is that, are they all sold? I was really hoping to get another pair.'

She wanted pair, *another* pair at six bob a go? Becky felt the swift pang of envy.

Katrin Hawley was allowed to keep half of her wage, so she said, and considering the style she kept herself in there was no denying it. Envy bit again. She could afford a pair of them stockings every week while Alice and Becky needed to save sixpence a week out of their pocket money and in the time it took to reach the price of one pair they had long gone.

'It must be great being able to wear them every day.' Becky sighed wistfully.

Katrin took a deliberate moment, savouring the knowledge that neither Becky Turner nor Alice Butler could afford to wear stockings such as these except perhaps once in a blue moon. Disguising the pleasure the thought inspired, she said matter of factly. 'It is nice, you should do the same.'

'I wish.' Becky sighed again. 'But they come too pricey.'

'Mm. They are expensive, but then quality never does come cheaply and Kayser Bondor Fully Fashioned Pure Silk are the best, so if that is what you want then you have to be prepared to pay, no matter that the price may be rather high.'

'And you certainly done that, seeing who it was you bought them stockin's from. They come by way of Freda Evans; tell me if I'm wrong.'

Lowering the hem of her fashionable straight knee-length grey worsted skirt Katrin met the stare of a young woman entering the washroom.

'Don't bother,' Alice Butler went on, 'I know it's true. You weren't the only one purchased from the black market. There are other wenches here bought stockin's but they likely won't get the next pair as easy, least not from Freda Evans they won't.'

'Lord, it was so awful Freda being caught, if only . . .' Becky bit her lip.

'If only what?' Alice asked sharply. 'If Freda hadn't brought them stockin's here? Then her would have sold them some place else, there are always some ready to buy no matter what's offered nor no matter the price asked.'

Was that a dig at her, a reference to not only pure silk stockings instead of lisle but also her stylish new coat? That could hardly have gone unnoticed. But then she would hate to think it had. Katrin smiled to herself. Any advantage she could boast, any emotion she could effect in Becky Turner and Alice Butler: envy, resentment, inequality, all or any of those feelings were sweet to her, and Katrin Hawley had a penchant for all things sweet. She turned to the wash basin. Eyeing the tablet of coarse brown soap, its uninviting appearance rendered more so by streaks of oily black left by its previous user, she let it lie, simply holding her hands beneath the running tap. These two had forgotten that day in the school playground, forgotten words thrown in childish anger. Shaking droplets of water from her fingers, Katrin watched them fall like tears . . . tears she had shed many times since that day. Yes they had forgotten, but Katrin Hawley had not forgotten. Nor would she ever forgive.

3

'Of course I didn't put a false date of birth, I'm not that stupid.'

'Not stupid but vain.' Ella Robson looked at her sister perched so nearly on the edge of a chair as to not be sitting on it at all. 'You've been that way from Jacob gettin' the job of manager along of Titan Engineerin', treating folk who've known you from being born as though they be beneath you. Remember Violet, walkin' with your nose in the air, talkin' as though pound notes grows on trees in your back garden don't make you no different, we all comes from the same stock though you likes to pretend otherwise, but vanity brings its own rewards and could be the reward you gets will be one you'll 'ave no liking for.'

Feeling the sting of truth, Violet retorted sharply. 'I did not come here to listen to talk like that!'

Ella's head lifted sharply, her glance noting the tight mouth, the eyes which did not slide away quickly enough to hide the flash of recognition.

'No you d'aint come to hear talk such as that, you come hopin' to hear the lies you needs to bring you comfort of mind.'

'Lies! Just what do you mean by that?' Her patience exhausted by long hours of the previous night in the air raid shelter, tired in mind and body, Ella rounded on her sister. 'Mean!' she snapped, 'I'll tell you what I mean, you be as noggin' 'eaded now as you was years ago, you be still daft if you think to pull the wool over the eyes of them sendin' that letter.'

'I'm not pulling the wool . . .'

'Oh for God's sake Violet!' Ella banged the teapot onto the table. 'I said a minute since it were vanity has you act the way you do but I were wrong, it be stupidity. But I warns you, keep your 'ead in the sand, refuse to face up to reality an' sooner or later you'll get your arse kicked.'

'I can't be forced!' Violet's mouth snapped like a clam.

Drawing a long breath, Ella poured tea into two heavy pottery cups using the moment to suppress an anger she found more difficult to combat with her sister's every visit. 'No I suppose you can't,' she said at last, 'but the consequence of refusal could be just the straw needed to break the camel's back.'

'You think you be so clever, but talking in riddles is as useful as a sty with no pig in it.'

Ella stirred the few grains of sugar she allowed herself from the weekly ration into tea as spared of milk, then looked at the figure on the opposite side of the kitchen table. Violet was regarding the heavy cups with undisguised dislike. But then cups given by the rag and bone man in exchange for a bundle of old clothing, or a tin pot with so many holes it could double as a colander, was not the only thing Violet Hawley found distasteful. Truth was another, but like it or not, she was going to hear that now.

'Then let's put the pig back in the sty. You think that pretending not to have received that letter is all it be goin' to take. But that be a blindness of the sort you suffered from twenty years gone, a blindness you be sufferin' still if you thinks Jacob ignorant of the fact that by marryin' you he walked a trodden path. Oh no, he weren't told by any of the family but by the man who put a child in your belly, the child old mother Hanley took from you with a long knitting needle, almost takin' your life the same time she took that of the babe. Yes, Jacob knew of your lying with a man who refused to wed you, just as he must have known it was no miscarriage you had twelve months after his taking you to the altar. Your so called loss was a pretence to cover the fact you could never again carry a child, that your backstreet abortion had deprived him of a family.'

Violet was attempting to hold the cup with little finger affectedly raised.

'That's a lie.'

'Then why not bring him here to this house, have him stand at this table while I repeat what I've just said. Let me ask him if he was on the verge of leaving you when you were both asked to take the child of a dying woman, to be father and mother to it; it were that child kept Jacob Hawley at your side. It was duty, you hear that Violet, he felt it his duty to care for and rear that child, a child he came to love. You tricked Jacob Hawley but be warned, others might not fool so easy, and that could mean not only the loss of a husband but also a daughter and that be the root of your fears don't it Violet? Deep inside you knows that once the girl be married and gone from your house then will Jacob leave it and with his going so will go the lifestyle you've built for yourself. It be this knowledge has you dress that wench like a band box, only the best for the daughter of Violet Hawley . . . except it don't be the girl you be thinkin' of do it? It be yourself, yourself as it has ever been. That were why she went to grammar school while every other kid in the street went to the council school. That's why you pays a fortune for clothes from Jim Slater and his black market friends, why you scheme to ensure her were given no job workin' on a factory floor but were taken on for office work. That way her stands a better chance of bein' noticed by them as has money, a better chance of landing a fish wealthy enough to keep Violet Hawley in her trumped up little world. It be your future you be lookin' to Violet, your future, not that of the wench and that be a truth even you can't deny.

As the third bus, already packed to the seams, passed the long queue of would-be passengers, Alice Butler tutted her vexation. The day had not gone well, a broken die had meant her machine lying idle for more than half the morning until the part could be repaired. 'We don't 'ave no spare.' The tool setter had been crusty as a fresh baked loaf. 'I can't go puttin' in what don't be 'ad, I ain't no magician.'

He was no Clark Gable either! His rat-like features and whining voice made even Peter Lorre look like a sex god. Half a morning! She shuffled restlessly, her eyes in search of the next bus. Half a morning she had been forced to log as day work, the flat hourly rate which paid half that she could earn at the newly introduced piece work; with piece work the more she produced the more money went into her pay packet, but for all the extra she worked her heart out, she saw no more of it than the regular half crown. 'You don't never miss what you ain't never had.' Her grandmother's saying whispered in Alice's mind but the answer was a shout in her brain. She did miss what she never had! She missed the pleasure of drawing pure silk over her legs, of seeing herself dressed in expensive fashionable clothes instead of those she wore now, government controlled Utility, drab things which might well have been designed by Methuselah.

Casting a furtive, beneath the lashes glance at the figure next in line in the queue, a figure who could have stepped straight from the pages of one of those woman's magazines she herself only ever glanced at in the newsagent's shop, Alice felt the hot rise of envy. Why? Why did Kate Hawley have so much while she had so little? How come her clothes even now were ultra smart? They were certainly not bought from Peacocks or Appleyard's draper shop.

Alice's covetous glance ran over the smartly tailored camel coloured coat, the brown leather bag slung across one shoulder, a gloved hand grasping the box containing a gas mask. She felt bitterness join with envy. Young 'uns! Why have as many kids as her mother had borne, as most women in these parts seemed to have? Kids older brothers and sisters had to work to help feed and clothe. She loved every one of her family, of course she did, but that didn't mean she ought to have to finance it quite so heavily.

'About time!' An exasperated voice heralded sight of another bus. 'My feet be singin' and it don't be no Vera Lynn toon.'

'What do they be singin' then Edie . . . "Underneath the Arches"?'

Edie shook her head over the ripple of laughter. 'Don't know about "Underneath the Arches", Bert,' she answered, 'but I'll 'ave fallen arches if I be standin' 'ere much longer.'

Caught by the shuffle of bodies pressing forward as the double-decked vehicle approached the stop Alice stumbled slightly. Murmuring an apology to the person she had knocked against she saw the fully laden bus sail past once again. 'Lord, we ain't never gonna get home!'

'We ain't if we depends on them there buses!' The woman who moments before had complained of aching feet shook a fist in the wake of the bus. 'What do the government be doin'? It be damned sure they ain't standin' in no bus queue after a ten hour day sloggin' away like a Trojan. It be one thing bein' called up, conscripted into factories and the like doin' the work of a man; doin' our bit they tells we and God knows we all be happy to, but the least them lot sittin' along of the House of Commons could do is mek sure there be buses enough to get women home o' nights.'

'Well I'm not standing here any longer.'

'Me neither.' Making to follow Alice, Becky Turner cast a glance at the girl behind. 'What about you Kate? Could be half a dozen more will pass before you get one with space enough for a fly; you far better walk with Alice and me.'

This was the last thing she wanted, to be seen walking home with girls who worked in a factory, girls dressed in clothes the rag man might well refuse, girls with scarves tied turban fashion over curling pins. Katrin Hawley gauged her situation. Refusal would no doubt offend, not that offending either Alice Butler or Becky Turner would worry her unduly, but for a while she needed to remain on speaking terms with both.

'Seems you may be right Becky.' Smiling, Katrin too vacated her place in the line of hopeful travellers.

'Edie Jones was only saying what everybody else is thinking; folk shouldn't have to walk long distances after a hard day lifting bars of steel and mauling heavy machinery.' Alice seethed.

'I don't dispute that.' Becky answered. 'But a long walk home is better than a short walk back into a prison cell and that is the only walk Freda Evans will be taking for many a night yet . . . I know which I'd rather have.'

'It was a shame what happened to Freda.' Katrin's reply broke the short silence Becky's words had induced.

'It's a shame all right,' Alice said, vehemence emphasising every syllable, 'a shame the real culprit weren't sent down.'

'Real culprit?' Katrin looked perplexed.

'Ar, real culprit. But that one got away with it, he

kept quiet letting Freda carry the can for what was his doin'.'

'I don't understand. Are you saying someone other than Freda should have answered to the charge of black marketeering?'

'That be exactly what I'm saying.'

'Careful Alice!' Becky cautioned. 'You know what the posters say, "Walls Have Ears". You never can tell who might be listening.'

'Let 'em listen.' Alice's head lifted defiantly. 'I'm only saying what is true, that idle fossack Jim Slater was behind it all and it were him said nothing while Freda went to gaol; what a boyfriend for any wench! I'd rather be courting a snake!'

'Jim Slater was dealing on the black market?'

'Was?' Alice ignored Becky's 'Shhh.' 'He still is, the sticky fingered swine. God only knows how he gets what he gets, same as only God knows the reason he don't get caught. I tell you, Kate, be wary of that one, keep clear of him if you want to stay this side of a prison wall.'

'But Freda must have known what she was doing, she must have realised . . . I mean when things are not to be had in the shops . . .'

'Of course her realised them stockings had been pinched, what her didn't reckon to was what Slater had slipped inside the packet sent along for Maudie Hopkins. Had it been only stockings the cops caught Freda with, then she wouldn't have been no more than fined, but Maudie was after buyin' ration books as well, and being in possession of them was what got Freda five years.'

'Ration books?' Katrin's glance swung quickly to the girl keeping step beside her. 'But how . . . where . . . ?'

'Where be easy.' Alice broke off as the three of them negotiated several lorries flanked by the ever present flurry of bicycles, continuing only when they reached the other side of the busy road. 'You must have read the newspaper of that break-in along of the Town Hall some months back, it reported several dozen food ration books and a number of clothing and petrol coupons had been stolen. I reckon Jim Slater were a party to that; as for how, even as a kid he could break in where castor oil couldn't get and I don't see him being any the less able now.'

'But how can you be so sure it was Jim Slater put a ration book in with the stockings?' Katrin queried. 'It could have been there when he bought them.'

Alice sniffed derogatively. 'Pigs will fly before Slater *buys* anything he can get by swiping it from the back of a lorry, and it were not one ration book but two Freda were caught with. And I know it was him pinched them cos he offered a couple to my mother.'

'Eeh Alice, he never did!'

'Cross me heart and hope to die. Mother might have took 'em except her didn't have the five quid asking price.'

'I never had a deal of liking for Jim Slater and now I dislike him even more.'

'You and me both Kate.' Alice's tone was scathing. 'But one I detest even more than him is the one who tipped off the coppers about Freda.'

They had reached the junction of Holyhead Road

and Dudley Street, the point where Katrin must go her own way to Hollies Drive while the other two continued on, Becky to Queen Street and Alice to Cross Street. Who was it Alice referred to? Who had informed the police of Freda Evans' black market dealings? The urge to have these questions answered had Katrin ask, 'Do you know who that man is?'

Alice Butler turned to look at the young woman and a trace of envy pricked warm in her throat. Kate Hawley could not be called a beauty, certainly she was not as pretty as Becky, but there was something about her that caught the eye. Not the hair, though that was thick and shone like polished copper. The figure then? No. She was no more shapely than Becky or Alice herself yet . . . the eyes. Alice halted in mid thought, it was Kate Hawley's eyes. Looking into them now she saw something deep and almost hidden. Yet not quite: a hint of it showed low in those green depths, gleaming like a candle flame amid darkness. Uncertain as to what her brain was telling her Alice was silent, only Kate Hawley's repeat of her question breaking what felt like a trance.

'No.' She blinked, clearing her mind of what she could not fathom. 'No, I don't know who that swine is or where he might be found but this I swear. So sure I do find out, so sure I hear a whisper of him, then he and Jim Slater will go down, but not before our Rob and a few of his mates have finished with him, he won't go shoppin' nobody else not for a long time!'

* * *

'*No, I don't know who that swine is . . . so sure I hear . . .*'

Claiming tiredness she did not feel had provided a plausible excuse for Katrin to retire early. Now in the privacy of her bedroom, she laughed softly at the words in her mind.

'*. . . He won't go shoppin' nobody else . . .*'

Alice Butler had vowed vengeance on the one who had informed against Freda, had as good as said her brother would give the man a beating should it ever be discovered who was the person responsible.

'Don't forget to put your gas mask handy, and lay your dressing gown across the foot of the bed.'

A breath of irritation filling her lungs, Katrin frowned resentment at the call that came from the top of the stairs. Her mother had called that same thing every night since the war had begun, had repeated those words so often it seemed they emanated from the very walls of the house; Lord, was she still a child who needed constant reminding of every least thing? '*Don't come home by yourself . . . if there is a raid while you are at work don't go sitting next to those girls from the factory workshop . . . if you are caught in a raid while on the way home then for heaven's sake choose a respectable looking house to ask shelter of . . .*' the list went on and on.

Forcing down the surge of annoyance and adopting a mumbling half-asleep tone designed to persuade her mother not to enter the room, Katrin replied that all was as instructed then clamped her teeth hard on the tut of exasperation as the nightly practice continued. 'I've made each of us a sandwich and the flask is ready for filling, it is all on the tray in the kitchen; them there

German bombers don't leave time for doing much once they be here so it's best to be ready to run. And, Katrin, remember; shoes for the air raid shelter not bedroom slippers.'

'Yes mother . . . shoes.' Letting it drift dreamily Katrin listened with bated breath. Her mother might yet come in, to ensure all of her instructions had been carried out; more than that, seeing her daughter still awake would evoke more enquiry as to her day at the office. Every question was aimed at learning one thing, had her daughter perhaps caught the attention of senior management, senior meaning Arthur Whitman, the owner of Whitman Engineering? But what could catching the attention of the boss achieve? Promotion . . . senior position in the typing pool? No, that was not what Violet Hawley was angling for, she was fishing for the main catch and the fish she hoped to land was Arthur Whitman.

Beyond the closed door a slight clink released the tension holding Katrin's mouth. That was the torch her mother placed each night on the small table on the landing, ready to light their way to the air raid shelter – her final act before going to bed. Assured at last she would not be disturbed Katrin slipped from the bed and listened several moments.

There was no sound from the landing. Releasing a breath she had not been conscious of holding, Katrin eased back the dark cloth with which each window of the house was covered in order to comply with black-out regulations. War! Touching a finger to the pretty flowered curtain the drab material had hidden, she stared into the moonlit softness. War was cruel, it scarred so many lives, yet war could not be blamed for the scar on Katrin Hawley's life. That blow had been struck years ago, hurled at her by angry children in a school playground. It was a scar only revenge could remove and Katrin Hawley would have that revenge.

4

'You tricked Jacob Hawley . . .'

'. . . others might not fool so easy . . .'

'. . . the loss of a husband . . .'

Like insistent bluebottles of thought, her sister's words buzzed in Violet Hawley's brain, words which had plagued like a thorn in her flesh since her return to Hollies Drive, words which even now, sitting in her gleaming sitting room, refused to be silenced.

'Jacob knew of your lying with a man who refused to wed you, knew your backstreet abortion had deprived him of a family.'

Staring at patterns of sunlight trickling through windows criss-crossed with brown sticky tape, a precautionary measure against glass shattered by bomb blast, Violet heard other words, words spoken some twenty-one years before.

'. . . He told me of the child you carried, the child he were father of.'

Jacob had stared at his pain.

'. . . he laughed on saying I'd been hooked like a fish, taken in by a wench no better than her should be.'

'. . . Jacob that is a horrible lie. . . !'

In the space of a moment the look of pain so vivid in his eyes had become cold anger then disgust.

'No Violet, the lie is the one we have lived this twelve month, the lie of believing we can have a life together, now that lie is ended, tomorrow . . .'

Violet's eyes followed the dancing gold of afternoon sunlight. What might Jacob have gone on to say of that tomorrow? What was his intention?

He had not said, not that night nor at any time since; but instinct told then what passing years had confirmed, whatever love Jacob Hawley may once have held for her was dead.

Caught in the web of memory, Violet saw again a young fair-haired man, grey eyes regarding her across a dimly lit room. They held no trace of righteous anger, no look of disgust nor the dullness of pain, the eyes that looked at her were devoid of emotion: empty, soulless, robbed of life.

'Tomorrow . . .'

He had begun to speak again. To say what she had kept hidden in her own heart these twenty-one years? To tell her their marriage was ended? That the next day would see him gone from the tiny terraced house? It had not been said yet nor had it been foregone or renounced. Ella had been right. Jacob was biding his time, simply waiting to see his daughter wed and then he would leave, turn his back on a life he had no pleasure in, on the wife he held no love for. And Katrin? Violet drew a long breath. Surely the child she had taken and reared as her own would not leave, she would not turn her back on the mother who had given her everything. Katrin had not been born of her body, but that would prove of no consequence! Violet shrugged away the sudden coldness touching her insides. Katrin loved her, that was evident in every aspect of the girl's behaviour and marriage would not alter that.

So what if Jacob left her?. . . Life would not be so very changed. From the day he found out about that pregnancy, discovering she had married him not for love but for security of name, they had not lived as man and wife. They shared a room but not a bed, he had provided food and home . . .

Jacob had provided a home! He had taken her from the smoke-blackened two up two down, tiny back to back in Cross Street, one of a long line of terraced houses each sharing a garden privy with four other families. Jacob had taken her from that drab dark house and brought her here to Hollies Drive, to Elm House, a tall detached villa with its own garden, a private toilet and running water piped directly into the house.

Hollies Drive! A flush of pride warmed away the last lingering vestige of cold in her stomach. A house here was a status symbol in the town, it carried the mark of a man's success, it commanded respect of the kind due Jacob Hawley as manager of Prothero Steel and Tube manufacturers. And it commanded the respect due his wife. Yes, she was respected by the shopkeepers of Wednesbury, she was held in esteem.

Elm House was her pride and joy, no other member of her family could claim such. That was the true reason for the snide remarks thrown at her by Ella; her sister was jealous of what Violet had, of Jacob's rise in the world; they were all of them filled with envy. They had expected her to remain as they still were, living in those tiny grime-covered terraces, but they had all been proved wrong. Violet's lips spread in a satisfied smile. They had thought Jacob would leave her when he found out about her past; they had not expected him to keep up the pretence of all being normal between them and certainly not to provide her with a home in so prestigious an area as Hollies Drive; Jacob had provided.

Until now! How much longer would that provision continue? He had stayed on for Katrin's sake, but now Katrin was capable of taking care of herself; there was no longer anything to hold Jacob here.

But what if he were not the one to leave?

What if he turned *her* from this house? If he disowned her as his wife?

The shame of that, the embarrassment of people talking, sniggering as she passed on the streets . . . how could she live with that?

Alice's resentment flared fresh and bright as she bit into the slice of cold toast she must eat while still operating her machine: no ten minute break now the country was at war. Half a bloody crown pocket money! And that wouldn't be long in her pocket, not with her mother going through them once she had left for work. Not that the hours away from the factory afforded much opportunity to spend her money, time was another thing snatched by her mother.

'. . . them there bedrooms wants a turnin' out . . . the windows needs be cleaned . . . blacklead the grate . . .'

Her mother's non-stop instructions beat in Alice's head, keeping rhythm with the slap of drive belts powering the many machines.

'. . . I don't get the time to do it all . . . what with the cookin' an' the washin' . . . it ain't easy what with the little 'uns . . .'

Always the same moans and excuses! Of course it were no easy job seeing to a family day in and day out, but then neither was her own job easy, certainly it was no less tiring, but try telling her mother that! She had never seen the inside of a factory, much less wrestled with a machine large enough to almost fill their living room. But she would not be wrestling with it for much longer. Alice fed the cutting tool into the revolving steel, slicing off one more gleaming silver bolt. She had made up her mind. Knowles Street was not so far away, she could run there during her dinner hour, enquire at the Labour Exchange Office on how to apply to join the Women's Forces and be back here at the factory before the afternoon shift began.

There was only one flaw in her plan. It had been Becky had voiced it. *'A girl can apply to become a member of the Women's Forces at eighteen years old, but eighteen don't be twenty-one, you'll need to show your birth certificate.'*

With the familiarity born of repetition, Alice's hands seemed to work independently of her mind, which ranged over the conversation she had held with Becky on their way into work.

'That'll be no trouble,' she had answered, *'all of them sort of papers be kept in a box in mother's bedroom, I can take mine out next time I clean, she'll never know it's gone.'*

'I've no doubt you can get a hold of it, but you can't go alterin' the date, that'll be breakin' the law, you'll get sent to gaol same as Freda.'

Alice's teeth clenched. She had not reckoned on having to produce a certificate. It was obvious she was fit enough for the forces, and wasn't she already doing the work of a man? Lord, what more could the authorities want?

Becky had the answer: parental consent!

'You'll need . . . hand them recruiting officers a letter . . . proving your father and mother gives permission for you to go leavin' home, they won't take you without that. I knows cos Lucy Phillips from our street had to take a letter signed by her folk afore she was accepted for the ATS.'

A signed letter! Alice wrestled with the dilemma Becky had raised in her mind. She could smuggle her birth certificate from the house but as to a letter of consent . . . ? Could she write one herself, sign the names of both parents? That was as much a crime as changing the date on her birth certificate, maybe not one which would have her sent to prison but certainly one her mother would not let pass easily.

'Tekin' money from the 'ouse . . . robbin' the little 'uns of food an' clothin' . . .'

Her father would consent, he would understand she wanted to do more to help her country than work in a factory. But her mother? No, she would not be pacified by the promise of forces pay being sent home, nor would she be duped like her husband. She would view the business of joining up for what it really was: a chance to escape the monotony, to escape her mother's domination. More than that, she would see herself doing all the chores she demanded her daughter do: that alone would have her refuse consent.

Yet there might be a way. The works' hooter signalled midday break and Alice thrust her time card into the clock before sprinting across the yard to the washroom. There might be just one way.

'So sure I finds out . . .'

Sitting at her desk, the letters she had typed awaiting only the Whitman signature, Katrin Hawley smiled.

Alice Butler had meant every word of that threat, but first she had to find the one who had committed the offence. And Alice Butler would never know who had informed against Freda Evans, never discover who had given the information which had led to the girl's imprisonment. Nor would Freda herself ever know. Shuffling the typed letters into a neat pile, Katrin allowed the smile to spread. She had achieved the revenge she had so long promised herself, but only in part; as yet just one of those who had jibed at her in that school playground had been made to pay. Five years! Katrin tasted sweet satisfaction. But as Becky Turner had said, those five years would not end with Freda's release; the stigma of having been convicted and gaoled would walk with Freda Evans the rest of her life. Yes, one girl had paid. The smile vanished as Katrin's fingers tightened on the sheaf of papers.

It had been so easy. All it had taken was a telephone call to the local Office of Information. She had not needed to say who was making the call and she had not, she had simply given the name of the suspect, Freda Evans, and the added tit-bit of the girl's place of work and probable place where a transaction was to be carried out. Freda had been caught, ration books and all.

One had paid. The sweetness of satisfaction became the tart bite of revenge. One had paid but there were two yet still to pay and one way or another they would.

'If you have finished those letters I will take them into Mr Whitman.'

Katrin looked at the woman standing at the desk, one hand already reaching for the sheaf of papers. Fifteen years as Arthur Whitman's secretary had other employees treat the woman with careful civility, a civility Katrin also observed, if only on the surface.

'They are all done, Miss Simpson.' Her mouth curving in a superficial smile, Katrin handed over the letters and watched the plumpish figure tap on the door marked 'Managing Director'. Harriet Simpson was sixty if she was a day, why didn't the woman retire? She was like a starving dog who had found a bone, nothing would separate her from it. There had to be some way of getting that woman to leave, there had to be a reason somewhere, it was simply waiting to be found. Switching her glance to a separate pile of papers taken from her in-tray, Katrin appeared not to pay attention to the fawn clad figure emerging from the inner office but beneath the apparent lack of interest her mind seethed. So long as that woman remained at Whitman Engineering there would be very little prospect of Katrin Hawley's promotion from office clerk.

Simply waiting to be found! Katrin's teeth clamped behind firm set lips. Katrin Hawley was quite competent at finding a means to an end.

5

A prayer answered!

Touching a kiss to the cheek of both parents, her slightly wan 'Goodnight, God bless' holding to the pretence she had practised for days, Katrin retired to her own room, where she let the curtain of deception lift from her face.

What had happened had been a blessing, though not bestowed by God so much as His adversary.

Taking time brushing her hair she smiled at her own reflection. So many people condemned Mister Adolf Hitler but Katrin Hawley had cause to thank him, for it had been his bombers that had led to this satisfactory state of affairs.

Setting aside the brush, she removed pale blue artificial silk cami-knickers. Her mother had frowned at this new form of underwear declaring 'it would never have been allowed in my young days'. But these were not her mother's 'young days', this was nineteen forty one and Katrin Hawley would decide her own underwear. Placing the cami-knickers with other clothing for laundering, Katrin wrinkled her nose at the flannelette pyjamas on her pillow. These were not to her taste but for now she would comply with her mother's instruction and wear them; she deemed pyjamas preferable to a flimsy silk nightgown 'in case of having to take to the air raid shelter; you never know as to somebody on the street asking to take cover with us, they can't very well be refused.'

Katrin's mouth assumed the tightness it had held upon watching Harriet Simpson come and go from Arthur Whitman's office. Like that woman her mother had jurisdiction, but neither of them would enjoy it for much longer. In fact the plump Harriet had already been temporarily relieved of her authority, now it remained only for 'temporary' to become 'permanent'.

It had been late evening when she was ready to leave the office, having agreed to Harriet Simpson's request she stay on to finish some urgent orders. Her coat half on, Katrin had grabbed for her bag as the siren had blared warning of an imminent raid.

'*You can't go home now girl . . .*' Harriet had almost shouted, her hand grabbing Katrin's wrist, '. . . *we must go into the factory shelter.*'

The perfect opportunity!

The offices were equipped with blackout curtains, while less used areas of the administration block including corridors had windows covered with black-painted paper. Very low-powered electric light bulbs, set at wide intervals, were their only illumination, and these were turned off once the staff had left for the night. An air raid AND the building in darkness. Fortune had chosen to favour Katrin Hawley a week ago: she had been granted its blessing.

Harriet had taken a small torch from the drawer of her desk and, keeping the misted beam playing on the ground inches in front of their feet, had hurried them from the room.

'*Darkness blinding when emerging from that lighted office . . . trying to run when they could barely see to walk . . . ! Fear of an explosion trapping them in the building when possibly no one knew them to be there making them hurry . . . !*'

She had sobbed these and half a dozen more reasons for the accident, had acted the part of a frightened, distraught young woman, but most of all one condemning of herself.

She had dashed into the factory screaming over the noise of the machinery that men and women insisted on keeping working regardless of all German bombers might do, shrieking for someone to help.

'*I should have led the way . . .*' She had cried against the shoulder of the work's night foreman while trained First Aid Personnel, their white helmets and satchels containing field dressings a gleaming contrast against dark uniforms, had bent over the unconscious Harriet, '*. . . I should have been first onto the stairs . . . I could have broken her fall . . . it's my fault . . . it's my fault . . .*'

She had refused to be comforted, all the while careful to keep her face pressed to the shoulder of the foreman, then covering her face with her hands when he gave her into the care of the First Aid Volunteers. They had seen her home, advised her mother she be given a hot sweet drink to help recovery from shock.

But she had suffered no shock. Nor had Harriet Simpson's headlong fall down those stone steps been an accident.

Would the woman claim that . . . ?

Katrin slipped into bed.

Maybe, but claim and proof were poles apart. Harriet had been unnerved by the prospect of the building being struck by a bomb, she had tried to take the stairs at a run and in the panic had tripped. That would be her answer to any claim that woman might make, and there was nobody could attest the fact it was a lie.

No, there was no witness to verify it was the foot she had deliberately thrust out as they had reached the head of the stairs had sent the older woman toppling.

A prayer answered.

An obstacle removed from Katrin Hawley's path.

'Now be sure you do as granddad tells you.'

Covering the meal with a plate to prevent the food drying out completely Miriam Carson slipped it into the oven and lowered the gas to minimum heat.

'. . . and be certain to turn the oven off when he takes out his supper.'

'I know mum, you don't have to worry about me.'

But she did worry. Miriam cast a quick look at the lad sitting at the kitchen table, slips of paper spread like a chequer board across one half of it. How could she not worry? He was all she had of Tom, the husband she had adored, who this war had stolen from her.

Turning to the sink with its soiled dishes, she hid the tears rising to her eyes.

A Step Too Far

Their marriage had seemed like weeks rather than years, not a day passing without them both whispering their love for each other; now that was ended and it had seemed her own life had ended too. How had she lived after receiving the War Office telegram? Only by the gentle love of a father. Why had she lived? Only for her son. It had been so hard without Tom: the nights she had reached for him only to find the bed empty beside her; the days she had needed his support when childhood ailments had her fearing for their child; the other children they had both wanted and were now denied her. 'You are young yet, wench, you'll marry again, you'll see.' She had heard those words many times over the months, words meant to bring comfort. But there had been no solace in them, they brought no relief to a heart that was dead.

Her son and her father. Miriam swallowed the tears. . . . They were her life now, she must live for them.

'Leave the dishes mum, I'll do them when I've finished my homework.'

'Thanks luv,' Miriam answered her son, 'they are done, but you could see to washing granddad's plate once he's eaten.'

'We do that together.'

Those deep blue eyes, Tom's eyes! Miriam's throat thickened as she met the boy's smile and she had to force her reply. 'Granddad washing dishes? That I would have to see.'

'We do a lot of things together.' Reuben's smile widened to a grin. 'He also tells me a lot about when you were young, about the tricks you got up to.'

'Tricks?' Mock effrontery drawing her mouth into a line, Miriam draped the drying cloth over the line strung above the kitchen stove. 'I'll need to have a word with your grandfather!'

'Best make it tomorrow mum, it's twenty minutes to six, you will be late for work if you don't leave now.'

Night shifts were the hardest of all for any of the mothers working to help the war effort. Being parted from family during an air raid took every ounce of willpower not to run from the place of work and dash home. Yet hundreds of mothers held in their fears and worked on.

Having hugged her son, leaving him with yet another instruction about going into the garden shelter should the warning siren sound, Miriam ran along the street, her heart pounding when she saw the bus already at the bus stop. It wasn't so much the thought of being quartered, though losing money was far from unimportant in the Carson household, it was thinking how many shells remained unmade by folk coming late into work had her run the faster.

'Seen you comin', wench.'

Putting a steadying hand to Miriam's elbow as she skipped onto the platform, the conductor smiled and rang the bell for the vehicle to resume its journey.

'Can't 'ave you locked out can we? That would serve to mek the little Führer 'appy and that be the last thing me and Sam there would want to be a doin'.'

'Tell Sam I'm very grateful.' Breathy from her run Miriam's answer brought another smile, the elderly conductor nodding as he issued the twopenny ticket.

'Sam be sensible, he don't go pullin' away when he can see there be a body racing along a gettin' of the bus; and what matter be a few seconds set alongside what you women be doin'? It be you keeps our fighting forces supplied with what be needed to put the little Führer in his place; be sure the country won't never forget the efforts you all be mekin'.'

As the coins dropped into the leather bag slung from the conductor's waist, Miriam turned her gaze to the window. Beyond, the world seemed to lie in darkness, no shop showing a glimmer of light, no street lamp casting a pool of gold on the satin blackness; only a dark emptiness echoing the emptiness of her heart.

Efforts! Miriam caught her lip between her teeth. Women had worked alongside men since time began. It was not their efforts brought them heartache, it was the sacrifice . . . the losing forever of their loved ones, that was the burden could never be lifted from their hearts, the shadow which would never pass entirely from their soul. She had made that sacrifice once, please God she would never be called upon to do the like again.

She had the necessary papers. Alice sprinted the last few yards to the factory gates. That clerk along of the labour office had been very helpful explaining all that was needed to do.

Calling a quick 'tell you later' in reply to Becky's enquiring glance she hurriedly switched on her machine as the vigilant eye of the foreman settled on her. As she watched the silver ribbon of steel curve away in a spiral, Alice's lips drew together in a wry line. That woman had explained what it was she must do in order to join the Women's Services, but *getting* it done was something else again. It wasn't going to be easy; in fact, getting her mother to agree to allow her to leave home would be no less than fighting another war. But she would fight it!

Alice gave free rein to her imagination. She could run away from home . . . no, that wouldn't do, for she still would have no parental consent on the document nestling in her coat pocket. So it must be the way she had planned earlier, a withdrawal of labour. She would simply refuse to do any of her chores: Alice Butler would go on strike.

'Strike!' Becky had giggled while listening to her friend relate her lunch time visit to the Labour Exchange Office but now hearing the conclusion Alice had determined earlier, the laughter faded.

'Strike!' she repeated, 'you can't do that, you can't leave your mother to do all that extra housework herself.'

That was exactly the thoughts her mother would have. Alice's smile died. Her mother would not be beaten that way, she would simply set Mary to do the tasks she refused. Alice caught her lip on the guilt. Although not quite fourteen, Mary it would be and not one of their brothers. Though older and stronger they would not be called upon to lift a finger in the house; 'men went out to work, they earned the bread, they could not be expected to do a woman's work.' So what the hell was *she* doing?

Alice felt chagrin rise hot in her throat. What was she and thousands like her doing if not a man's work? Wasn't she in a factory day or night as shifts called for? Didn't she stand as many hours, produce as many bolts as any man? Yes she bloody did, and still she was expected to do half the household chores when she got home.

'If you refuse to help out at home might your mum refuse to give you pocket money?'

There was no 'might' about it. Alice recognised the flaw in her plan. Half a crown was nothing compared to the pocket money Kate Hawley got but it was the one means Alice had of expressing herself, the one and only way of deciding for herself the things she could have; the very occasional pair of silk stockings, the even rarer bottle of perfume, the lipstick, all of the treats her mother decreed as being 'frippery, a waste of good money'. Well, self expression she could live without until she came of age, after that her mother would have no hold over her. But in the meantime Mary would carry the burden she laid down. It was wrong to do that to her sister. Guilt flickered again in Alice.

Having led the way from the factory, blowing a cheeky kiss to the elderly gatekeeper as they passed, Becky resumed her cautionary advice.

'You should think a bit longer about what to do,' she said joining the interminable bus queue, 'I mean, even given the money we are allowed to keep we can't buy all the things we would like, but not having anything, that'll be awful!'

'It won't be pleasant.' Alice felt in her pocket for the return bus ticket she had bought that morning.

'Then don't do it, the factory isn't that bad.'

'*The factory isn't that bad!*'

Lying in the bed she shared with Mary, Becky's words rang in Alice's mind.

'. . . *isn't that bad.*'

She sucked in a long hard breath. The constant noise of machinery, the stink of slurry, that mixture of oil and water which clung to the air, which tasted on the tongue, seeped into every pore of the skin 'til it felt you were wrapped in a foul smelling shroud . . . that wasn't bad? Maybe not for Becky, but there was better for Alice Butler and she had to try for it.

The Women's Land Army. Memory flipped her back to the Labour Exchange Office. The woman she had spoken to there had said that division of the Voluntary Services was crying out for girls to join, maybe they wouldn't bother about parental consent. But the Land Army, that had been rejected even as it had been mooted and Alice rejected it again. Shovelling animal muck and grubbing in fields, where was the glamour in that? The ATS, the Auxiliary Training Service? Better than the Land Army but not so appealing as the WRNS or the WAAF, those uniforms were very fetching, she would look good in either.

But there would be all that yes ma'am, no ma'am business, all that being ordered left, right and centre for two shillings a day all found. Two bob a day! That amounted to almost six times what her mother allowed her and she could keep the whole lot to her herself! Fourteen shillings . . . and all hers. It was a heady thought. So much money and a uniform so sexy it had the head spin.

Money! Alice's half-closed eyes jerked wide. There was her answer, the solution to her dilemma. If she sent home, say, ten shillings every week, ten shillings not a penny of which would have to be spent on her keep, that might have her mother sign on the dotted line. Yes, her mother would go for that! Relief bringing a smile, Alice returned to her fantasy. Which should she go for, the WAAF or the WRNS? Light blue or dark blue, both uniforms were mouth watering but . . . eyes closing in sleep, her smile became one of pure content. Navy blue trimmed with gold braid, the Women's Royal Naval Service, that was the service she would join.

Dare she? Violet Hawley looked at the carefully folded lavender silk scarf lying in a drawer of her dressing table. Five pounds she had paid, five pounds for what Jim Slater had said was a bargain. But how much of a bargain if she could not use what she had bought?

As he stood on her doorstep, Jim Slater's small wide apart eyes had flicked along the street with the quick nervous motion of an animal under constant threat of being hunted.

'. . . *this be more than a bag of sugar or half a pound of tea but you 'ave to make your mind up now . . .*'

More than tea or sugar . . . then what? She had stared uncomprehendingly. He carried no bag, no newspaper-wrapped parcel, so what could he be offering?

'*. . . I ain't standin' here all day . . . either you be interested or you don't. If you are then I steps inside, if you says no then I'll be away, but this I'll tell for free, you won't go gettin' another chance like I be offerin' now, not in a long while you won't.*'

She had asked him in!

Violet stared at the scarf but saw only a pair of small eyes glinting back at her.

'*This'll make a big improvement to your life.*'

He had reached into an inner pocket of his too flashy coat, bringing out an ordinary brown envelope.

'*. . . what I 'ave in this packet can act like magic, certainly it can make your life much easier . . .*'

He had handed the envelope to her urging her to look at the contents.

'*. . . Didn't I say life could be easier?*'

Already thin lips had narrowed to a vulpine smile, sharp eyes never leaving her face.

'*Think of it,*' he had urged again, '*think of the benefits that can bring, I ain't sayin' it will 'ave life the same as it were a few years back but with what you holds in your hand it can certainly be a lot more comfortable, and at five pounds I reckon that to be a bargain you can't pass up.*'

She had not passed it up.

Lifting the scarf from the drawer, Violet placed it on the table top then peeled back the layers of soft lavender to reveal the slim buff coloured books, bold black lettering stating their purpose, the vacant space waiting for names to be added.

'Ration Book.'

The words had seemed to spring at her.

Double everything ... with these she could have twice the amount of food allowed now. Eight ounces of meat in place of four would mean a meat meal more than once a week, the same of bacon; a double ration of tea, sugar, butter, milk and even eggs which ever stricter rationing had reduced from one a week to one each fortnight, she would have two in place of one! She could have more of them all, all of the basics she missed so much.

'*Well if you don't want them . . .*'

It had taken no more than a moment for the ultimatum to sink in, no more than his outstretched hand for her to say yes . . . yes to buying something she had not dared bring into the light of day.

6

Harriet Simpson would not be returning to work.

Katrin's murmurs of sympathy hid the cream of satisfaction. Harriet's badly broken hip would be months in the mending and, given the stairs leading to the offices . . . she could not return to the office for quite some time.

'You worked with her for a while.' Arthur Whitman looked at the young woman seated on the other side of his desk.

'Almost four years, I joined the firm on leaving school. Miss Simpson thought I would be best placed working alongside her rather than in the general office.'

'Harriet had a good eye, she could be trusted to spot a worthy trainee.'

Maybe, but not good enough to spot a foot being thrust in front of her own.

'Miss Simpson was very kind, she took time and patience in teaching me the way of management in the office.' The quiet voice was touched with the right degree of regret, the calm eyes revealed nothing of the jubilation running in her veins. Katrin rested her glance on hands placed demurely in her lap.

'That is the reason I wish to speak to you, Miss Hawley. You ran things very well after Harriet's accident, I was impressed, not to say grateful, when I returned from my business trip.'

'Thank you, Mr Whitman, but it is Miss Simpson should have your thanks, anything I did is a result of her training.'

'That is as maybe, but putting that training into practice as smoothly as you did and under such circumstances, well . . . ! Once more you have my gratitude Miss Hawley.'

Gratitude! Katrin forced her fingers to remain loose though her insides clenched. Gratitude was all well and good but she wanted more, she was *entitled* to more. She had kept the wheels turning, she had been the go-between passing government requests for armaments to the various factory departments, she had seen to the ordering of steel, persuading foundry managers into extra deliveries, which was something even the excellent Harriet had been unable to do. But then Harriet Simpson had not been young and attractive with a figure to match; she had not the smile of promise glistening in her eyes.

'Harriet's unexpected retirement has placed me in somewhat of a quandary.' Arthur Whitman shook his head, a frown coming to nestle between straight black eyebrows. 'The employment office tells me they have no one of her experience. In fact they have no more workers to offer for the factory floor either.' The frown deepened. 'The government is taking men and women into the forces more quickly than they can be replaced by youngsters leaving school, and heaven knows every man and woman capable of walking has already returned to work. Those in Whitehall seem not to know . . .' He shook his head again, 'If the drain of employees goes on then the whole factory will come to a halt, and not only this one, but many more in Wednesbury and Darlaston. We all want to do our best but without the manpower our best will not be good enough to win this war. Sorry!' Arthur Whitman's tired eyes smiled from a face lined with weariness. 'I didn't mean to go on like that, I meant only to say thank you for a job well done.'

A job well done! That was it? She had hoped, she deserved to become Harriet Simpson's successor, yet Whitman had applied for someone else to fill that position.

Anger catching at her throat, Katrin kept her glance several moments longer on her hands. She would not let him see the resentment now icing inside.

'I am glad I was able to be of help, Mr Whitman.'

It had all been for nothing! Returning to her desk, Katrin fumed inwardly. She had been every bit as efficient as Harriet Simpson, foremen of both the day and night shifts had remarked upon deliveries coming on time, of shipments smoothly collected, in fact everyone had congratulated her on her management of the office side of it all, but congratulation was insignificant compared to what she had intended. She had opened the letter from the Employment Office and read the contents before carefully resealing the envelope, so she had known there was no candidate for

Harriet Simpson's post. Yet even with the assurance that she could do the job equally well, Arthur Whitman had not offered it to her. Why? Unless Arthur Whitman already had someone else in mind.

'Jacob Hawley, Violet Elizabeth Hawley.'

Violet looked at the books lying on the kitchen table. Her husband did not know she had bought stolen ration books; no one did, except for Jim Slater, and he was hardly going to tell anyone. But registering for meat and groceries in Wednesbury would be risky, she might be observed going into different shops. No, she must take these books out of town, Bilston maybe, or Darlaston. That was the nearer, she could register with Peark's or the Maypole for groceries and with Frank White or even Boynton's for meat. Yes, she would go to Darlaston.

The decision made, Violet slipped the precious books into her bag and carried it into the hall. She need not wait any longer, the hue and cry over that theft from the Town Hall had long since died down and with the imprisoning of that girl Freda Evans police enquiries had ceased. Five years! Violet felt her blood chill. Five years locked away in gaol, the disgrace of it! But it would be the derision of neighbours, the acrimony of those who had once been friends would prove the hardest to bear. Poor girl, she had probably been the pawn in some man's game, that man being Jim Slater or another he was in league with. And what of herself? Was she not as guilty as Freda Evans? Yes, every bit as guilty but there was one difference between herself and that girl: Violet Hawley would not have kept silent on where and how she had come by those stolen books. She would have made sure Jim Slater went down alongside her. But that danger was passed, now she could begin to reap the harvest her five pounds had sown.

Reaching for the coat that hung from a lovingly polished brass hook, Violet's hand stilled at a sharp knock to the door. Slater? No, he had been once today he would not risk a second visit. Jacob then, or Katrin, had an accident befallen either of them, had the factory sent a messenger to fetch her? Anxiety replacing conjecture, Violet opened the door, her heart retching into her mouth as she saw who stood there.

'Sorry to have to call on you this way.'

Violet felt her whole body chill.

'Might I step inside, Mrs Hawley, it will be more private.'

Private! Violet's brain jerked from its stupor her glance raking the windows of the houses opposite. Who had seen the man now standing on her doorstep?

She motioned the tall figure inside, closing the door sharply behind him. He was from the Civil Defence, someone with a message for Jacob. That's what she'd say to anyone who might enquire about her visitor. Violet's mind supplied the plausible answer. For a moment her world settled back into place, but that illusion shattered as he eased the strap from beneath his chin then removed the definitive helmet from his head, a helmet whose badge proclaimed him a member of His Majesty's Police Force.

The police! They must know what had lain hidden in the house, what was now in her bag!

Violet's agitated glance slid to the handbag on the hall table. Would he ask to see the contents? Would he search the whole house? Of course he would, those ration books could be the only cause of his coming here. But who had informed the police of her purchase? Not Slater. His informing against her would not only put an end to his highly illegal business but would see him behind bars for a very long time.

Dread shivered its way along Violet's spine. Freda Evans was behind bars. Had she talked? Had she decided not to bear the brunt alone? Had she divulged the name of a customer her fickle boyfriend had also supplied with stolen ration books?

She could deny it! The only proof lay in that bag, if she could get rid of the books then the police have no grounds upon which to base any charge. But to do that the policeman must be led away from the hall.

'Come . . .' The frightened quiver of her mouth strangled the effort to speak. She coughed then began again. 'Come into the sitting room.'

'No need for that, Mrs Hawley,' the policeman said politely. 'This business will only take a minute.'

Violet swallowed the sour taste of sickness rising in her throat.

'It has been reported to the station . . .'

Reported! Someone had informed against her!

'. . . therefore it is my duty . . .'

Drawn as though by a magnet, Violet's trapped gaze followed the hand raised to release the gleaming brass button of a pocket on his dark blue uniform.

'. . . in accordance with this . . .'

He held a fawn envelope.

'. . . I must ask you to accompany me to the station.'

7

Alice had delivered her ultimatum; allow her to volunteer for one of the Women's Auxiliary Forces or have a complete withdrawal of labour on her hands. Immersed in her thoughts, Alice paid no attention to the night foreman carefully measuring the dimensions of a screw she had cut from the length of revolving steel.

The reaction had been as she had expected. Her mother had refused in no uncertain terms. 'No daughter of mine be goin' to live along of a load o' men; there's never been a trollop in the family and it don't be a child o' mine be breakin' the mould.'

The words had been flung at her, her mother's face red with anger. But anger at what? Alice fed steel through the jaws of the machine, clamping them fast with a vicious push to a lever. At losing a daughter? No! More like losing a slave; the hours spent cleaning and polishing, ironing the mountain of laundry she had helped wash, getting older brothers' bait tins packed of a morning with sandwiches and bottles of tea to take with them to work and seeing younger ones washed and into bed of an evening: that and the wage packet she brought home each Friday.

Isaac Eldon touched her shoulder, an upraised thumb signalling approval of her work before placing the screw he had scrutinised into a box on one side.

At least somebody was satisfied!

Isaac replaced the micrometer in the pocket of his brown overall and pointed to the watch on his wrist. 'Five minutes.' He mouthed the words, exaggerating each in order to convey them clearly over the noise of machinery, repeating them once more before moving on to the next machine.

She would get what she wanted. Alice felt a swift surge of determination. Her mother could continue to withhold her pocket money, she could continue with her threats of 'not another stitch d'you get wi' my buyin', not another thing 'til y' comes to your senses.'

I won't be missing much! The mental retort had Alice's clenched teeth press harder with frustration. She hadn't had anything except what she bought for herself since she was fourteen years old so what was there to miss? What else could her mother deny her?

Slurry oil spilled onto revolving steel showering a thousand milk white droplets. Alice stared at the delicate snowy ballet dancing over the metal, each pearly drop leaping back into the air like some tiny gossamer-winged creature. Choice. Choice was what could be denied her. Until she was twenty-one choice was what her mother decided; she could and would exercise that in a manner to suit herself. Control! At fourteen she had to work for her living, at eighteen she must play her part in fighting this war yet not for another three years could Alice make decisions for herself.

A Step Too Far

At the nightly signal denoting completed armaments were to be removed from the factory, Alice switched off her own machine. In one minute the rest would fall silent. Shaking her head at Becky's call to come into the canteen, she wiped her hands on a cloth already stained with oil then took her packed lunch to where she could watch the proceedings. This was a saving grace of working through the night; here she would watch a dance of a different kind, a lumbering yet somehow graceful dance.

Alice's spine tingled. This was as good as going to the pictures, it was better than watching any gangster film.

Biting into her bread and margarine – canteen lunches cost money her mother said they could not afford – the blood in her veins chilled into delicious ice. There in the almost blackness came the sound of something moving, something which growled deep and ominous.

Perched on her wooden crate, Alice pressed into the shadows. If Isaac Eldon spotted her he would order her away to take her lunch break with the rest of the workforce in the canteen.

At the further end of the workshop, veiled in mysterious darkness the sound of movement came again.

Almost afraid to blink lest it be heard above, that harsh whoosh of breath drawn into massive lungs, that deep animalistic threat as it was exhaled, Alice felt her senses jar. Bread sat unswallowed on her tongue. Soon would come that slithering swish which in her mind became the sliding of some gigantic reptilian body, a gorgon such as she had trembled at when listening to the story of Medusa, a grotesque demon capable of killing her with a glance. Fuelled by fantasy, an exquisite thrill of fear rushed through her. Yes, this was definitely the equal of sitting in that flea pit of a cinema unrealistically called 'The Odeon'. Odeon! She giggled almost choking on a lump of bread, odious would be far more apt.

A few yards away Isaac Eldon called an instruction and moments later came the creak of doors being pushed open. Despite herself, Alice drew a sharp breath. It always affected her this way. It seemed the whole end wall of the workshop slowly vanished allowing moonlight to cast its magic over silent machines, to touch levers and pulleys until they appeared to float in a world of silver, a world revealed to her only through the darkness of war.

Sandwich lying forgotten in her hand, Alice slipped into a half forgotten world of softly silvered stillness, the world of childhood, of sitting at a bedroom window staring into the hush of a summer night, breathing the scent of sleeping gardens that for those precious moments overcame the smell of coke-fired furnaces and factory smoke. It had been a world of hope, the years ahead a blank canvas on which she would design a beautiful life.

'All set this end.'

The call acted swiftly on Alice, winging her from childhood into the present.

Turning her glance from the velvety patch of moon filled sky she peered into the depth of shadow clouding the opposite end of the dim lit workshop.

Now! It would be now!

'Right Harry . . .'

Isaac Eldon's quiet instruction echoed on the following moment of silence, on a peace she knew would soon be shattered.

'. . . bring 'er up.'

Then she saw it. Looming out of the shadows, red eyes blinking, lungs belching, a huge body dragging toward her. For a long, heart-stopping moment it seemed the red eyes looked directly at her, that the growl of approval was a threat intended for her. The delicious thrill suddenly became genuine alarm. Any interruption in its progress would bring Eldon to find the reason and that reason would be her! That would lead to more than a telling off: she could possibly be sacked. Isaac Eldon was a fair man in his dealings with the factory hands, he had a ready smile and a cheering word, sometimes even turning a blind eye to some prank, unlike his counterpart Bert Langford; but safety regulations were something he would not suffer to be flaunted and her being here right now was a breach of regulations.

The sack! What would her mother have to say about that? About the shame of having a member of the family dismissed from their job?

This could have proved one caper too many, putting her job at risk simply to observe the 'steamboat' in action. Alice allowed herself a smile of relief. The creature of her lurid imagination was none other than the 'steamboat', the huge steam-operated crane used to lift and carry crates of large shell forgings and cartridge cases out onto waiting transport. Shrouded in secrecy, the removal of armaments taking place only at night under the protective cover of darkness had earned the works the unofficial title of 'Shadow Factory'. That secrecy was paramount if German spotter planes were not to discover the location of the town's heavy industrial plants, and secrecy was the more observed by workers being required to take their longer meal break at the time of equipment transportation. 'What was not seen could not be talked about' was the criterion by which the 'Shadow Factory' was run, and it would be better for her should Isaac Eldon not find out what Alice Butler had seen.

She had not told Jacob about being taken to the police station nor had she mentioned it to Katrin. Now she would not have to. Back in her living room Violet looked at the letter on her lap. It was no use trying to deny having received it: that trick had brought a visit from the police. Try it again and she would go to prison. Those had been the words of the magistrate she had been summoned to appear before.

'*I recognise the distress appearing before this Bench is causing you . . .*'

Iron grey hair, horn-rimmed spectacles which he had peered over more than through, the magistrate had looked at her from a table set on a dais, his voice firm yet not without sympathy.

'*. . . I understand your anxiety . . .*'

How could he possibly understand how it felt? What being taken to the police station by a uniformed policeman did to a woman like her, the wife of a works manager. She had tried not to see the stares of people they had passed on that walk along Spring Head, tried to ignore the gossip as she had crossed the Market Place, but every step had been utterly humiliating. Then, a week later she had been summoned to attend the Magistrates' Court at Wolverhampton.

'. . . *now you too must understand . . .*'

Words which had burned like living flame in her mind flared again.

'. . . *you have three times been notified of compulsory registration for ancillary duty, for work outside of your home and which for reasons we need no further discuss you failed to do. Therefore, it is now my duty to inform you, Mrs Hawley . . . that should you fail to comply with the order issued by this court then I will have no other option than to have you confined to prison for the duration of the war.*'

The order had come yesterday. Violet touched the envelope lying in her lap.

'. . . you are ordered to report . . .'

Each word was like some physical entity imprisoning her limbs so she could not move. There was no mistake.

'. . . you are ordered to report . . .'

There was no need to check again, the words of the official document danced on her vision.

'. . . to the Personnel department of . . . TITAN ENGINEERING, DARLASTON.'

How could the government send her there? How could they expect her to work in a place that would have her clothes stinking like those of women she was sometimes forced to stand alongside when they had dashed from the factory to the shop during their midday break? It was intolerable. But to reject this order would result in a far more dreadful penalty.

Perhaps she should explain, should write to the magistrate asking to be assigned some other place of work, to any factory other than TITAN ENGINEERING, the factory where her husband was manager.

8

Isaac Eldon! Temper lending speed to her feet, Katrin walked quickly along Lower High Street.

Why had Arthur Whitman thought to bring that man to management?

She almost spat the question aloud.

'*You have done a valiant job, Miss Hawley.*' Arthur had smiled at her across his wide-topped desk. '*But it is one I cannot ask you continue.*'

She had done a valiant job but she could not continue!

Had he seen the consternation in her eyes? That sense of shock turning to anger, a cold vicious anger which deepened when he had gone on to say . . . '*the responsibility is too much for a woman as young as yourself to carry and with the continuation of war then the burden can only increase, therefore I have asked Isaac Eldon to take on the post of works manager.*'

The rest of what Arthur Whitman had said had barely registered over the turmoil seething in her head.

Isaac Eldon would be works manager: he was thoroughly conversant with every aspect of the forging of steel; he would take responsibility for production but even with that load removed from this office he was loath to ask she replace Harriet Simpson.

'*Why?*'

It might have seemed like anxiety at the prospect of being told she was no longer required, but its progenitor had been the demon she had long served, the demon of bitterness. But she had kept that hidden, merely asking quietly if her work had proved in any way inferior to that performed by the older woman?

Deep brown eyes had flashed quick apology. She had proved admirable in all she had done, but he paused, a hand flicking through hair that daily became more liberally sprinkled with grey, Harriet had years of experience.

'*But,*' she had answered swiftly, '*you have said Miss Simpson will not be returning; as for experience that comes only from being allowed to try and that is what I ask, Mr Whitman, that I be allowed to try.*'

She had the benefit of Harriet's tutoring . . . she had managed exceptionally well on her own . . . had taken up the reins . . .

He had mused aloud, fingers pressing worriedly at his temples, then in a tone remorseful as that quick glance, '*If you are sure, Miss Hawley, then you have my gratitude.*'

Gratitude! Gratitude but not trust. Katrin Hawley was not to have quite all of the authority the blessed Harriet had enjoyed, rather she should refer to Eldon on those occasions Arthur Whitman was absent.

She paused at the kerb of the busy road, waiting to cross to where an imposing coyned building marked the corner of Hollies Drive. There was an assortment of vehicles: lorries with their loads concealed beneath tarpaulin sheets, vans with names and logos painted out, all were devoid of reference to street or town, nameless of origin or destination, they simply passed anonymous and unrecognised.

But she would not go unrecognised. No, the name of Katrin Hawley would become well known at Prodor. But for the time being she must accept the fact of Isaac Eldon becoming works manager. Oh yes, she would defer to Eldon, only not in the manner he or Arthur Whitman expected.

The thought brought a smile as she darted across the road, but on reaching the turning for Hollies Drive, she was flung backward, her shoulder hitting the wall of the graceful building as she collided with a figure emerging from its entrance.

Some sixth sense had prevented her posting that request to the Magisterial court, some desperate last-minute warning sounding in her brain as she had sealed the envelope.

'It will be seen as one more refusal and you will be sent to prison.'

Leaving the bus at Darlaston Bull Stake, Violet Hawley breathed deeply, trying to still the trembling.

'Prison! Prison!'

Why had he not listened? Why had he not understood a woman such as she, the wife of the manager of a large engineering factory, could not possibly be sent out to work? She had explained the social implication, but the man had merely shaken his head, saying everyone alike must play their part in fighting this war, even the wife of a factory manager.

How could she go there? Think of the humiliation not only for herself but for Jacob. What effect might it have on his position, having a wife working on the factory floor? But there was no alternative.

Caught in the maelstrom of her thoughts, only half aware of the constant noise of traffic following the road which ran on into Walsall, Violet rested her glance on a building opposite. Dark with soot, serene with age, the church of All Saints seemed to stand aloof from the happenings around it.

There! Violet almost cried her relief, she could go into that church, sit in its quiet peace, there she would be given the help she needed, there everything would sort itself into place.

It had been such an ordeal walking with that police constable through Wednesbury town, knowing every eye turned to her, every tongue spoke of her.

Her prayer finished, Violet huddled in the corner of a deeply shadowed pew, her mind treading again that shame-filled path.

Then had come the court appearance. She had been so terrified, so sure someone had revealed her dealings with Jim Slater, that she was being called to answer for buying black market goods, for illegally holding two extra ration books, even though she had destroyed them the moment she had returned from the police station.

It had lifted a weight from her heart when that had not been mentioned, but the weight which lay now on her shoulders was just as heavy.

A Step Too Far

There had to be a way!

At the end of a long aisle a white draped altar graced with a tall cross at its centre gleamed in the late afternoon sunlight.

Please God show her the way!

You should have told Jacob of the letters. Answer echoed back from the sunlit altar. He could have intervened; had he asked then maybe you would have been placed elsewhere, perhaps one of the Civil Restaurants.

Helping to serve meals, that would not have been so awful, at least it would not involve getting her hands and clothes smeared with dirt. Tears for what might have been spilled onto Violet's cheeks.

'*But even that you thought beneath you.*'

The voice was suddenly that of her sister. '*You couldn't bring yourself to do that, same as you couldn't bring yourself to tell Jacob o' them letters, o' your thrusting them back o' the fire, oh no not you, Violet Hawley knowed best . . . well look where that best brought you, you be standin' outside o' prison gates.*'

Violet jerked upright as the bellow of air raid sirens sounded the alert.

She had to take shelter. When caught on the street you had to share the protection of the nearest house, that was the official directive. But that might be someone just returned from the engineering works, or even an iron smelting foundry, who hadn't time enough to have washed and changed their clothing!

Repulsed by the prospect Violet shrank back against the wooden seat; she wouldn't do it, she wouldn't!

But then she didn't have to.

Nobody knew she was here.

She could stay until the raid was over. It was safe here, this building was strong as any garden shelter.

And her appointment with TITAN?

That would keep. Violet smiled toward the glistening altar. There could be no qualms at lateness caused by an air raid.

'Mr Eldon said I could come.'

Mr Eldon had given permission! Biting back the acrimony the explanation stirred in her, Katrin smiled at the young woman before her desk.

'I wanted to see you on your own, I . . . I didn't want Becky knowing . . .'

Katrin waited out the pause.

'. . . it be this,' Alice held out a paper. 'Mother changed her mind, her said as I could join the WRENS, seeing as how I'd set my mind to it, though between you and me I think my saying her could take all of my pay 'cept for a shilling was what decided her.'

'Well whatever spurred her decision I'm pleased for you Alice; you can leave those forms with me, I will see Mr Whitman gets them.'

'I ain't come to hand them in, not yet.' Beneath the turban scarf tied about her head, Alice blushed an embarrassed pink. 'There be some questions I don't be too sure how to answer and I thought . . .' she swallowed, obviously finding it hard to admit the rest, '. . . I thought you with your grammar school education . . . well I hoped you'd help.'

Katrin's smile revealed none of her pleasure at having the girl who had called her a cheat ask for help. Would it feel even more pleasurable to refuse? No. She took the paper from the other girl's hand. There was more enjoyment yet to be got.

'Of course.' She laid the document on the desk. 'Glad to do anything I can. I don't have time to go through it right now, is it all right for me to take it home?'

'Thanks, Kate.' Alice beamed. 'I won't forget, and if there be anything I can do for you then you need only ask.'

Katrin's smile deepened. There was nothing that girl could ever do for her, and as for this – she slipped the paper into her bag – Alice Butler would certainly not forget.

9

'I thought they would have explained all of that when you collected the application form.'

Katrin glanced at the crestfallen Alice. She had anticipated this moment from reading the forms the other girl had asked her to check over, but anticipation had not matched the satisfaction coursing through her at this moment, the sheer gratification of watching disappointment register on the oil-smudged face.

'You see,' she went on, elation expertly submerged beneath the parody of sympathy, 'to join the WRNS requires you hold certain qualifications and you do not have them. I'm sorry Alice, truly I am.'

Truly! Katrin disguised her glee with a rueful smile. Nothing could be further from the truth.

'What qualifications might they be then? Oh don't bother to tell me.' Alice rejected her own question. 'If I ain't got them then I ain't. I should have known it took more of an education than I had, thanks anyway Kate, but . . .' she hesitated, 'if I don't have the necessary for to join the WRNS, then mebbe's I should try for the WAAF.'

'You can try, of course.' Katrin nodded, 'But it seems they also have certain requirements.'

Alice shrugged resignedly. 'I suppose the ATS don't be any different.'

She could leave it there, let Alice Butler walk back to the workshop; but that would be to curtail the pleasure, and why would she do that?

Katrin watched the figure turn to leave then said, 'The ATS does have some exceptions, there are two branches of that Service which require no qualifications.'

'What branches do they be?'

Delight transformed the other girl's face, delight which Katrin Hawley could dampen at a stroke.

'They may not be quite what you wanted, Alice, they call for volunteers for Orderly Duties.'

'Orderly Duties!' Alice's features registered disillusion. 'Does that mean what I take it to mean? They're asking for folk to go cleaning up after others?'

'I think it would incorporate that, possibly along with kitchen work.'

'You mean skivvying! Cooking and bloody cleaning!' Alice's turbaned head swung side to side. 'I get that at home, no need to go running off to find it, but there again Kate, at home I get my mother grumbling at everythin' I do. At least Orderly Duties ain't going to include looking after kids.'

'Does that mean you wish to apply? I left the forms blank just in case.'

'Too bloody true I wish. Thanks, Kate, you be a real friend.'

A real friend! Katrin's glance dropped to the papers in her hand. Then it was to be hoped Alice Butler did not meet with a false one.

Venom hidden with that expertise years of custom had bestowed, she glanced again at the girl she could so easily deceive, her smile a continuation of duplicity.

'Do I take it, then, I should go ahead and fill these in, or would you rather do that yourself?'

'You do it Kate, please, you're better at that sort of thing than I am.'

'The ATS it is then, Miss Butler. I will have these done for you as soon as I can.'

Not that time would make the slightest difference. With her help Alice Butler would most definitely *not* be joining any of the Women's Auxiliary Forces, in fact she would never get to the asking point.

Alice had regaled Becky and herself with complaints about her mother a dozen times over. Now she would discover parental consent was not all that was needed; Katrin had noted the relevant paragraph and it had brought a genuine smile.

'. . . where the applicant could be released from present employ . . .'

The government had made it so easy. That one stipulation provided a way of retribution which could in no way reflect upon her.

Smiling down at the papers Katrin took up a pen.

This was the weapon with which she would strike.

She had trodden the path carefully. Her first act had been to make a count of male employees due for conscription within the month. Then she had looked up the number of youngsters having applied for employment with the end of the school year and discovered one in no way compensated for the other. She had rung the Labour Exchange Office asking did they have notice of men or boys needing employment? The answer being no had added beneficially to her plan yet she had continued those enquiries directing them at the various schools throughout the town and again fortune had smiled. There were no pupils of an age to leave education who were without firm promise of a situation within industry.

Looking at the figures she had recorded, Katrin's inner glow was that of congratulation. Deficit between men being called to the forces and the availability to replace them was an ever widening gap, a gap which must be filled by women.

Sure now she had overlooked nothing, she tapped at the door of Arthur Whitman's private office.

'The new intake, pass them along to Isaac Eldon.'

Katrin felt a moment's irritation.

'Of course, Mr Whitman.' She replied smoothly not allowing vexation to colour her answer. 'But then he will need refer back, so I thought showing these to you beforehand might save time.'

'Oh? Let's see them then.'

He scanned the results then threw the papers down with a short breath of exasperation.

'How the hell am I expected to keep up production when I continue to lose manpower? Do they think I can manufacture workers the way I manufacture armaments? Twelve men going,' he dropped his head into his hands, 'and eight to take on their jobs and no lad older than fourteen, they can't possibly manage the heavier machinery! What do I do? Without folk to work then we will have machines lying idle.'

'I realised that problem when getting the numbers ready for Mr Eldon, which is why I ventured to ask your decision on another issue before handing those papers on to him.'

'*Another* issue, well why not?' Arthur Whitman's laugh was pure dejection. 'The barrel will always take one more apple.'

'One of the girls is applying to join the Auxiliary Services, she needs employer consent.'

'One more leaving the sinking ship!'

'Very probably more than one, Mr Whitman.' Katrin launched the first of the reserve of lies she had drawn up. 'There are several others of the same mind, I have heard them discussing it.'

'These others, who are they?'

'I'm sorry, Mr Whitman, do not ask me to reveal names, it would be a breach of confidence, I would feel I was letting friends down. However, I can tell what Mister Eldon will corroborate: all the girls of an age to join the Forces are employed in the production of the heavier armaments.'

'I appreciate your not wishing to name your friends Katrin, it is to your credit . . .'

He had taken to using her Christian name. One more step in the direction she determined to lead him!

'. . . but the fact remains, the more labour drained from the factory the less equipment we can provide for use at the Front. Those women wanting to leave must surely see they are paying Peter by robbing Paul; no matter what they may be called upon to do, it cannot possibly compare in importance to what they do here: the Army can't fire bullets they don't have, Naval guns are useless without shells and the same applies to the Air Force, they can fly their planes but without ammunition how can they attack or defend? No!' He slammed a hand onto the desk. 'We have to get our priorities right and if that means refusing to release women from the factory then so be it!'

He had refused. So much for Alice Butler and her dreams.

Katrin took the papers to the general office, handing them to a junior clerk with the instruction they go to Isaac Eldon. He could be the one to pass on the disappointing news.

Freda Evans and Alice Butler. Two she had dealt with. But one yet remained.

It had been this way for over a week. Miriam Carson threw on her coat, buttoning it as she ran.

There had been virtually no let up, no respite from the threat of planes throbbing overhead, of the thud of bombs which seemed to shake the very earth and through it all the constant harrowing fear for the safety of loved ones.

Reuben! She drew a ragged breath, tasting smoke from a burning building. He would have been at home when the alert sounded, alone in the house; a boy of scarcely twelve years old alone while hell broke loose around him. She fought back a sob. Why did it have to be like this? A mother should be with her child in time of danger.

She flinched as a distant thud echoed across the night. War was the reason, war was the culprit and people its victims; men who had no choice but to fight, mothers who had no option but to leave their children to the care of others, as she was forced to leave her son.

'Get off the street, get into a shelter!'

Ignoring the ARP warden, Miriam sped on. She would take shelter when she had Reuben safe in her arms.

Would he have done as he was told when the sirens warned of a raid? Would he have joined next door in their garden shelter?

Yes, yes Reuben would be with neighbours. Forced to slow to a walk by the stitch snatching at her ribs, Miriam felt a moment's comfort. Her son was a sensible boy.

But what if Reuben were not home? He had taken to visiting the library after school, spending hours there working on some project. She had questioned why he could not work at home the same way he had always done his homework.

'*Can't mum.*' He had smiled his father's smile, that gentle half grin. '*Not for this. The books I have to look at can only be used for reference, they can't be taken out. But that's okay, I quite like working in the library.*'

But that meant he would have been made to evacuate the building when the alarm was given. Had he decided to head for home? Was he somewhere out on the streets, was he maybe . . . ?

'You oughtn't to be on the street.'

The policeman turned away, the brittle clang of fire engines and crashing masonry calling his attention.

Fire! Buildings falling in on people, bombs screaming at them from the skies, horror they could hear, terrors they could not see; only pain . . . pain to leave them maimed, death reaching for them in the darkness.

'Oh God!' Miriam cried aloud, 'not for Reuben, not for Reu . . .'

A sudden mind-shattering explosion ripped the air like no thunderstorm she had ever witnessed, and the blast hurled her to the ground.

Winded, her senses reeling and her ears ringing, Miriam felt herself being lifted to her feet.

'You'll be all right, no bones broken, but best you be taken to a First Aid Post.'

Miriam frowned. Was it her father speaking?

'Come on,' the voice said again, 'better have you looked at, could be a bit of concussion.'

Not her father. Tom then, was it Tom?

'That were a big one.' The attempt to reassure, to comfort continued. 'Seems the Gerries have got wind of the steel foundries and heavy munitions factories, that's what them bombers be after, knock them out and it leaves this country worse off than ever. But I reckon they scored a blank with that one.'

Miriam found herself walking, though her limbs seemed made of water. Not Tom. Miriam's mind fingered the darkness hovering over it. Reuben, it must be . . .

Reuben! Mind and body flashing together in unison she shook off the supporting hands. She had to get to

A Step Too Far

Reuben! It had been a bomb! A bomb so near it had thrown her off her feet! But where had it struck?

Then she knew.

Anguish tearing the soul of her she stared.

Ahead, in the direction she must go, a great vivid sheet of orange flame ripped along the skyline.

Fear lent her strength to run on, ignoring the bite of pain beneath her ribs, mindless of the crash of tumbling walls and roof slates, oblivious of all but one thought: Reuben, she must get to Reuben!

The house was still standing. Sobbing with relief Miriam hurled herself along the terrace darting into the entry that gave access to the house she shared with her father.

Reuben would be there, his grandfather would be with him, they were both safe.

'I be sorry Miriam, wench . . .'

Numbed by shock Miriam made no answer.

'. . . the lad said he were goin' along o' the library, said he would come home along of yourself and that bein' so, I didn't come to fetch 'im to the shelter when the bulls blew. Had I knowed there were goin' to be a raid then o' course I wouldn't have let him go to the library; but that be the trouble, there be no tellin' when them bombers be goin' to come and you can't keep kids chained up, they need some freedom if they're goin' to be sane at the end o' this war.'

Even in her fear Miriam recognised the truth of her neighbour's words.

'But the library would have closed.' She turned to the woman who had come into the house on hearing her return, 'He would have come home, he promised always to come home, to go into the shelter, Reuben would not break his promise.'

'The shelter!' The woman's face drained of blood, 'Oh God, wench . . . we never . . .'

'Reuben!' Miriam's scream trailed behind as she fled into the garden and saw, in the reflected glow of the burning sky, the garden shelter buried beneath tumbled brickwork of the high boundary wall.

10

The police constable had come late that evening, asking to see her father.

Katrin stared at an enamelled box, its colours glinting in the light from a window.

Her father was not home, she had explained; he undertook volunteer duties each evening.

'My mother also is not at home,' she had continued, 'perhaps I might be of assistance.'

Helmet under one arm, the constable had slipped open the button on the breast pocket of his uniform, drawing from it a pencil and a slim notebook, juggling them awkwardly in his attempt to write.

'Might you know your mother's whereabouts?'

'I might not.' It had been clipped, precise, cold as the frost in her eyes.

He had glanced at the clock at the foot of the stairs, asked her to inform her father of his having called, then left.

Her father had looked haggard and drawn on his return from the police station, shock written deep across his face. Was that how she had looked when opening this box for the first time? Yet there had been something other than shock in the glance he had lifted to her, there had also been guilt.

Guilt! Katrin lifted the lid of the box she had taken from a drawer. Was that look in his eyes caused by what he too had known lay here? She had not asked then, she would not ask now.

Returning the box, drawing back into position the scarf which had covered it, she walked from the room.

'Ashes to ashes, dust to dust.'

Miriam watched the group of people gathered at the graveside, women dabbing tears of sympathy, men glancing surreptitiously at wrist or pocket watch. Absence from work was not lightly taken, even to attend a funeral, for it meant loss of wage to family and loss of production vital if the war was also not be lost.

Watching the coffin being lowered gently into the ground, Miriam shuddered. War had claimed so many lives, taken the hearts from so many more.

'Steady girl.' Isaac had felt the shiver. 'It be all over.'

Tears stinging her eyelids, Miriam clutched the rough hand closing over hers. Would it ever be really over, would the pain ever fade?

Looking at the girl visibly fighting an inner battle, Isaac's own heart tripped. They had come to a church, to a house of God, to ask mercy for the dead and a blessing for the living but it was hard to see mercy among so much suffering.

'You'll both be comin' for a cup of tea.'

'It needs be a quick one.' Isaac answered his sister. 'I

said I would be back to the factory as soon as the funeral were done.'

'That were Jacob's answer.' Ella Robson shook her head. 'He says he must go straight off but I wouldn't 'ave thought the wench needed do the same, it ain't as if her work be on munitions.'

'We all be needed.' Isaac's answer was conciliatory though his thoughts matched those of his sister. The girl would likely have been given a full day.

'Ar, some more'n others judgin' by the speed that one be goin'!' Ella glared toward the receding figure of Katrin Hawley. 'Remind me to back 'er in the Derby once horse racin' be on again.' Following up with an irritated 'tut', she turned to Miriam. 'Violet fair ruined that wench, brought her up to think herself better than the rest, but no good comes of that, mark my words, no good comes of that.'

'Aunt Violet acted as she thought best.' Miriam too was conciliatory.

Isaac glanced at Jacob, who followed a few steps behind his daughter, then back at Miriam. 'You go on with the others, I want a word with Jacob.'

'Ar wench, you come along home, a cup of tea be what you needs.'

No, she needed more than tea. Miriam looked at the mound of freshly turned earth, deserted now of mourners. That was all that was left of a life, a life ended by the impact of a bomb.

'I . . .' She swallowed hard, the grave with its flowers swimming in an ocean of hot tears, '. . . I'd like to go back into the church for a few minutes.'

Sitting alone in the graceful sandstone church of Saint Paul, Miriam gave herself up to the silence, to the memories so ready to envelop her.

She had run until it seemed her lungs would burst, run while her brain pounded one thought: she must get to Reuben, she must be with her son. When at last she had reached the house, every room was empty.

'. . . I be sorry Miriam, wench . . .'

She had heard no more, her screams drowning the rest of Isaac's words as she had thrown herself onto the heap of rubble, ripping it away with her bare hands. She felt nothing until strong arms had pulled her to her feet, holding her against a heaving chest. Breathless from his own running, her father had held her as close as on the day that fatal telegram had arrived.

But his voice could not penetrate the anguish in her brain, could not quell the torment of a soul once more ripped apart.

Neighbours had come from all around, working frantically to remove the fallen brickwork, but there had been no body pulled from beneath it, no boy inside the shelter.

Eyes still closed, Miriam looked on the scene showing like a film in her mind.

It seemed the world had stilled, the night had become silent except for one sound.

'*Mum.*'

It had been so quiet. The murmur of a child drawn from sleep.

Caught by the horror of those past minutes, she had clung to her father, desperate to throw off the trick her mind was playing. He had put her gently from him pointing to where a shape, dark and solid, loomed in the sudden brilliance of fresh flame scorching into the sky.

She had not wanted to look, had wanted only the comfort of her father.

'*Mum.*'

One simple word that rocked her senses. Then a gentle push from her father and she had run to the dog kennel, to where her son was crawling out, a puppy held in his arms.

'*Sorry I didn't go into the shelter . . .*'

Reuben had smiled sleepily.

'*Spot is frightened to go in there and I couldn't leave him on his own.*'

Miriam opened her eyes and stared at the cross centred on a plain white covered altar.

'Thank you,' she murmured, 'thank you for saving my son.'

He had returned from that police station his features grey and drawn, his head slumping onto his chest when Katrin had asked what was wrong. He lifted his eyes to hers and she had seen the guilt.

Those ration books missing from the drawer, had her mother taken them with her to use? Had he known? Was that the reason for the look of guilt? If she had been caught, there was only one consequence.

Prison!

Katrin's whole body had tensed.

Her mother would be sent to prison!

As she lifted dresses from a walnut inlaid wardrobe, Katrin flinched.

Jacob Hawley would be pointed at, shunned by colleagues and friends; but the same would be directed toward Katrin Hawley.

'*. . . folk round here won't want no truck with a wench convicted of dealin' on the black market . . .*'

Words said about Freda Evans rang in her mind.

The repercussion would be the same for her. As the daughter of a convicted criminal, she would be ostracised. But having the like of Alice Butler and Becky Turner, of the Eldons and the Robsons turn their back was of no significance. the danger lay in the position she had engineered for herself at Prodor. Arthur Whitman would break the links she had so carefully forged between herself and him, sever them easily as he had those moulded by Harriet Simpson.

Her mother had been a fool, a fool to buy those ration books and even more of a fool to try to use them!

'*Mother is . . .*'

Tea had spilt into her saucer as her hand shook with rage.

'*Not at the Robsons'.*'

'*. . . nor was she with the Eldons, the police checked at both houses.*'

'*But I thought . . . when she was not home when I came from work . . . I thought she was shopping later than usual.*'

Despite the resentment that burned like coals, some inveterate self protection made the lie slip out.

A Step Too Far

Jacob had reached for her hand, clasping it a moment, then had gone into the hall, returning with a dust-covered bag.

'*The police gave me this.*' He had swallowed hard, struggling to bring out the rest. '*That is how they came to call here, the address was inside.*'

She had looked at the bag. Her mother was so very meticulous about her belongings.

Maybe she had not been arrested.

An accident then, there could be no other reason for her mother not being home; the police had thought it prudent the husband be first informed.

She had not been so flippant then, careful to mask the reassurance already cooling the flames of anger, the satisfaction of once more feeling herself secure. Inflecting a note of trepidation into the questions, she had asked where was her mother, had she been hurt?

She was found in Darlaston. There had been an air raid, the church of All Saints had been bombed. It was thought no one was inside and then . . . someone found that.' He had looked again at the battered handbag, his voice cracking as he went on. '*A few minutes later they found her, she . . . she . . . she was dead.*'

Her mother was dead.

It was Violet Hawley they had buried in Wednesbury Cemetery.

Violet Hawley was dead.

But Violet Hawley was not her mother.

11

They had sat beside her in the church, stood alongside her at the grave, commiserated with Jacob upon the loss of his wife. Violet's family, her sister and brother, had gone through the motions – their grief genuine enough, their sympathy also. But sympathy and truth had not gone hand in hand. They had not once spoken of that truth Katrin had carried so long inside, despite calling Violet Hawley her mother.

Would they have told her? Had that been the purpose of Ella Robson and the Eldons calling to herself and Jacob as they had walked from the cemetery?

Unconscious of the pen twisting in her fingers, Katrin listened to the questions in her mind. What had the three of them talked about there at the cemetery gate? Had it been Katrin Hawley they had discussed or had they used some other name? Had they mulled over the pros and cons of acquainting her with what they, their sister and her husband, had kept hidden?

Why had she not told them? Why had she not thrown their so carefully concealed secret in their faces?

The pen slipping from her fingers, Katrin smiled.

That was Katrin Hawley's secret!

'I couldn't take it in when Isaac Eldon said it'd been rejected.'

'Eh Alice, after all the time it took persuadin' your mother an' everything.' Becky Turner's look reflected disbelief.

'Huh!' Alice half laughed, 'Eldon shouldn't have the say of what we wenches can and can't do, it's our life after all.'

Shaking droplets of water from her hands Alice crossed to the communal towel, stained with oil and dust, on the wall of the washroom.

'Is it? I often wonder about that; if it ain't your parents telling you what you can't do then it be the government, and if not them then it's the folk you work for.'

'Well I think you should go tell Eldon that!' Becky's blue eyes gleamed affront.

Alice slipped the turban-tied scarf from her head. 'Wouldn't do no good.' She ran fingers through the wealth of brown hair. 'Seems it don't be Eldon's decision.'

Becky was indignant. 'Well if it don't be Eldon saying no then who is it, who else has joined the queue?'

A fitting description! Wasn't that what life seemed to hold for her? A long queue of people all wanting to direct her life, all so eager to tell her the wrongs of it, all more competent at running it than she was? She stared

A Step Too Far

at the colourful paisley design of the scarf in her bag. Her life was like the pattern on that cloth, its colours like her actions, following a line only to come up against another solidly blocking its progress.

'Well!' Becky demanded of the silence. 'So who is it has said you can't?'

Alice answered dully, 'It was Mr Whitman.'

'What!' Becky's exclamation brought glances from several other women washing their hands prior to leaving the factory. She lowered her voice. 'You reckons it were Whitman?'

'I don't have to guess, seeing it was his signature on the paper Isaac Eldon showed me.'

'I don't think you should take what Whitman says.' Becky waved goodnight to the gateman in his cubicle. 'You should go see him, tell him he's got no right to object . . . ain't that so Kate? I was saying as how Alice ought to go see Whitman, tell him boss of Prodor he might be but that don't make him boss of us girls, it ain't up to him to tell any woman her can't go leavin' the factory.'

'Sorry!' Katrin said, a small frown lending illustration to her voice. 'I don't know what it is you are talking about.'

'Whitman!' Becky answered hotly, with fresh outrage at what she saw as an insult to her sex. 'Men can go, oh yes, he can't go refusin' them, but let a wench ask and it be a different story.'

So Alice Butler had been given the verdict, informed of her rejection. A rejection whose grounds had been so carefully construed by Katrin Hawley.

'I don't understand, Becky.' She answered quietly though triumph shouted in her brain. 'What has Mr Whitman done that has you so annoyed?'

Clambering onto the loaded bus, juggling with handbag and gas mask while holding onto an overhead metal rail, being jerked almost off her feet as she felt for the return ticket in her coat pocket, Becky let her irritation ride. 'Done!' she snapped. 'He's turned Alice down flat, that's what he's done.'

Katrin glanced at the silent Alice.

'Mr Whitman has turned you down?'

'Tell her Alice, go on . . . tell Kate what he's done, tell . . .'

'Turk's Head!'

The three of them squeezed past other standing passengers until they were free of the vehicle.

'Ain't good enough!' Becky declared emphatically. 'Ain't as though we was kids at school, they need be told what they can do, but shouldn't be the same for a wench who is eighteen and more, what do you reckon Kate?'

The cover of blacked-out streets hid the smile curving Katrin's mouth, but she carefully maintained her previous act of innocence as she answered. 'I really can't reckon anything seeing as you have not yet said what appears to have gone wrong.'

'It be my application,' Alice blurted. 'The one to join the Forces, it hasn't been granted.'

'But you can't know that. C'mon Alice, you didn't complete the forms until yesterday, they can't possibly have been processed by the recruitment centre and returned to you already.'

'Ain't the recruitment centre, they couldn't have found any fault, you know that Kate. It were you filled out them forms, you seen everything I said was true.'

But not everything Katrin Hawley had said. Alice Butler had been so very thoughtless, so trusting. She had accepted all that had been told to her, all she had been led to believe.

Led! Katrin hugged the word. Alice Butler had been led along a painful path and Katrin Hawley had held the halter.

It was all becoming too much for him. Miriam Carson looked at the figure slumped in an armchair, weariness written in deep lines across his face. It had been a kind thought on the part of Arthur Whitman: promotion to works manager had been a vote of his confidence in her father, but with promotion had come problems. Arthur Whitman ought to have foreseen that. He knew Isaac Eldon for a man who would not forego one task in favour of another, but would do both. That was what he was doing now, two jobs at the same time. She had tried reasoning, tried to get him to agree he was overworking, but he had simply smiled and shaken his head.

Going into the kitchen, Miriam added salt to the potatoes she had peeled earlier and set the pan to boil.

'*I have no liking for bein' tied all day in some office.*'

He had admitted that much, so why had he consented?

'*Just for a while. It be difficult finding somebody suitable what with so many men being called up; but not to worry yourself, I'll manage until Whitman can find the man he wants.'*

So her father believed, but managing two jobs was wearing him out . . . when would he believe that? Shredding cabbage, Miriam blinked against her own weariness.

'. . . not to worry yourself . . .'

Words so easy for a man to say, but how easy for a woman to accept when her every day was filled with anxiety for those she loved, when every hour held the possibility of war depriving her of them?

Crumbling an Oxo cube into a half cup of hot water, Miriam stirred it into a pan of fried onion.

War! She watched the mixture brown and thicken.

War was the Devil's instrument, a multi-purpose tool designed to persecute; and how many ways he used it. Bomb, shell, bullet they were all his bringers of death, but death was finite, an ending of pain. So when that was not the outcome? When fire and falling buildings burned and crippled the body, when heartbreak and worry tortured the mind, when desolation maimed the soul? That was when the Devil smiled.

'Shall I set the table, mum?'

She wanted to take her son into her arms, to hold and not let go.

To hold and not let go. Smiling through her tears, Miriam looked at the lad taking cutlery from a drawer. What would Reuben say to that!

'Just you and me mum, granddad said to put his meal in the oven.'

'Oh did he!' Miriam glanced toward the living room. 'Well you just tell your granddad he is to come eat it now, with us.'

'Can't mum, he's already gone.'

'Gone?'

'Two minutes ago. Said he had to go back to the factory.' Setting condiments on the table Reuben gave a puzzled look. 'When I asked why, seeing he had been there all day, he didn't answer . . . have I done something has made him angry with me?'

'No . . . no, of course not.'

'But granddad always talks to me, yet tonight . . .'

'Granddad is tired.' Miriam replied quickly.

'Then why go back to work? Why not stay here and rest?'

Why indeed? Miriam returned to the pans bubbling on the stove. She knew war was driving everyone to do their utmost, but what was driving her father beyond that point?

What was it had Isaac Eldon at Prodor all day and much of the night? After the meal, Miriam sat beside the fading living-room fire. As much in short supply as every other commodity, coal was too precious to allow holding fire in the grate any longer. She reached for a blanket always kept ready against a night raid and drew it about her shoulders.

Reticence, withdrawal into himself, reluctance to be drawn into conversation – Reuben too had noticed the change in his grandfather.

Was it the death of his sister? He had grieved for months for those two brothers killed at Ypres during the Great War, two whose photographs hung on a wall in his bedroom. Two brothers dead on the same day. How could he forget? Now that sorrow was added to by fear of his son risking his life in an equally horrifying war. That she could understand, it was an agony ate at the heart, hadn't she suffered the same? That fear which rose afresh when letters from her brother did not come.

But she sensed this was a new cause of concern, one he could not bring himself to speak of her father's sadness had been obvious when standing at Violet's open grave. It had been made abundantly clear Violet Hawley's relatives were not there with the blessing of her daughter. Though Isaac and Ella had been brother and sister to Violet, it appeared quite plain the invitation to attend her funeral found no favour with her daughter. It had been Jacob Hawley had met with them at the church, Jacob who had talked with them while the girl had kept a cool distance. She had spoken to none of her mother's family, had not acknowledged them by so much as a nod, then as the priest finished the final invocation she had turned from the grave and walked away with no glance in their direction.

She had seen the hurt flash its signal across her father's eyes. Miriam's fingers clutched the corners of the blanket. Even as a young girl Katrin Hawley had shown no affection toward her mother's kin; now she was a young woman filled with spite, a vindictiveness it seemed she was ready to vent upon anyone. Jacob and Violet had reared her with all the care they could give, but it was to be regretted they seemed not to have taught her that malice and spite has a way of bringing its own reward. One day Katrin Hawley would find that out for herself.

12

'Eh Alice, I'm sorry you was turned down, it's a right shame, really it is.'

Katrin smiled remembering the words she had heard Becky Turner say as she had left the two to walk home. So it was a shame Alice would not be free of her mother, would not get to wear any glamorous uniform; but then Alice Butler should never have accused another girl of being a liar and a cheat.

Table cleared of the meal she had prepared for her father, she glanced about the kitchen. Everything was in its place, tidy, ordered, dealt with just as she had dealt with Freda Evans and Alice Butler. They had hurt the feelings of a young girl but had given a great deal of pleasure to a young woman.

She checked her father had locked the front door when leaving for his fire watch duties then went upstairs to her room.

Yes, repaying those two had been very pleasurable and it was an experience she would enjoy again.

'Eh Alice, I'm sorry . . .'

Catching her reflection in the mirror of the dressing table she stared back into eyes hard as stone.

'Don't waste all your sympathy, Miss Turner,' she murmured, 'save a little for yourself – you are going to need it. But you will not be alone in that, there are others also will know the way Katrin Hawley repays a slight.'

Pulling open a drawer, she touched a finger to a lavender silk scarf then drew the delicate fabric aside to touch the box it had covered. These two things were all that remained of Violet, the only personal possessions of the woman she had called mother. The rest, clothing and shoes, had been packed into boxes and donated to the Civic Centre where volunteers could hand them out to people who had lost everything to bombs and fire; but the scarf and the box she had kept.

As a memento of Violet Hawley?

She rippled the fine silk through her fingers.

No. She smiled, watching the cloth move and shine like water reflecting the pale mauve of early evening. No, she had not kept them in memory of Violet, but rather of what she and others were responsible for.

'No, *mother*! That memory will never die . . . but it will be avenged.'

She drew aside the heavy blackout curtain and allowed the clear moon to light the bedroom, then lay watching the reflection of breeze-tossed leaves dance their graceful movements on its walls.

Her father's cherished silver birch. Memories as soft as the silvered beams pirouetting to the silent music of the night whispered in Katrin's mind. He had planted the tree on the day she had come to them; he had nursed her beneath it, soothed her to sleep with the branches swaying in unison with his gentle words.

'Katrin's tree.' That was what her father had called it. Every birthday for as long as she could remember a prettily wrapped gift had hung from its branches and each Christmas Day he had gone with her to stand beneath it while he lifted down the special present left for her by Santa Claus.

Special days. They had been special days. It was before her teen years she had realised that only on those days, in the shelter of that tree, had the haunted, unhappy look disappeared from his eyes, a look they held even now on the rare occasions his mental guard slipped. It had slipped the evening he had returned from identifying his wife's body, the look she had taken to be that of guilt.

Guilt? Unhappiness? A mixture of both with one being responsible for the other? Whichever, the outcome was the same: Jacob Hawley was a man plagued by the past.

And his daughter?

She also was acquainted with that demon but it was a relationship she had at last begun to destroy.

Knowledge had been a wine too delicious to swallow in one gulp, it had needed to be sipped a little at a time, savoured, the sweetness captured in the throat before letting the delight of it seep into the soul.

But now the tasting was over.

She had put down the glass but the bottle was not yet empty. It still held the ambrosia of revenge and Katrin Hawley would drink deeply.

She had given no name, given no identification when making that telephone call. The government made some things so easy. You needed only to voice your suspicion; the name and address of the security conscious citizen was no requirement. That was how it had worked when she'd reported Freda Evans' black-market selling and it would work again this time. But there was one difference.

The consequence of that call would not be a five-year gaol sentence. Treason was a serious crime at any time, but betrayal of your country during war could only be counted the *most* serious and therefore bring the ultimate sentence.

One difference! She breathed long satisfaction. Execution constituted one very big difference!

She had worded the call carefully, injecting the right amount of uncertainty into her voice. '*I really don't feel . . . it might be just me imaginin' . . . I don't want to be a' gettin' o' nobody into no trouble . . .*'

She had hesitated over every fumbled sentence, wavering, seemingly unsure if she should continue, But there had been nothing she wanted more.

'*I don't be a one to go a' tellin' o' no lies . . .*'

She had gone on, local vernacular lending its disguise.

'*. . . but seein' them there papers . . . them drawrins . . . I means what wi' secoority the way it be, a'tekin' away o' every street sign an' all . . .*'

Had it been her mention of drawings, of security? Certainly when she had said those words the voice at the other end of the line had developed a deal more interest.

'*. . . I ain't a'wantin' to be no noosance.*'

The man urged her to go on, that it was right to inform him of any irregularity, and so she had.

The snare was set.

She would watch the rabbit walk into it.

'Oh God!' Miriam Carson's hand flew to her throat. 'Oh God no, not Robert!'

'Robert is your son?'

Fear choking her, Miriam's voice trembled. 'No . . . he . . . he's my brother.'

The tall, spare framed figure, a dark trilby hat covering most of his grey hair, stood on Miriam's doorstep and watched her reaction with cool assessing eyes.

'Is . . . is Robert . . . has anything happened?'

There was genuine anxiety in the question. 'I have not called about your brother.'

Relief burned bright tears in Miriam's eyes.

'I should have realised, you aren't holding a telegram.'

'No, Mrs Carson, I bring no telegram.'

As perplexed as she had been afraid, Miriam hesitated to invite her visitor into the house. He was not the bearer of that dreaded telegram, he did not wear a uniform, so who was he? Why was he here?

'Perhaps this will explain.' Taking a slim leather wallet from his pocket, the man held it toward Miriam.

It bore a card with an identity photograph.

'Mrs Carson, I am here about your son . . .'

Reuben! Something had happened to her son, he

had been injured! This was one of the teachers from his school come to tell her.

'. . . Please,' the man went on, seeing the anxiety in Miriam's stare, 'could we talk inside.'

What did Reuben do after school? What were his interests? Did he go out in the evenings? So many questions. Why all the interest? Had Reuben done something he shouldn't have? Why didn't this man explain? A mother's protection suddenly hot and fierce she snapped.

'Hold on a minute! You show a piece of card any schoolboy could come up with and expect it to give you the right to come to this house asking as many questions as you can put tongue to, well let me tell you . . .'

'Mrs Carson . . .' His interjection was as calm as the stare in pale grey eyes.

'. . . I am sure if you look carefully you will see this card is not the work of a schoolboy, you will also agree it provides me with the legal right to ask as many questions as I think fit and of every member of this household. Now,' he took back the wallet returning it to his pocket, 'please tell me . . . what time do you expect your son home?'

'I can't see anyone right now Katrin, tell whoever it is he will have to make an appointment.'

'He was very definite he must speak with you.'

'They always are.' Arthur Whitman banged his pen agitatedly against the desk. 'We must have more of this . . . there is a vital need for more of that. Always more, can't they get it into their heads I can't conjure munitions out of thin air!'

'What shall I tell him?'

'Tell him to bug . . . Sorry, Katrin.' Arthur Whitman let his head fall back against his chair his eyes closing for a few seconds before adding, 'Better get it over with. Ask him to come in.'

He was not a man she recognised. The man she had shown into her employer's private office had not called here previously. But he had not intended leaving without first talking to the person he had come to see, that had been very clear. More demands to be made of Arthur Whitman? More weight added to his shoulders? Hopefully, yes. Katrin removed a letter from the typewriter and placed it to one side to await signature. The more pressure on Arthur Whitman the more he would look to someone to alleviate it.

Would that someone be herself or would it be Isaac Eldon?

He was turning more and more to that man. Each day had that man consulted over one thing or another, 'Eldon is the man to sort that out' was becoming the standard cry.

Works manager! Why had he been given that position? Wasn't it patently obvious that he spent all his time in the workshop doing exactly as he had always done, working alongside fitters adapting machinery to a different purpose, replacing broken or worn parts when tool setters had been busy elsewhere? Didn't that prove he wanted nothing of work which tied him to an office? She had heard him say as much but it had been brushed aside. Eldon was the man for the job. The words had become Whitman's creed.

But not her creed.

Placing a second letter with the first, Katrin nursed resentment.

She would not subscribe to a doctrine she had set her faith in destroying.

A quiet buzz called her attention.

'Katrin.' Arthur Whitman paused as though reluctant to speak. 'Isaac . . . Mr Eldon,' he corrected himself, observing protocol in the presence of a visitor, 'would you tell him I wish to speak with him?'

Eldon again! Irritation submerged beneath a nod, Katrin affected a smile. 'I will have someone fetch him.'

'No!' Whitman answered quickly. 'I want you to go yourself, and Katrin . . . no word to anybody else.'

No word. Katrin frowned making her way down the flight of stairs. What was there to talk of when all she had heard was an instruction to fetch Isaac Eldon? What was so important that she must not speak except to Eldon himself? It could not be that Whitman wished the presence of the man in his office kept secret, his arrival had to have been recorded by the gatekeeper and witnessed by several others as he walked along the corridors leading to her office. Yet the instruction had been clear. She was to speak to no one other than Isaac Eldon.

Ignoring the appreciative glances following her through the various workshops, her breath shallow from the effort not to breathe the odour of slurry oil, Katrin was relieved to see the brown overall-covered figure bent to examine a batch of large mortar shell cases. The man standing at his elbow nudged Eldon, who immediately came towards her.

What was the sense of appointing this man to a managerial position? She watched him pull a rag from his pocket and rub it over his hands and disapproval became derision. This was all Isaac Eldon was, all he was qualified to be, a worker on the shop floor. One day Whitman would realise that. But not yet. Having him learn too soon could mean another man taking Eldon's place and that was not in her scheme of things. No, Whitman must be allowed his mistake a while longer. Time she would use to her advantage. She would let him know who saw to the management side, disclose the fact it was she did Eldon's paperwork, but only when she had entrenched herself so deeply it was impracticable to replace her.

'Katrin . . .'

Isaac Eldon's colour drained leaving pale patches between dark oil smears on his face.

'Katrin . . . is it Robert? Is it my son, is he . . . ?'

Had Robert Eldon met with an injury? Was his ship torpedoed? Was he lost at sea? Was he dead? Katrin met eyes filled with dread yet felt no pity. Isaac Eldon did not deserve her sympathy and neither did his family.

'Mr Eldon.' Cold as the glacier in her eyes, Katrin's reply cut the query hovering on lips caught firm against emotion. 'I am to ask you go to Mr Whitman's office at once, and Mr Eldon . . .' she paused, her glance chiselling his, '. . . please address me as Miss Hawley!'

13

'My machine were switched off waitin' of a new drill to be fitted, that be 'ow I come to hear what were said.'

'But why would her say that?' Drying her hands on the washroom towel, Becky Turner cast a glance at the woman standing with fingers held beneath a running tap.

' 'Ow would I know!' The woman shook water from her hands. 'But I do know what I 'eard and it were that wench tellin' Isaac Eldon . . .'

'Who's tellin' what to Isaac Eldon . . . ? But don't say 'til I've been to the lav'.' Alice dashed into the washroom and disappeared into a cubicle. Minutes later, trying without success to build a lather from the tablet of coarse brown soap, she rephrased her question.

'It be like I were tellin' Becky, I 'eard that there Hawley wench put a flea in Eldon's ear.'

Alice pulled the towel on its wooden roller searching for a dry spot. 'I reckon you've got that wrong,' she said 'I don't see nobody giving Isaac Eldon a flea in the ear.'

The retort was tart. 'Well you reckon what you will but I knows what I 'eard an' it were that wench say clear, "Mr Eldon," her said, "Mr Eldon, please address me as *Miss Hawley*!"' The woman sniffed disapproval, 'If that ain't a flea in the ear then tell me what is!'

'Do you think that is really what Kate said?' Becky asked the question she had been forced to hold until break.

Newspaper-wrapped sandwiches tucked under her arm, Alice glanced about the machine shop emptying rapidly of workers. She didn't really want to chat right now whatever the topic, this was the time she enjoyed, watching the huge crane lift crates of shells easy as lifting an empty cup.

'Can't believe anythin' Nosy Nora says,' she answered dismissively, hoping to end the conversation and for Becky to follow the others to the canteen.

'But her seemed sure enough.' Becky seemed not to notice Alice's offhand manner. 'Her face dropped a mile when you said you couldn't see anybody giving Isaac Eldon a flea in the ear.'

Why couldn't Becky leave it? Why didn't she go along with the rest of them? Any second now they would be spotted by the night foreman and that would put an end to any chance of indulging in fantasies of monsters and fire-breathing dragons. 'Sure is one thing, but truth is another and how much Nosy Nora tells of one and how little of the other is anybody's guess; we all know how ready that one is to call the kettle black.'

'Mmm.' Becky nodded. 'Like my mum says, gossip and lies often share the same bed, but . . . well I can't help but wonder whether there might be something . . .'

Hearing the deep rumble which heralded the approach of the steam driven crane, Alice caught at her friend's arm drawing her to crouch in a well of darkness between machinery.

'Alice we shouldn't . . .'

Alice gave a warning shush. To be caught by this particular foreman would result in a more serious dressing down than that Isaac Eldon might give. Feeling Becky resist she leaned closer, murmuring there was nothing to worry over provided they remain still and silent. But the words froze in her throat as Alice stared at the feet of the man come to a halt before their hiding place.

Isaac Eldon was no longer works manager!

Notepad on her knee Katrin felt the words push against her brain.

Isaac Eldon had been relieved of his post!

'I haven't said anything until now, Isaac had always been . . .' The explanation ended abruptly, Arthur Whitman's look indicating regret. 'Katrin,' he cleared his throat, 'the workload here in the office will, as a result of what has happened, increase substantially and it will probably be a week or two before I can bring in trained help.'

Katrin's mind cleared. Help of any kind was the last thing she wanted.

'We have had this conversation before,' she said quietly. 'The answer I gave then was "let me try", my answer is the same now.'

His deep brown eyes reflected relief. 'I was hoping you would say that . . . selfish, I know, but I was hoping. But I'll take in Isaac's paperwork,' he paused. 'Oh yes, he told me who it was saw to that . . . you have my gratitude, Katrin.'

Isaac Eldon had admitted she kept the wheels of his department running smoothly. Was she surprised? Katrin looked down at the pad on her knee. Strangely she was not.

'The man who came to see me, the one who asked I send for Isaac, he was from the Ministry.'

The Ministry! She had expected the police to come for Eldon, but this . . . this was so much better.

'. . . *is it Robert . . . is it my son?*'

She had so wanted to throw her reply back at him, to answer no, Isaac Eldon, it is not your son, but you will feel pain, pain of a sort you never expected, it is your turn to suffer! But she had kept her words for a time when the pleasure of speaking them would be even more intense.

She asked, with a show of concern, 'Is Mr Eldon in some kind of trouble?'

'You know as much as I do, Katrin. The fellow just asked Isaac to accompany him and they left together. No doubt there is speculation, I can't prevent that, but I prefer not to be a part of it.'

'*You know as much as I do, Katrin.*'

Katrin gave herself fully to the jubilation in her soul.

But he didn't know as much as she did. Arthur Whitman did not know the arrest of Isaac Eldon could only be the result of her phone call.

Providence had truly smiled the evening she had collided with that figure coming from the library. He had been so apologetic, blaming himself for not looking where he was going. She had wanted to hug him. On seeing what was strewn across the narrow pavement, she had realised this was her chance.

'This looks interesting.'

She had made it sound no more than politeness, seeming to give only a cursory glance to the sheet she had picked up. But interest had been very real indeed.

'What is it for . . . ? Oh sorry, I'm being too inquisitive.'

Had it been innocence or had he simply been too involved in gathering his belongings to recognise the ploy? Whichever, he had replied with a smile that the papers and books he juggled into the crook of an arm were to do with a project he was working on.

'It must be very complicated judging by those maps.'

'I get a lot of help,' he had said taking the last sheet of paper from her, 'My grandfather helps me.'

His grandfather. Katrin smiled contentedly. His grandfather, Isaac Eldon.

'I ain't never going to do that again. It scared the you-know-what out of me. Next time we are on night shift I'm off to the canteen at the first flicker of them lights. You want to play hide an' seek with the foreman then you play on your own.'

'Oh c'mon,' Alice laughed. 'You know you enjoyed it.'

'Enjoyed!' Becky exclaimed. 'I enjoyed it about as much as I enjoys being caught in an air raid. I tell you, Alice, seein' that foreman standing no more than a yard away . . .'

'Two feet.' Alice laughed again. 'You seen his two feet.'

'It weren't funny.' Becky giggled in spite of herself. 'I thought he had to hear the way my heart was pounding.'

'He couldn't hear anything over the racket that crane makes. Has me wonder why they take out them shells only at night; I mean where's the benefit of waiting for the cover of darkness when that crane makes so much racket it's probably heard by any Gerry plane that happens to be around.'

'Shush! You never know who could be listening. Let Isaac Eldon catch you and you'll be for it.'

'Speaking of Eldon,' Alice changed the subject glibly, 'it were not to be given word of Robert that he was called into Whitman's office. But why is he not workin' at Prodor any more? I asked Kate but seems her knows no more than we do.'

'Do you think his going has somethin' to do with what Nora says her heard Kate say, y'know callin' her *Miss* Hawley?'

Sandwiches eaten, Alice folded the sheet of newspaper and slipped it into her bag, mindful of the edict that every scrap must be saved toward the war effort. Though quite how it was used evaded her.

'I think now what I thought then.' She picked up the mug of tea purchased from the canteen counter. 'Kate Hawley wouldn't say no such thing, her wouldn't hurt anybody's feelings.'

'Still, I can't help but wonder . . . Nora was so positive.'

'Huh! You know about folk on a soapbox, if they goes on long enough and loud enough then there's them who'll believe what they say no matter how crackpotical, and nobody has a soapbox bigger than Nora's.'

'Then you don't believe what her said.'

'O' course I don't and neither will you if you have any sense!' Alice retorted. 'Kate Hawley couldn't be unkind if her tried; look how upset her were over Freda Evans being sent down, and what about the way her helped me with applying for the Forces, her took it that bad when it turned out I couldn't get in you would have thought it were all her fault.'

'You're right.' Becky nodded. 'Whatever it is has Isaac Eldon sacked it won't have anything to do with Kate.'

This was the second time he had come to the house. Miriam Carson looked at the man on the couch. He had already spoken with Reuben, her son had answered every question, so why was he here again?

'We have to check everything very carefully.'

Almost as though her questions had been spoken aloud! Miriam set down her tea. Did the official-looking card he showed enable him to read people's minds along with the rest of the privileges it seemed to hold?

'Reuben wouldn't keep anything back.'

The man met Miriam's glance. Defence, attack, all the characteristics of the female defending her young . . . well, good for her.

'I am sure he wouldn't.' He gave a brief a placatory smile and stirred milk into his cup. 'He has been most helpful.'

'So why do you have to talk to him again?'

The man she had come to know as Philip Conroy paused, then, as though coming to a difficult decision, said quietly, 'Mrs Carson, the information we were given regarding Reuben was . . .' he paused again, '*is* . . . a matter of national security.'

National security! He thought her son was some sort of spy? But, how could he be? Reuben was just a boy, what would he know of spies and national security?

'Try to understand, we have to investigate wherever and whenever suspicions are voiced even though the suspect is quite young.'

Suspect! Then he did think Reuben was a spy!

'Is,' she forced a reply, 'you said *is*, does that mean . . .?'

'Mrs Carson,' Philip Conroy interrupted quickly, 'it means only that information is being acted upon.'

'And who is it supplied you with that information? Who can dislike Reuben so much they accuse him of spying?'

'I'm sorry, I cannot answer that.'

'You can't tell who it is doing the accusing?' Miriam snapped. 'You can protect them yet subject a young lad to all kinds of questions? That's what you call security? Well I call it downright sly. You bring your informant here, let whoever it is tell his mother Reuben Carson be a threat to national security!'

He wouldn't give tuppence for the informant leaving the house in one piece!

'That is something else I cannot do.' Philip Conroy hid his appreciation of the woman stating her challenge. 'But this I will tell you, the information was given by telephone.'

'Telephone . . . ! But who? I doubt you'll find any man in Cross Street knows how to use one.'

It had been no man, a female had made that call; that too he could not reveal to this woman.

'Mrs Carson,' he began again, 'the material found in your son's room, what can you tell me about it?'

'You know what it is, Reuben told you.'

'Yes.' Philip Conroy's fair hair caught light from the one electric bulb allowed to illuminate the living room.

'Yes,' he nodded. 'Now I am asking you.'

She had gone over it again, trying to recall everything Reuben had told her, but only now did she realise her son had told her virtually nothing apart from the papers he was writing and sketching were his homework project. She had not looked closely at them! Why would she?

Had the sharpness of that reply been due more to her feeling of guilt at not showing deeper interest in Reuben's school work than irritation at questions repeated over and again? Miriam knew it was. But where could she find time? How often she had wanted to sit and talk with Reuben, to share his interests as she had once done . . . as Tom had done. But her wants had to take second place to those of the factory. And her son's needs? They also must play second fiddle in the orchestra of war.

'Miriam . . . Miriam, you be all right?'

Absorbed in thought, Miriam had not heard the tread behind her.

'Dad!'

Seeing the worry leap into his daughter's eyes, Isaac Eldon took her into his arms. 'Nothing be wrong.'

But there was something wrong. Why else would her father be home so soon? He worked longer hours now than he had at Prodor.

'Reuben?'

Miriam stepped free. 'Yes, he went straight upstairs on coming from school and hasn't come down since.'

'Conroy?' Isaac glanced toward the living room then at Miriam's further nod led the way there.

'Mrs Carson, Mr Eldon,' Philip Conroy began as father and daughter were seated, 'I apologise for calling at this hour but . . .'

'But darkness be a better cover than camouflage.'

'It does help not to be seen.' Philip Conroy smiled. 'Loose tongues and all that.'

'Ar, there's been one o' them waggin', spreadin' muck. Be that why you're here again, been a few more shovelsful throwed your way, has there?'

'No, Mr Eldon.'

'Then why do you be in my 'ouse, and why bring me away from my work?'

'We have our reasons.'

'Reasons!' Isaac's tone hardened. 'Then you'd better tell 'em to me afore I throw you out.'

'That is my intention.' Philip Conroy's smile faded. 'But first Mrs Carson, will you call your son.'

'Reuben, where did you get the information you have recorded on these maps, who did you ask to help you?' Philip Conroy watched the face of the boy, watched for any flicker in the clear eyes, any nuance of uncertainty across the features.

'I told you, I had no need to ask 'cos I knew all of that already.'

'When we spoke before, didn't you say your grandfather had helped you?'

A quick smile at the man sitting beside him. Philip Conroy mentally listed the observation.

'He did, but not with drawing maps. Granddad's no hand at drawing.'

'And with the descriptions . . . the names of various premises, the products they make, maybe he helped with that?'

'Wasn't no need, I've known those places since I was little.'

'That do be my doin'.' Isaac intervened. 'You see, I don't 'ave a deal o' book learnin', no sooner I turned twelve than I was put to earnin' a livin', workin' to help rear them younger than meself. That bein' so I had little to pass on to my son 'cept what I'd learned out of the classroom. I could only teach him what I had taught myself, to have an interest in all around him, it became the same with my grandson.'

'That's right.' Reuben beamed. 'Granddad and me often went for walks on Sunday, or sometimes he took me fishing, that is how I know names and places, Granddad pointed them out, I'm sure I got them right.'

Philip Conroy glanced at the briefcase he lifted to his lap, then looked again at the boy. 'Reuben . . . have you discussed this with anyone?'

The smile was wiped instantly by a frown and the answer was no longer that of a boy.

'Mr Conroy, my dad said I was never to break a promise if it were in my power to keep it and my mum says always to tell the truth. Well, I am doing both. I am telling the truth in saying I kept the promise I gave you, I haven't spoken a word of your coming here, not to anybody.'

'And your homework?'

A slight pink tinge crept into Reuben's face. 'That . . .' he looked at his mother, 'that were a bit of a lie, but that were cos you asked me to say it wasn't finished.'

'Thank you, Reuben.' Philip Conroy smiled. 'Now with your mother and your grandfather's agreement there is one more thing we would like you to do.'

14

Isaac Eldon had been given the sack. So went the rumours circulating the factory, folk asking why? What had he done to get himself dismissed?

They could ask. Katrin slipped into her grey worsted skirt. They could gossip all they liked but only she had the answer. It was more than the sack. Eldon had not been handed his cards then given leave to walk from the premises alone as would be the normal way of things, he had been escorted by a man dressed in a dark suit . . . a man Whitman had said came from the Ministry. Not a uniformed policeman, but someone from the government. Meeting her own eyes in the mirror, Katrin smiled in satisfaction. Everything had gone just as she would have it.

What she had seen fall from that boy's hand – the maps drawn with pencil, and coloured with wax crayon, squares and rectangles, names of factories, steel works, railways and canals marking each – had stared their promise at her.

And she had availed herself of it.

'*I don't want to be a gettin' o' nobody into no trouble . . .*'

Shrugging into a matching grey jacket, she let recollection trickle through her mind.

'... *it were a seein' o' all them maps ... factories an' the like, all drawed wi' names to 'em an' what it be they meks, well it d'aint seem right to me ... 'specially seein' as every name were blotted out wi' paint the minute war were declared, I means to say, where be the use in a doin' o' all that, o' paintin' all o' them places wi' that there camelflaarge if'n kids can walk around wi' maps a markin' o' every one?*'

'A child, you say it was a child had these papers?'

The answering voice had developed a note of uncertainty. Katrin had harboured no desire to linger, street telephone kiosks were too public, anyone using them drew attention, more so when there appeared to be no obvious emergency. But opportunity had been too good for it to be lost for want of another minute.

'*Weren't no babby!*' Her mind had worked rapidly. '*Were a lad near enough to leavin' school judgin' by the size o' him.*'

'Can you tell me his name?'

'*No.*' She had smiled at the lie. '*But I've seen 'im afore, seen 'im wi' a man by the name o' Eldon.*'

'By the name of Eldon.' Katrin purred the words aloud. It had not taken long to find a man named Eldon, one who lived in the same house as a young boy.

So what of Isaac Eldon now? If she heard he was rotting in hell the news would be pleasant. The boy? She took out the lavender silk scarf and held it to her throat. He was young, he would forget. And his mother, would she forget?

Twisting her shoulders Katrin watched the play of light touch the fragile silk highlighting the delicate colour against the grey of her jacket.

A Step Too Far

Why spend a moment worrying for Miriam Carson? Removing the scarf, she placed it back in the drawer.

Miriam Carson and Isaac Eldon.

Two birds with one stone.

And there were more stones yet to throw.

'Thank heaven that's finished.' Thrusting her card into the time clock Alice depressed the lever with a jerk of annoyance. 'Two more hours on top of what we already do, I tell you this government think we be the machines.'

'I don't suppose they do it out of choice.' Stamping her own card, Becky smiled placatingly.

'Huh! Then whose bloomin' choice is it? I know it ain't mine!'

'I wouldn't think anybody chooses, it's just what we have to do.'

'I bet I wouldn't have my work day extended by two hours were I in the Forces, I'll wager they don't get put on like we do, extra time here extra time there 'til you don't never know what time you get to leave this place.'

'Well, if you don't want to be invited to stay another couple of hours I suggest we leg it afore he gets here.'

Following Becky's nod, Alice frowned at sight of the approaching foreman. 'Just let him ask,' she ground between set teeth, 'he'll be told what he can do with his invitation and I'll even help with the shovin'!'

'D'you think he heard?' Having sprinted halfway to the factory gates, Becky stopped to fasten the buttons of her coat.

'Who cares!' Alice tossed the reply carelessly. 'Can't do nothing if he did.'

'Reckon he could ask Whitman give you the sack same as Isaac Eldon.'

'The answer might be more polite but I reckon the outcome would be the same, if Whitman couldn't let me leave on grounds of insufficient workforce then he ain't likely to do it 'cos old sore arse complains I was rude.'

'Seems everybody be puttin' extra time in tonight,' the watchman called as the two girls passed. 'Even the main office be workin' over, I've just said goodnight to Whitman's secretary, like as not you'll catch up to her.'

'Mebbe Kate has some news regardin' Eldon.'

'No, I haven't heard anything more since he left.' Katrin answered the question put to her in the bus queue.

'Seems funny to me,' Becky put in. 'I mean you would expect to hear of his being took on some place else but there's been nothing, least nothing Nora has got a whiff of or we would all know.'

Alice's retort was sour. 'Now there's a woman should be given a new job, I reckon her be enough of a gasbag to fill every barrage balloon that's made! Let's put that to Whitman.' She turned a glance to Katrin. 'Speaking of him, why keep you so late?'

'Mister Whitman was called away last night,' she answered. 'I was given the message when I arrived at the office this morning. His wife has been in Coventry for some months now looking after her mother.'

'That be where he's gone then?'

A Step Too Far

About to explain that he would be absent no more than a day or two, Katrin was forestalled by the wail of sirens.

'Bugger!' Alice exploded. 'Extra hours, rain and as if that ain't enough 'Itler sends his bombers, what more can a lucky girl hope for?'

Toward the front of the line of people standing huddled against the rain a voice called laconically. 'Her can queue forra bus but her won't get one, not afore the "all clear" her won't!'

'Well, I ain't going back to Prodor not if it rains bombs!' Alice hitched her gas mask decisively. 'I've been in that factory all day and part of the night, I certainly ain't spendin' the rest of it in no bomb shelter.'

'But . . .'

'Don't tell me no buts,' Alice retorted quickly, 'you go back if you want to, Becky Turner, but Alice Butler be going home.'

Katrin glanced hopefully along the street, though she knew no buses ran during an air raid. There would be very few people taking shelter, maybe the gatekeeper and a few of the labourers, but the others, the machine operatives, the tool setters and foreman, they always opted to carry on working. Even so she had no fancy for sitting in close proximity to any factory hand.

'You going back to the shelter, Kate?'

Her decision made, with a brief shake of the head Katrin slipped from the queue.

Of similar mind, other people began to hurry away, their figures suddenly lost to the night.

Becky followed, her steps quickening to a run as a rapid drumbeat of sound echoed in the distance.

'Oh Lord.' She caught Alice's hand. 'That . . . that's pom poms.'

Despite her earlier display of bravado, Alice's insides trembled.

Anti-aircraft guns! That meant bombers coming this way. Maybe it had been wrong not returning to Prodor but now wasn't the time for reflection. If they kept to a run maybe they could get home, things would be better once they were all with their own folk. Alice gasped against the breathlessness of running, 'You . . . you best come home with me, Kate, you know . . . case your dad be still at work.'

Go with them to Cross Street, share a garden shelter with either of those families! Aversion sweeping her, Katrin made no answer. Her father would almost certainly not be home, he stayed late at his work so much more these days. But she would rather be alone than take the alternative.

Accepting Katrin's lack of reply as a reflection of her own trepidation, Alice ran a few steps then was suddenly jerked to a halt.

'Oh Lord,' Becky was staring upward, 'Oh Lord Alice, look at that, look, there must be hundreds.'

Looking up into a night sky rendered brilliant by gleaming ribbons of light, Alice and Katrin gasped on seeing what had Becky transfixed.

Sound beat in their ears, a great throbbing swell of sound which seemed to press on every part of the body, to drown out the mind, to force the eyes to close.

But their eyes did not close, wide open they gazed at the spectacle playing overhead. Aeroplanes lit by the criss-crossing of searchlights seemed to flit and dart among the long slender shafts like huge dragonflies, their great grey bodies flying so low they might almost be touched, droned on, a great swarm following endlessly wave upon wave.

'Oh God Almighty!' Becky instinctively touched a finger to forehead and breast making the sign taught from childhood. 'Oh God, please . . .'

The request got no further, snatched away by the noise of a tremendous explosion. Out of the distance it rushed in on them, the tumult swallowing them then spitting them out against a high walled building.

Crouched in its shadow, fear bonding them close the three girls listened to the thunderous drone of aeroplanes accompanied by the continuous thud, thud of anti-aircraft barrage.

When would the next bomb drop?

Where would it fall?

The whole world seemed to shake; roll upon roll it thundered, rippling through the darkness, successive crashes of tumbling masonry and breaking glass bearing witness to some terrific impact.

'Oh, oh my God!' Becky rose first, her face white and frightened in the glow of fire.

'Seems to be Wood Green way. Somebody's had a direct hit.'

'We should go there, people will be needing help.'

'No.' Alice caught Becky's arm as the other girl made to run. 'The fire engines and ambulances will already be on their way.'

'Alice is right,' Katrin added. 'Those people are trained where we . . . we would probably be in the way.'

'I should have joined the Civil Defence,' Becky whimpered, 'I could have helped.'

'Well, you d'ain't and you can't!' Sense overriding shock, Alice answered with familiar bluntness. 'Ain't no use standing here moithering over what you could have done, it's what you need do now should be botherin' you.'

'What Alice is saying is that it is not safe to stay here, we need to find a safer place.'

Head drawn into hunched shoulders, Becky could not repress a cry as more explosions thundered, the vibration of them rocking all three on their feet.

'Where, Kate?' she asked, tears of fright in the question, 'Where is any place safe from them Gerries?'

Glancing at the wall they had crouched against, Alice called over the shouts of air raid wardens, over the noise of motor vehicles hurrying through the town, of crashing brickwork and splintering wood, of glass falling all around.

'What about here?'

'I don't advise that.'

'I don't see why not, Kate,' she retorted testily. 'We are told to take shelter anywhere when a raid be on, and this be one hell of a raid or my name ain't Alice Butler!'

'I agree,' Katrin nodded. 'But bad as our situation is, it could become a lot worse should we try getting into there.'

A Step Too Far

'Crikey!' Alice's half laugh sounded hollow as she read the name illuminated by the luminous red of flame. 'I sees what you mean. Lloyds Bank – break into that place and it will be a case of move over Freda, I'm here to stay.'

'Over there then, we should be all right in there.'

Looking to where Becky pointed, Alice felt no comfort from the tall spire rising black against the silver tracery of searchlights. Saint John's Church, a house of God; you would think to be protected in there but a church had not protected Violet Hawley.

'Not me,' she answered resolutely. 'I'll be lyin' in a churchyard soon enough. I'm going home!'

'You be going into a shelter is where you're going.'

Alice had stepped from the shadow of the bank straight into the arms of a policeman.

'No.' She pushed free. 'I have to go home, my mum needs help with the little 'uns.'

'Does her now?' The deep voice rose over the strident jarring of structures threatening to fall. 'Well, your mother's going to have to manage on her own.'

'You don't understand . . .'

'Neither it seems do you! Tonight don't be Guy Fawkes' night, them lights be pretty to look at but they don't be fireworks, they be shells bursting and that glow you sees don't be your usual garden bonfire, but people's homes and work places burning. Now you three young ladies have a choice, either you goes into a public shelter or I arrest you for loitering with intent.'

'Intent?'

'That's what I said.' The constable glanced at the building they still stood beside. 'This here is a bank and unless I am mistaken, which I'm not, then you three were loitering and that is a serious charge when you be found hanging about a bank, especially when doing so under the cover of an air raid.'

A public air raid shelter! Repugnance a quiver along her spine, Katrin joined the others, following after the policeman across the junction of Bridge Street and Holyhead Road.

'He'll leave us here.' Alice whispered to Katrin as they approached the police station. 'That'll be our chance to scarper.'

Her brain busy, Katrin made no reply. Just a few yards further on would bring her to Russell Street and then into Lower High Street; once there it would take only a few minutes to run along Spring Head and across into Hollies Drive.

Drawing level with the police station, the constable halted.

This was it. This was their chance. The moment he disappeared through that door they would run.

'I have to make my report.' He paused, a fresh shower of bursting shells studded the sky with diamond points of shimmering light. Then, as if reading the thought passing through Alice's mind, added. 'But first I'll just see you three safe in the shelter.'

15

Would she ever feel really clean again? Eyes closed, Katrin lay in the bath whose water she had scented with the last of Violet's precious *Les Parfums de Molinelle* 'English Roses'. Not her preferred choice, but much more preferred than the scents of slurry and machine oil.

How many hours had she been forced to sit in that shelter? So many she thought they were never going to end. Situated opposite the Municipal buildings, they were intended mainly for people from those offices but last night they had been filled with people who had had to leave public transport: men from iron and steel foundries, their hands and faces streaked with sweat-caked dust, and others who, though having washed, still smelt of oil and grease.

So many bodies, and all so close together. She settled lower in the water, drawing the fragrance into nostrils and lungs in which the odour of factories and oil-stained clothing still lingered. She would rather have faced the blitz, run home despite the danger of shells bursting overhead.

Was that how Freda Evans felt? Did she long to walk free of her 'shelter', to breathe air that was not stale with perspiration? Katrin smiled. Freda Evans would not walk free for quite a time. Maybe she should visit, wear the smart costume she had worn to the funeral, teamed with the hat she had chosen for that day – a jaunty chenille astrakhan, its grey and fawn giving the effect of tweed. The outfit had drawn several envious glances. She rubbed soap onto a flannel and smoothed the cloth over her breasts. Yes, she would visit Freda Evans, remind her of what she was missing by being imprisoned, give her a glimpse of the type of clothing she had never had.

A Cross Street girl! A convicted criminal! Katrin creamed scented lather along her arms. Freda Evans would never be more than that, never more than a factory worker in a soot-grimed Black Country town.

But Katrin Hawley was no Cross Street girl and, like the woman who had reared her, she had no desire to live the rest of her life in Wednesbury. Had Violet thought that one more fact the young girl had not recognised? Had she mistakenly believed it was hidden along with that other secret?

The flannel slipping from her hand, she slid lower into the water. No, mother, she murmured, your daughter knew them both.

'You heard them, didn't you Kate, you heard them girls talking?'

Yes she had heard them, possibly half the people in that public shelter had heard them.

'It sounded great didn't it?'

A Step Too Far

'Sounded more like the circus to me,' Alice answered, 'all that jumping and twisting, you'd need be a contortionist to do half what they reckoned to be dancing; what was it they said it were called, Kate?'

'Jitterbug.'

'The jitterbug!' Becky's blue eyes gleamed. 'It must be so exciting. Lor, I'd give a week's pocket money to learn how to do that.'

'Don't need no learning.' Alice shot a conspiratorial wink at Katrin. 'Just go along to them houses the Corporation be demolishing along Lea Brook way, the bugs you pick up from one of them will have you jump and twist more than any dance them Americans can teach.'

'Not only Americans, there were others, Continentals,' Becky smiled dreamily. 'They sound so . . . ooh.'

'More than "ooh" considering the giggles that were going on, I'd say a few of them wenches had been given lessons in somethin' more than jitterbuggin'.' Alice folded the newspaper which had held her margarine spread sandwiches. 'My advice, Becky Turner, is stick to your church social.'

'Huh!' Becky sniffed disparagingly. 'A cup of tea and no man younger than your granddad to dance with! I'd better not go too often, I don't think I can take the excitement.'

Alice picked up her teacup. 'Mebbes not,' she said, taking a sip. 'But one thing there ain't no mebbes about, seeing the photos being among them girls I'd say them fellas ain't no granddads.'

The shelter had been dimly lit but she had caught glimpses of the photographs courtesy of a torch held by a girl next to her. Katrin looked into her own cup. There was a saying, 'A picture speaks a thousand words.' She was hearing them now and each word held a promise.

'I'd say they was the very opposite of granddads,' Alice said again, 'but even if they wasn't I'd take me one any day.'

'I wouldn't refuse, they all looked . . .' Becky giggled self-consciously, '. . . you know what I mean . . . attractive ain't the word for them, they was gorgeous, and them uniforms so smart they had them looking more like film stars than pilots. Imagine.' Becky's dreamy look returned. 'Dancing with an aeroplane pilot.'

'You wouldn't be, least not right off.' Alice was matter of fact. 'Going on what was said, them Americans come to Cosford bringing planes sent over from America while them from the Continent be there to train as fighter pilots.'

Aeroplanes were not all they brought. Katrin remembered giggling whispers of 'stockings so fine y'can hardly tell a wench be wearin' any.'

'Did you see the stockings one of them wenches took out of her bag? They was like nothing I've ever seen, talk about pure silk, they was finer even than that, more like gossamer; said the fella offering them to her called them . . . ? I can't remember . . . I know it were a word I've not heard before.'

Feed the enthusiasm, give Becky all the rope she needed. Katrin answered. 'It was nylon, Becky, the girl said the stockings were called nylons.'

'Well, whatever . . . I'd give my eye teeth for a pair.'

'A week's wages for the teaching of the jitterbug and now your eye teeth for a pair of stockings, wonder what it be you'll go offerin' next.'

'Oh you!' Becky expostulated, 'You always sees things as don't be there Alice Butler!'

Perhaps. Katrin answered silently. But this time Alice was not simply imagining, this time there was definitely something to be seen, all it needed was an outlet . . . maybe she should provide that.

Innocence personified, Katrin smiled. 'Why not both go on Saturday, that way you can determine for yourself whether or not these girls were . . .'

'Shootin' a line!' Becky put in quickly. 'That's what I heard one say the Americans called tarting up the truth, he said it were "shootin' a line".'

'Huh!' Alice retorted. 'You've already got the lingo without being nowhere near that dance hall.'

'But we could, we could go Alice,' Becky leaned excitedly across the scrubbed bench of a table. 'So shall we?'

Alice shook her head. 'Depends,' she said doubtfully.

A breath of exasperation adding to a frown nestling between carefully plucked eyebrows, Becky demanded, 'Depends on what? There's neither of us working after six on Saturday.'

'Not so we've been told up to yet.'

'All right, then if we don't get called for extra hours will we go?'

'Going be one thing, but Wolverhampton's no two minutes away, how do we get back? You know buses run far less frequently after nine o' clock at night and if there's an air raid they don't run at all.'

'We will just have to do what them girls do.' Becky's determination was not to be outdone. 'Make sure we don't miss the last one, and if there's a raid we either waits it out or leg it back to Wednesbury, either way it'll be worth it.'

Worth a pair of stockings? It would be worth much more to Katrin Hawley if the promise of those words which had echoed in her mind became fulfilled.

'There is one more thing we would like you to do.'

Miriam Carson's insides fluttered at the remembered words.

How could anyone ask such a thing of a boy? Yet Philip Conroy had asked and the glance he had shot to her on hearing the answer had been one of quiet congratulation.

'Mum, granddad . . .'

Reuben had looked at them both with eyes that tore her heart. '. . . *before dad went away he told me always try to face up to things, never to run away. I don't want to run away from this, please let me do it, let me do it for my dad.*'

She had looked to her father for support in saying no, but the same tears of pride had glistened in his eyes as had glittered in her own.

'If there was any other way then we would not ask Reuben to take part . . .'

We. Just how much thought had the so secretive 'we' put into finding some other way?

'... *believe me Mrs Carson, had we reason to think your son would be in danger* ...'

How could he not be in danger! Miriam's mind snapped accusation. It was so easy for Conroy, it was not his son being asked.

'... *let me do it for my dad.*'

As she nodded to the man adding her work to the large container, Miriam blinked against tears misting the gleaming brass cartridge cases into a glittering golden stream.

Tom! Deep in the silence of her heart she had cried to the husband who could not help, called to a love which could not hear. Yet in that same silence had come an answer. Trust him Miriam, it had whispered. Trust our son.

And so she had said yes.

Philip Conroy had smiled that brief smile which seemed to say he understood her fears; but he didn't understand, how could he? How could anyone other than a mother know the fear of having her child walk into danger? This was no game he was about to play, no chat with a school friend. If discovered, then retaliation would be no tap on the wrist.

Trust our son! It was as if Tom had spoken to her. Tom telling her he had trust. And so she had kept her fears locked inside.

'*Before I say what it is we would ask you to do, let us go over things one more time.*'

'It was not like the little 'uns in junior school do . . .' Reuben had smiled at Conroy. *'. . . you know, they collect newspapers, and depending on how many they bring in, are awarded a paper badge which says "corporal, sergeant" or whatever. Well, we were no longer juniors, Mr Browne said, collecting newspapers was not proof of quality of leadership. An officer, a good officer, needed knowledge of terrain, of what it held and where. If it were an industrial town what was its major source of industry? Where were those sources located? How were they transported? How well were they defended? Mr Browne said knowledge of geographical location was an important aspect, one any officer would familiarise himself thoroughly with when out on field expeditions, and though we couldn't do that, we could, by means of a project, demonstrate our ability for leadership as a school prefect. I wasn't all that interested until he explained that for the duration of the war the term "prefect" was to be replaced by similar rank of officer in the armed forces . . . and like I told my dad I wanted some day to be a lieutenant. I wanted to be like him and this seemed a good way to start so I did a project on Wednesbury.'*

'That is the one we have here?'

The signal for the end of her shift sounded over the noise of machinery and Miriam murmured goodnight to the young woman waiting to take over, but her mind did not so easily relinquish its hold on the past, did not blot out the question pointed at her son.

Reuben had shaken his head.

'No, Mr Browne said the work I handed in was good, good enough even for Sergeant Major but if I could put a

little more into it then it could warrant commission as lieutenant.'

'Did Mr Browne suggest what form those additions might take?'

'Yes.' Reuben had answered immediately. *'He told me to consider, should rail or road transportation be impeded, was there some other way materials might have of reaching their destination. That was when I remembered the canal and thought how the "Shadow Factory" must be shipping stuff out.'*

'Shadow Factory!' Concern and curiosity had combined in Isaac's exclamation. *'Where did you hear that?'*

'It's what folk are calling Prodor.' Reuben had looked at his grandfather. *'They say it's on account of it being so well camouflaged that from above it must seem like a shadow on the land and what with bringing armaments out only at night . . .'*

'Oh my God!'

Washing her hands, Miriam looked at the grease-stained lather but saw only her father's troubled look, felt her heart miss as it had missed when he had asked were folk talking of that also?

'I haven't heard anybody say, and I certainly haven't asked.' Reuben had smiled.

'Then how do you know?'

'That stuff is brought out at night?' Reuben had glanced at Philip Conroy, then at herself and his grandfather, before lowering his eyes and confessing sheepishly. *'Sometimes at night, when you've both been on night shift I . . . I've left the house; I know I shouldn't but it somehow felt safer in the places I'd been with granddad,*

especially our fishing spots, they felt peaceful and friendly, it was while sitting in one of them I saw Prodor's doors open and the crane load huge cases onto narrow boats drawn up on the canal that runs along the back of the factory.'

Miriam shrugged into her coat, Philip Conroy's next question the same lance in her heart it had been when asked.

'And these narrow boats, did you know where they took their load?'

A moment's silence had followed, a silence driving into her with the ferocity of any bullet she might make. Leaving her own place of work Miriam looked at the darkened sky. Peaceful and friendly . . . when would the night ever feel that way again?

'I guessed . . .'

Reuben's gaze had lifted, his clear honest eyes begging forgiveness and understanding.

'. . . but I wanted to be a lieutenant, mum, and I knew guessing would not be good enough so . . . so I followed the boats down along the canal. Nobody saw me, I made sure of that.'

'And did those boats go to where you had guessed they might?'

Walking through the unlit streets Miriam followed the conversation in her mind.

'Mmm.' Reuben had nodded.

'They went along to Friar Park, they offloaded there.'

Conroy asked if Reuben had any idea of why those narrow boats should offload after a journey of so few miles?

'I didn't know for certain what the loads were so that time I just had to guess.'

'So what was your guess?'

It had not been Philip Conroy's question had held breath in her throat, it had been Reuben's answer. Passing along the narrow Kings Cross alleyway leading to Cross Street, Miriam saw in her mind her son's face, the candid sincerity, the same integrity . . . she had seen the image of Tom, heard his strong truthful voice in the reply.

'Whatever was being put onto them canal boats had no wheels so it was unlikely to be motorised transport of any kind. At the same time I reckoned they were not guns, least not the anti-aircraft type seeing the size of the crates so it seemed fairly safe to assume they were shells.'

'And?'

It had been asked so calmly yet Philip Conroy's watchful stare had been riveted to that of Reuben.

Reuben's half laugh had carried that note of slight embarrassment, the apology of attempting to 'teach his grandmother to suck eggs'.

'. . . it's . . . well, everybody knows shells are useless without the explosive to set them off.'

He had halted there, but when neither listener made comment he proceeded.

'It was fairly certain that those boats ferrying shells would be taken to a place to be filled with gunpowder.'

'Royal Ordnance Factory.' Isaac had met the glance switched to him. *'There be a branch along of Friar Park, the shells we machine at Prodor all goes there to be filled.'*

Had Reuben been too observant? Had his agile mind led him a step too far? Dread which had hung over Miriam the whole day became heavier with the thought. The 'we' behind Philip Conroy must be very powerful people, powerful enough to take her son from her if they thought him the least threat.

'*One more thing,*' Philip Conroy had accepted the explanation. '*Tell me Reuben, and please think very carefully, tell me again what you overheard on the afternoon you took your project along to that room; are you certain who it was you heard? And more importantly, the exact words spoken.*'

'*I know it was Mr Browne I heard, he has such a . . . a thick voice is the best way I can explain the way he sounds . . . and having heard no reply, I reckoned him to be speaking on the telephone.*'

Reuben had paused, frowning as he puzzled to recall every detail.

'*. . . The door was shut as always but with everybody except myself gone home the school was silent . . . I had been given permission of my teacher to stay an extra half hour to finish off my project and it seemed the sensible thing to do to hand it in there and then, so I went to Mr Browne's room and that was when I heard. I couldn't catch all of what was said but the way he emphasised some of the words they came clear into the corridor; I wasn't eavesdropping, mum, honest I wasn't!*'

'*The words that were emphasised, Reuben?*'

Philip Conroy had brought Reuben back to the question in hand.

'I heard them several times, he repeated them like he sometimes does when he wants to be sure one of us lads has got the point but . . .'

The frown returned, displaying Reuben's reluctance to get something wrong, but at his grandfather's reassuring nod he had gone on.

'I'd decided not to disturb him, that I would hand my project in next day and had begun to walk away when I distinctly heard him say, "Raygenskerm" he stressed that very much and the same with the next thing, "Fine at Price", and then "Corn". He wanted whoever he was talking with to be quite sure of what it was he wanted, though I don't know any corn called Raygenskerm, do you granddad?'

Had it been an echo of her own fear she had seen in her father's eyes as he had given that negative shake of the head? Was he also afraid Reuben might be taken from them? She had prayed Philip Conroy would leave without asking any more of Reuben. But not every prayer received the longed for answer.

'Thank you Reuben. Now, this is what we would like you to do . . .'

Miriam's mouth trembled against a volley of sobs. Philip Conroy had smiled as if inviting Reuben to a game of chess.

But it wasn't chess!

Miriam winced at the sharp stab of fear.

Oh Lord . . . it wasn't chess!

16

The works' canteen was not her favoured choice of meeting place, nor was the company desirable, but she must put preference aside if things were to go as she wanted; she would pretend friendship just as long as it suited her purpose. Glancing at the clock on the wall of her office, Katrin reckoned the minutes from hearing the factory hooter announce midday break. Those two were never slow off the mark, they would have collected their drinks and be sitting at one of the tables. Katrin's nose wrinkled. Slurry oil had a way of donating its unpleasant smell to the clothes of anyone coming into contact with it and the overalls of the factory girls always carried it. But how else, short of inviting them into her home, could she get to talk to Alice Butler and Becky Turner? That was even more undesirable than speaking to them here. So why speak with them at all? Glancing again at the clock, Katrin walked from the room. Why? Because every inner sense said it would prove to be of benefit for Katrin Hawley.

'Hey, Kate!'

Leaving the serving counter with a cup of tea, Katrin gritted her teeth. Did the girl have to shout, couldn't a wave of the hand serve the same purpose? Ignoring stares and none too quietly observed comments regarding the dismissal of Isaac Eldon, she wove her way between tables to Becky and Alice.

'We was just saying what a great time me and Alice had on Saturday; eh Kate, it were smashin', I wanted it to go on all night.'

'You tried enough to make it last all night, we got that last bus by the skin of our teeth.' Alice unwrapped a sandwich which had been promised a sliver of cheese and then the promise forgotten.

'Oh, but it were worth it.' Cornflower blue eyes glistening like azure stars, Becky hunched her shoulders, hugging the memory. 'It were the best night I ever had.'

'Yes, but did you learn to jitterbug?'

'Not what you would call learn, Kate.' Becky laughed. 'Though the fella that danced it with me said I would pick it up proper with a couple more lessons.'

'Was that "shootin' a line"?'

'Fancy you rememberin' that.'

She remembered more than that. She remembered the giggles and suggestive nudges, the half guilty looks which had passed between those girls in that underground shelter.

'I don't think he was,' Becky answered, 'he seemed too nice to be saying anything he didn't mean.'

'He?' Katrin forced a smile in to her eyes. 'Did you dance only with one man?'

'No.' Becky's turbaned head shook once. 'There were others, me and Alice didn't sit one dance out but . . .' she paused, colouring slightly, '. . . but Earl were different, he was so polite, called me ma'am, every time he asked me for a dance. I tell you Kate, them Americans leave our fellas standing when it comes to manners.'

'Weren't only lessons in how to jitterbug you was treated to.' Alice looked over her slice of bread. 'Show Kate what else you was given.'

'Not only me!' Becky was defiant.

'No, not only you, but it be you and not me have brought your'n with you. So . . . show Kate, show her what them Americans give us.'

Carefully shielding her bag from any inquisitive gaze, Becky drew out a small paper bag. 'I couldn't believe we might be given some of these.' She drew out a pale mist of tan, letting it float across the back of her hand. 'Nylons, Kate,' she whispered reverently, 'ain't they marvellous?'

'Pity you didn't come, Kate, you would have been sure to have been given a pair; and you would have enjoyed the dancing. Why not come with me and Becky next time?'

Becky's pretty mouth drooped. 'Who said anything about next time?'

Tingles of alarm flickering in her veins, Katrin put in quickly. 'But I thought you had enjoyed going.'

'Don't pay to think.' Alice shoved her folded lunch paper into her bag. 'Neither does it do to go setting store by anything 'cos you be like to find somebody'll tell you no, and that's what your mother's done I reckon, told you you can't go again! Is that right, Becky?'

Becky stared disconsolately at the sheer mist of stockings before gently returning them to the bag. 'Mother don't know I went to Wolverhampton,' she said, 'her thought it was the social at Saint Mary's, her would have a fit if her found out I'd been to the Civic, and if her catches sight of them nylons then Lord only knows what will happen.'

'So tell her you be going to the church social again this Saturday.'

Becky's eyes had lost their gleam. 'Can't,' she said miserably, 'it's only held once a fortnight, and even if it were more often who wants to go there to dance to records after dancing to a live band? And then there's the chance of mother hearing on Sunday morning that I hadn't been at the social at all, her would be wearing my innards for garters.'

'That be it then,' Alice returned philosophically. 'I suppose going to that dance once were better than not going at all, at least we knows what we be missing, and we can stick with using sand in place of nylons, least 'til we be twenty one.'

It must not take that long! Alarm sparked like fireworks in Katrin's veins. This was the opportunity providence was holding out to her, the chance to take revenge on Becky Turner. Lose it and it may not be offered a second time. Suppressing the sweep of concern she said, 'There could be a way, supposing you wanted to go badly enough.'

Becky sniffed her disappointment. There was nothing she wanted more.

'What way would that be?'

A Step Too Far

Katrin breathed silent gratitude for Alice's question. But still she must move slowly.

'I don't really feel . . .' she paused, an air of false rectitude making it appear she was reluctant to continue, then went on, 'No . . . no it's wrong of me even to think it.'

Alice frowned. 'Is thinking something else we shouldn't be doing! What with government restrictions and a mother telling you no to everything you want to do, we wenches be stifled so tight it don't really need old Hitler's bombs to finish we off, the job is already being done well enough!'

'I was really looking forward to Saturday.' Becky seemed not to have heard Alice's irascible remark. 'You'd understand if you'd been there, Kate, it was so nice having somebody treat you like a lady and not just a factory girl, somebody who called you ma'am, spoke to you polite instead of ordering.'

Somebody like Earl! Chewing her lip, keeping the pretence of moral reluctance, Katrin said quietly, 'Becky, there might be a way but . . .'

'But what? Stop running all round the Wrekin, Kate, if there be a way then tell it!' Alice's impatience was a benediction, a sanction on the idea which had fast developed in her mind.

'It is only a suggestion, Becky, but . . . well I thought should you ask your mother could you come spend the evening at my house, keep me company while my dad is on fire watch duty.'

'Great!' Alice thumped her cup onto the table. 'Your mother wouldn't say no to that.'

No, Mrs Turner probably would not say no. Katrin watched the two girls leave the canteen as the factory hooter recalled the workers. The woman would have no idea of her daughter's escapade. Should it become known, Katrin Hawley would claim her involvement was no more than fabrication on Becky's part.

They would follow her suggestion. Alice Butler and Becky Turner would follow exactly where she guided, and for Becky Turner that could be straight into hell.

Arthur Whitman would not be returning as planned. Replacing the telephone on its cradle, Katrin's mind ran the call through again. The evening of the raid which had forced her to spend the night in that public shelter had been heavy enough here in Wednesbury but the full fury of it had fallen on Coventry.

'*It was the worst night I have ever lived through.*'

Arthur Whitman's voice had trembled as he had talked.

'*. . . a third of the city has been devastated, the centre of it utterly destroyed, pounded into the ground by wave upon wave of enemy aircraft, the sound of them, oh Christ, Katrin, the sound! Roll after roll so low overhead the throb of engines drummed the brain until the world spun, and the screech of falling bombs, the thud of their hitting target after target, the crash of falling buildings blown apart . . . it was like living through a nightmare, a nightmare intensified by fires raging from exploding gas mains, from burst underground water pipes flooding streets until they resembled rivers . . .*'

He had stopped speaking, only a ragged indrawing of breath signifying he still held the telephone. She had asked then was he all right but his answer had been one of a man still caught in the trauma of shock.

'*It was the people . . .*'

He had murmured like someone half awakening from a dream. '*. . . men . . . women . . . crying, bleeding, scrambling in the wreckage calling the names of loved ones, fighting off police and civil defence trying to lead them away; and the injured, Katrin, the injured carried by rescuers to hospitals which no longer stood . . . it seemed the Devil had risen from hell and taken dominion of the earth and the burning skeleton of the Cathedral bore witness to his victory.*'

But living through that ordeal had not ended the nightmare, the rest, it had turned out, was yet to come.

Was it sympathy she felt, compassion, pity for the man? Or was it elation for the woman fate had chosen to endow with its favour. It had given Katrin Hawley the gift of becoming indispensable to the running of this office and now it was offering another, one which promised so very much more.

'*It must have been terrible,*' she had sympathised, '*but thank Heaven you are unhurt . . .*'

The laugh coming hard on her words had been sardonic. '*Oh yes, I'm unhurt.*'

'*Mrs Whitman and her mother,*' she had asked, '*will you bring them back with you? They might be more comfortable here in Wednesbury, if you wish me to make any arrangements . . .*'

His reply had rung with a withering self indictment.

'It was my fault,' he had said, *'I should have been with them but no, no I had to go outside, I had to offer my help . . . Oh Christ, Katrin . . . the bomb! It landed directly on top of the house!'*

17

'With deepest sympathy.'

Katrin murmured the words on the card accompanying flowers she had sent to that funeral, a card tactfully inscribed, 'From all at Prodor.'

Sympathy? It had not been sympathy had swept Katrin Hawley when taking that telephone call, it had been the invigorating flush of opportunity. She could not have planned it better, Fate was again holding out a gift and she would take it. But taking advantage must not be rushed. Choosing the sensible grey flannel suit her mother had bought for her to begin her job at Prodor, Katrin buttoned the slim straight skirt. Violet would have pushed, would have had her throw herself at Arthur Whitman, urged her to land him before he knew he was being fished, and the bait? Violet would have had no qualms about using any worm which would see her daughter become the wife of a man of money, and Arthur Whitman would be no exception.

Turning the collar and lapels of her dusky pink artificial silk blouse over those of the suit jacket, Katrin glanced at the lavender scarf nestling in the halfway open drawer.

But Violet's way was not hers. That would be clumsy, too overt; far better it were achieved quietly, indirectly and seemingly without intervention, exactly as she had dealt with the problem of Harriet Simpson.

There was a crisp November chill but bright sunlight made the morning pleasant. She had enough time to walk to work.

At the end of Hollies Drive was an imposing cream stone building. The library. It had been a stroke of luck colliding with that lad. Those maps falling from his hands had provided the moment she might otherwise have waited years for, her chance to strike a blow against the man she loathed. Her one regret was that she could not be present when he was accused of assisting a minor to betray his country. Yes, that was the one disappointment, but it was mollified somewhat by the fact the woman too would suffer and so would her son. Having a spy, a traitor for father and grandfather would not sit well with them, should the people of the town discover the truth . . . and though that aspect of revenge may have to wait its turn, it would be told.

They would be ostracised, rejected by all who had once called them friend; they would be forever the daughter and grandson of a quisling and Katrin Hawley would rejoice in the outcome, revel in the knowledge, the silent knowledge, of who it was had made everything known.

It would have to be silent. Passing through the factory yard, Katrin climbed the stairs leading to her office. It would not do for the world – the world and

Arthur Whitman – to learn her secrets. But she would not deny herself completely. One day she would tell Isaac Eldon who it was had him arrested.

Hanging her coat on the branched coat stand in a corner of the room she glanced at the door of the inner office.

He had been taken from there, escorted away by a man in a dark suit. No uniform, nothing to mark him as anything other than the usual businessman, but she had known the man who had escorted Isaac Eldon from that room had been here on a business very different from that of making gun shells.

Little had been said then and nothing since. Arthur Whitman had given no indication of the reason for that abrupt departure.

'. . .*you know as much as I do, Katrin* . . .'

No, Mr Whitman! Katrin Hawley knows a great deal *more* than you.

But even so she had thought to hear something, whispers on the grapevine, gossip running around the factory. None of it could be factual but nevertheless it would be interesting and maybe instructive in helping solve the puzzle of what had happened to Isaac Eldon. Of course the apprehending of a spy would be kept quiet, but even the Ministry had their work cut out preventing the like of Nora Bates ferreting information and passing it around. Yet even that woman had nothing to say other than, ''*Ow come nobody don't see nuthin' o' Isaac Eldon no more? Don't even a'hear 'im shoutin' to folk to put a light out. It be a right mucker an' no mistek!*'

But it was not confusing to Katrin Hawley.

She knew the reason of the man not being seen. She knew he might never be seen again!

He looked so tired.

Closing the door behind her father Miriam felt the tingle of anxiety cold against her spine.

He had not spoken of the reason for his leaving Prodor, nor of what had virtually robbed him of his home and family, of the reason he returned only for a few hours, leaving and returning always at night. Why? Miriam felt the question lodge in her throat. She had tried asking but he had brushed aside any question saying it was nothing, that she was giving way to imagination. But was it imagination had the marks of worry deepen on his face? Was it illusion on her part have him sit for most of those brief visits locked in his own thoughts?

Ought she to have tried to persuade him to stay home this evening? Perhaps plead she felt unwell. But that would add another straw to the burden he carried, one more worry to set beside that Philip Conroy's visit had left behind. One more secret!

Unable to quell the sharp rise of fear, she set about placing blankets and coats on the sofa in preparation for raids which were an almost nightly occurrence, then fetching the bucket of sleck, small particles of coal and coal dust doused with water and left ready in the scullery, she banked the living-room fire, it would slumber all night, keeping the room tolerably warm.

She should go to bed, rest while chance presented itself. But rest did not come easily, sleep could not combat memories of Tom, of the love they had shared, darkness could not dispel sight of that beloved face nor drown the voice speaking in her head.

'This is what we would like you to do . . .'

Clear, incisive as though the man sat opposite, the words echoed in Miriam's mind. Miriam reached for yet another pair of socks in need of mending but try as she might she could not banish what Philip Conroy had said.

'. . . we want you to be certain, Reuben, absolutely certain you can carry this off.'

Staring into the dulled fire, Miriam followed the scenes memory unfolded.

Reuben's head bent over the paper Philip Conroy had placed before him on the table.

'This is the area in question.' Conroy had pointed to the paper. *'We want you to mark this on your diagram as a possible source of armament manufacture.'*

'But there is nothing there, it used to be the golf links but nobody plays there any more, that's right, isn't it, grand-dad?'

'We are aware of that, Reuben, and because it is unused land it suits our purposes so well.'

'But the lad be right!' Isaac had protested. *'There be nothing there . . . least not to my knowin'.'*

'Which is exactly why it must be inserted into Reuben's project bearing a question mark; it must have no name ascribed to it, it must not even be given the pseudonym "Shadow Factory" as that other is signified.'

'Then if it 'as to be so secret how come Reuben is reckoned to know of this . . . factory?'

'*I think Reuben has already provided us with the answer to that.*' Conroy had smiled briefly. '*Did he not say that sometimes he left the house at night, that it was during one such escapade he observed crates being brought out from the "Shadow Factory" and loaded onto narrow boats? This will also be the way he discovered the operations taking place on the golf links, materials being taken away under cover of darkness.*'

Miriam saw again the quick lift of her son's head, the frown preceding the question: with no building present on that land, how was it to be supposed any existed?

'*It is not unknown for quite extensive construction to be placed underground,*' Conroy had returned, '*we need only to remember London's Underground Railway system.*'

'*. . . This is what we hope will be believed from your sketch,*' Conroy had continued, '*We want it thought that beneath that expanse of empty land there is a factory so secret no evidence of it must be seen to exist, a producer of materials so vital to the outcome of the war they can only be brought out at night. If . . . no . . .*' he had shaken his head, '*. . . when you are questioned . . . and we can have no doubt you will be . . . you must say you could find nothing more, that when you asked your grandfather he got angry, told you to stop asking questions and warned you stay away from the golf links. You must sound convincing, Reuben, so much depends on you achieving that.*'

'That'll be no problem, sir.' Reuben had grinned. '*I'll need only to mention the strap, the teachers all know the respect us lads have for that.*'

Reuben had left the living room saying he would re-draw his plan of the town to include Conroy's asked-for addition. Then their visitor had turned to herself and her father.

'*Mrs Carson, Mr Eldon,*' he had said, his voice kept deliberately low, '*the Ministry recognises you deserve an explanation, a fuller understanding of the happenings which have led to asking Reuben's continued assistance, but before I can give that explanation, I have to ask you both to sign the Official Secrets Act.*'

Isaac nodded agreement to the request.

'*You understand.*' Conroy had returned the signed documents to his briefcase. '*Nothing of what you are about to hear must pass beyond these walls.*'

'*Reuben?*'

The sharp question had been her own.

'*Your son has already demonstrated the fact of his dependability.*' Conroy had answered. '*We are convinced it is a quality he will retain. Reuben is a sensible lad, Mrs Carson, you can be proud of him.*'

Sensible! Miriam rose from her chair. What sense was left in a world where children were called upon to do such things?

She would see him again tonight, see Earl, the American pilot who called her ma'am, who rose from his chair when she left her seat to go to the Ladies. Caught in her own romantic dream, Becky Turner walked alongside her mother. He would ask her to dance, hold her in that special way, close against him yet gentle as if she were some precious thing he valued above all else. Then in the interval, that half hour of the band taking a break from playing, he would suggest a breath of fresh air; that was the part she liked most. Heart lurching at the thought, Becky hid it with a small shake of her shoulders, as if the sharp promise of frost pervading the afternoon reached through her coat. Her mother must not suspect! Hiding a tremor was easier than hiding the bloom of colour thoughts of Earl always sent rushing to her cheeks. Thank heavens today was cold, her mother would see that as responsible for any blush.

'Best go get the groceries first. Lord, another queue!' Her mother's irritated remark went unheeded until she pushed ration books into Becky's hands. 'You stand an' I'll go see if there be aught at the butchers as don't be needin' o' no coopuns.'

Tonight the dream could come true. Wedged into the line of women patiently waiting their turn to be served, Becky slipped back into her reverie. Earl would take her out of that hot crowded dance hall, away from the press of people; he would find a secluded spot shielded from prying eyes and there he would draw her into his arms, whisper her name as his mouth closed over hers . . .

'If you don't be in no 'urry to get served then shift y'self outta the way an' let others be seen to!'

Accompanied by the jab of a finger between her shoulder blades, the woman's words rang around the shop. Stammering apology, Becky handed the ration books across the counter. One day all of this would be over, war would end, rationing, standing in endless queues for everything would be no more than a memory and she . . . Becky breathed against the delicious trickle invading her stomach . . . she would be in America.

'*You're so pretty with those gorgeous blue eyes and lovely smile, any man would be proud to have you for his wife.*'

Becky nodded to the shop assistant, watched the woman's lips move but it was Earl's voice she heard, the husky whispered words as his mouth had brushed her ear.

He had held her against him, his arms tightening his voice harsh with pent up emotion.

'*. . . I'd sure as hell be proud to take you back with me to the States but . . .*'

But! How that word, that pause had hurt, how it smashed into her hopes, shattered her longings and then . . .

'*. . . I couldn't do that to you. I couldn't ask you to leave everything you have ever known, your home, your family, I . . . I think too much of you, Becky, to cause you the pain that would bring, yet if . . .*'

Becky's number nine cloud floated higher. Earl thought too much of her. He loved her, Earl *loved* her!

Ration books returned, groceries packed into the crude Hessian bag, its plaited string handles biting into her palms, Becky left the shop.

Would there be stalls lining each side of the street in Earl's home town? Miami. Becky hugged the name to her.

'*Miami.*' He had smiled. '*Beaches blonde gold as your hair, fringed by an ocean blue as those luscious blue eyes and sunshine, sunshine every day of the year; you would love it there Becky, I just know you would.'*

He had sat that first evening of meeting her, his own deep brown eyes gleaming softly, his tone quiet almost reverential as he described the place he had come from, a place so different from Wednesbury. And now he had said he would be proud to take her there, except for its causing her the pain of parting from her home, of leaving the town she had grown up in. But what was there to grieve over by leaving Wednesbury? Glancing again over the assortment of market stalls huddled beneath smoke palled skies, skies made darker by threat of leaden snow, Becky knew her question needed no answer; leaving this town for Miami, exchanging her home for that which Earl would give would cause her no pain at all.

She would take such delight in telling him so tonight. He would ask her tonight, he would say, those few precious words which he would have said last week had Alice not called her to leave.

'Be you a' listenin'!'

Laced with aggravation, her mother's irate question snatched at the dream, scattering it like snowflakes on the wind.

'. . . Twice I spoke to you, twice, an' no answer neither time, where be that head o' your'n I'd like to know!'

Taking the extra shopping bag thrust at her, Becky followed the figure darting with the certainty of an arrow toward O'Connel's greengrocer stall. Should she tell her mother where her head had been? Tell her where the rest of her daughter would be in a few weeks' time? Tell her of the man who tonight would ask her to be his wife?

The past few weeks had been fortunate in her and Alice being able to swap late evening shift on Saturday for double shift on Sunday. But she would not be doing that much longer, she would be spending all of her Saturdays and Sundays, every single weekend of the year, lying with Earl on the sun drenched beaches of Miami.

'That were a stroke o' luck, another couple o' minutes an' there would 'ave been none left.' Stuffing several onions and a swede into the bag Becky held, her mother gloated triumph. 'Go nice wi' that bit o' liver I got from the butcher, that be supposin' I can find it, be that little; but I wouldn't have got even that hadn't I seen him slip a packet across the counter to that fancy piece along o' Russell Street. He thinks folk don't know what be goin' on 'tween 'im an' that one, but we ain't everyone o' we blind and we ain't dumb neither.'

Thoughts warm and golden as the imagined sun, Becky's glance fell on the window of Boot's Chemist shop. Maybe, just maybe, she would be lucky enough to find a lipstick or even a bottle of Amami Wave setting lotion.

Daydreaming had caught her off guard. Her mother wanted to know why Becky hoped to buy cosmetics. 'I . . .' she faltered under the questioning stare, 'I . . . told Kate I would try to get some for her, and take them with me when I went to her house tonight.'

'Won't be no goin' along of the Hawleys' tonight, I needs you to sit along o' the little 'uns!'

18

'*I needs you to sit along o' the little 'uns.*'

The bell of doom rang in Becky's' head, sounding the end of everything, of hopes and dreams.

Tears of disappointment gathered thick in her throat. Earl would think her not turning up at the dance was because she didn't want to see him. But she *did*! She wanted to be with him more than she had ever wanted anything in her whole life! The cry loud in her heart, Becky bit it back from her tongue. Her mother would not understand, she would not believe a couple could fall in love so quickly; but Becky knew it was the real thing and Earl's eyes, whenever he looked at her, showed he knew it too. They loved each other, it wasn't fair they be kept apart, that the few precious hours they could be together was taken from them so she could child-mind. She had waited all week! She thought of it the whole time at the factory, talked of it with Alice as they ate their sandwiches in the canteen, and again while they made their way home together. That was nearly as much a delight as actually being there in the dance hall, both of them giggling at the charade played out before ever arriving. They had to make it look as though there was no more to the evening than passing it with Kate Hawley, which meant leaving Cross Street with faces scrubbed clean, best dress hidden beneath an everyday one, almost irreplaceable rouge, face powder, lipstick and eyebrow pencil and her cherished nylons secreted in a brown paper shopping bag and dropped into the yard from a rear bedroom window to be collected as they left the house, then dart quick as their legs would carry them away along the Holyhead Road. But the transformation had to wait until the safety of the Ladies room allowed for everyday dresses to be removed, make-up applied and finally hair (which had spent the day tightly bound in steel curling pins beneath turbans) to be combed and coaxed into a preferred style. Becky brushed hers to fall long and loose to her shoulder with one deep wave sweeping down over the brow, seductively half covering one eye exactly as worn by the American film star Veronica Lake. But it was the dresses they dreamed of most, dresses they imagined themselves wearing, gowns beautiful as any those screen stars wore but which she and Alice could only dream of. Becky sniffed back tears. That was all it could ever be so long as she remained here in Wednesbury, imagination and broken dreams.

She could refuse to babysit! She could follow Alice's example and flatly refuse, give her own mother the same ultimatum that had been given Mrs Butler.

But Alice had not been subjected to the restrictions of church.

Becky felt the surge of resolve melt away.

It would have been much easier for Alice to deny her mother, to tell her 'no' for Mrs Butler did not have the reinforcement enjoyed by Mary Turner, that of a priest backing her every word.

'*It is the duty of the child to obey the parent.*'

She had heard those same words from earliest childhood, heard them with each weekly visit the Father made to the house, listened to them every Sunday in Saint Mary's Church, it had even been given as a reminder upon completion of her Confession though all she had felt the need of owning to had been the fact she had nothing at all to confess.

But what of now!

Guilt poured fresh waves of colour on Becky's cheeks. What of the deceit she was practising? The pretence of spending Saturday evenings at the Hawley house when in truth she was visiting a dance hall, and more than that – she shivered against the cold touch of sinfulness suddenly fingering her spine – she spent those hours with a man, a man who kissed her, a man whose emotions, whose affection for her spoke in his every smile, the tenderness of his feelings glowed soft in his eyes, and the love, the love she felt throb strong and hard when he drew her close in the privacy of those dark obscured corners.

Was this what she should ask forgiveness for?

Was this what life demanded . . . forgiveness for being in love?

'Hello luv, 'ow you keepin'? Eh I was so sorry to hear of your mother, bad do were that, it be sad enough when folk goes natural but a bomb . . . an' on a church! Lord, what do the world be a' comin' to!'

It had taken a moment for her mother's voice to penetrate the cloak of thought Becky had drawn about herself. As she looked to the person addressed, alarm flashed like electricity sparking from every nerve ending; Kate Hawley! She caught her breath. Oh Lord! Don't let her mention those Saturday evenings.

'It be 'ard for you, wench, I knows 'cos I've bin through it, seems your 'eart won't never know the mendin' . . . but God's good, though we might not always think it . . .'

Let Him be good to me, please let Him be good to me. Becky's soundless prayer added fervour to the statement.

'. . . He sends His comfort one road or another. But what o' your father? Eh 'ow he must miss 'er . . .'

A shake of the head emphasising her feelings for the loss father and daughter had suffered, the older woman continued.

'. . . he 'as my sympathy, tell 'im that, wench, tell your father he 'as the sympathy o' the Turners.'

'Thank you, Mrs Turner,' Katrin replied politely. 'That is most kind, I know my father would wish me to thank you on his behalf also.'

'Ar well,' Mary Turner's head swung again, 'ain't much a body can do 'cept sympathise but you tell that father o' your'n, you tell Jacob 'Awley be there aught the Turners can 'elp with then it need only be asked.'

They could move on now. Her mother had given her condolence now she would say goodbye.

Becky met Katrin's glance in mute appeal.

She was afraid! Deep inside, Katrin Hawley laughed. Becky Turner was afraid her secret would be revealed for her mother to see. Should she do that? Should she take her revenge now, see the girl shamed before her mother? It would be entertaining to see her squirm. But it would be a pity to bring the curtain down before the play ended, and going by the accounts both girls shared with her after each Saturday night entertainment, the confidences concerning those covert moments they whispered in the factory canteen, then it was certain this particular production had not run its length; there would be several Acts yet to come. Katrin basked in the sense of power coursing like flame. Several Acts! She would watch them all.

'What be all the to-do over your way? I 'ear the police moved everybody outta their 'ouses.' As she sat with several women enjoying the ten-minute teabreak, Miriam Carson's nerves jumped at the query. So it had happened!

'You 'eard right,' a second woman replied. 'Wouldn't tek no for an answer; bloody thoughtless I calls it turfin' folk out, not givin' 'em a minute to collect so much as a pair 'o bloomers.'

Easing her bottom on a hard wooden crate that served as a seat, one more woman joined the conversation, asking loudly, 'An' why would you be wantin' of a clean pair o' bloomers, Elsie Partridge, be it a fella you was meetin'?'

'Ask him!' Elsie laughed, 'Ask Simeon Cartwright about my bloomers, he's had the seein' of 'em near as often as my old man.'

'Be that right, Simeon?'

'Be what right?' Simeon Cartwright's lined face lifted over the rim of the large container half filled with cartridge cases.

'What Elsie 'ere just said.'

'An' what be that?' Obviously knowing he was to be the subject of some good natured tease, Simeon played along.

Coyly lowering her gaze to the tin mug in her hands the woman continued the pretence. 'Elsie says as how you gets to see her bloomers near as often as her old man.'

'Eh Elsie!' The lined face frowned mock distress though rheumy eyes twinkled. 'You said as nobody'd ever know, you said as 'ow it were our secret, what'll I do should my Sarah find out?'

'You can come stay wi' me.' It was the woman who had first questioned Elsie. 'I could do wi' a few nights of 'ows ya father, tek me mind off this bloody war.'

'Careful, Maude,' Elsie's turbaned head shook warningly, 'there be a lot more to Simeon Cartwright than you be seein' at this moment.'

'That's what I be countin' on.' Maude's laugh rang out. 'Seein' a lot more. You be ready forra night o' passion, does you, Simeon?'

Pushing flat cap back from his brow Simeon scratched thoughtfully at his head. 'Passion?' He pulled a wry grin.

'Yeah passion, I wouldn't 'ave thought a fella like y'self to go a' forgettin' o' what passion be.'

'Forget! I've not only forgot what it be, I forgets 'ow I comes to get it.'

'Well, I can put that right quick as I can mek one o' them bullet cases, you just come outside wi' me along o' finishing time.'

'I'll do that Maude,' Simeon's wicked smile spread wide, 'but only if I gets to bring Elsie's bloomers.'

Glancing conspiratorially about the workshop Simeon leaned closer, whispering, 'Passes 'em to me every time her comes into work, they be vital to defence. Old Hitler knows about our guns, our ships an' about our aeroplanes but he don't know about Elsie Partridge's bloomers; they be our secret weapon; should them Germans invade then we waves Elsie's bloomers an' they'll run like buggery all the way back to Berlin.'

The old man's chuckle echoed behind him as he shuffled further along the line of machinery. The conversation returned to its starting point.

Pouring more tea into the cap of her large vacuum flask Elsie sipped several times before speaking. 'I was wonderin' the same meself, I means it be expected you come out when them bombers calls a payin' o' their respects, but when they ain't . . . well it 'ad me fair flummoxed I don't mind tellin' you.'

'But they must 'ave said a reason,' Maude chipped in.

'Oh they said all right. They said as 'ow it were a fractured gas main, that they couldn't be tekin' a chance on its explodin', though I never smelled no gas and neither did anybody else shoved along to wait in the church hall or in them school rooms; you ask me I says it be a load o' codswallop, there ain't no broken gas pipe.'

'Well they must 'ave believed summat!'

'Ar they believed!' Elsie answered disparagingly. 'They believed as we all 'ave brains like coddled eggs, soft enough to swallow what they tells wi'out the thinkin', but Elsie Partridge be no noggy'ead, her be sharp enough to know that lot all be bigger liars than old leatherin' arse an' he got kicked out o' hell for tellin' lies.'

'Well it be no lie my sayin' you lot will be short in the pay packet if you don't get them machines goin'.'

Casting a calculating wink at her companions, Elsie turned to the man come to stand beside them. 'Eh Fred, you looks done in; why don't you find a corner down the end o' the shop an' 'ave y'self a quiet hour?'

Well used to banter, the foreman smiled good humouredly. 'I would Elsie, but I knows how much you wenches would miss me.'

'Oh Lord!' Maude groaned, ''ere we go again!' Rising as one the group of women looked to the roof, as the blare of sirens sounded an air raid.

She could have told them. Miriam returned to her work, ignoring the alarm as did all of the others. She could have said what Philip Conroy had told herself and her father.

'*We will say the constant vibration of bombs hitting the ground may have resulted in an underground gas pipe becoming cracked; that in the interest of safety the area has to be vacated until it can be dealt with.*'

Until it could be dealt with! Miriam worked the spinning bar of brass with uncomprehending mind.

A Step Too Far

When would that be? When would this be over? When could she be sure her son was safe from . . . ?

Safe! Hands becoming still, she stared at the rapidly turning bar, seeing nothing of the golden darts glancing from beneath the play of overhead electric lights. Reuben *could* be safe now, she could forbid him to go through with what Philip Conroy asked, it wasn't too late.

'Be you all right, Miriam, wench? You looks like you seen a ghost.'

'I . . .' Miriam tried to answer but tears were suddenly in the way.

Reaching for the stop button, the foreman cut the power to the machine then gently drew Miriam aside.

'Get y'self a few minutes.' He lowered her to sit on an upturned box. 'Don't do no good tryin' to carry on while you be feelin' poorly, accidents won't 'elp win no war.'

'Her needs to be at 'ome.' Elsie Partridge observed over her own machine. 'The wench be near to breakin', any but the blind can see that; what wi' losin' 'er man to this bloody war then seein' 'er father bein' sacked from Prodor for what be no reason, it be a marvel 'er ain't broke afore now: you teks my advice, Fred, you'll send 'er 'ome, ain't like her will be mekin' many more cartridge cases afore knockin' off time anyway, not wi' the state 'er be in.'

Glancing toward the large wall-mounted clock, the foreman thought quickly. Less than an hour to shift change, he could work the machine until the next woman clocked on, that way there would be no loss of production.

'Reckon Elsie be right.' He returned his glance to Miriam. 'You get along 'ome and rest.'

'But I can't leave before the end of my shift!'

'You let me worry about that.' The foreman smiled at the protest. 'There'll be no shortfall in the number o' cases, you 'ave my word. Now will you be all right on your own or does you want I get somebody from First Aid to go along of you?'

She had not wanted any person to walk home with her.

Tying a cotton paisley-patterned scarf beneath her chin, Miriam glanced along the street. Houses she had known from childhood, tiny, smoke-caked homes huddled together in friendship as in structure, now watched like strangers beneath the dank grey sky.

'*You get along 'ome and rest.*'

But it was not home she wanted, nor was it rest; she wanted her son safe in her arms. That was how it was going to be! Miriam's mouth set in a determined line . . . and not all the Philip Conroys in the world would prevent it.

Resolution marking her steps, Miriam turned swiftly from the Alma Tube Works toward the High Bullen, where she paused, looking at the clock tower of the ancient soot-blackened spire of Saint Bartholomew's Church. Its clock showed ten minutes to four o' clock. Forty more minutes and the schools would empty for the day. Should she wait? Miriam hesitated. Had she let worry get the best of her? Hadn't Philip Conroy promised he would let no harm befall her son? But that man could not be with Reuben every minute of the day, he was not with him now, so what good was that promise! Argument ebbing and flowing, reason countered by reason running through her mind, Miriam mumbled an apology to a drab, harassed-looking woman attempting to steer a deep bodied pram around her. She brought it to an irate halt in front of the low window of a small shop, tutting loudly about 'life bein' 'ard enough what wi' shops empty o' anythin' wi'out 'aving to work your way about folk who 'ave naught better to do that stand a' gawpin'!'

Miriam struggled with the uncertainty growing in her mind.

Reuben had not hesitated, he had simply agreed to all Philip Conroy had requested . . . and she had allowed it! *She* . . . and no one else . . . *she* had sent Reuben into danger, for without her consent none of this could have taken place.

' . . . trust him Miriam, trust our son, let him do what has been asked of him.'

No, Tom! This time you are wrong! Resolution renewed she crossed the High Street turning left into Earp's Lane following it to emerge into Church Street.

It was quiet after the sounds of the Bullen with its cross flow of traffic. Ahead of her, the stone church rose dark against the sky. It was normally quiet in this backwater but today the silence was strangely ominous. She shivered as she watched the man coming toward her.

19

Closing a file marked 'Secret', Philip Conroy leaned back in his chair. Tomorrow he would return to London, his report would go to the head of the department; but would that see the end? Would there ever be an end . . . ? He breathed a long breath of exhaustion. The answer to that question was, there was no answer, as long as man fought against man there would be infiltrators, those working against a country from the inside. 'Bloody quislings' as Isaac Eldon had spat angrily, but Godfrey Browne was no quisling.

It had been something of a miracle. There had been a report of maps displaying geographical locations of some town he had never heard of. He had felt little interest in the information passed to him – a young lad, coloured crayon on bits of paper, probably a school project, certainly not worth time following up. But of course bureaucracy demanded he give it a passing glance. He had thought that was all it would take, until he checked the name of the town. Wednesbury! Even now he felt tingles of alarm race along his spine. The town was small, insignificant on the map, but set where it was in the centre of the industrial Midlands, producing what it did, munitions vital to this country's existence as a sovereign nation, then those maps had suddenly taken on a very different face, and with the face had come a body.

It had been known to the Ministry of Defence for some time that Luftwaffe photo reconnaissance aircraft had made a series of passes over Coventry, Birmingham and Wolverhampton, no doubt assessing what anti-aircraft defences they boasted. Assessment had paid off. It had cost England almost an entire city; four hundred and sixty nine German bombers all raining their payload onto Coventry. Christ, how had anybody survived?

There had been some indication of a special operation being planned by the enemy. The Code and Cipher School housed at Bletchley had decoded a signal laying down procedures for something they termed 'Moonlight Sonata'. The target was not named but the word '*Korn*' had been mentioned. That had been on the eleventh of November and on the twelfth another decoded transmission listed target 51 '*Einheitpreis*', target 52 '*Regenschirm*' and target 53 and again that word '*Korn*.'

Not a lot of use as it stood; without knowledge of what those targets might be, the Ministry's hands were tied. In the quiet of his office, Philip Conroy relived the feeling of utter hopelessness. All that next day the sense of impending disaster had haunted him, the thirteenth! It seemed destined to live up to its reputation. It had been the evening of that same night that capricious Lady Luck had seen fit to change her mind. A captured German pilot had been overheard telling a cellmate of a massive air attack planned to take place between the fifteenth and twentieth of November. He mentioned the same words that had been in that earlier decryption, *Regenschirm* and *Einheitpreis*. It had taken but a moment for someone to say '*Regenschirm is German for umbrella*' and another to add whimsically that '*perhaps they had been talking of England's Umbrella Man, that is what Neville Chamberlain is nicknamed, isn't it? On account of his always being seen carrying an umbrella.*'

Not Neville Chamberlain, those German prisoners had not been discussing the trait of England's erstwhile Prime Minister! Understanding had rushed in like a flood. They must have been speaking of his home town, of Birmingham! One of those predetermined targets had to be that city. But what of that other word, what of '*Einheitpreis*'?

'*Say it quickly enough and you could be saying "all at one price".*'

A colleague quipped, '*That would be the Sixpenny Store, Woolworth's to you ignoramuses.*'

The laughter stopped. Birmingham was a city of heavy industry, could that other target also be a part of the vital heartland, another of the larger towns? It had to be. But which, Coventry or Wolverhampton? Eventually they had settled for the latter.

Lady Luck had smiled yet her kiss had been the kiss of Judas. The very next evening Coventry had been almost wiped from the earth and eight days later had come Birmingham's date with destiny in an air attack which severed three vital water mains, leaving the city without water with which to fight the fires. The destruction had been harrowing, as had been the worry of where and what was *Korn*? The question had remained to plague, could that be Wolverhampton or some other place entirely? Days brought no solution and it had seemed they never would; but then had come information regarding a boy and several hand drawn maps.

It had fallen to him to come to Wednesbury and as his train approached the town he had wondered just why it was so important. There was virtually no visible evidence of its coal mining history, no colliery winding wheels as he could see, yet the part it played in the war effort was so crucial that the powers that be had seen fit to despatch him there, his brief to interview a boy. He had felt a fierce aggravation. What could a boy tell him? A boy would most probably pee in his trousers at the first question!

But Philip Conroy had reckoned without Reuben Carson.

The lad had not peed his trousers. He had shown no sign of fright when questioned by a stranger but gave each reply clearly and directly.

'*The maps are for a school project.*' That answer had confirmed his theory. The whole thing would be a waste of time. Then the boy had spoken of a 'Raygensherm' and it was that had the tingles running along his spine, turning to icicles when Reuben had gone on to mention 'fine at price' and finally 'corn'.

The boy's pronunciation had been incorrect, but it had been near enough to match with the information gained from intercepted enemy transmissions.

Intelligence had reported radio transmissions emanating from somewhere in the Midlands, transmissions feeding information to the enemy. Could they be coming from this town?

Similarity had been too close to ignore. Philip Conroy remembered the leap of his veins. What he had supposed would be a complete waste of time had suddenly promise to be what Special Branch were searching for . . . an enemy agent!

Lord, if only the connection had been made sooner, maybe they could have been ready for the raids which had decimated Coventry and Birmingham. But the milk had been spilled and it was no use crying over it. Two names, two cities, but the third 'Korn', where was that destined to be? They had found no similarity for that, no indication of what it might imply.

He had reported his findings, emphasising his belief that neither the boy nor his family knew anything beyond what they had told. It had been at that meeting he had learned of a new project, one which was the reason for the enemy's heavy bombardment of the Midlands. They knew what, but they didn't know where; that at all costs must remain a secret.

All costs meaning a boy's safety!

Philip Conroy's teeth clenched. War was a dirty bloody business!

The boy could not be told of any threat yet it had been certain he knew, it had shown in his quiet reply when asked would he take one further step. He had shown no trace of fear, no sign of reticence when requested to undertake what for a man would have been termed a mission. He accepted immediately. Not quite so readily the mother and grandfather, but then their reluctance had been understandable as had Miriam Carson's desire to take her son from that school.

She had been intercepted, asked would she go home willingly or be escorted there by a policeman?

What must the woman have felt? What were her feelings now, supposing the lad had told her what had gone on inside the school? Somehow he felt the boy had not revealed how he had been summoned to the headmaster's room, detained there after the rest of the pupils and staff had left the premises. He had also likely not spoken of the man opening a cupboard and taking out what appeared to be, in Reuben's own words, *'something like my mum's wireless set except she doesn't talk to hers. He pressed a switch and said something I did not understand into a microphone in his hand. My mum doesn't do that either so I guessed the machine must be a way of talking to people, you know, rather like a telephone, not that I have ever used a telephone.'*

The boy had later confided the conversation privately, adding *'I would rather you don't repeat this to my mum, Mr Conroy. She has enough to worry over without my giving her more.'*

Again that concern for others. Reuben Carson was a young man deserving of his 'lieutenant' status.

'You have been most helpful, Reuben,' the headmaster had said. *'Your map has shown very clearly the spot my friends have been searching for.'*

'Friends?' Reuben had queried convincingly.

'Let us say my countrymen.' Browne had turned again to the transmitter. *'Now it is time to give them the information they have been seeking.'*

'*You mean the golf links?*'

The man had depressed the switch again, spoken into the microphone then, flicking it off once more, had turned again to Reuben.

'*Of course the golf links. Or rather, what is beneath them. It was very clever of you to have found out they hide a secret underground armaments factory. Not that secrecy will be of any importance for much longer; the Luftwaffe will wipe it out once my message is received.*'

'*I was certain then, Mr Conroy,*' Reuben had explained, '*that the machine was a way of passing information to the Germans and that should he tell them about the golf links, even though there was no truth in what he said, they would bomb Wednesbury like they bombed Birmingham. I couldn't let that happen, not if I could help it, so that was when I grabbed the inkstand and hit him with it.*'

How could one so young have such presence of mind, so much courage? He thanked God for it, for the time it allowed for himself and the officer of Special Branch to reach that room.

The blow had taken the man by surprise, leaving him dazed but by no means incapable. He had snarled as they had entered the room and in that same moment snatched the lad, holding him with one arm across the throat, the other hand touching a revolver to his temple.

'*Make no mistake,*' he had said, pressing the gun against the young face, '*I will shoot. I will kill the boy. Allow me to leave, make no attempt to prevent or follow, then before I leave this country I will set him free; on that you have my word.*'

'The word of a traitor!'

'The word of a patriot,' Browne had answered the accusation. *'The word of a man loyal to his own country. Allow me to introduce myself; Gottfried von Braun, former officer of the Wehrmacht.'*

'In other words a bloody spy!'

'If you wish.' Cold with menace, the pale grey eyes had glinted. The gun swung to meet the police officer surging toward von Braun; the bullet it spat threw him to the ground where he lay unmoving.

There had been a moment of silence. A silence intense and heavy, a moment of disbelief.

'Now,' von Braun had said matter of factly, *'I must leave.'*

Only then had the boy moved. Muttering, *'You're not going anywhere,'* at the same time he lifted one leg and brought his foot down hard on that of his captor.

It could only have been the hand of God that prevented von Braun pulling that trigger, but the gun had fallen from his hand as he screamed with pain.

'I knew as that would take his mind off leaving.' Reuben had grinned as other officers had rushed into the room placing von Braun in handcuffs.

'You see, Mr Conroy, I noticed he was wearing a slipper, that meant his gout was playing up again. We all of us lads knows of his gout, that sometimes his foot gets to be so painful he can scarce walk on it; so it was my guess that, could I stamp on that foot, it might have him drop the gun and give you the chance to grab him.'

Pulling the file toward him, Philip Conroy opened it at the last page to read again the words he had written as a footnote. Words describing the bravery and selflessness of a young boy.

'A boy the country will never learn of,' he whispered. 'England will not know the debt she owes you, Reuben Carson, but I know . . . yes, I know.'

20

What would Becky Turner have said had her secret been revealed? Would she have denied she had ever visited that dance hall? Perhaps, but would her mother have believed that denial?

Placing underwear she had laundered into the drawer of her dressing table, Katrin Hawley smiled at her reflection in the mirror.

'Why did you not tell Mary Turner of her daughter's visits to Wolverhampton? Of the man named Earl? Was it because you value Becky's friendship?'

The smile remained as if painted on the surface of the glass, but the eyes took on the hue of ice. Becky Turner had not valued the friendship of a girl she had helped humiliate in a school playground. It was probable she never thought of that incident, but Katrin Hawley thought of it and that was the reason of that confidence remaining unbroken. To have informed Mary Turner would have afforded some little gratification, but that little could be nurtured, helped to blossom and grow until it reached the point of ultimate satisfaction, the moment when revenge would taste its sweetest. So the charade would go on, she would continue to assist in the achieving of Becky's dreams, but one day payment would be taken, Becky Turner would awaken to a nightmare.

Can you be so positive? The reflection seemed to ask its own question.

Slipping into a chocolate brown skirt that fastened easily about her slim waist and teaming it with a cream blouse, she looked again into the mirror. 'Oh yes,' she breathed, 'I can be positive . . . one way or another I will make it happen.'

Her father would be working with Isaac Eldon!

Katrin Hawley watched the man on the opposite side of the large desk but her mind refused to leave the words he had just spoken.

Isaac Eldon would be working with her father!

It had to be a mistake, Arthur Whitman had not intended to say Isaac Eldon, it had been a slip of the tongue.

'I see you are surprised.' Whitman smiled, catching the frown settling on his secretary's face. 'I suppose quite a few will feel the same way once the news breaks on the factory floor. Isaac and Jacob,' he laughed, 'aptly named, wouldn't you say Katrin, seeing they will work so close together.'

'*I don't understand.*' Katrin seemed to talk to herself. 'Eldon, he . . . he was arrested, he is in prison.'

'Arrested! In prison! Good Lord, Katrin, whatever gave you that idea?'

'The man who came to the office, the one who had Eldon called from the factory, he was from the Ministry . . '

'That's right.'

Her mind oblivious of the interruption Katrin continued in the same dazed half murmur, ' . . . it had to be because of those maps, it had to be.'

Arthur Whitman frowned. 'Maps,' he repeated sharply, 'what maps would they be?'

The sudden cut of his voice or instinct? Whichever, it had Katrin snap alert. She had made an error speaking of those maps.

'Sorry.' She glanced at the pad on her knee then back to the man. 'What was that, Mr Whitman? I'm afraid I didn't quite catch that last word.'

'Maps!' Enunciation precise, Arthur Whitman replied. 'You said it . . . Eldon's arrest . . . had to be because of some maps.'

'Did I say that? I must have got my tongue in a twist, what I meant to say was p'raps, perhaps it was the rumours which circulated after Mr Eldon's leaving so abruptly had me thinking he had been arrested, rumours hinting at his passing information about the work done here at Prodor.'

'That's the last thing Isaac Eldon would do! Whoever spread those rumours best pray God they don't make the mistake of saying them in front of me; that man came from the Ministry of Defence with a special project they wanted Isaac to work on. There is to be a new system of heavy shell manufacture and the project is to be carried out in conjunction with Titan Engineering of Darlaston. Isaac and your father have devised a method of shell forging that requires no internal machining, a method they have termed 'finished cavity forgings'. This will prove invaluable in terms of production of heavy artillery, increasing the number of twenty-five pound shells for the Howitzer Gun and the three point seven Anti Aircraft Guns, it might even double the number made at present as well as significantly adding to the numbers of all the rest of what is made here at Prodor once the new plant is installed.'

Her father and Isaac Eldon had devised a new method of shell production! Back at her own desk, Katrin contemplated what she had heard. Eldon had not as she thought – as she had hoped – been arrested . . . but those maps? She had seen them with her own eyes, detailed drawings of Wednesbury showing areas of industry, maps carried by the grandson of Isaac Eldon! The authorities could have found no evidence of those maps, how otherwise could Eldon have avoided a charge of treason? A charge which, if proved, could have him if not hanged then at least imprisoned for a great many years. But he was not imprisoned. Katrin's fingers tightened over her pencil. Isaac Eldon was free as he had ever been.

They would not let her into that school.

Standing at the window of the home she shared with her father, Miriam Carson stared at the street through a misty sheen of rain. She had gone to Church Street, she had almost reached the school when a man had stepped in front of her.

'*Sorry,*' he had said, barring her way when she had made to walk around him. '*Sorry, Mrs Carson, but I can't allow you to go any further.*'

He knew her name, knew why she was here . . . Reuben! Fear which had dragged at her the whole day became ice blocking every vein. This man must have come to the school for the same reason she had, to take her son!

'*Reuben!*'

She had cried the name and pushed at the tall dark-suited figure, but it did not move. Square in her path he had said quietly.

'*Please Mrs Carson, I do understand your being afraid but to let you into that building could be to put you and your son in danger.*'

'*I want my son!*' She had tried to dart past, to run to the squat grey stone building that was Saint Bartholomew's School for Boys, but the man caught at her before she had taken a step. Holding her firmly by the arms he had spoken quietly as before.

'*Mrs Carson . . .*'

Somehow the words had breached the fear pounding like waves in her head.

'*Mrs Carson, screaming can only draw attention, which could affect what both of us know is happening in that building.*'

'*Reuben!*'

It was the sob of a mother terrified for the safety of her child.

'*He will be unharmed. You might see only myself in the street, but I assure you there are others and we all have the same goal, to see this business over and your boy home. We do realise the strain you are under, but we must insist on your returning home; you can do so with the assistance of a police constable should you so wish.'*

Drawing together the rough cotton blackout curtain, Miriam turned from the window. *We.* It was the same word Philip Conroy had used, that all-effacing *we*; it had also been said with that same quiet authority Conroy displayed, a firmness that conveyed the certainty he would brook no refusal, and the offer of police assistance had been no offer but a veiled proposition. She had been left with no alternative, but every step back to Cross Street had been a knife in her heart.

'This is the BBC Home Service. The news at nine o'clock with Alvar Liddel reading it. There has been more heavy fighting . . .'

Reuben had turned up the volume on the small wireless set she was buying on hire purchase. *'A tanner a week, waste o' money be what it is, you gets the news just the same wi' the newspaper!'* Her father had protested and sixpence a week could, she had admitted, be spent buying extra vegetables from the allotment when gardeners had some to spare, it could be saved toward a bag of coal. She would have foregone the wireless had not her father smiled and said to go ahead. And she was glad she had, for by listening each evening to the news she felt somehow closer to those far from home, men risking their lives for people like herself, closer to women who as she had done, sat in dread that the next report would involve the area in which their own loved ones fought.

The broadcast over, she switched off the wireless, told Reuben it was time for bed and reached for the socks her son wore through quicker than she could darn.

'Germany continued its advantage.' It might not have been reported quite so bluntly but that had been the thread underlying the latest bulletin. So many men, so many lives, so many Toms with life snatched away before it could be lived, death finding them in places so far from home, each man killed by another whose face he never saw.

But enemies were found not only on foreign ground. Letting the mending fall to her lap, Miriam stared into the fire.

'*We knew information was being passed,*' Philip Conroy had explained, '*but we did not know exactly how or from where. It was in order to obtain proof that we asked Reuben take a further step.*'

That could so easily have proved a step too far.

''Night, mum.'

Lifting her face for her son's goodnight kiss, she vowed silently, never again. Never again would she allow him to do anything so dangerous, no matter it had gone without a hitch.

'*It was okay, mum,*' Reuben had laughed at her anxiety. '*I was never in a moment's danger, it was all a bit of a let-down; Mr Conroy and another man came into the room and Mr Browne just shrugged his shoulders, said he was ready to go and that was it . . . finished!*'

Watching him hug his grandfather goodnight, Miriam felt a pull at her heart. It had been like listening to Tom, he had always downplayed the worrying side of things, he would never have a mountain made out of a molehill; father and son, they were so alike. Tears sudden and hot rose to her throat, she should thank God for the safekeeping of her son but she could only cry her reproach at His taking her husband.

Reuben hesitated at a rap to the door. The front door! It would be no neighbour; no one from Cross Street or those streets in close proximity to it ever used the front door, they invariably came to the rear of the house, giving the door a tap and calling 'it be me . . . be you in Miriam, wench?'

Isaac laid aside the newspaper and went to open the door.

'I apologise for calling so late . . .'

Philip Conroy! Miriam's blood froze. No! She threw aside the sock she was mending. No more . . . ! He would never use her son again!

Ushered into the tiny living room, Philip Conroy smiled at the lad, his hand already extended in greeting. The boy's bravery deserved recognition, but how many brave souls received that reward?

'I felt I had to call . . . I was hoping to speak to Reuben, to offer my congratulations . . .'

'It was nothing!'

'Nevertheless, I wanted to give my personal thanks, catching up with that fellow would have taken a lot longer had it not been for you; I also wished to apologise personally to you Mrs Carson, I'm sorry we could not allow you to go into the school, I hope you understand the problem that could have caused.' She couldn't know the problem was a likely bullet in the chest and another in her son's head!

'As I said to you afore, Mr Conroy, I don't 'ave the learnin' o' some so I asks your patience wi' my failin' to fathom the involvin' of a lad.'

'Things had to appear normal, Mr Eldon.' Philip Conroy answered Isaac. 'So very much depended upon that. Believe me, we thought long and hard before making a decision.'

'That decision bein' to use my grandson!' Isaac's pent-up emotions ground the exclamation.

'I didn't mind, granddad, I wanted to help. I had to do what was best, you see that, don't you?'

'Ar I sees that, I be proud o' you, lad.'

Miriam's own pride was overshadowed by question. Had Reuben realised the potential danger? Could a boy of fourteen reason fully what it was he was being asked to do? *Had she?* Miriam's senses flared. Had she entirely comprehended what she had agreed to, the situation she had allowed her son to be placed in?

She looked at the man opposite: well-kept hands, neat dark suit and immaculate white shirt a vivid contrast to her father's well worn trousers and once blue shirt faded to grey as a result of boiling to remove the grease of factory work. So many differences, but beneath them both men were the same, both did what was necessary in fighting this war; and so did she in her way. Like Tom, she was willing to give her all, but that did not grant her the right to gamble with the safety of their son, to consent to his exposure to such risk. If she had lost him!

Miriam fought the tide of fear that still accompanied that thought. Hardly able to disguise it even now, barely able to hold the tears pressing against the dam of her reserve she glanced at the clock, trying to smile as she asked Reuben be excused, adding as a salve to teenage feelings that so many nights disturbed by air raids compelled people to take advantage of sleep while they could.

Once more the father shone in the son. Miriam's heart expanded with pride as Reuben thanked Conroy for his visit, replying quietly to the man's repeated thanks that it was no more than his father would have wished. Then shaking hands and wishing Conroy goodnight, he had turned to her and in that moment she had seen a cloud cross his face, the bright glint of tears before they disappeared beneath a smile that hid a deep unhappiness.

'I didn't get it, mum,' he said softly. 'I didn't get to be lieutenant . . . I'm glad dad didn't have to know.'

21

Isaac Eldon had not been arrested!

Bitterness a gall in her throat, Katrin stared from the window of the train carrying her to Birmingham.

Why had he not been arrested? Why not charged? Those maps she had helped retrieve from the ground might have been crudely drawn but she had seen what they depicted: factories, chemical works, railway depots, sensitive material compiled, the boy had said, with the aid of Isaac Eldon. Yet nothing had happened to that man, no action had been taken against him even though she had reported what she had seen. It could only be that the boy had told him of bumping against a woman and repeated the short conversation which had followed. That would have alerted Eldon. The man might be no more than a factory hand, he might have only a basic education, but that did not make him a fool. He must have realised the possibility of a report being made to the authorities, of some investigation being instigated and so had destroyed the evidence, had probably burned those papers while impressing on his grandson the need for secrecy.

But what he did not know was the identity of that woman.

Leaving the train at Snowhill Station enmeshed in rancour, Katrin paid little mind to the bomb-damaged properties, the fire-blackened buildings rising like skeletons from graves of rubble and broken concrete.

Isaac Eldon did not know who had spoken with his grandson. Nor did he know her vengeance! Let him rejoice in his security, let him wallow in the idea nothing could befall him, nothing would spoil his mundane working-class life; but Katrin Hawley would. One method had failed but there had to be another, sooner or later the chance to destroy Isaac Eldon would arise and when it did Katrin Hawley would grasp it with both hands.

Her father had returned to Prodor, he was back in the job he loved, in the place he had worked since leaving school a lad of less than thirteen years of age. But he had not returned as department manager.

'That don't be for me wench. I don't be one for paperwork; give me a job wi' metal, the mekin' of it or the forging of it into whatever be wanted; ask me about the designin' of new machinery or set me the problem of how to produce two of anythin' in the time it had teken for the makin' of one and I'll do my best in the solvin' of it, but management and paperwork don't be for me.'

Looking at her father sitting with his newspaper, the sense of relief Miriam had felt on hearing of his rejoining Prodor lived another brief moment.

She had worried so much when she'd learned of his 'being sacked'. He had 'been marched off', 'teken away afore even the shift ended . . .', 'be said he's

A Step Too Far

been a tittle-tattlin' about what be made at them works.'

Those had been some of the hushed remarks, but they had not been so hushed she could not hear. They had been meant to be heard, said by people who knew nothing of the reason behind her father's being dismissed and cared less for the hurt their gossip caused.

She had asked her father the reason, of course she had. But he had said only she should not fret. Not fret! How could he have imagined she wouldn't have fretted? How could he have left her to worry? But that was unfair! He had not given the true reason because he had been bound by the same Act had bound them both on the business of Philip Conroy . . . the Official Secrets Act; her father had been given a job of vital importance, one he would not speak of even to her. Was it the outcome of that job, the project he and Jacob Hawley had worked on together, the revolutionary new method of producing shells without having to separately machine the inside of the cavity? That much he had since been able to share with her.

Had something of that project leaked despite precaution? Was that the information Philip Conroy said was known to have been passed to the enemy? The man had not confirmed that of course, but it did not take a mastermind to construe its being the reason of the hoax concerning the golf links.

'. . . they said as 'ow it were a fractured gas main . . . I never smelled no gas . . . you ask me I says it be a load o' codswallop, there ain't no broken gas pipe.'

Elsie Partridge had complained of the evacuation of nearby houses claiming it a nuisance, but what would have been her complaint had Wednesbury undergone an all out air attack?

'D'you think there really would have been a raid, I mean one deliberately aimed at the golf links?'

Reuben could have been reading her thoughts.

'No, just the golf links, son . . .'

Miriam watched the pair, Reuben at his grandfather's feet, face upturned to the grave look of the older lined one. 'Not simply that place.' Isaac shook his head. 'I reckon had it not been for you the whole of Wednesbury would 'ave suffered what Coventry went through; once the Germans had wind of where that new plant was supposed to be then this town would 'ave been wiped out completely.'

'It was a big risk Mr Conroy took, wasn't it, granddad? I mean letting me hand in my project.'

'Ar lad.' Isaac replied touching a hand to his grandson's head. 'An' it were a risk you ran in tekin' them maps to that bloody spy! I don't know what I were a thinkin' of lettin' you go through that!'

'I wanted to do it granddad, I wanted to help same as my dad helped.'

Miriam's heart lurched. Glancing at her father, she saw, that his heart was asking the same question as her own. What if Reuben had paid the same price, if helping protect others had cost his life as it had cost Tom's?

'You done that lad, you helped, and I know your dad would've been proud, he'd 'ave been like a cock wi' two tails; had *you* been a man you'd 'ave been awarded a medal, but as it is, you get naught, not even an official thank you.'

'I don't want any thanks, granddad, I'm satisfied knowing that German agent was captured.'

Isaac's look was grave. 'Ar,' he nodded, 'we all gives thanks for that, but I finds meself wonderin' 'ow the hell he got that post along of the school; when Anthony Eden called for men to volunteer for local Civil Defence, applicants was vetted in order to weed out potential Fifth Columnists, so 'ow come that bloody Nazi weren't weeded out, 'ow come he slipped through the net, an' to be appointed 'eadmaster no less?'

'Philip Conroy explained . . . as much as he was allowed.'

'Oh ar, he explained!' Isaac was not to be mollified. 'He said as the man were a retired schoolmaster, that he lived along o' Dartmoor but had volunteered to return to teachin' when so many were forced to leave the profession due to conscription, but that don't explain his gettin' away wi' pretendin' to be English; it be bloody careless on somebody's part, most like couldn't be bothered to check his background or they would have found 'im to be a German immigrant an' he would have been put in internment camp same as other foreigners.'

'That must be what happened to the Peoli family.'

'Who?' Isaac frowned.

'The Peolis.' Reuben looked up from his books. 'They are Italian, they have a sweet shop in Darlaston, it has a small café at the back serves tea and delicious ice cream . . . or they did up until a couple of weeks back, seems they just left giving no reason.'

'And how does Wednesbury's very own oracle know this?' Arms crossed over her chest, Miriam regarded her son.

Reuben grinned. 'Simple mum, Bobby Walker told me. He's a boy at school, lives in Dangerfield Lane, that's near to Darlaston shops so he gets to go there with his sister who keeps house for his dad since his mum died . . . so the news of the Peolis . . .'

Isaac glanced at his daughter. 'Who needs the Express and Star when they have a news reporter livin' in the house?'

'Mmm.' Miriam dropped her arms. 'Well, that particular reporter had best be careful over exactly what news he communicates.' Then she said seriously, 'Remember Reuben, you gave Conroy your promise to say nothing of what was said in this house nor of what happened at school.'

'I remember.'

Reaching for the coat she had laid ready alongside her gas mask, Miriam shrugged into it. 'There is something else it'll pay you to remember Reuben Carson,' she said, buttoning the coat, 'that is the promise you gave not to go on any more night wanderings. If the alarm sounds you are to go with next door into their shelter.'

'Mum, I'm nearly fourteen!'

'So you are . . . but it'll be when you're forty you can argue with me!'

'Best give up, lad.' Isaac smiled over his daughter's curt reply. 'You gets nowheres arguin' wi' a woman.'

'Reuben . . .' Miriam began warningly.

Reuben held up both hands. 'You win,' he laughed, 'but just you wait 'til I'm forty!'

He had laughed, but then why shouldn't he? He couldn't realise her heartache of having to leave him, of knowing he was alone in the house once her father returned to his work at Prodor.

'*I knows what it be like for you wench, but it 'as to be done . . .*'

Her father had sympathised. '*. . . but the lad be sensible . . .*'

Sensible! Could her father call it sensible for a young lad to roam alone at night? Lord, he could have been thought a spy!

Passing a word with the watchman at the gates of the Alma Tube Works, Miriam entered the machine shop and stamped her time card in the large wall clock.

A spy! But wasn't that what Reuben had been suspected of? The accuser had believed those maps not to be a project set as homework but something injurious to the safety of the country.

Indeed, given to that headmaster they could have proved just that. Wednesbury and probably near enough the rest of the Black Country would have been annihilated.

Miriam donned her overall and crossed to her own machine. Whoever it had been helped recover those papers had not intended harm to Reuben; the person had foresight enough to see what a young lad had not, that such information should not be in his possession.

Even so ... Miriam stared at the bar of brass waiting to be turned into gleaming carriers of death ... that person could have come to Cross Street, have spoken with her personally, have enquired of what Reuben was doing with those maps; that way the shock of it all could have been lessened, she herself would have taken Reuben and those papers to the police station.

It could only be that that person didn't think at the time, then when realisation dawned Reuben was already gone, so it was too late to ask where he lived, or could the person come to the house with him?

That was the answer. She set the machine in motion. There had been no malice in the action, no hurtful intent; information had been given solely out of concern for public safety and in that had possibly safeguarded Reuben.

Who are you? The thought whispered in Miriam's mind. Maybe one day I will know, one day I can say thank you.

He had gone back to the factory. Katrin glanced at the meal her father had scarcely touched. It was not the fault of her cooking, she had been taught cookery at school, lessons augmented by her mother with results appreciated and complimented upon by her father. And Violet had taught her much more than how to prepare a meal. Unwittingly she had taught patience, how to wait and watch for that right moment. Violet had not known she was guiding a young girl along that path, that her own evasive answering of questions put so long ago, her long-held silence concerning secrets held in a box, was paving that path.

Plate and cutlery washed and put away, Katrin glanced at the table. It had become a ritual with her mother, placing gas masks, torch, matches and candle together with flask and blankets on the table last thing before going to bed; ready, she would say, in case of an air raid. Now Katrin followed that same ritual, preparing for a dash from the house to the shelter in the garden. But she set out those things only to reassure her father, to have him believe she would go into the shelter in an emergency.

Her father and Isaac Eldon spent so much of the day together. Will o' the wisp, Katrin's thoughts flitted. They spent so many hours talking, testing and re-testing parts of new machinery, nursing it into position with all the care you would give a newly born child, barely leaving it long enough to take a meal in the factory canteen.

But that suited her. Snapping off the light she cast a quick look into the living room. Satisfied her father had positioned the mesh fireguard across the fire he had banked for the night, she walked upstairs. She did not mind being alone. No. She smiled at the reflection that jumped into the mirror as she flicked on the light. Being left to her own devices suited Katrin Hawley very well, especially so at Prodor.

Her father and Eldon were not the only ones devoting almost every minute to that new project; Arthur Whitman was there with them, there on the factory floor and not in his office.

'*That is most acceptable to you, is it not, Miss Hawley?*'

Katrin laughed the reply. 'Very, it is very acceptable.'

She had thought that Eldon would be reinstalled as manager on his return to Prodor, but that had not transpired. Nor, as yet, had Whitman done as he proposed and hired a man to act in that capacity. While he was so engrossed in seeing machinery installed, in getting that enterprise up and running to government specification, he was likely to leave more and more administration of affairs in the hands of his secretary.

'Your capable hands, Miss Hawley, that is the way it must remain.'

Right now Arthur Whitman depended upon her only as his secretary, but that would be remedied. She would get the other half! After all, he had been a married man, had known the comfort of the marital bed, comfort he must be missing.

Crossing the room, Katrin picked up the carrier bag she had deposited on her bed when returning from Birmingham. She emptied its contents and touched a hand to the cloud of sapphire silk chiffon spilling onto the cover.

This was one more thing Violet had taught. Use what you have to your best advantage. This dress would help her do that. Holding it against her, Katrin turned again to the mirror. The sales woman had seemed reluctant to let it go, had said there would probably be nothing of its quality until the war was over . . . and the price, could madam . . .

She had not said more. Katrin's sharp retort that cost was irrelevant cut the woman short. It had not been completely truthful. But that was of no consequence. Her glance sliding to the drawer of her dressing table Katrin laughed softly. 'That would not have been a bother to you, would it, mother?' she said. 'Truth was never a strong contender against Violet Hawley getting what she desired.'

Nor would it be a hindrance in her daughter achieving the same. The delicate dress shimmered in the light of the bedside lamp as Katrin twirled, exulting in the swish of its softness about her legs.

The time would come; sooner or later Arthur Whitman would recognise he needed more than a secretary and when he did, Katrin would be on hand, wearing a dress which embraced the body, enfolded it like the arms of a lover.

'You would have approved, mother,' she murmured drawing the delicate fabric through her hands. 'It was what you intended, wasn't it? That your daughter marry money.'

Arthur Whitman was not the wealthiest of men but the factory he owned was already enlarging, the products it made becoming so vital to the country that there had been talk of expansion, of setting up more factories in other areas. More factories more profit. Katrin smiled. More wealth for his wife to share.

22

'Oh God, I tell you me heart were in me mouth, I thought for certain mother were about to find out.'

'You should've known better.' Alice Butler's mouse brown hair hung in wet strands about her neck. 'You ought to 'ave known Kate would never give the game away.'

Dividing off a section of her friend's damp hair then winding it onto a steel curling pin, Becky Turner answered, 'You're right o' course, but you know how it is when anythin' takes you by surprise, you just don't think straight.'

Alice's reply was faintly disparaging. 'I hardly think seeing the wench out shoppin' be a cause for not thinkin' straight.'

'Well it were for me!' A touch of annoyance had Becky wind the next pin with a tug.

Wary of yet another scalp-snatching tug to her hair, Alice grabbed comb and curler, completing the task for herself while saying, 'I don't see why, ain't Kate showed her can be relied on? You ask me, Kate Hawley be a real nice wench, her wouldn't do nobody a bad turn; just look how her tried helpin' me when I applied to join the Women's Forces, couldn't nobody 'ave done more and it goes wi'out saying wouldn't anybody cover for you the way Kate has, tellin' your mother you be spendin' Saturday nights up at The Hollies when all the time you be off to Wolverhampton . . .'

'Shhh!' Becky interrupted fiercely her glance going to the doorway connecting kitchen to living room. 'Don't say anythin' about that, my mother has ears a bat would envy whenever there be somethin' her ain't intended to hear.'

'Like my mother.' Alice shrugged the towel from her shoulders. 'That one could hear a moth fart a hundred yards away, especially if the stink be somethin' can be gossiped over for weeks.'

'Such as marryin' an American.' Becky's voice dropped to a whisper. 'Lord, won't that give Cross Street plenty to talk about?'

'Not only Cross Street, but King Street, Queen Street and 'alf the other streets in Wednesbury, except there be one thing you've forgot.'

'Forgot?' Draping the towel about her own shoulders Becky cast a quizzical glance.

'Oh it ain't a big thing,' Alice replied as the other girl took her place on the plain wooden kitchen chair. 'It's just you 'aven't been asked yet.'

'But I will be, I just know I will.'

'Oh yes, just as surely as you know day will follow night!'

Becky's eyes, alight with happiness a moment ago, dulled with Alice's remark. It was true Earl had not proposed, but he would . . . he would! Hadn't he said how much he loved her? Hadn't he talked of her going to Miami? That was proof positive Earl intended asking her to marry him.

Alice combed the hair she'd had to wash with soap and rinsed it with vinegar to restore the shine.

'Becky, don't you think this has all happened a bit too quick?'

'No, I don't!'

'Well, I do!' Alice answered snap with snap. 'You are talkin' of marriage with a man you know next to nothin' about.'

'That's not true, Earl has told me lots about himself.'

Winding a long strand of blonde hair onto a steel curling pin, Alice could almost feel the emotions riding her friend. Becky had been wound like a spring for several weeks and the cause had to be Earl Feldman. Working long hours, having to make do with little or nothing of everything was long familiar to most folk of Wednesbury, so only one thing could possibly account for these unusual mood swings and that had to be the American. Alice dipped the comb into the chipped cup kept for mixing a stolen spoonful of sugar and hot water for use as setting lotion and drew it through another strand of hair. Questions would not be exactly welcomed, but questions needed to be asked.

'So,' she took the plunge, 'he's told you lots about himself . . . like what family he has, whether he lives with them, what he does for a living?'

'He doesn't need to.'

'Doesn't need to!' Alice stopped winding. 'Lord, Becky, listen to yourself.'

Snatching her hair free of Alice's fingers, Becky twisted about on the chair, her blue eyes ablaze.

'It's you needs to listen,' she spat, 'you don't know Earl like I do!'

'No, I don't.' Alice answered flatly. 'But I know you and I'm tellin' you not to set store by a man you've known such a short while. Becky . . . meetin' a fella once a week, spendin' all of a couple of hours together, gives no time to get to know him, I mean really know him.'

'I know enough!'

Alice looked at the girl. How much was enough?

'Earl's family,' she asked, dividing off another strand of hair, 'do they know enough, has he been as honest with his parents as you've been with yours?'

Towel bunched to her mouth, eyelids pressed hard down, Becky squeezed back the tears. Almost all of what Alice said was true, Earl had told her virtually nothing. But he'd said he'd be proud to take her to the States.

The words echoed in her mind.

'. . . *I'd sure be proud* . . .'

What more needed saying?

'Excuse me.' Katrin looked coldly at the man who had stepped up to her.

'For what? You 'aven't done anythin' . . . yet.'

The slight pause jangled Katrin's nerves, but she knew she must not let that show; to think her afraid of him would be to his advantage.

'I've been wantin' to talk wi' you for some time.'

'Really.' Mouth tight, head held high Katrin's glance was pure disdain.

'Yes,' The man stepped closer. 'I been watchin' you, y' be a smart lookin' wench . . .'

'Look,' Katrin's nerves flared, bringing a hot reply to her tongue, 'whatever it is you want to speak with me about, please say it and go.'

'Ooh I like that.' Small, wide-apart eyes glinted, 'Got a bit o' go in you, that can be very nice, make the finish to an evenin' more interestin'; an' that be what I want to talk about, an evenin' out on the town, you an' me, shall we say tomorrow?'

She could hit him with her gas mask box, but unfortunately that would have no lasting effect. She could cry out, call some passer-by, but that would draw attention. Discarding both ideas Katrin answered freezingly. 'Let us rather say never.'

Katrin saw the hands curl and stretch, the rat-like eyes gleam, a smile like a snarl settle on thin lips, the reply squeezing past them. 'You tellin' me no?'

It had been said with the semblance of humour but Katrin heard the threat. Derision her only weapon, she deliberately hesitated, allowing a small frown to settle between her brows before answering coolly.

'Forgive me for expecting you to understand; let me put it a little more simply. I do not wish to spend an evening with you, in fact I do not wish to spend one more moment talking to you.'

'Oh you don't!' He spat savagely. 'P'raps you'd rather spend a few hours along o' the cop shop talkin' to a copper.'

The police? Katrin's affected frown became genuine, but this time it was not fear of the man but rather of what he knew. Something not propitious for her, that showed in the flicker of sly cunning in his eyes. Was it to do with Freda Evans? Had he somehow discovered who had informed against her? No, she dismissed the thought, for the police that was a closed case, and in any event passing information of that sort was not an offence. But attempting to incriminate! Katrin's heart kicked in her chest. Could he have found out about her part in the Isaac Eldon affair?

'I see that's took some of the starch outta your drawers.'

Insidiously soft, the low laugh seemed to stroke its spite against her skin.

'Now, p'raps you'll be a bit more pleasant.'

She had to fight back, give her brain time to think.

'I really see no reason why . . .'

'Then forgive my not expectin' *you* to understand!' He grabbed her arm. 'Let me put it a little more simply, either you be pleasant, and I mean that in more ways than talkin' nice, or I tells the coppers about a couple of extra ration books in a house along of Hollies Drive.'

'Extra ration books?' Katrin strove to keep relief from her voice.

'Don't come the old soldier with me! Remember who it be you're talking to, you know very well what ration books.'

'Oh, those books.' Katrin's smile was cracked ice. 'If you are referring to the illegal ones sold to my mother then I must disillusion you, they were burned long ago, and as for her own, that was handed back to the Food Office. You may enquire there for yourself, you will find their records verify what I have told you. In fact, if you really desire my company I will go with you to that office, *they* will be most interested to learn who supplied the illegal ration books and so, I am sure, will the police.'

He would not risk that. The hand that flung her away smoothed sand-coloured hair already slick with Brilliantine, the eyes sparking malice. Jim Slater was not fool enough to venture the business of black marketeering. He didn't want that and the questionable reason of his not being conscripted into the Armed Forces undergoing a thorough investigation.

'Bloody smart-arsed bitch!'

He had gone.

Katrin turned toward home.

But was that the last she would see of Jim Slater?

'It's gone better than expected. Thanks to your "baby" the production of shell has increased significantly, the Ministry extends its appreciation as I am sure one day the nation will.'

'It is these should be thanked.' Arthur Whitman answered a stockily built middle-aged man who stood watching women machinists riveting base plates to large shell cases. 'God knows the men here work hard enough, but without the women we could not produce anywhere near what the Ministry asks.'

'Which brings me to a further reason for our visit here today.'

You guessed right! Arthur Whitman smiled grimly to himself as he followed the stocky man and his dark-suited retinue out of the noise-filled machine shop. This 'thank you' came with a 'but' at the end of it.

'As I said . . .'

In Whitman's office, the stocky Ministry official glanced at the young woman carrying a tea tray, his sentence hanging in the air until she left the room.

'As I said,' he repeated, taking a cup and adding sugar and milk, 'production has increased thanks to the process designed by you, but if we wish to win this war then that output has to be further added to.'

'Sir.' Arthur Whitman's manner cooled visibly. 'You and your colleagues have seen the way people are working here, the sheer physical effort that work involves, effort continued with day and night shifts, a twenty-four hour cycle done willingly on the part of women and of men. What they are achieving is already *more* than can be asked, yet you ask for a miracle.'

'Yes.' The near-bald head nodded sombrely. 'We are asking for a miracle, and believe me when I say it is only a miracle, a miracle performed by people like those working in your factory can save this country.'

'But they can only do so much!'

'The Ministry recognises that and of course offers technical assistance wherever it can.'

Technical assistance! Arthur Whitman's thoughts were scathing. That meant dotting the 'Is' and crossing the 'Ts' on other people's brain child!

'The man who proposed Finished Cavity Forgings, does he work here still?' The matter of fact tone did not disguise the keen observation of the man doing the asking, nor did it fool Arthur Whitman. These men would have made every possible investigation before coming to Wednesbury, they would know the names of every man and woman engaged at Prodor.

'Isaac Eldon.' He nodded. 'Yes, he is here and so is the man who worked on the project alongside him.'

'Jacob Hawley, an employee of Titan Engineering of Darlaston.' Sharp eyes watched over the rim of a teacup.

So they did know! Then perhaps they should know the offer of assistance for what it was really worth.

Looking deliberately at the face of each of the men, his voice calmer than his emotions, Arthur Whitman returned levelly, 'Both are here. Isaac Eldon, the man who construed the whole idea, and Jacob Hawley, who helped design and construct the machinery necessary for the production of Finished Cavity Forgings, between them seeing the whole thing up and running *without* the assistance of any government department, technical or otherwise. Would you care to speak with them? Who knows, they may be able to accomplish the miracle you spoke of.'

His smile still bland, he watched the flinch of eyes, the uncomfortable shuffle of cups on saucers. The dart had hit the board, and with no insignificant result!

'If that will not be an impediment.'

Arthur Whitman raised a patronising eyebrow before depressing a button on the intercom. 'Not at all, we are well used to interruption, and equally well used to dealing with it.'

★   ★   ★

'It be a lot to ask.'

Isaac Eldon ran a hand through hair not totally protected from dust by the flat cap he pushed back.

The Ministry officials having taken their leave, he stood with Arthur Whitman and Jacob Hawley, the three of them poring over machinery blueprints spread across the desk.

Whitman's answer was almost apologetic.

'They knew that, Isaac, but they had to ask it all the same. Of course, if it can't be done they will understand, there will be no blame.'

'D'aint say it couldn't be done.' Isaac bent to the blueprints. 'I reckons if we made modifications 'ere,' he prodded the paper with a finger, 'and another 'ere then it's possible to give the Ministry what it be callin' for, what say you, Jacob?'

Today was not the first time Isaac Eldon had pondered this particular question. Stepping aside, Arthur Whitman watched the two figures bent over his desk. Isaac had pinpointed where improvement could be achieved too quickly not to have already thought long and hard on the problem; and Hawley had agreed, adding his own ideas on how existing machinery could be adapted while entirely new ones were being made. Had they discussed between themselves this very question of a possible increase in production? Whitman smiled at the naivety of the thought – of course they had.

'There be a problem.' Isaac turned from perusing the blueprints. 'Least there be one from my point o' view an' I thinks Jacob sees it an' all.'

The two of them saw a problem. Why then had they

not broached it while those Ministry representatives were here? Holding the question inside, Arthur Whitman glanced toward the papers spread across his desk.

'Aint nothin' to do wi' that.' Isaac's glance followed to the blueprint. 'That be easy enough to alter . . . it be the other stuff they be wantin'.'

'What Isaac is saying,' glancing at the other man, Jacob Hawley took the brief nod as agreement to continue, 'what we *both* are saying is every request the government makes for a new type of weapon needs its own particular range of projectile. This requires the adapting and re-tooling not only of existing machinery but the designing and installing of new ones, itself no mild headache, but it is the accommodating of that new machinery will be the major problem, here at Prodor there is not space enough.'

'I see.' Whitman nodded. 'That is a problem, but . . .'

'Can't be no buts!' Isaac put in flatly. 'Them rockets we've been asked for can't be made in no corner an' neither can the launchers needed to fire 'em! What be needed is another factory, one given over entirely to the production of heavier armaments.'

Lower lip caught between his teeth, Arthur Whitman thought for a moment. 'There might be a place – you know it, Isaac, the New Crown Works.'

'Ar!' Isaac nodded. 'That could do nicely, there be several buildins to the place, all of which can be made suitable to 'ouse plant and equipment.'

'I'll get a surveyor over there in the morning, have him draw a map of the area.'

'No maps, they leads to trouble!' Checking his slip of the tongue, Isaac went on quickly. 'What I means is that which don't be set to paper can't be said to be what it ain't.'

'I don't follow, surely a surveyor's map . . .'

'Will show not only where New Crown Works be situated, but the proximity of others, this one among 'em!' Isaac interrupted sharply. 'What we be makin' at Prodor be vital, we've all been told that, so vital the Gerries be tryin' their best to see it destroyed; the number and severity of their raids proves as much. It would only take one wrong sort to get 'old of a copy of a map such as the one we talks of to send its information to the enemy . . . I don't need tell you the rest.'

'I doubt we have one of the wrong sort in Wednesbury,' Arthur Whitman chuckled, 'but then secrecy is paramount. I will contact the Ministry, ask their views before going ahead.'

Would they tell him? Returning to the workshop Isaac's thoughts ran on. Would the authorities allow Philip Conroy to reveal to Arthur Whitman the fact of a young lad's homework being utilised by a headmaster who turned out to be a retired officer of the German *Wehrmacht*, an officer turned spy? Would they let Conroy tell of enemy communications citing the Black Country as the base for the target they searched for, the factory responsible for producing finished cavity shell forgings? A factory not, as that spy had been led to believe, hidden beneath the golf links, but here at the 'Shadow Factory' . . . here at Prodor.

23

He had been there again today. More angry than afraid, Katrin stared blankly, her mind seeing only the figure across from the town library, a figure which turned to watch her as she walked along Spring Head, then followed her across the Market Place and along Lower High Street until she reached the White Horse Hotel. There the figure had remained while she continued along Holloway Bank to Prodor.

It had proved the same every morning and evening. Jim Slater waited for her to pass just as he had waited that first time, except as yet he had made no attempt to speak to her, merely followed. No doubt it was his way of scaring her, of frightening her so much she would concede to his demand she be 'pleasant' to him.

Never! She breathed the disgust rising inside. Jim Slater had more chance of seeing pigs fly! But on the other hand she had to do something, find some way of putting an end to what had fast become a nuisance. But what way? None as yet had presented itself.

She could stay on here at the office, wait until her father was ready to leave; but that could be well on into the early hours – he and Isaac Eldon regularly stayed late working on their latest project.

Eldon! Thoughts veering off at a tangent, Katrin remembered a boy smiling at her, at herself handing him a sheaf of papers, then at a woman in a public telephone kiosk, her head and shoulders hunched, shielding her face from any curious passer-by, one hand held half over the mouthpiece adding to the indistinctness of the disguised voice. It should have worked! Katrin pushed the pictures from her mind. It *should* have succeeded but somehow it had not. And failure was not something Katrin Hawley would accept.

She shrugged into her coat. As with the nauseating Jim Slater so with Isaac Eldon. She would find a way of dealing with both.

'Hey, not thinkin' of doin' a bye turn are you, Kate?'

'If 'er is then 'ers got more go in 'er than me, I be that dummocked I couldn't do another hour not if 'n the Devil hisself fetched me!'

'Me neither,' Alice answered. Then to the woman just inside the factory compound who had put the question, 'We all be worn out, Kate be doin' what we all do, tekin' a breath before runnin' for the bus.'

'Then you'll needs be quick for it's almost 'ere, but it'll like be already full an' so will the next 'alf dozen.'

'Like as if I didn't know!' Alice's dour reply followed the stream of workers passing through large gates daubed in the drab colours of camouflage.

'Might as well start walkin'.' Taking from her pocket the scarf which had served as a turban all day, Becky Turner drew it protectively about hair tossed by a lively breeze.

A Step Too Far

'Nosy Nora weren't right was 'er, Kate? You're not thinkin' of stayin' late?' Having walked a few yards, Alice turned to look back at the girl who had not moved.

He was there. Waiting across the street from the factory! How long would he make do with merely watching, how many more mornings and evenings would this fiasco go on before he tired of the tactics and changed to a more physical approach? She did not need two guesses to figure out what that would be. Slater wanted sex, and whether it followed a night 'on the town' or was the result of dragging her into a hedge, it would make no difference to him.

'Hey, Kate!' Alice had returned to stand beside her, 'You look like you've seen a ghost, you feelin' all right?'

It was no ghost, she only wished it was!

'You do look pale.' Becky had come to where they stood. 'Would you like Alice an' me to take you to the Ambulance Room?'

Still silent, Katrin shook her head. Medical assistance was not the sort of help she needed.

'What about 'er dad? Should we fetch him? He was in the machine shop when we left.'

'N . . . no!'

Anger made the reply tremble but with Becky's quick, 'Hey, you look absolutely terrified', Katrin realised it had been taken for the trembling of fear, and with that cognisance came another, one which could put an end to Mr Jim Slater's unwanted attentions. Swallowing hard, releasing breath in tiny gasps, forcing just enough tears to make her eyes glint wetly,

Katrin whispered, 'It . . . it's nothing, I . . . I'll be all right.'

'Like bloody hell it's nothin'! Becky's right, you do look terrified, an' if it's down to nothin' then I'd hate to be frightened by summat . . . hey!' Alice came up short, 'Has somebody in the works said somethin' they oughtn't, 'cos if they 'ave then they'll 'ave Alice Butler to reckon with!'

Katrin shook her head and pressed a clenched hand to her mouth, holding back a shudder of feigned sobs.

'Just when you think tomorrow will never come it's yesterday.'

The words her father had said so many times to a young girl anxious for a special day to arrive spoke in Katrin's mind. So it was now. What she had thought might be a while in presenting itself was already taking her hand.

'Not . . . not in the works.' She kept up the charade.

'Can't be your dad, I mean . . . well, he looked—' Becky stumbled over her possible blunder. 'Eh Kate, I hope there be nothin' wrong there.'

Katrin measured a pause long enough to feed concern then said, 'Thank you, Becky, it is nothing to do with my dad.'

'Then what 'as it to do with?' Alice demanded. 'An' don't say it's nothin' 'cos we can all see it is, so let's get it said or else *I* fetches your dad an' he can sort it.'

'There is nothing you can do, Alice, really.'

''Ow d' you know when you 'aven't said what it is?'

The shift changeover completed, those whose stint

was finished gone their various ways, others who had come to begin work having disappeared into the building, Katrin judged the moment perfect to reveal her 'fears'.

'I . . .' she hesitated, must not appear too ready to divulge her worry, 'I'm being stalked.'

'You're bein' what?'

'It means bein' followed.'

Piqued by her understanding being at issue, Becky's reply was tart. 'I knows what it means Alice Butler, I ain't daft. What I don't know is what leads Kate to think such a thing.'

'That does.' Permitting herself a brief nod in the direction of the street, Katrin turned her head away. 'He follows me here every morning and at night he follows me home.'

'Who, why?' Becky queried again.

'I know who, an' why can wait 'til later.' Hackles at full tilt, Alice was through the gate and crossing the road despite the blare of horns from traffic moving in both directions.

'You!' She marched up to the figure who as yet had made no attempt to move. 'What the hell d' you think you're doin' followin' after Kate Hawley!'

The snarled reply carried a lethal warning but Alice paid it no mind, retorting instead, 'Naught but a pile of muck when I be talkin' to Jim Slater!'

Slater's lips curved in a snide imitation of a smile.

'Very ladylike!' he said, contempt in every syllable, 'but then what can be expected of a Butler, not one of the family would know what a lady was.'

'Mebbe they don't,' Alice flashed back, 'but every one of 'em knows a toerag an' that's what you be, a nasty dirty little toerag.'

A threat burned in Slater's eyes.

'You need be careful!'

'Of what!' Alice tossed her head. 'Of being followed by a rat?'

'No, of being bitten by one.'

'Oh, you mean the way Freda Evans were bit; you'll slip a couple of illegal ration books in my bag an' get one of your cronies to tip the wink to the police? You wouldn't do that yourself, not Jim Slater, he wouldn't do the dirty on nobody – except to wipe it off himself. That's what you did to Freda, you used her to keep your own stinkin' self clean, well let me tell you the smell ain't gone an' ain't never likely to. Folk hereabout hold their grudges for a very long time.'

'Some of us don't need to carry a grudge, some of us can settle 'em right away.'

'Alice, Alice, leave it please!'

The two girls had crossed the road to join them. Slater nodded. 'Better do as Kate asks, take your nose outta what don't concern you.'

'You'd like that, wouldn't you Slater? It'd suit you fine for me to walk away an' leave Kate to your pesterin', but I don't be no Judas, I don't turn my back on a friend.'

A bus trundling its way past the quartet shed little illumination: its headlights were shielded by caps that trained their light downward to prevent detection by aircraft. But it was enough to highlight the animalistic glare Slater turned on Alice.

'Then don't never turn it on an enemy, 'specially . . .'

'Especially *you*.' Alice's retort snapped sharply across the advice.

'C'mon Alice, do like Kate says an' leave it, he won't go botherin' her no more, not now we all knows about it.'

Shrugging away Becky's restraining hand, Alice stormed on. 'I wouldn't turn my back on a snake an' though I ain't never seen one I reckons Jim Slater comes close!'

Katrin smiled to herself. This was going perfectly, but she must make it seem she deplored the whole thing. Inserting a deliberate tremble in her voice, Katrin said imploringly, 'Alice, please, I think I have been mistaken, I apologise Mr Slater.'

'Apologise!' Alice's scornful laugh echoed on the gathering night. 'You don't apologise to vermin, you gets rid of 'em!'

Slater turned his glance to Katrin. 'Folk try,' he said, 'but tryin' don't always succeed.' He returned his stare to Alice and added, '*You* should bear that in mind, an' remember this while you be about it, Jim Slater don't take kindly to bein' threatened, anybody daft enough to try it soon finds that out.'

In a move too quick to be avoided, he grabbed the cotton of Alice's coat and spun her around slamming her painfully against the wall of a small nut and bolts works.

Dripping with venom, he snarled between barely parted lips, 'Seems as 'ow the Butlers don't 'ave brains enough to know when they'm bein' warned so p'raps this will knock sense where there be none.'

The hand not pressed against Alice's throat slapped her brutally across her face.

'I'm sorry, I'm so sorry he slapped you. I never should have told you.'

'Keepin' silent wouldn't get Slater off your back.' Alice and Becky had insisted on accompanying Katrin to her door.

'But now he will be on yours! Maybe next time it will be more than a slap! Oh Lord, Alice, I'm so frightened for you.' It wasn't true but it sounded good. That slap had been precisely what she had hoped would happen.

'Ain't no call for you to be frightened.' Alice smiled despite her cut lip. 'Slater be the one needs to be scared when mother sees this lip an' the bruises on my back! Heaven an' all its angels won't be enough to save Jim Slater from a lampin'.'

'No!' Katrin kept up the pretence she had practised all the way to Hollies Drive. 'Alice, your mother must not attempt . . .'

'Ain't mother will be givin' Slater a good hidin', nor will it be no attempt, it'll be done good an' proper an' not just wi' a cut lip an' a bruise or two to show for it.'

Katrin caught the other girl's hands in her own. 'Nor your father, Alice he must not . . .'

Alice shook her head. 'Won't be 'im neither.'

'Then who?' Katrin forced back a laugh. She knew very well who, but ignorance was the dress best chosen to wear.

'It's our Jack be who! Dad taught his kids one creed, that should anybody lay a hand on one Butler they laid it on 'em all, an' our Jack don't be one to 'ave any man touch a hand to 'im; Jim Slater will be findin' that to his cost, an' knowin' our Jack the price won't come cheap.'

Katrin stepped into the house calling one more goodnight, her laugh jubilant at the words '*The price won't come cheap.*'

Good. She slipped from her coat, hanging it in the hall. The more the odious Mr Slater was made to pay, the better she would like it.

She had seen her opportunity and Alice Butler had allowed her to grasp it; brother Jack would deal with the problem of Jim Slater while Alice and Becky would continue to believe, mistakenly of course, that Katrin Hawley was a true friend.

Letting her skirt fall to the floor, Katrin caught her reflection in the mirror. Smiling back at it for a moment, she crossed to the dressing table and took out the box, stroking a finger across the exquisitely soft lavender cloth.

'Playing both ends against the middle is a rewarding game,' she mused. 'But then you would know that, wouldn't you, mother? After all, you played it for years; but not with the skills your protégée has acquired.'

24

'I meant to thank you for not telling mother about Saturdays, I'd intended to say it the other evenin' but it went clean out of my mind, what with all that to-do with Jim Slater.' Becky Turner smiled at Katrin as the three girls sat at the lunch table.

Forcing a smile in return, Katrin thought that this must be like eating meals in prison, all seated in rows! But she would not have to endure it for much longer; Arthur Whitman had mentioned a new dining room saying it would be preferable for offering visitors hospitality instead of having tea and sandwiches in his office, and of course it would be available for staff use.

'You've 'ad no more trouble from that direction, 'ave you?' Alice asked.

Katrin shook her head.

'I doubt you ever will again, he won't chance his hand a second time, not with Jack Butler wise to his game,' Becky chipped in.

'He . . . Alice's brother . . . he didn't . . .'

'Like hell he didn't!' Alice touched the tip of a finger to her partly healed lip. 'Not even one of them Churchill tanks would 'ave had the stoppin' of him once he clapped eyes on what that toerag Slater did to my face; our Jack went after him that same night.'

Becky changed her mind about taking a further bite of her sandwich. 'I can't say as to how much be truth an' how much be a bit of icin' on the cake, but as I heard tell Jim Slater won't be botherin' nobody for a long time. I were hangin' out the washin' . . .' glancing each side for possible eavesdroppers, Becky lowered her voice before going on, 'and next door's husband were standin' at his pigeon loft talkin' with a fella from higher up the street; I paid no heed until the name Slater were mentioned an' . . . well, after what had 'appened between him an' we three . . . well, it were only natural I would listen. Somebody's belloiled 'im all right, got a fizzog a dog would be feared to lick . . .'

Katrin interpreted the local vernacular to determine Jim Slater had received a beating which had left his face severely cut and bruised.

'. . . said it were every shade o' the rainbow,' Becky was continuing, 'an' judgin' by the way 'e be a' walkin' seems 'is ribs be caved in.'

'Did they say who 'ad done it?'

'No.' Becky pulled at the turban that covered the curlers fastening her hair. 'But the fella doin' the tellin' said, there be a good few in Wednesbury would 'ave liked to do what were done an' good luck to whoever it be; Slater be a crafty fossack, he be so crooked he couldn't lie straight in a bed, not that he'll be able to do that for a week or two even were he innocent as a babe.'

'But if the man is so injured, will he not go to the

police, have his attacker arrested?' Katrin judged her moment.

'Not Slater.' Alice's reply was confident. 'He knows he's only 'ad a taste of our Jack, same as he knows goin' to the police will mean his bein' treated to the full meal next time. No,' she shook her head, 'Jim Slater's sly but he ain't daft, the police won't be hearin' from him.'

The police would not be hearing! Katrin bathed in satisfaction. Should every shell find its target with the efficiency of the bullet fired from Katrin Hawley's arsenal then war might last no more than a week!

'It's all settled, the go-ahead for the new plant and the site 'as been approved, so Arthur Whitman informs me an' Jacob.'

'Should you be telling me this, dad, shouldn't it be kept secret?'

'What'd be the use o' that?' Isaac Eldon looked across at his daughter as she set a wicker basket of freshly dried laundry on the floor beside the living room table.

'It's just . . . well, you know what it can lead to when secrets are leaked.'

Yes, he knew, he knew only too well. Silent with the thought, Isaac stared into the glow of the fire. Miriam knew the threat to this town had that spy managed to pass information regarding a supposed factory beneath the golf links, but she did not know fully the danger her son had been in, nor must she ever know. That had been the promise extracted by Philip Carson. The man had wrestled with his own conscience, fought in his own mind the rights and wrongs of breaking a promise. He had promised Reuben on that final visit he would say nothing to his mother – but he had not given any word regarding his grandfather.

They had stood together in the shrouding darkness, the door of the house closed to prevent any chink of escaping light. He had felt the hesitation in that normally confident figure, an uncertainty Conroy had not shown on any previous visit to Cross Street. Had there been something else, something he was keeping back? The arrest? Had it after all been too late? Had something of what von Braun had wanted to divulge been already transmitted? All of these questions had raced in his mind as he had wished Conroy goodbye. The man had not turned immediately away, but stood, face upturned, playing a long look over a star-filled, frost-bitten sky; then he had said quietly, '*I wish to share something with you, Mr Eldon. It is not a professional thing to do but right now I think professionalism can take a back seat. Maybe,*' he had turned his glance from the sky, '*seeing I, myself, am breaking a confidence I should not request you hold this conversation as private between us, yet that is what I am doing. I ask that you say nothing of it to your daughter, principally because Reuben desires I should not.*'

'Reuben! He'll do nowt else so don't ask, this time I puts my foot down!'

Isaac had felt rather than seen the quick smile, heard it when Conroy had spoken again.

'*It is to do with your grandson, Mr Eldon, though not in the way you are thinking.*' Conroy had paused, drawing on his gloves before resuming in that quiet voice, '*I gave Reuben a promise, a promise I am about to break.*'

'Mr Conroy.' Staring into the crimson glow, Isaac recalled his reply. '*It's ever been my way to respect another man's rights an' I hold the same to my own. What you do wi' regard to promises be your concern, break or keep 'em as you feels you must, but any promise Isaac Eldon gives be kept, an' supposin' this be naught as will put my wench an' her lad to any risk, then you 'ave my word.*'

Overhead the large bodies of several barrage balloons hovered like ships caught on a windless sea, their bulk blotting out the stars. It had been so still, so calm, a world where war was not even a memory; then Conroy had spoken of what had transpired in that headmaster's room, of Reuben's brush with death. Shaking hands prior to walking away, he said, '*Your grandson deserved his lieutenant's insignia; I only wish it had been awarded.*'

'Dad, you say this new plant has been approved, is that all there is to it – for you, I mean?' Taking the heated flat iron from the trivet drawn close against the fire to smooth creases from the shirt she was ironing, Miriam glanced at her father.

Isaac shook his head, trying to drive away from his mind pictures of a boy lying dead, a black hole where his temple should have been.

'Eh?' he frowned.

Miriam spat on the hot iron. The resulting sizzle testifying to its readiness, she took it to the table. 'This new factory, will it mean changes for you?'

' 'Ow d'you mean, wench . . . changes?' Isaac frowned more deeply.

'I mean who will be running the place? Arthur Whitman can't be in both and you . . . well, you hated being in the position of manager. If anybody deserves to be in charge then it's you, but I wouldn't want you with that worry again.'

'Won't be me tekin' the job on so you sets your mind to rest.'

'But refusing will mean keeping you down, spending the rest of your working days on the factory floor, I shouldn't ask you to do that.'

'The choosin' don't be your'n.' Isaac smiled into eyes filled with concern for him. 'The work place be where I'm 'appiest an' that be where I'll stay; you don't fret y'self, Arthur Whitman be already advised o' that decision, and that be atwixt Hawley and Whitman.'

Changing irons, testing the heat before setting it to a nightgown worn almost to a thread, Miriam smiled. 'But you think he's the man for the job?'

'Stop your ferretin'!' Isaac set aside his newspaper. 'It were the same when you were a little 'un, kept on 'til you got what you wanted.'

'But you do, don't you?'

Isaac felt the familiar surge of his heart. She was so like her mother; that smile, that quiet gentle way of asking, a way that could fetch the ducks off the water.

'Ar.' He nodded. 'Ar wench, I thinks that Jacob Hawley be deservin' o' the job.'

'Mr Hawley is a nice man.'

Miriam's next words echoed in Isaac's mind as he left the house to take his turn at fire watch. Hawley had always been a decent chap, he deserved more than life had dished up for him; he should have had a wife who had married him for love and not solely to suit her own ends. Yet . . . ! The age-old query returned, haunting him as so many times in the past. Was Violet the only one to have availed herself of Jacob Hawley's good nature?

She had thought several times during the course of the afternoon, ought she to make some excuse? Tell Becky and Alice not to come to the house, that she would bring the dresses to the factory for them to look at? Yet each time some inner voice had seemed to warn *that* would be the backward step. So she had let Alice's self-invitation ride and now they were here.

'It's real good o' you, Kate, offerin' to give Becky a frock.'

Forcing a smile as the girls stepped inside the hall, Katrin answered lightly, 'Wait to see what is offered before saying thanks, you might well think the dress should have been thrown out – not just when the old king died, but with his great grandmother's passing.'

'Old Queen Victoria.' Alice grinned impishly. 'I think it were one o' her frocks me mother bought last week from a jumble sale.'

Joining in the laughter, Katrin took their coats and hung them on bright brass pegs set beside the door.

'Eeh! I've often wondered what these houses be like inside, you know, whether the insides matched the outside.'

It couldn't have been made more plain had Alice asked for a tour of the house. Biting down on her chagrin, Katrin issued the invitation. Showing them briefly into sitting room and kitchen, their oohs and aahs clucking like excited hens, Katrin felt an inward smile. Whatever would Violet Hawley and her precious pride have made of having factory workers parade through the house? Girls who still carried a faint odour of slurry oil.

'They do match, don't they Alice, the inside an' the outside?'

'Match? What do you mean Becky?'

'Huh!' Alice laughed cynically, 'You'd know right enough if you lived in Cross Street, them houses matches alright, the insides don't 'ave room enough to swing a cat and outside be little better, houses joined in a row, their brickwork black from smoke and soot! Oh yes, Kate, you'd know the difference if you lived in one o' them.'

Making no reply, Katrin led the way upstairs. She bypassed her father's bedroom using the shaded light of the landing to guide them through the darkness of her own room and drew the blackout curtains across the window, covering them in turn with the pretty chintz so beloved of her mother before switching on the bedside lamp. With another bevy of 'oohs' sounding behind, she turned toward the wardrobe her mother had lavished so much time and care on polishing; but then she had doted on every stick of furniture in the house as if they were the Crown Jewels. Katrin returned to the jest made downstairs. 'Your mother bought you just one of Victoria's cast offs, Alice, my mother bought the rest.'

'I doubts that,' Alice said quietly. 'I remembers you from our bein' in the babbies class and on right through to our leavin' school. I remembers the way your mother had you turned out, you was always the best dressed kid at Saint James'.'

Katrin effected a tight swallow before replying. 'My parents did not have other children to feed and clothe.'

'That must 'ave been as much a heartache for them as it was for you.'

Katrin almost laughed aloud. Becky's answer had held true sympathy. But then they were both so easily deceived. They swallowed lies like cats swallowing cream, they had believed that lie as they would believe those yet to come. She had been contemplating the next, the one which would say she had no idea how Nora Bates had found out about those Saturday night jaunts to Wolverhampton, about Alice Butler and Becky Turner dancing with foreign men at that Civic Ballroom.

It would be so easy. A word said a little too loudly in the works' canteen or the ladies' toilets, a word taken back to the workshop and repeated within earshot of Nosy Nora, that would see it spread like chaff on the wind, reaching Mary Turner in less time than it took to tell. Yes, it would be easy. A dress in her hand, Katrin paused on the thought. Angry as that would make Becky's mother, would it be revenge enough? Talk of Becky Turner's liaison would last only until the next juicy bit of gossip hit the collective tongue, then it would be over and forgotten. Katrin's fingers tightened. Easy, but not satisfying for Katrin Hawley!

'Eh Kate, you don't know how lucky you be havin' such a lovely home,' Alice was enthusing again. 'You've so many nice things – and a room all to y'self. Lord, what wouldn't I give to 'ave a bedroom all to meself!'

Katrin's sad smile highlighted her lie. 'You have brothers and sisters, that is what I call lucky. What wouldn't I give to have a sister to share this room.'

'Be careful what you wishes, Katrin!' Alice retorted ironically. 'You could 'ave been like me, saddled wi' too many brothers and sisters, I'd swap any one of mine for a tanner!'

'Sixpence!' Becky laughed. 'You don't do things on the cheap, d'you?'

'A girl has to keep up appearances!'

The quip struck a chord with Katrin. Keeping up appearances was exactly what she was assisting Becky Turner in doing.

It had been during the lunch break. Talk of Jim Slater had waned as both girls lost interest and she, herself, had made no attempt to revive the topic, letting it appear that she had laid that business to rest.

'*It would be this week Mrs Haywood has to be taken poorly. Doreen says it means her lookin' after the kids, so that knocks my Saturday night on the head unless I can find somebody else willing to trade shifts with me; if I can't . . .*' she had shrugged ruefully, '*. . . then I just won't be able to make it to Wolverhampton. I didn't really want to go on Saturday anyway.*'

It had been patently obvious from the way Becky's glance had dropped to the thick pottery mug twisting in her hands that what she had said was untrue. Her back toward the girls, Katrin's inner smile deepened. Instinct kicked in. For the keen student of jitterbug, for the girl so smitten with her American dance partner to say she really didn't want to attend the looked-forward-to Saturday evening dance, then something was wrong.

It had not taken long to emerge. This coming Saturday was to be a special evening. Some of the men were moving on to different units and others in the camp had decided to give them a special send off and Earl had said he so much wanted Becky to be there.

'*So then, why do you not want to go?*'

Her enquiry had sounded innocent enough but there had been none of that virtue beneath the asking. Becky had tried to hide her embarrassment but her cheeks had blushed a deep shade of pink. It had been left to Alice to explain. '*It's her frock, her's worn it every time we've gone to that dance hall. Like meself, Becky has to take a back seat where clothes be concerned, it takes all the money and all the coupons to keep the little 'uns clothed, and well . . . with this bein' a special do, Becky don't want to be seen wearin' the same old frock.*'

'*Ain't just a special do for the men that's leavin'.*' Becky had tried to keep disappointment at bay but tears had glistened in her eyes. '*Earl said there were somethin' he wanted to ask me, somethin' he said he'd wanted to ask for some time but had needed to get permission from his C.O. first.*'

Permission of a Commanding Officer! Katrin's instinct had deepened by several degrees, but none of it had shown in her reply.

'But if Earl has something he wants to ask, something he has already implied to be of importance, won't it be hurtful to him if you don't turn up?'

'Not near as hurtful as a smack in the face,' Alice had replied, 'and that's how it'll feel supposin' Earl don't say anythin' and Becky feels he won't once he sees her in that frock her's worn every time they've met, her fears he'll not want her after realisin' just how rich her family ain't.'

'But surely if he loves Becky, lack of money will have no influence?'

'*He does love me!*' Becky had retorted. '*And I love him, I love him too much to humiliate him in front of his friends, probably in front of that C.O. he talked of; I won't 'ave him shamed by my wearin' a frock that has more years to it than me mother has.*'

A deep primeval feeling surged its message through Katrin's veins. This moment must not be ignored!

She had leaned across the table, touching a hand to the red-faced Becky. '*Please,*' she had murmured, '*please don't take this the wrong way, it is not meant as a slight in any way, but I have several dresses I'm about to send to the Welfare Centre, perhaps . . . well, perhaps one of them . . .*'

The rest had been submerged beneath the blare of a klaxon recalling both girls to work but as they had left the table Alice had called back, '*We'll come up to your place tonight if that's okay.*'

'I'll be keepin' up appearances and no mistake.' Becky's comment recalled Katrin to the present. 'Come next month I'll be livin' in a big house, it'll have its own garden and even a pool you can swim in, Earl says . . .'

'Earl says a lot o' things!' Alice snapped. 'I've told you, Becky Turner, you wants to be very careful where that one be concerned, y' shouldn't take every word he says as gospel!'

Becky snapped back, 'An' I've told you, Alice Butler, you don't know Earl the way I do!'

'Yes, you 'ave told me, so now p'raps you'll tell me what it is I be missin', what is it I don't know about Earl Feldman?'

'You don't know how gentle he can be, how tender he was when we . . .'

Alice was not about to relent. 'How tender when you what?'

Glancing over her shoulder, seeing the bloom of pink becoming a high tide of scarlet, the lowered eyes and twisting fingers, Katrin put her own question. Was Becky Turner playing the game she herself intended to play with Arthur Whitman, given half a chance? Had Becky Turner already succeeded? If so, then she might well be leaving for America next month as she claimed. Where then would be Katrin Hawley's long-desired revenge?

Katrin carried the dresses to the bed, placing them beside Becky.

'These are what I had sorted to go to the Welfare Centre.' She forced a smile. 'But remember, I said they are far from new so don't feel you have to accept any of them.'

'Eh Kate, you must be crackers to even think of givin' stuff like this away!' Alice had bounded across the room, her busy hands lifting one garment after another.

'It would be more foolish to leave them hanging in the wardrobe when perhaps someone might find them useful.'

'Well, Becky and me knows you've never gone short of clothes but . . .'

'I will not be wearing any of those again.' Katrin cut away Alice's protest.

'Ohh!'

Becky's sigh of admiration took their glances to the wardrobe, its open door admitting a glow which shimmered over sapphire silk chiffon.

'Kate.' Alice breathed appreciation. 'That's beautiful, the colour, the shine . . .'

'It is the last dress my mother bought for me.' Katrin swallowed hard on the lie. 'She too loved the colour, she said it would be perfect for celebrating the end of the war.'

Eyes soft as the silk she stared at, Becky's reply came from a scene only she was imagining. 'Or a wedding,' she murmured rapturously, 'a bride would look lovely in that.'

The two girls left the house, the dresses along with them, and Katrin returned to her room.

'A bride! A bride would look lovely in that.'

'Yes, Becky,' she murmured. 'Arthur Whitman's bride will look lovely.'

25

Coming into the office, Arthur Whitman looked at the desk – document trays empty, typewriter cover in place – then to Katrin, her coat fastened, gas mask case slung over one shoulder. 'Good Lord!' He frowned abstractedly. 'Is it that time already?'

'It is almost seven, Mr Whitman.'

'Lord, so it is.' He glanced at the watch strapped about his wrist.

'I stayed . . .'

'Oh hell!' With a rueful smile he went on, 'I didn't put that very well, did I? Sorry Katrin, I hadn't meant to imply you were skipping off before time, it's very much the reverse with you, I know; you stay late more often than I have the right to ask, sorry . . .' he apologised again. 'That's me, I just don't think.'

Taking up her bag, Katrin smiled. 'It's all right, no need for apology.'

'That's the first time I've known you make a mistake.' Whitman's deep brown eyes held a moment of teasing laughter. 'You are mistaken and I am an ill-mannered lout. There is every need for me to apologise and I do so again in all sincerity. Forgiven, Katrin? I lose track of everything when I'm in the workshops,' he went on, seeing Katrin's nod, 'and this latest request of the Defence Ministry has me not only forgetting time but my manners as well.'

'And also food,' Katrin remonstrated. 'Missing meals won't see that project completed any more quickly.'

Watching him now, his eyes closed, neck and shoulders stretched back to ease a weariness she had come to see more and more often, Katrin acknowledged one more thing: her chance of becoming Mrs Arthur Whitman could easily be lost to this damned new project. Her employer was wearing himself out.

He walked to his own office, tiredness bringing a stoop to his tall figure. Why? The door closed behind him and the questions which had occupied her mind on previous occasions rose again. Why was Arthur Whitman driving himself so hard? Pressure of work? Katrin stared at the door, unadorned except for a brightly polished brass handle. War had increased the burden on everyone, but was it only that had him so changed? Or was it more personal, was he punishing himself for the death of his wife, blaming himself for leaving her and her mother alone in that shelter? No, that aura had been there before. Something had been missing from Arthur Whitman's life long before that bomb took his wife.

The comforts of the marriage bed! A smile curving her lips, Katrin removed her coat.

Arthur Whitman watched the girl preparing to leave his private office. Chestnut brown hair gleaming in the glow of the overhead light, hazel green eyes darting a smile, slender without being thin, Katrin Hawley was an attractive young woman. Given those looks, that well educated manner and her ability to deal with people, she was an asset to the business.

'You didn't have to stay, and you certainly didn't have to do what you have.'

'I haven't done anything I didn't want to do.' Katrin smiled across the desk.

She had *wanted* to do it. How long had it been since the same had been done willingly for him? Years.

'Is there anything else you would like me to do before I leave?'

Unaware he had closed his eyes, already half asleep, Whitman jerked upright.

'What?' He blinked, electric light brilliant against tired eyes. 'What? No . . . no Katrin, thanks, I . . . I'll be leaving myself shortly.'

'Will that be before you have finished with that folder or after?'

'Something else I forgot.' He drew the folder to him, 'Lord, the Ministry will want my guts for garters.'

'Is it that important?' She had read through the folder earlier in the day, but Katrin maintained a false air of concern.

'Important?' he answered. 'Only if we want any chance of winning this bloody war!'

'Well we both want that and no doubt the Ministry wants the same, so if I might make a suggestion . . .'

Whitman ran a hand through greying hair made greyer by a liberal coating of foundry dust and sighed. 'Suggest away, I'm ready to listen to anything that might get this business done and shifted off to London.'

'I can't help with the technical side, but typing up of the finished report is something I can do, so why don't I stay and work with you? My father has a favourite saying, one appropriate to this present situation. He says, "Doing what you can today leaves tomorrow free for something else."'

Whitman pulled a wry mouth. 'Free for what? More of the same!'

'Probably,' Katrin replied perkily, then, on a more serious note, 'no, not probably – definitely; but at least what is waiting in that folder will not be a part of it. One more consideration.' She smiled, 'Doing it tonight means it can go by first post in the morning, thus saving a whole day . . . oh, *and* your guts, let's not forget those.'

'Lord, Katrin,' Whitman shook his head, 'what would I do without you!'

He was not going to have the opportunity of finding out! Not, that was, until she was ready.

In the outer office she glanced at the tray on a small table. Canteens had to open for set break times during the night as well as the day and the cook had gladly found sandwiches and hot tea for 'the gaffer'.

Arthur Whitman had been so grateful to her for bringing that meal. Taking up pencil and notepad, she turned back toward the inner office. If fortune smiled, then Arthur Whitman might be helped to more than a sandwich!

★ ★ ★

They had worked together, he dictating, she taking notes then typing them up before returning them to be signed. Hour after tiring hour, the process had been repeated and through it all he had barely looked up from his desk. Finally, the last document sealed in its envelope, she had brushed aside his thanks with a smile while her mind raged. Each time she'd handed him papers, she had bent close, her shoulder touching his. She had even ensured, accidentally of course, that his hand had brushed across her breast when he had reached for a letter. All that, yet nothing achieved but a 'goodnight and thank you'.

It had been a futile exercise. Bottling the acid of failure, Katrin had been reaching for her coat when the first wail of the air raid alarm had sounded.

Was Fate giving her one more go at the prize? The thought had glanced like lightning and like lightning she had acted upon it.

Thank heaven she could force tears whenever they were to her advantage, and last night they had fulfilled their purpose. She had not screamed, but stood frozen as marble, her hands gripping her coat as if in terror; the only real fear had been of Arthur Whitman's rushing down to the factory in search of help. But he had not, and she had silently thanked the Fates for their munificence.

He had called from the doorway to his office, '*Katrin, leave the bloody coat! Go to the shelter.*'

Even when the urgency of the moment made him grasp her arm, not a flutter of an eyelid, not a whisper of breath moved in her, only the tears she had squeezed from her eyes ran silently over her cheeks.

His voice softened into compassion.

'*Katrin . . . Oh Christ, you're terrified . . .*'

No, not terrified Simply a very good portrayal of terror.

'*Leave it Katrin, come with me.*'

Not yet! Not yet! Caution had counselled loud in her brain.

'*Katrin, you have to take shelter.*'

He had continued to coax while the siren died away, urging the need to go downstairs to the factory air raid shelter. But that had been nowhere in her intentions.

The sound of an explosion, the rumble of it shaking the building, he had lifted her from her feet, sending the coat stand tumbling.

That had been her moment. As if awakening from some horrifying nightmare, she had released the coat on to the carpet then twisted in his arms, pressing her body tight against his.

'*Don't leave me.*' She had trembled convincingly. '*Please, please don't leave me.*'

His arms were around her, his mouth touching the side of her face buried in his shoulder.

'*We shouldn't stay here, we need to go down to the shelter.*'

Need had echoed in his voice, but it had not been the need he had spoken of. Intuition had guided her as surely as it had guided Eve.

'*No! No . . . I can't! I can't . . . I'm afraid, don't make me . . . please don't make . . .*'

A bevy of heartrending sobs said the rest.

'*It's all right Katrin,*' he had soothed, '*we won't go to the shelter.*'

'*You.*' She had made it seem to take every ounce of her courage to say, '*You must go to the shelter, you must not stay.*'

A second crash reverberated through the room, rattling taped windows, tipping chairs and throwing things around as though caught in a cyclone, flinging her to the floor, his body covering her own.

He had murmured her name then his mouth had come down on hers. She had returned the kiss, lifting her mouth for more as his hand pushed aside her bra to caress the soft mound of her breast, and she dreaded him coming to his senses and moving away from her. That could not be allowed to happen; with a soft moan she had arched her body, pressing her stomach against him. His long quivering breath testified to the battle raging in Arthur Whitman. It must be now, or probably never. She allowed her tongue to slide, moist and warm, across his lips. He stiffened as though touched by a live electric wire, then his hand had left her breast.

Groaning with the sweet torture of soft flesh beneath him, he ran his palm along her taut hip until his fingers reached into the cleft of her thighs and released the tiny buttons of her cami-knickers, pushing away the soft silky fabric.

'*Katrin . . . Oh Christ, Katrin!*'

As his hand touched against the soft downy vee, she had sought his mouth again, opening her own seductively to take his tongue, her legs parting in that same unspoken appeal. It had not been denied. He had groaned once, a deep animalistic sound, a cry of purely carnal desire then he had thrust into her the hard column of his roused flesh driving deep inside until, passion spent, he had rolled away from her.

Back in the present, in the privacy of her bedroom, Katrin glanced at the drawer holding the box and scarf.

'Game, set and match mother.' She smiled dispassionately. 'Game, set and match.'

He had not come to the office. Katrin walked steadily across the factory yard toward the gate. He had phoned to say he had caught the morning train to London, that he would be away all week, could she manage to hold the fort? No mention of his making love to her, but then she had not referred to it either. But not speaking of it did not mean it had not happened. Arthur Whitman would be made quite aware of that fact.

'Kate! Kate . . .'

Katrin turned to the girls running to catch up with her.

'Oh Kate, I've been dyin' to tell you.' Becky Turner bubbled happiness. 'Saturday night, oh I'm dyin' to tell you . . .'

'Well, tell her before you drop dead.' Alice fell into step on Katrin's other side.

'Oh, it was grand . . .'

'That weren't how you felt when we got to that dance hall, you were ready to walk straight out.'

Unaffected by the sarcasm, Becky's laugh trilled on the night. 'That were when I thought Earl wouldn't be comin'.' She glanced at Katrin. 'Alice and me 'ad gone all out to look our very best. I wore that white dress you gave me, I swapped Doreen Haywood five Woodbines for a blue belt—'

'Let your dad find out about them fags and you won't be needin' of no belt, he'll tie your entrails around your waist.'

'He ain't about to find out though, is he Alice?'

Unless someone not totally deaf were walking behind! Katrin declined to share her observation while Becky went on. 'Anyway, it were me got them cigarettes, not me dad.'

'So you did,' Alice returned. 'But like I says, don't let him find you give him only five.'

'What if he does? After next month he can have as many cigarettes as he wants.'

Trying to sound flippant, Katrin gave a light laugh. 'Oh, is that when the war will end?'

'It's when mine will end, but let me tell you from the beginning.'

Katrin bit back the irritation Becky's chatter was building.

'Alice decided on the yellow dress, the snood her'd crocheted was just the same shade and they looked real glamorous together; but I didn't wear anythin' on my hair, Earl loves it loose, says it feels like silk.'

The bus, full to capacity, sailed past their standpoint and Katrin's displeasure surged anew. A low tut expressing her irritation, she began to walk away, hoping they would remain at the bus stop for another bus. She wanted to be alone to muse on that episode in Arthur Whitman's office.

'I were just about to get my coat and leave when there he was . . .'

Bubbling like a running brook, Becky's account of her latest amours flowed on, she and Alice walking one each side of Katrin.

'Eh Kate, I wishes you'd seen him, he looked so 'andsome.'

'Never mind the way he looked, tell Kate what he said,' Alice chipped in testily.

'He said I looked real beautiful in my white dress, just like . . .'

'Oh for God's sake!' Alice snorted, 'Kate don't want to listen to you goin' on about how you looked.'

How right Alice was! In fact Kate didn't want to listen to either of them!

Becky continued joyfully.

'It were durin' the interval, Earl took me to our special place and it were there after we'd . . .' she paused with a sudden attack of shyness, but with Alice urging her on she continued, 'Well, it were there Earl told me he'd been called in to speak with the Commandin' Officer, that were the cause of him bein' late gettin' to the dance . . . so that's what I'll become next month . . . a bride!'

Like stones rattling against glass the words rapped against Katrin's brain, slipping through her mental defences. The other two turned down Holyhead Road, leaving Katrin to make her way along Lower High

Street, and she dug deep in her mind seeking the rest of what Becky Turner had disclosed.

'*He'd been given permission to marry, but first a check needs be made back in the States, seems they 'ave to be certain all be the way Earl says it is. They 'ave to make sure he don't already 'ave a wife!*'

The trill of laughter suggested the absurdity of the very idea.

'*Earl said that would take no more than two, maybe three weeks and then we will be married. I shall wear that white dress, and you two will be my bridesmaids.*'

Becky Turner was to be married. In four weeks she would be left from Wednesbury!

Crossing the almost deserted Market Place, Katrin's brain thundered with the revelation. Becky Turner would be gone, so where would be Katrin Hawley's revenge?

Four weeks! So little time. Would it be enough to make Becky Turner pay that long-held debt?

Maybe now was the time to have Mary Turner learn of her daughter's carryings on.

She would have preferred something more damning, something that would follow Becky Turner through life as that prison sentence would always overshadow Freda Evans.

Think! Katrin's brain stabbed its own command. There has to be some . . .

Half formed thought and breath were lost in the gasp of pain and fear as Katrin felt herself hurled viciously against a wall.

26

'Now if this ain't my lucky night! Never thought to get what I wants so easy as this.'

Winded, her sight fuzzy from knocking her head against the brick, Katrin fought to stay back from the brink of the void waiting to swallow her.

'Y' should 'ave walked by way o' the town, there be folk comin' and goin' there, too many for me to go takin' chances, but you chose this way and that be my good fortune.'

Katrin would have fallen had not hands caught roughly at her shoulders.

'No, not here!' A low and menacing laugh carried briefly on the empty street.

'I 'ave a better place for you to lie down, one where we won't be disturbed; there you'll spread your legs an' I can take time to enjoy what you 'ave to offer, but then,' the laugh sounded again, 'offer be the wrong word since you don't be gettin' no chance to refuse.'

The bite of cold night air or the gentle drift of snowflakes touching her face? Katrin could not tell, but suddenly her mind was sharp and clear. Slater!

'You refused an offer once afore, one which were made civil an' polite. But the one makin' it were not grand enough for the hoity-toity Miss Hawley to be seen along of! Well, this time he'll be takin' no refusal.'

'Wait.' She eased her head back from alcohol drenched breath. 'I realised later I had been hasty, I made a mistake.'

'Too bloody true you made a mistake refusin' of me, same as you made a mistake in gettin' Jack Butler to give me a pastin'.'

'That was none of my doing, it must have been Alice.' She had hoped he would step away, but the grip on her shoulders remained firm, another cloud of alcohol fumes blowing into her face.

'Don't make no odds who done the tellin' 'cos all three goin' to do the payin', that loud-mouthed Butler wench and the other one that's always with her, they'll get theirs. Oh, not both at the same time – that might give rise to question, no . . . no,' he smirked, 'a bus . . . a dark night . . . a tragic accident . . . that poor Butler girl; then some weeks on the other one will be found floatin' in the cut or mebbe her won't be found at all, there be many a coal pit ain't yet been sealed, her won't be the only wench ever to go missin' and the reason of it bein' put down to a dissatisfied client not gettin' all he paid for. And Jack! Money'll take care of that problem; he'll never use his fists nor his legs again. But first there be you . . .'

She must not antagonise him further. She must try to appease him, make him believe her truly sorry for her behaviour the evening he had invited her out.

'Please.' She forced herself to relax beneath his hands. 'I'm sorry I was so abrupt, constant air raids and a heavy day at work had me on edge.'

His grip lightened, his fingers no longer bit into her shoulder, but she must not move yet.

Trying to close her nostrils against the assault of foul breath, she leaned her body into him, purring softly. 'I was so tired, but I'm not tired tonight, maybe we could go now for that drink and then . . .'

She left it deliberately, a provocative worm to catch her fish.

He snapped at the bait. 'Then you can prove how sorry you be.' Releasing her, he delved a hand into a pocket of his overcoat, bringing out an object wrapped in paper. Swaying uncertainly, he waved it in triumph. 'Ain't no need to go to no public house,' he slurred. 'We 'ave a drink right 'ere; it were meant for a customer but I reckons we'll enjoy it more. Good old Johnnie Walker, he can warm the cockles of your 'eart and Jim Slater'll warm the rest.'

A lewd laugh mixed with the distant sound of traffic. No one had passed along this street from her entering it and it was highly probable no one would. Glancing at the Chapel rising dark at her back, Katrin cursed the luck which meant there was no service being conducted there. Deliverance had to be found!

The gentle fall of snow had ceased and a high full moon spread its silver cloak. In its light she watched him tear the paper away and drop it heedlessly to the ground.

'There, you get y'self a swig of old Johnnie.'

He thrust the whisky bottle forward, his half stumble betraying an already over indulgence of whisky.

'Go on, take a shwig,' he slurred 'then y' can 'ave a good old shwallow of the other delight I've got for you.'

Revulsion swept Katrin. His use of language was as odious as his person; yet pointing that out would serve only to revive his anger.

'You first.' Placing a hand on the one holding the bottle, she guided it to his lips, saying laughingly, 'Call that a drink? I would have thought Jim Slater could do better than that.'

'Better!' He threw off her hand. 'O' coursh 'e can do better, Jim Shlater be better'n any man at anythin'.'

Katrin watched the bottle lift, watched it press to his mouth, heard the noise of liquid gulping past his throat. He had taken the lure, but how to make certain he choked on it.

'Thash,' he grinned, 'thash be takin' a drink, now . . . hic . . . now it'sh your turn.'

His speech was becoming more distorted, the sway of his body more pronounced, but he was not yet incapable of harming her.

'One more for you, just a little one,' she wheedled.

'You . . . hic . . . you 'ave shome.'

The bottle almost hitting her face, Katrin knocked his hand away. The sudden movement made him stumble forward and strike his forehead against the mounting block, moaning as he dropped to his knees.

This was her chance, she could be safe at home by the time he recovered. But that would not prevent him claiming she had given herself willingly to him. How damning would that be in the eyes of Arthur Whitman? What chance would she have then of becoming his wife?

Her mind ice cold, her brain perfectly in control, she bent to retrieve the broken bottle.

She must not lose that chance.

Weighing the moment, waiting until he was nearly to his feet, she called his name. Then, as he lifted his head, she stabbed the jagged bottle into his throat.

'Mother took a faintin' turn, the kids were cryin' and dad, well we had to pull him off that copper afore he throttled the poor bloke.'

Alice Butler was talking of the arrest of her brother.

'The police knowed of that shemozzle 'tween Slater and our Jack.'

Slater! Katrin's heart leapt. This was to do with Jim Slater; was he alive? Had that broken bottle in his throat failed to kill him?

'They knowed Jack had peeled Slater's onions a while back.'

Katrin's fingers clenched white beneath a table in the refurbished works canteen. Did they also know who had tried to kill him? Would the police come here to the factory, arrest her with everyone looking on? Lord, why had she not stayed long enough to ensure he was dead? She had felt the bite of glass against flesh, felt it rip as she drove it deep, heard the choking gurgle of blood bubbling into the throat, had seen his eyes glitter in the moonlight as he had reached a hand to his neck; then she had run.

'So they thinks it be our Jack has done this'n an' all.'

'The police, 'ave they arrested him?'

'Carted him off this mornin'.' Alice answered Becky's concern. 'Asked would he mind goin' along to the station to answer some questions. Mind!' Alice's voice rose angrily. 'O' course he'd bloody mind, but objectin' would make no difference, he'd still 'ave gone to the station, only he would 'ave gone in 'andcuffs.'

The police had taken Jack Butler in for questioning. Katrin's pulse beat like drums in her wrists. How long before they did the same with her?

Notepad on her knee, Katrin wrestled to keep from her mind thoughts of what she had heard in the canteen.

'Katrin, are you all right?'

'What? Oh, yes, sorry, I was miles away.' Katrin glanced at her employer, his fingers fiddling nervously with a dark blue patterned fountain pen.

'Katrin, I . . .' Arthur Whitman cleared an imaginary frog from his throat, 'I've been meaning to speak . . .' the pen rolled across the desk, his fingers scrabbling after it. He began again, though his glance remained on the pen. 'Katrin, about what happened between us, I'm sorry and very deeply ashamed, I . . .'

'Please.' Katrin rose quickly to her feet. 'It's me should apologise, I was to blame for being so silly when those air raid sirens sounded.'

'You were not being silly.'

'I was,' Katrin blurted. 'There have been so many air raids, I should be used to them by now, but with my mother—'

'I ought to have realised, but I allowed my own feelings to get in the way.'

Soft curls swinging with the shake of her head, Katrin flashed a brief smile. 'We were both under a lot of stress and I suppose we each looked to the other as a means of relieving it; what happened, happened and there is no way of changing that, so couldn't we just forget about it?'

The look of relief on his face was quickly dismissed, but not so quickly it was not caught by Katrin. Enjoy it Mr Whitman. Enjoy your reprieve while you may, for it won't last very long!

'I thought it might be less of an embarrassment if we spoke in your own home rather than the station.'

It would be less embarrassing were she not 'spoken' with at all! Keeping the thought submerged beneath the briefest of smiles, Katrin led the way into the neat living room before saying, 'That is very considerate but why do you need to speak to me at all?'

The Police Inspector ran a finger around the grey trilby hat he had removed on entering the house before asking. 'Is your father at home, Miss Hawley?'

Katrin frowned. 'I thought from what you said in the hall it was me you wished to speak with.'

'That is correct.' The man nodded. 'But you are not yet of age, Miss Hawley, and therefore you need to be accompanied by your parents. The law, you understand.'

Here was the opportunity to rally the composure this man had sent haywire. But she must not appear too confident. The tremble of a sob in her voice, she said quietly, 'I'm sorry, my father is not at home and my mother was killed in a bombing raid.'

She had achieved the desired result. Katrin acknowledged the murmured sympathy then went on. 'My father may go straight from work to complete his duty as a Fire Warden, in which case it will be quite late before he gets home.'

The hat rotated several times while its owner pursed his lips as though seeking the answer to some virtually impossible problem. The Inspector nodded. 'Then maybe he will call at the station, and you with him, of course, Miss Hawley.'

That was not what she wanted. Too many people saw the comings and goings at that police station and Katrin Hawley preferred not to be among those observed. Thinking quickly she said, 'Inspector, I know the law says a parent should be present at any discussion but might I ask the reason of your coming to this house? If I can tell my father then he will not have a possibly sleepless night worrying what this is connected with.'

The Inspector shook his head. 'Best not, Miss, the law be the law and needs be abided by.'

'Of course.' Katrin assented with a smile she felt no affinity with. 'The law states a child can work for its living from fourteen years old, that boys can and must fight for their country on being eighteen and as for girls and women they can become auxiliary members of the Armed Forces from that same age while others up to the age of forty must work in engineering, agriculture or allied trades. Yet the rule of law ordaining that is the same rule of law which deems a person must reach the age of twenty one before they are seen to be responsible for themselves; a little ironic, don't you think, Inspector?'

'We might not all agree with the law, Miss Hawley, but we must all adhere to it.'

His eyes held a slightly amused look. Like an argumentative child, Katrin felt she had been treated to a timely slap on the wrist.

She had been showing him to the door when her father had arrived home unexpectedly, explaining he had wanted to ensure his daughter was prepared for any air raid. The Inspector nodded understandingly and agreed to stay and conduct the interview there rather than have them call next day at the station.

'On the evening of the . . .'

The Inspector consulted a notebook taken hurriedly from his breast pocket then continued, *'were you approached by Mr James Slater?'*

Alice would have said as much during his visit to Cross Street; so she replied yes, then gave an account of what had passed between them, an account which made no reference to illegal ration books.

'You should have told, told me about Slater, Katrin, I would have dealt with him.'

Taking her silence as evidence of distress, Jacob had passed a comforting arm around his daughter's shoulders.

'Did you at any time after that evening . . .'
'I did not meet with him.'

The Inspector said he had a witness who claimed otherwise, that Slater had been seen outside the Prodor works.

'*That is not entirely correct,*' she glanced at her father as though seeking assurance, then with his brief nod continued. '*The term "meet with" implies a face to face encounter or perhaps a mutually agreed assignation. This did not occur between myself and Mr Slater, though for several mornings I saw him on my way to work.*'

'*You saw him? But you did not speak with him?*'

'*That is what she said!*' Jacob intervened angrily. '*And that swine Slater better not try bothering her again or he'll find out what dealing with a man can be like.*'

Sharp black eyes switched to Jacob. '*Have you met with him? Warned him against approaching Miss Hawley?*'

'*No!*' Jacob snapped. '*But that doesn't go to say I wouldn't have had I heard of this before tonight.*'

'*Miss Hawley, why did you not tell your father of Slater's accosting you?*'

'*Inspector,*' she answered quietly, '*my father has had a great deal to worry over for some time now, his employer will corroborate that; I had no wish to add to that worry.*'

The Inspector returned the conversation to the matter of his visit.

'*Was that the only time you saw him?*'

A shake of the head added emphasis to the unhesitating reply

'*No. I also saw Mr Slater one evening. He was standing across the way from the entrance to the Prodor factory. I was with two friends, Alice Butler and Becky Turner. I did not speak to Mr Slater, though Alice did. She went to talk with him and I believe he got angry and struck her across the face.*'

'And after that, the three of you walked home together?'

That was to be his *tour de force*, or as local idiom would put it, 'a crab to catch an apple'.

'Only as far as the White Horse...' She named the Hotel which had long stood as a local landmark. *'Alice and Becky went on along Holyhead Road leaving me to follow Lower High Street, to the Market Square.'*

She deliberately left off her explanation at that point, waited for the question she knew would come.

'From the Market Square you then proceeded along Spring Head?'

Her simple 'no' had been met with a quizzical frown. *'But doesn't going the way of Spring Head cut the journey to Hollies Drive quite considerably?'*

'Certainly,' she replied coolly. *'And I would normally take that way during daytime but at night it is not so frequented by people and so I prefer to come home by way of the High Bullen.'*

'I understand.'

'And understand this,' Jacob added. *'I will be speaking to Slater.'*

Rising to his feet to intimate the interview was at an end, the Inspector levelled his gaze at Jacob.

'That be your right and privilege, Mr Hawley, but don't go expecting any answer; you see, James Slater is dead.'

27

The office which had been assigned to Isaac Eldon as works manager, yet been all too rarely put to that use was to be redesigned. For a new manager? Had Arthur Whitman finally got round to appointing someone to that position when he had been in London? Certainly he had held no interview here at Prodor.

'I thought it would serve the purpose very well, what do you think, Katrin?'

She had thought that office, that job, as good as hers! Hadn't she proved herself as good as any man at handling the business of the factory, hadn't she been every bit as efficient in the running of the office as Harriet Simpson had been?

'Not so big as to be daunting yet large enough to accommodate a fair-sized table and chairs; yes, I think that office should fit the bill all right, don't you?'

'Maybe I could answer if I knew what the "bill" is you are talking about.'

'Sorry.' Whitman gave a brief shake of his head. 'I thought I'd told you. Christ, there are so many things to think of a man can lose his reason trying to keep track of them.'

Hence the newly appointed manager! Maintaining a smile which inside held all the warmth of an arctic winter, Katrin replied, 'Well, if you tell me now then it will be at least one thing hasn't got itself lost.'

All she needed was the name of the man who had landed himself the position she had thought would be hers. A man! What if it were not a man, but a woman? What if he had appointed a woman as works manager? It was not inconceivable. And was Arthur Whitman bringing her here to Wednesbury to fill a vacancy other than that at Prodor? Was she coming here to fill the position of Arthur Whitman's wife?

'It's the staff dining room, I'd thought it could wait but given the circumstances . . . having the works canteen re-vamped seems more important, help to keep up the workers' morale.' He shuffled the papers lying under his hand. 'But with government representatives coming her more and more often I realise the need not only for a quieter area for them to eat, but one where sensitive issues could be discussed more privately, in other words a board room. Seems a bit grand for a small engineering works, but Prodor will not always be small, nor will it only be here in the Black Country; it will grow and grow and with it the integrity of its name and the reliability of its products; Prodor will be recognised the world over.' He laughed. 'I'm rambling on, but then you listen so well, Katrin.'

Listen and learn. The tension of those earlier minutes drained from Katrin. There was to be no newly appointed manager.

A private dining room for visitors and staff. Katrin smiled down at the keys, her fingers pressing with rapid confident movements. And Katrin Hawley was still virtually in charge.

'Look 'ere Mr Whitman, I knows these folk from the Defence Ministry be important, but so does the work bein' done 'ere an' I prefers to get on wi' that 'stead of standin' around talkin', more so when the folk I be talkin' to don't 'ave no more understandin' of what it is bein' told 'em than they 'ave o' flyin' in the air wi'out wings.'

'I understand how you feel Isaac, but needs must when the Devil calls.'

'If you says so!' Isaac Eldon snorted exasperatedly; 'But don't you go a'bein' surprised if you hears me tellin' o' the Devil where he can go.'

Nothing would surprise him less. A smile hovering about his mouth, Arthur Whitman glanced at his watch. These last few days had not been easy; lying was not something he agreed with, nor was it his particular forte; it would be a hell of a relief when this particular 'Devil' was lifted from his shoulders.

'I have to say I agree with Isaac, we are both of more use in the workshops, that new machinery—'

'Can wait! Oh Christ, Jacob I'm sorry, I didn't mean to snap.'

'Forget it, we have all been under a lot of stress.'

Why had it been decided they need come here? Arthur Whitman glanced again at his watch, a nervous harassed move. Disturbance to the working day was a hindrance in time of peace, but in wartime hindrance became a hazard, a danger that time lost in producing armaments allowed the enemy that much more time to increase its stranglehold on the world. Would it not have been more convenient to have Isaac, Jacob and himself travel to London, to meet with people there? No! His brain answered immediately. Most folk of Wednesbury considered themselves fortunate to get an annual day outing to Bewdley, to sit beside the river with a home-made sandwich and tea from a flask; or maybe a trip to Clent to walk among grass not turned black by smoke and grime from the chimneys of a thousand iron and steel works, where the daytime sky was a canopy of blue dotted with milk-white cloud, not the grey poured into it by the issue of those same chimneys. No. He glanced at the two men locked in discussion. To suddenly whisk them off to London would create a stir, whys and wherefores would not remain within the confines of this factory. Despite being reminded by placards plastered over walls that 'Loose Talk Costs Lives', human nature being just that – human – talk of a trip to London would have spread across the town as unstoppable as the very smoke that choked it.

'Mr Whitman, you asked me to remind you of the time.'

Turning to thank Katrin as she entered his office, Arthur Whitman smiled grimly. This was one moment he would never need reminding of, one a frontal lobotomy would not have him forget. A retinue of cars swept through the factory gates as he muttered, 'I wasn't at liberty to tell either of you about this beforehand, it all had to be done under the tightest security! It was all so strictly hush-hush I was afraid to let myself even think about it!'

'It be as well you said naught for 'ad I known o' this then neither the Devil 'isself nor all the cohorts o' hell would 'ave fetched me 'ere today.'

Isaac spoke through gritted teeth as he watched the procession of uniformed men, acres of medals flashing bravely across each left breast, follow behind one whose decoration outshone the rest.

'Then what would I have told our distinguished visitors?' Whitman murmured, shifting anxiously foot to foot.

'That would 'ave been your worry.' Isaac's mouth dried as the parade moved nearer. 'You and Jacob be better at talkin' wi' folk than I be, so if there be questions asked then you answer 'em.'

'Mr Eldon and Mr Hawley, the designers of the machinery and method of producing Finished Cavity Shell Forgings.'

Isaac heard the introduction as if from a distant place. Then his hand was taken by the foremost member of the group.

'Ah yes. An achievement to be proud of. We are most thankful to you both. Please, might I ask to be shown this new method of production.'

'There were never a word o' it spoke, not to me not to anybody, Arthur Whitman's mouth had been closed tighter than the vaults along o' Barclays Bank; I tells you, girl, I was bothered as a bum baillee in an empty 'ouse when I seen who it were offerin' of 'is hand.'

Her father flustered? The man who had dealt so calmly with problems brought to him? The quiet, sensible man who, unlike some, had never raised a hand against anyone? A father she, Robert and—stopping herself short of finishing the thought, she took the used plates and cutlery across the small cramped kitchen to the sink. She must forget that terrible day, she must never allow herself to think of it. Yet the spectres would, in the darkness of night, creep into her mind, phantoms which played over and again the happenings of those terrible days, ghosts whose cries of agonised sorrow called in her brain until she felt she too must scream.

'You should 'ave seen the faces o' the workers when they walked into that factory along o' Jacob an' me, weren't one of 'em you couldn't 'ave knocked over wi' a feather, the King of England askin' Isaac Eldon an' Jacob Hawley to show 'em how shells be made!'

'It wasn't just the King, though, was it, granddad?'

'No lad, weren't just the King.' Isaac smiled fondly at his grandson. 'The Queen were there right alongside o' him; weren't no airs an' graces about 'er neither, wouldn't 'ave no fuss but went atwixt them machines with no thought o' muck or grease touchin' of her clothes: smiled an' spoke a word wi' every one o' the women in that workshop while the King done the same, passin' a word wi' each man, eh!' he breathed, 'this'll be a day long remembered in Wednesbury.'

'Why would the King choose to come to Wednesbury?'

'Why?'

Reuben's delighted laugh rang along the cheap metal saucepans set on a shelf across from the gas stove. ' 'Cos Wednesbury is the only place has the technology.'

'What?' Miriam frowned.

'He means it be only Prodor 'as the knowin' o' how Finished Cavity Forgin' be done.' Isaac answered his daughter. 'The young bugger knows a deal more'n he should.'

'And whose fault would that be!'

It was true he talked to his grandson more than he ought, but he had made no mention of that process of shell manufacture. Isaac heard the remonstrance in his daughter's tone. He had drummed into the lad the need to keep silent on the subject when Reuben had confided the talk he had overheard when walking home behind several workmen from one of the town's steel mills.

'It wasn't granddad.' Reuben's defence followed swiftly on the heels of her accusation. 'I heard it talked of in the town.'

Miriam hung the drying cloth over a thin rope strung across the room and answered firmly. 'Then mind you don't go repeating any of it beyond this house.'

'Mmm, I agrees wi' you, Miriam, wench.' A covert wink directed at his grandson, Isaac rose from the table. 'I be advisin' o' him to keep a closed mouth on the rest o' what 'appened today, that he don't go tellin' you no more'n you've heard already.'

What more was there to hear? 'All right you two, you win. I know when I'm beaten, so what is it I haven't heard?'

Isaac mused quietly. 'Don't know as I'd go a'tellin', seems to me a woman who gives no credit to a lad for the keepin' o' a quiet mouth shouldn't go enquirin' o' him that which he needn't tell.'

'You are right, granddad. Like Mr Conroy said, it's my secret.'

Miriam turned sharply to her son. 'Mr Conroy!' she demanded. 'What has he got to do with this?'

Recognising that the teasing could be that step too far, Isaac glanced at the boy trying desperately to hide his own smile.

'Best tell 'er, lad, we don't want that elastic to go bustin' outta 'er drawers!'

'Mr Conroy came to the school.' The words burst eagerly. 'I didn't know 'til the headmaster sent for me, I thought I must have done something wrong, that I was in for a telling off, but no, he said a visitor wished to see me, that visitor no other than Mr Conroy.'

Her blood chilling rapidly to ice, Miriam's teeth barely allowed words to pass. 'Reuben,' she half choked, 'Reuben you haven't agreed to – you haven't said you will do anything!'

Deep brown eyes laughed into hers, eyes so like those others, eyes which in those lonely hours speared her heart. Miriam's soul called in its fear, 'Tom, protect our son, protect him from himself.'

'Relax.'

A Step Too Far

It was not Tom speaking, but it was Tom's voice she heard.

'There is no need to fret. Mr Conroy did not ask those things like last time, in fact he didn't ask I do anything at all.'

Thank you, Tom. But why had she not been consulted, her permission sought before her son was approached? She would have words to say to that headmaster!

Aiming to reduce the tension, Isaac smiled at his daughter. 'Let them porcupine bristles lie 'til you hears the all o' it. I were spoken to on your behalf.'

'I've been able to speak for myself since I were fourteen!'

'Ar wench, an' d'aint we know it, me an' your mother both. But this were different, you couldn't be fetched from your work an' no tongues wag, it were for that reason I couldn't be asked to go along o' the school an' tek Reuben from it.'

'Take Reuben from school! But he said . . .'

'Miriam!' Isaac interrupted. 'Why not sit you quiet an' let the lad tell his story.'

'Mr Conroy explained why you were not with him, he said he had talked with grandfather at Prodor before coming on to the school. He said he was not free to say more except the choice of whether I went with him or not was mine to make.'

So he went! Miriam sighed.

'I asked where it was we were going,' Reuben talked on joyfully, 'but Mr Conroy wouldn't be drawn, he said wise heads carried a still tongue. He took the towpath along the canal and turned into Prodor the back way, into the offices. I was scared then granddad had met with an accident, one so bad they thought you shouldn't see. Mr Conroy guessed what I was thinking for he assured me nothing was amiss, that in a few minutes I would know what it was all about. I thought I must be seeing things. I was completely tongue-tied, my mind not believing what my eyes saw; it was the King, mum, can you credit it, the King right there in that room! He looked so smart, his uniform gleaming with medals.'

Reading his daughter's puzzled look Isaac supplied, 'Uniform of Marshal of the Royal Air Force, or so I were told.'

'He spoke to one or two people stood along of us in the boardroom,' Reuben passed over the interruption, 'then his eye caught us and he came direct across asking was I the young man he had heard so much of. When Mr Conroy said yes, he took my hand. The King!' Eyes gleaming with pride switched from mother to grandfather. 'You saw it, didn't you, granddad? You saw the King shake hands with me.'

Isaac Eldon's heart swelled with the pleasure of the moment. He had seen England's King congratulate one of Her young sons.

'He said I had been very brave and that I could be proud of what I had done to preserve the safety not only of the factory and town, but of the country as a whole. It were then he took this from a man stood just behind him. He said he were sorry it were not presented at Buckingham Palace, war placing many restrictions, but that it were given in no less gratitude.'

Miriam looked at the box Reuben laid open on the table, a box in whose blue velvet heart nestled a silver medal inscribed 'For Bravery'.

'That's not all, mum.' Reuben met the eyes glittering with tears.

Her heart would not take any more, it was already filled to breaking. Her son, hers and Tom's, had been honoured by the King.

'The Queen talked to me as well. Oh mum, I wish you had been there to see. She looked so beautiful in her pale blue dress and matching coat that was trimmed with a creamy white fur collar, its tips reaching down over the hips; and her hat . . . it was exactly the same colour blue with a fur cockade slanted to the front of the brow, it all matched mum, blue leather gloves, shoes, handbag all of it even to the creamy roses pinned to her shoulder . . . I didn't know you could get roses in winter.'

I didn't know I had a son quite so poetic. Miriam smiled to herself.

'But it wasn't so much her outfit or the pearls around her neck struck me most, it was her eyes, they were so very blue and they smiled as much as her mouth, I'd say if stars were blue then the Queen has stars for eyes.'

'She smiled at you, did she?' Miriam asked.

'More than smiled wouldn't you say, granddad?'

Shaking his head Isaac responded. 'I be sayin' naught lad, this be your tellin'.'

'It was after the King had moved on.' Reuben required no exhorting to continue. 'The Queen came to where Mr Conroy and myself were standing. She smiled and asked would he mind if she spoke to me alone. Well, he couldn't refuse, could he mum, he couldn't go saying "no" to the Queen of England. Anyway he moved off and after convincing herself no one was close enough to overhear she said, "Will you keep a secret if I share one with you?"'

'I bowed.' Reuben grinned. 'Then said I could keep a secret along with the best. "So Mr Conroy informed us," she laughed. Then, bending closer she whispered, "His Majesty has graciously given his permission for me to tell you that arrangements have been put in place whereby once you are of age, and should you be of a mind, then a place has been set aside for you at Sandhurst. If it is still your wish you will be trained as an officer of His Majesty's Army and when you emerge you will be a *real* lieutenant."

'Think of it, mum, a real lieutenant. I only wish dad could have known, it would have pleased him, wouldn't it?'

Everything about their son would have pleased him. Tears burning along her cheeks, Miriam stared into the past, at a soldier kissing his son goodbye, a soldier whispering to the wife he loved, '*While you have Reuben you and I can never be parted, we are together in him.*' Together! Reuben was her life. But he could not take the place of the husband her heart cried out for.

28

'Eeh, it be that cold I be piddlin' icicles!'

Seeing the thin woman who dashed into the toilets, faded yellow headscarf tied turban-fashion over protruding steel curling pins, Alice grabbed Becky's arm and pushed her into an empty cubicle. 'Don't go comin' out, not 'til Nosy Nora be gone, let her see you in that state and it'll be all over the factory afore knockin' off time.'

'I thought Becky Turner were along o' you, it were 'er I seen I be sure.' Leaving her cubicle, Nora glanced around the washroom.

'In the lav.' Alice nodded toward a closed cubicle.

'Don't 'er be well?' Nora Bates' internal antenna snapped into operation.

Hands held beneath a running tap, Alice answered nonchalantly, 'Be her period, Becky always has a lot of pain with that.'

'Don't be no pleasure in that for any wench.' Nora's faded yellow turban swung back and forth. 'But be a lot less pleasure when it don't come, I knows for ain't I got six kids that be the provin' of it?'

'Be like my mother says, Mrs Bates, if you don't want the puddin' you shouldn't do the mixin'.'

Shaking water from her hands, Nora walked across to where the oil-stained towel hung on its roller. 'Your mother be right, but try a' tellin' that to my old man an' like as not you'd greet the mornin' wi' not just a belly full of child but a pair o' black eyes along wi' it.'

Reluctant to leave the wash basin, Alice turned off the tap then made a show of shaking excess water from her hands. Nora Bates would recognise she was dawdling and that recognition would not lie wasting on a still tongue. Praying Becky would guess the reason of what she said, she called, 'We'll 'ave to get a move on Becky, the big picture starts at half seven.'

'Goin' to the pictures then?' Nora made no attempt to leave.

'Mmm.' Becky and me are goin' to see *Gone With the Wind* at Darlaston.'

'Darlaston!' Nora's brow rose questioningly. 'Wouldn't it be better for you to wait 'til it be shown 'ere in Wednesbury, save you goin' all the way to Darlaston?'

For God's sake, Becky, answer! Anxious her friend's silence would arouse the very suspicion she was trying to allay, Alice said quickly. 'Ain't no certainty the Gaumont will 'ave the film, there's been no advertisin' of it as I've seen; besides I'd walk a lot further than the four miles it be to Darlaston to see Clark Gable, ooh!' She leaned her face dreamily against the damp towel. 'Clark Gable, he's a man could fetch the ducks off the water, I'd leave 'ome for one like him any day of the week.'

'Ar,' Nora snorted, 'an' be back a few months later groanin' in agony pushin' out that he'd run off leavin' you to fend for!'

Alice closed her eyes, displaying emotion which in truth she was far from feeling. 'Not Clark Gable,' she murmured, 'Clark would never do a thing like that.'

'Hmph!' Her sniff pure disparagement Nora retorted stonily, 'Clark, Tom, Dick or 'Arry they be all the same, mark my words you let a man 'ave what brings 'im to market afore the ring be on the finger an' it'll be the wench as pays the price; you think on that Alice Butler an' tell Becky Turner to think on it an' all; remember an ounce o' advice be better'n a ton o' sympathy.'

As Nora departed Alice called the all clear to Becky.

'Christ, you look awful!' Alice gasped. 'Oh my God! You 'aven't . . . ? Becky, you ain't . . . ? Oh Lord, say you ain't pregnant!'

Her dark-circled eyes stark against an ashen face, Becky bent heaving over the basin.

She was! Alice tried to think clearly. They both had their 'monthly' at the same time, it had been a sort of bond between them from its first occurring. That had scared the life out of both of them; their teacher had found them in the school toilets each crying they had some terrible disease, that they would be dead before ever seeing their mothers again. If only those mothers had forewarned, explained as that teacher had explained that what they were experiencing was perfectly natural and would happen every month, it was simply a part of growing up.

'It'll be the wench as pays the price.'

Nora Bates' words clanged loudly in Alice's mind but were as loudly rejected. Becky would not have to pay, she and Earl were to be married. She stared at the girl still retching into the basin. But should Becky's mother find out her daughter was pregnant then marriage, no matter how soon, would not save Becky from the woman's anger; and neither would that anger be lessened should the news be passed around Prodor and halfway around Wednesbury before reaching her. Thank heaven they had both finished their shift. Grabbing her coat, she flung it over the other girl's shoulder and dragged her out into the yard.

When they were clear of the factory gates, making sure nobody was within hearing distance, she asked quietly, 'How long?'

Sobs rolling in her throat Becky choked, 'Four weeks.'

Alice calculated swiftly. Eight months left, that was ample time, Becky would be in America long before the birth she could swear happened prematurely.

She shook the sobbing girl. 'Becky, it's okay, your mother need never know, you and Earl will be married.'

Becky shook her head. 'No,' she cried, 'no, we won't be married.'

Alice's confusion settled on her brow. Becky and Earl not be married! Why? Hadn't he said his Commanding Officer had granted the necessary permission? He had even told her they could go ahead whenever it suited her, so why now was Becky saying they wouldn't be married?

'You don't understand, Alice, Earl and me won't be marryin'. Earl is gone!'

'Gone? You mean he's been posted away from Cosford, sent to some other camp? Well, that don't mean nothin', he can be recalled or you can go to wherever it is they've sent him and get married there.'

'No.' Becky laughed a dull hopeless laugh which barely left her throat. 'No, I can't Alice, he has gone back to America, and even if I could follow him there, it wouldn't do no good. Earl Feldman already has a wife.'

Placing the last of the letters her employer had signed into its envelope Katrin glanced at the inner office, the voices of the two men inside coming to her in a low uninterpretable hum.

She had thought Isaac Eldon would have been imprisoned when it was discovered he and his grandson were in possession of maps denoting every steel mill, every iron foundry and every engineering works in Wednesbury, but that had not happened.

Why? She stabbed the letter vexedly onto the finished pile, scattering the whole lot across the desk. The information she had given would have had to be investigated very quickly, yet nothing had come of it. Nothing? She snatched up the letters. Isaac Eldon had been presented to the King, how could an honour such as that have been managed when an allegation of treason had been made against him?

There had been more to that day than handshakes and a tour of the factory, why else would Eldon have left the workshop minutes before the Royals? Why had he slipped away moments after being spoken to by a dark-suited official? Her father had of course been presented, he also had accompanied the King to explain the intricacies of Finished Cavity Forgings, yet no man had come to speak quietly with him, he had not been called away. What was it had Eldon treated differently to her father when both were equally involved in that project? But with the tour completed he had come to stand with her, had remained at her side while the King, Queen and their be-medalled gold-braided attendants had, to the cheers of the workers, proceeded out into the yard.

But they had not immediately left the premises.

Resentment kindled by suspicion flared a hot trail.

She and her father had followed from the factory but there had been brought to a halt. The cars which had brought the visitors were still in the yard but there were no people other than chauffeurs and police guards. The company must have gone into the office block, to the room Arthur Whitman had been so anxious to have completed in readiness for that Royal visit. Dining room and boardroom, that had been a cover for what it was really meant for!

But what other purpose had it served that afternoon? Prevented from returning to her own office by an apologetic policeman, she could only guess, but it was not guesswork as to who it was she had seen cross the ground at the rear of the factory.

The afternoon had been deceptively bright, the sun giving the illusion of warmth while in reality it masked a coldness, a chill in the air which had her shiver. Her father had said he must return to his work at Titan and that she should wait inside the works, stay warm until things returned to normal. But she had not wanted to be in any workshop, the factory was not the place for Katrin Hawley; so she had stood until the deepening chill had her walk halfway around the building. It was then, just before she was turned back by yet another policeman, she had seen two figures.

They had been walking away from Prodor toward the canal towpath which bordered the building. She had glimpsed them from the rear, one a little taller his flat cap and light brown foreman's smock signifying a workman whose slight stoop to the shoulders attested to his being so much older than the shorter figure. The shorter figure! She had mused on that. Had it been a lad enquiring after employment in readiness for leaving school, a lad being turned away in respect of those very important visitors? But then would it not have been one of the police officers who prevented that youngster entering the works, as she had been prevented entering the offices?

Instinct solidified into certainty as the hum of conversation within Whitman's office ceased, he and Isaac Eldon coming out.

It was Eldon she had seen going toward the towpath, Eldon and his grandson!

But why leave the back way? Why the secrecy?

Whatever it was, something had brought the boy to meet the King.

Both of them should rightfully be locked away, the man in jail and the boy in a secure Borstal institution, yet instead they had been rewarded, given the privilege of meeting Royalty.

How? Who had pulled the strings to clear them of an accusation of treason?

The Devil takes care of his own! The Devil was Isaac Eldon's guard and protector. The river of fire raging in Katrin turned rapidly to ice in her brain.

Guards and protectors, even the very best of them sometimes had their attention drawn away. But hers would not be diverted. Katrin Hawley's concentration and all of her detestation would remain centred on Isaac Eldon and each of his family until it destroyed them.

Letters scooped again into a neat pile, Katrin looked up at the young woman whose progress had been halted by the departing Eldon.

'I 'ave to see Kate . . . Miss Hawley, I would 'ave asked you, Mr Eldon, could I take a minute off but you wasn't in the machine shop nor any place else I looked.'

'There'll be time for talkin' after work.'

'But there won't, Mr Eldon.' Alice Butler shook her head. 'I be on the two 'til ten shift as you know and Kate won't want me goin' to see her that late at night.'

Obviously having heard the somewhat agitated voice, Arthur Whitman had come to the door of his own office.

'Is something wrong?' He looked from Isaac to the girl not yet allowed to pass.

'No.' Isaac's reply was terse. 'It be one o' the girls wantin' to see Kat . . . Miss Hawley, but like I've said there be a time for talkin' an' that time don't be durin' work hours.'

'Please, Mr Whitman, it'll take no more than a couple of minutes and I'll work through my tea break to make up for them.'

Meeting the pleading glance, Arthur Whitman smiled. 'Of course I will not override Mr Eldon should he insist you do not . . . er . . . transpose . . . a few minutes of your work time, but I am sure he will act as he sees fit.'

Recognising a nod was as good as a wink, and warning that five minutes was all Alice could have, Isaac left.

'Eh Kate, I had to come.' Alice crossed to stand at Katrin's desk. 'It be Becky.'

Becky? Placing the letters in the outgoing post tray Katrin frowned. What could be so important that Alice had come bounding in here?

'Her and Earl, they ain't gettin' married.'

'But it is all arranged, he has had permission and also clearance from the United States, hasn't he?'

'Ar.' Alice nodded agreement.

'Then why the delay?'

'It ain't no delay to that weddin', it be a definite ending of it.'

'Alice, how can it be ended when it has not yet been performed?'

'I'll tell you how; there won't be no weddin' for Becky 'cos Earl bloody Feldman be married already though he pays no mind to his wife nor to the four kids he's fathered on other women back home in America, nor will he pay mind to another one left 'ere in Wednesbury.'

'Becky?' Katrin's interest sharpened.

'Ar, Becky!' The answer whispered fiercely across the desk. 'Becky be pregnant, her be up the duff while that swine Feldman has got hisself sent back to them United bloody States where no doubt he'll play his filthy game on some other wench who don't have enough oil in her lamp to see what he be about, another wench who'll 'ave no more sense than to trust him.'

'How did Becky find out, about Earl I mean?'

'I couldn't go to Wolverhampton with her the last couple of Saturdays so her went to the Civic on her own. The rest of the Yanks we danced with were all there but not Feldman, he didn't show either time . . . and when Becky asked his mates where he was they told her he'd gone home to the States. But that weren't all what they told Becky, they told her about a wife and kids, said her could ask to see the Commanding Officer but doubted that would achieve anythin'; what that was meant to tell her was there could be no proof of Earl Feldman being the father.'

That was understandable. Katrin remained silent with her thoughts. If Becky Turner had lain with one man, who was to say how many more she had had intercourse with? Who could definitely place the resulting pregnancy at Earl Feldman's door?

Alice leaned her hands on the desk. 'Kate, I'm worried for Becky, worried what her will do to herself. The wench is terrified of what'll happen once her mother finds out about this, Becky says her will have her put away in some place never to be brought out again.'

'Surely not, Becky is foolish to think that of her mother.'

'No, Kate. You don't know Mary Turner, that woman be capable of doin' anythin' to keep her name from bein' talked about by so called friends, and her callin' herself Christian.'

'But putting some people away, putting girls into an asylum just because they become pregnant yet cannot marry? That doesn't happen any more.'

'Don't you believe it! My mother told me of it happening not a year gone, named names her did though I ain't goin' to repeat 'em. A young wench of sixteen were sent to an institution. The mother covering by saying her had a heart complaint and had died a month or so after; but you don't have a daughter die and not have a funeral. I reckons my mother had the truth of it, wenches can be put away and that be the fear I have for Becky. So I come to see you Kate, to ask is there any way we can help 'cos if we don't then Becky will surely kill herself.'

29

'I thinks it shameful the way your Jack were hauled off to the station, them police should be made to apologise.'

'Apologise, them! They'll be givin' no apology, think they be above that; but I told 'em, come knockin' at my door again wi'out rock solid proof of what they be there for and it'll be the piss pot emptied over the lot of 'em, bloody Inspector an' all!'

'Some folk believes they can get away wi' anything and bein' wrong don't seem to cause 'em no worry.'

'Well, I'll cause them coppers worry enough should they come for my lad again. He be no saint, that I knows, but he ain't no killer neither.'

Standing in the queue of women at the grocery shop, Katrin heard plainly the conversation going on a little ahead.

'Be that what the police thought? Be that why he were arrested?'

'That be the trouble, they d'aint stop to think!' Polly Butler's indignant retort rang across the line of customers, their own conversations put on hold.

'. . . It were Jack Butler had lamped Slater that other time so it must be Jack Butler done the deed this time.'

'Eh, Polly wench, that be terrible for you.'

'Well, it weren't no party I can tell you, but it be my lad had the worse of it, bein' fetched away from his work while 'alf of Wednesbury looked on and the other 'alf a' gloatin'. Yes, our Jack give Slater a hidin' but what brother worth his salt wouldn't 'ave done the same were it a sister of his got slapped. I tell you, Ginny, if our Jack hadn't done what he did then it would 'ave been him as well as Slater got a pummelling 'cos I'd 'ave given it him meself no matter he be grown.'

'And you wouldn't 'ave been doin' less than any mother would do, Polly.'

The queue shuffled forward a few steps as a customer left the shop with her groceries.

'I told them bobbies the same,' Polly returned. 'Told them straight out to their faces, a bloke who knocks a woman about deserves more than a hidin', he deserves gaol, and that for a bloody long time!'

'I agrees wi' all you say, but Slater won't be goin' to gaol.'

Katrin smiled to herself. Jim Slater would not be going to prison. He would be going to hell.

'That be the worst part,' Polly answered vindictively. 'That swine should 'ave lived long enough to tell it weren't our Jack set about him.'

How long *had* he lived? Katrin felt her nerves twang. The Inspector who had called to interview her had said Slater was dead but he had not said whether he had died prior to or after being found. If it were prior, had Slater said who had thrust that broken bottle into his throat?

'But they ain't still holdin' your lad, the police 'ave let him go, ain't they?'

'D'ain't 'ave no option.' Righteousness resounding in every note Polly Butler's response dominated the shop. 'My lad had the provin' that it weren't him had done for Jim Slater.'

'That be a blessin' Polly.'

Regret registered in Ginny's reply.

'Not so much a one for that Inspector and the rest of them bobbies, they was ready to lock my lad up and forget where it was they'd put him, but now they 'as to go on lookin' 'til they finds who it is be truly guilty.'

The words fell heavily on Katrin. Had the police got some lead, some information? Could that information possibly point to her?

'My lad had a witness!'

A witness! Jack Butler had someone backing his claim of innocence! Had that witness seen what had happened?

'Fact be he had more'n a dozen could vouch for him!'

'He told 'em, but them bobbies wouldn't listen.' Polly slapped a handful of ration books onto the counter. 'Kept him hours they did askin' of the same questions time after time. It weren't 'til he told 'em he'd answer nothin' more lessen they spoke to others that they finally done what he asked and talked to his mates. Three lads he works alongside of had gone together with my lad straight from the foundry when their shift ended, that bein' eight o'clock at night. They went straight over to the 'Ome Guard base where they was kept on duty 'til next mornin' when the four of 'em walked 'ome together. Our Jack weren't never gone from their sight nor that of the others of them 'Ome Guard lads not once. He were with them when Jim Slater got done in, that put the cobblebosh on that Inspector's reckonin', now he has to go lookin' for the real culprit.'

'Do the police 'ave any notion as to who that be? Did Jim Slater tell aught of who done it?'

An expectant silence fell over the shop and Katrin feared the loud throb of blood in her veins must be heard. Would Fortune smile again or would it turn its face away?

Polly watched several tawny coloured coupons fall to the counter. A warning note in her voice said firmly: 'The bobbies won't need no tellin' of who it be has done for you 'Arold Pearks if you cuts more of them coupons than you should, you'll be goin' home light of a few things and them things won't be no food coupons!'

Behind the counter Harold Pearks smiled, his bushy grey eyebrows lifting. 'I ain't never cut too many up to yet, Polly.'

'And you'd better go on not never cuttin' too many, fact be you should ought to cut less of them there coupons for a good customer.'

'Now that would bring the police to my door.'

'Ar well,' Polly answered his laugh with her own, 'I'd far rather they come a knockin' of your door than mine.'

A Step Too Far

The conversation drifting dangerously from the subject in hand Ginny shuffled her own ration books from the deep belly of a coarse hessian shopping bag.

'I hopes they won't come knockin' on account of Jim Slater tellin' it were Harold Pearks set about him.'

'Ain't likely, Ginny.' The elderly man chuckled. 'It be all I can do to set about me dinner these days.'

'I knows the feelin'.' Ginny returned. 'Ain't none of we got the energy these days, but saying that it seems somebody has got plenty, at least enough to set about Jim Slater; I only hopes he's told the bobbies who it be.'

Slapping a lump of butter between a pair of wooden pats before placing it on scales set to one side of the counter, Harold Pearks nodded affably, a grin deepening the wrinkles around his eyes. 'So do I, Ginny.' He removed the butter and wrapped it deftly in a square of greaseproof paper. 'Just so long as he ain't said it were me.'

Keenly as she had followed the cutting of coupons and the weighing of the butter, Polly watched the fine wire slice deftly through a block of cheese, severing a portion which would serve no more than three days' supply of dinner sandwiches and only then if it were cut thinner than moth wings.

'Bobbies would 'ave no mind to that,' she retorted, placing the cheese beside an equally meagre amount of butter. 'Your mother don't go lettin' you out after dark.'

The grocer handed Polly two dark blue paper bags, each containing one pound of sugar. 'Weren't you were spoke of . . .'

Needle pricks of alarm jabbed at Katrin's brain. Jim Slater *had* said something! Lord, why hadn't she made certain he would never speak again? She should have stayed long enough to see the job thoroughly done, to see Jim Slater totally dead. But it was too late for 'why', too late for anything other than concocting an alibi, one which must negate all that Slater might have said; but what . . . how?

'Them police d'ain't say of nobody's name. But then they wouldn't,' Polly was still speaking. 'Kept a tight mouth did them police when I asked who it were my lad been brought in to pay the piper for their wrong tune, oh no! That Inspector weren't answerin' of that, though it weren't in his reckonin' that every tongue might not be tight as his'n.'

'Does tha' go to say one has been a waggin'?'

'I do!' Polly's reply was emphatic. 'And what's more it be one as can't 'ave no arguin' with.'

Katrin's throat closed, sickeningly cutting off air from her lungs.

'. . . The men who found Slater on their way to work at 'alf past five that mornin' uses the Rising Sun in Meeting Street, they shares a pint with my old man – whenever there be a pint to be had, that is – anyway they told him that Slater were stone cold dead when they come across of him so he couldn't 'ave told the police who hit him.'

Jim Slater had been dead! Katrin's brain sang the words. The police had no information and she would need no alibi.

'Seems they'll 'ave to go on lookin' for that villain.'

Let them look, they wouldn't see what was beneath their noses. Who could possibly suspect the young, well educated daughter of the respectable Jacob Hawley to be a killer?

She could write off the episode of Mr James Slater!

30

Slater was dead! Elation in every step, Katrin left the grocery shop and crossed the busy Market Place, weaving between stalls so surrounded by eager customers it was virtually impossible to see the goods on offer. But it was not only greengrocery to be had from the market, some stalls offered a bare selection of household goods, candles and matches all quickly snatched up to be kept for use in air raid shelters, while others carried a variety of second-hand clothing and part-worn shoes, all no doubt obtained from pawnshops ridding themselves of unredeemed pledges. Some women, judging it more practical, bought second-hand to wear in factories, thereby allowing the saving of treasured clothing coupons for new clothes bought for a special occasion.

A special occasion such as the wedding Becky Turner had seen vanish before her eyes.

Alice Butler's agitated whisper floated in her mind.

'. . . *is there any way we can help, 'cos if we don't then Becky will surely kill herself.*'

Not yet! Her brain whispered. Becky Turner must not kill herself just yet!

What was it her mother used to say? 'When one door closes another opens.' That was exactly what had happened. The door had closed on her attempt to have Isaac Eldon gaoled but another had opened and the wedge she intended to use would ensure it did not close until she had seen that man crushed, his family along with him.

The method – neat, efficient and practical – had sprung perfectly formed into her mind, but she had said no word of it to Alice. Katrin Hawley must not be seen as a collaborator.

Having reached the house and stored the groceries in their various cupboards, Katrin read again her father's note. He would be the rest of the day and evening at Titan. It could possibly be very late before he returned.

Another door opens! Katrin walked upstairs to her room. Crossing to the dressing table she opened a drawer and withdrew the delicate lavender silk.

As with the gift of dresses to Alice and Becky, she had once again chosen to talk with them in her own home rather than the factory canteen; it was the only way she could be certain no other ears heard her proposal. When a timid tap at the door announced their arrival, Katrin ushered them through the hall and into the living room, Becky bursting into tears the moment her bottom touched the chair.

'Oh God,' she sobbed, 'what am I goin' to do?'

'First thing you be goin' to do is stop snivellin'!' Alice thrust a handkerchief into shaking hands. 'Cryin' don't wipe up spilt milk but it does make the eyes all red and puffy so unless you wants your mother to be asking questions you'll stop right now!'

'Alice is right, Becky, it is the sensible thing to do.'

Tension so long coiled in Becky released itself in the rush of words. 'Sensible!' she said, blue eyes flashing brilliantly through tears. 'Sensible! Since when was sensible the answer to pregnancy? To a child I d'ain't ask for and I certainly don't want?'

'I'm sorry, I didn't mean . . .'

'I know Kate, you only meant to help.' Becky pressed the handkerchief to her eyes. 'But there's nothing you can do, nothing anybody can do except for Earl.'

'An' he ain't comin' back!' Alice snapped. 'He be gone for good and the sooner you gets used to the fact the better. He weren't in the running for a wife, but simply out for all he could get.'

Which he had certainly got. Concealing the thought behind a falsely sympathetic smile, Katrin poured a conciliatory cup of tea.

'Your mother does not know yet?'

'Oh Lord, Kate, no! I dread her finding out, her'll have me put away that's if her don't kill me herself, either be preferable to her than have it broadcast all over Wednesbury her daughter be carryin' a bastard.'

'You could go away, some place in the country where you are not known.'

'My askin' to leave home would have the same result Alice got when her asked to join the Women's Forces, it wouldn't even be thought on.'

'Well, anythin' be a deal more useful than sittin' cryin' your eyes out!'

'Then what do you suggest?' Agitation had Becky's question flare into a demand. 'We all knows what be of no use so now you tell what *do* be of use! Well, what be of use, Alice?'

Alice could find no answer.

Katrin collected teacups onto a tray and carried them to the kitchen.

They could see no way. But Katrin Hawley had a way! She looked down at the prettily decorated china her mother had taken so much pride in. A few more minutes' distress, a little longer worrying would serve to reinforce the suggestion she would offer. The hurdle was getting Becky Turner to agree. But set that hurdle beside the insurmountable barrier that was Mary Turner and any objection would most certainly disappear.

'I hope your mother will not be annoyed with your coming here tonight, I know she relies on your help with your brothers and sisters.'

'Annoyed,' Becky sniffed miserably, 'that ain't what her will be feelin' once her gets to know I'm carryin'. The worst temper I've ever seen her have will seem like nothing more than a babby's tantrum in comparison to the explosion that'll bring.'

'I still don't understand how you could let things go so far, how you could be so daft!' Alice's patience snapped now. 'It ain't like you d'ain't know how kids be got. Christ, Becky, we've both knowed that long afore leavin' school. You knowed the risk so why take it!'

'Earl said . . .'

A Step Too Far

'Earl!' Alice spewed the name like acid from her tongue. 'Seems he said a lot of things you was fool enough to believe!'

Becky went on quietly, without tears, a young woman seeking refuge in confession. 'Earl said it were not wrong if we truly loved each other, the only wrong thing would be to marry without being absolutely certain we both wanted all that marriage entailed. He said it was sinful for a man and woman to pledge the rest of their lives together while not knowing whether that deepest most explicit act were a celebration of love, something both revered . . . I . . .' Becky faltered, 'I was afraid but Earl said there could be no fear where love was true; that if I loved him as much as he loved me there would be nothing immoral in my showing it, and so I let him make love to me. I believed him.' Becky looked with wide eyes at Katrin, 'I believed it when he said we would marry. Alice is right in saying I was stupid. Oh Kate, it's all so hopeless, it would be better all round if I were dead!'

Seeming to veer the discussion to a new path Kate asked: 'Earl, is he the only boyfriend you've had?'

'He's the only one whose . . .'

'No!' Katrin interjected swiftly, 'I don't mean is he the only man you have made love with, I meant is he the only man to have been attracted to you?'

'That be a definite no.' Alice compounded Becky's shake of the head. 'Don't be a chap in Wednesbury ain't had a fancy for Becky, her could have married any one of 'em. Not least Rob Eldon, he's still crazy about her, asked her to marry him afore he went into the Navy and no doubt he'd ask again were it not for . . .'

'For me bein' caught with another man's child.' Becky's laugh was pure despair. 'Well, askin' ain't likely now, is it?'

This was the moment. All she hoped for rested on the next step . . . it must be taken carefully. Katrin waited long seconds before saying, 'It could be.'

'Could be what?' It was Alice's question.

Prevaricating, using the ploy of uncertainty, Katrin said. 'I was thinking should Robert Eldon ask Becky to marry him, it would put an end to her problems.'

'Well, seein' as he ain't here, nor not likely to be so long as this perishin' war goes on, then I don't see the use in talkin'.' Alice dismissed more discussion.

'But he is here, or will be by tomorrow.'

'Rob Eldon be comin' home?'

Katrin nodded. 'That is what I heard just before you came into the office. Mr Whitman called to Isaac Eldon saying to give his regards and that Isaac should take a few hours away from work, spend some time with his son while he was on leave.'

'That be nice for Isaac Eldon, but I don't see how Rob havin' leave can help Becky.'

'It can if she wants it to. When Alice came to ask could I help then honestly I could think of no way. It was later I thought . . .'

'What . . . you thought what?'

'Nothing.' Katrin shook her head. 'It was nothing.'

Her glance hardening, Alice said, 'That be a lie, Kate

Hawley! I brought Becky here 'cos I thought you'd help but if you can't then say so but don't go givin' we lies!'

'Really Alice, it's crazy.' Katrin shook her head. 'I don't know how I could have dreamed such an idea.'

'Crazy or not can't be judged 'til it be told and any idea be better than none.'

Keeping to the illusion she would much prefer to say no more Katrin took her time.

'It was probably on hearing Robert Eldon's name mentioned had me remember, as Alice had, the crush he had on you and it flashed into my mind that should he still feel the same way it would be a simple matter to get him to ask again would you marry him.'

'Marry Rob! I couldn't do that!'

'Of course not. I told you it was a crazy notion, it's better you make a clean breast of things to your mother.'

Sharper than any nail, the point had been driven home. Becky Turner knew the outcome of confession.

'It will be hard for you, Becky, but you can't keep your mother from finding out.' Katrin added hammer to nail head, driving it deeper.

'Nor can you hide it from them at work, especially Nosy Nora – that one be suspicious already.'

'Oh God!' Becky dropped her head into her hands. 'What can I do?'

'You could marry Rob Eldon.'

Quiet as Alice's reply had been, it acted like a gunshot on Becky. Her head snapped up and she cried sharply, 'How can I marry Rob or any other man? I be pregnant, Alice, how do I tell him that?'

'You don't!' The bombshell was Katrin's.

'I be well over now.' Becky's face crumpled, 'How far along will I be by the time . . .'

By the time she was married to Robert Eldon? Katrin set the reply to words. 'There is government legislation which allows men about to leave on active service to apply for a special licence which enables them to marry three days later in a Register Office.'

'Not in church? Mother would never go for that.'

'A civil ceremony can be blessed in church.'

Alice agreed. 'The priest wouldn't refuse, seeing Robert will very soon be returning to action and if he agreed then surely no one would object.'

Katrin caught the look that crossed Becky's face, a look which said 'Could I?' Satisfaction smiled warm in Katrin. This was what she had aimed for. It would need only a touch more cement and the foundation stone on which her plan was to develop would be well and truly laid.

'Supposin' . . . supposin' I did marry Rob . . . and we, we . . .' Becky blushed scarlet, 'you know what I be sayin', it wouldn't hide the fact I were already pregnant when a child comes weeks sooner than it should.'

'Wouldn't be the first kid born premature.'

Well done, Alice, right on cue. Katrin's silence hid a growing sense of achievement.

'But should Rob find out . . .'

'Who's to tell him?' Katrin cut in, 'I won't and Alice won't, that leaves only yourself, and daft as Alice says you sometimes are, surely you wouldn't be daft enough to go telling him he is not the father.'

'It's a rotten trick to play on Rob.'

'Life be full of rotten tricks, and it keeps throwin' 'em. The one Earl Feldman has played on you be a clear example; thing is you 'ave to learn to throw 'em back.' Alice was brusque. 'Look at it this way, you needs a husband, the babby you be carryin' needs a father, marryin' Rob Eldon would take care of both and Rob would be gettin' the girl he's always wanted; what's more it would mean your mother be off your back and once this war be over and Rob back home you would be gettin' a place of your own so you'd be free of her altogether.'

Without realising it, Alice had delivered the ultimate reason. Becky Turner would accept any alternative if it meant not having to face her mother's wrath.

31

'There's no one else with the technical skills as yet, there hasn't been time enough to train them.'

Alone in the living room, Katrin stared into the fire her mind repeating what her father had told her before he returned for yet another long evening of extra hours at Titan. Signs of fatigue had shown clearly on his face, responsibility for designing a completely new method of shell production etching deep lines. She had tried to get him to stay home to rest at least for one evening; that was when he had said the Ministry of Supply, concerned at the high risk of Prodor and its sister factory New Crown Forgings being bombed, had decided to transport the necessary machinery to Australia and that he was to go there to supervise installation.

'But why you?' she had asked. *'Isaac Eldon has the knowledge, why can't it be him sent to Australia?'*

Her father had said consolingly, *'It will only be for a couple of months.'*

'Couple of months, couple of days, I still don't see why you should be the one sent off to the other side of the world!'

She had stared at the man who had cared for her as he would for a child of his own body, he explained patiently.

'*I am not being despatched without consultation. I was asked would I go and I consented.*' He had smiled at her bewilderment. '*Katrin, there comes a time when we all do what perhaps we might not do in the normal run of things.*'

Like stabbing a man in the throat with a broken bottle! The thought had reflected in her eyes.

Judging the swift gleam to be that of fear, he had come to sit beside her. '*Katrin, try to understand, this method of shell forging is the lifeblood of this country and possibly the whole of Europe. Without the means of continued production we cannot stand against the enemy, without comparable supply of armaments we risk our freedom; so you see, my dear, how very important it is we safeguard this by installing machinery abroad.*'

'*I do understand.*' She had countered. '*I also understood it to be a joint undertaking, you and Isaac Eldon together both equally necessary. What I don't understand is why now it seems to need only one to set it up, and why suddenly that one is you.*'

A gentle squeeze of the hand had accompanied his answer. '*Isaac offered to go, but it is vital one of us remain behind.*'

He had not needed to say the rest: that should both be lost, then, with the process not fully grasped by anyone else, hope of winning the war was placed on an even more precarious footing.

'*And that one is Isaac Eldon!*' She had said it scathingly, antipathy cold and hard as ice.

'*It could be no other way.*' He had shaken his head. '*I design the machinery but it is Isaac has the knowledge of metals, his knowledge is not so easily transferable. That is why Whitman agreed it had to be he and myself take the machinery to Australia.'*

Arthur Whitman was going also! There had been no hint of this from him.

Her father continued in that gentle tone she had known from babyhood. '*I know this is going to be difficult for you, especially so with your mother . . .*' he had paused then moved to stare into the fire. '*I wanted to tell you but Violet said you were too young to understand. Then as you got older she begged we leave it just a while longer, always a while longer, I gave in to argument, anything for a quiet life. But I was wrong!*' He had thumped a clenched fist against the fireplace. '*I should have insisted you be allowed to know . . .*'

'*To know what was hidden in a box mother kept in a drawer of her dressing table? What she maybe never intended I should?*'

He had turned to face her, regret dark in his eyes.

'*Yes,*' she had answered the emotion. '*I know. I have known for a long time. I found the birth certificate which showed Violet was not my birth mother and you are not my father.*'

'*. . . your folks d'aint want you . . .*'

Words from an angry tongue echoing back from her childhood, Katrin opened the box in her hands. They had known: Becky Turner, Alice Butler and Freda Evans. They and how many more had been privy to that which Violet Hawley had kept hidden from her?

'But it was not hidden so well as you would have had it, mother.' She touched the document with the tip of a finger. 'You should have known secrets have a way of biting their keeper, as yours would have had not a bomb deprived you of the experience.'

But there was no bomb had deprived those still believing Katrin Hawley ignorant of her adoption. Let them bask in their misconception. She snapped the box closed. Time added flavour to the dish of revenge and revenge was a dish she would eat well of. But not yet.

Replacing the box beneath its soft lavender shroud she returned to the living room.

There was something must take preference even over revenge.

Arthur Whitman frowned at the letter on his desk. What the hell had brought this on? Reading it again more slowly he tried to fathom the cause then rang for Katrin.

'You know what this is?' He waved the letter as she entered.

'Yes.'

'But why? Is it due to your father?'

'My father?'

'On account of his leaving for Australia.'

Of *his* leaving, not *our* leaving. Katrin noted the disparity. 'Why would my father leaving for Australia have any bearing on my resignation?'

'Well, it's not because of your going with him!'

'No.'

'Then is it so you can go stay with relatives somewhere, will travelling into work here take too long, is that why you are giving notice?'

'No, it is neither of those reasons.'

'Then for God's sake what is? I'm sorry, I didn't mean to blow, it's just this has come at a bad time.'

Could there have been a better time? No, Mr Whitman, I think not. Katrin had dwelt on that very question, pondered it well before writing the letter.

'The fact is, Katrin, this will make the move to Australia that much more harrowing by my having to take time every few minutes to explain the ins and outs of everything to a new secretary. If it's a question of salary . . .'

'It isn't!' Katrin's answer came quickly. It must appear she wanted no discussion, no real delving into her decision to leave Prodor.

'So what is it, Katrin, why are you resigning?'

This was the moment. Lowering her glance, fingers twisting together, she allowed silence to enhance an entirely fictitious air of misery.

'I have to. Please don't say any of this to my father, I don't want him learning . . .'

Whitman's frown deepened. 'Learning what, Katrin? Surely there is nothing a father should not know about a daughter he loves as Jacob obviously loves you.'

'That's just it!' With all the quality of an established actress, Katrin let her words rush on a broken sob. 'It is because he loves me I cannot see him shamed, I will not let my disgrace become his, that is why I ask you to let him leave for Australia without knowing.' Shoulders drooping a perfect emulation of despair, Katrin turned to leave.

'One moment.'

She paused. There was recognition in his voice, he had guessed the reason of her resigning.

'Katrin,' He spoke quietly. 'The shame you would not have your father suffer, is it the shame of pregnancy?'

A shudder of sobs her answer, he asked, 'The child you are carrying, is it mine?'

There had been no striving on her part to get him to believe her murmured yes, and no questioning on his, just a quiet acceptance.

Holding the blue dress against her, Katrin laughed softly. Deceiving Arthur Whitman had been so easy. She had wept a little, protested he should not have to answer for her mistake. But it had been no mistake; getting him to make love to her had been well planned. She would be Mrs Arthur Whitman.

He had asked was she prepared to marry him. No 'I love you, Katrin', no 'Please be my wife', no kiss, just a bald 'The child will need a father and a stable home, I am prepared to provide that, are you in agreement to marriage?'

He had not come to her side of the desk, made no effort to comfort her tears and made no claim as to fault lying with him; but as with running the everyday business of Prodor he had set wheels in motion by telephoning her father and asking permission to visit the family home that evening.

There had been no opposition from Jacob. He had accepted the story of his daughter and her employer having been in love for some time, that both wished to be married before he left for Australia and had happily offered congratulations. He added smilingly that his consent would not be needed in a few weeks, that Katrin would have come of age, but it was nice to be asked.

'*The child will need a father and a stable home . . .*'

'Yes.' Katrin's voice was as icy as the stare in her eyes. 'There will be a stable home, but not a father. You see, my dear Mr Whitman, your secretary is not pregnant.'

'I 'eard there's to be a weddin''

Quite distinct, the words floated to Katrin.

'Bit rushed an' all. You asks me there be more to it than 'as been said. Be my bet a weddin'll be followed by a christenin', and that won't be in no nine months time.'

'What you sayin', Nora?'

Katrin tensed. How had word got out? Whitman? That was unlikely, he was too wrapped up in the forthcoming trip across the world to have indulged in talk of his marriage. Who then? She had told no one other than her father. That must be it; he had been like a cock with two tails, so pleased and proud at the marriage his daughter was making. He had probably shared the news with the people at Titan and from there it would reach Wednesbury faster than any train.

'What I be sayin' is, there be a babby in the belly, why else would things be rushed?'

Katrin smiled. The oracle was wrong this time; Nora Bates' tasty gossip would prove to have no foundation.

'Best not let Mary Turner 'ear you talkin' like that, her won't be pleased.'

Mary Turner! Those women were speaking of Becky.

'Pleased or no, time'll prove whether what Nora Bates says be true or otherwise.'

'What do Isaac Eldon 'ave to say?'

Katrin listened attentively.

'Ain't been able to find out.' Nora was obviously peeved at the gap in her knowledge. 'Isaac Eldon don't be a man given to talkin' overmuch, not that is 'cept a body don't get a job exact to his likin', then 'appen he goes on summat chronic.'

'What about that wench of his? Surely her'll 'ave said summat?'

Pausing only to rebuke a woman complaining the tea break hardly allowed time to drink a cup without it being shortened by the queue being held back while folk gossiped, Nora went on. 'Like yourself I expected Miriam Carson to 'ave spoken, ain't every day you 'ave a brother gettin' wed now is it, but seems her be keepin' as close a mouth as does her father.'

So Becky was to have her wedding.

It would be told first hand, once Becky and Alice finished night shift and returned to daytime hours; in the meantime she could think of the effect word of her own marriage would have. Sipping the hot sweet tea Katrin smiled. Nora Bates had propounded gossip with relish; that of her employer marrying his secretary would have the woman in raptures.

But her wedding was not to be conducted in the office of the town's Registrar, hers was to be no rushed affair. Nora Bates would undoubtedly look for a hole in the corner reason, the one quoted for Becky; but she would find no babby in the belly accounted for Katrin Hawley's marriage.

Arthur Whitman and Nora Bates; swallowing her tea, Katrin smiled into the cup, they were both in line for disappointment.

32

Becky and Robert Eldon were married. Katrin had spent a week wondering would the idea she had put that evening be accepted, would it be carried through or dismissed? But now it was an accomplished fact, Becky Turner was Mrs Robert Eldon.

She had not attended the wedding. Becky had protested her disappointment but accepted that Katrin had to be present at a meeting in Birmingham. That too had been a lie.

Isaac Eldon would no doubt be aware there was no such meeting scheduled. But then he knew also her dislike of him, and that that dislike would deter her from being a guest at any function he and his family attended.

'*Becky didn't wear her white dress.*' Alice had reported in the few days her friend had stayed home with her new husband. '*It wouldn't have been right. She said "White be for purity, it means a girl ain't never done what I done afore being wed, it says her be pure. But I ain't pure, I sinned and to wear a white frock would be adding to that sin in the eyes of God, it would be the same as lying to Him and I won't do that, I won't!"*'

'*But did her mother not ask why Becky would not wear white?*'

'*Didn't 'ave to.*' Alice had grinned. '*Becky couldn't go wearing a white frock which had a dirty great ink mark splashed across it. Seems the two little 'uns had found a bottle and were painting pictures with it and like always they began to squabble and just at that moment Becky brought her white dress into the living room so her could iron it the bottle were flung across the table.*'

Fabricating a frown she had commiserated. '*Oh how awful, poor Becky.*'

'*That ink went nowheres near that frock.*'

'*But you said . . .*'

'*I knows what I said,*' Alice had replied. '*Havin' throwed that bottle the two little 'uns took off like Gabriel's Hounds were barkin' at their heels. They d'aint wait long enough to see where that ink landed so it were easy enough for Becky to place the frock in a patch of it then claim it were done by the bottle droppin' right on the skirt.*'

'*I still can't help but feel sorry for Becky.*' Once again she had fabricated sympathy. '*She did so like that dress, it is a shame she could not wear it.*'

'*I d'aint say her d'aint wear it.*' In answer to Katrin's puzzled look she had gone on. '*Her mother come into the room just as Becky lifted the frock from the table, her took one look, grabbed it, took it into the kitchen and soaked it in cold water. It took some time before the stain faded and even then the whole frock finished up a shade of blue; but I reckon it took more time afore the arses of them little 'uns lost their redness, seems Mary pasted 'em good and proper.*'

So Becky had married in blue.

And Robert Eldon!

'*Eeh Kate,*' Alice had gushed as though the thought had been spoken aloud, '*it be a pity you couldn't be there to see, Rob looked so 'andsome in his Navy uniform; Becky be lucky, there's many a wench in Wednesbury would 'ave parted with her eye teeth as well as drop her knickers had it meant marryin' Rob Eldon, and him, well a blind man could see he thought Becky were naught less than an angel.*'

Katrin met her own reflection in the dressing table mirror.

So Robert Eldon thinks he has married an angel. What would he think when he saw that angel was fallen?

But how could he be got to see? He could be told of Becky's former lover, told of the American who had fathered her child but where would be the proof of that?

Without that proof she had not truly taken revenge on Becky Turner, nor would the hate she held for that girl's father-in-law strike as she had hoped. So was it to be left there? Was the desire of years to remain only part achieved? Lips white with pressure, Katrin walked from her bedroom. She could not let it rest there, she would not! Of all the people her heart cried vengeance on, Isaac Eldon was the one she would hurt most. Somehow she would find a way, see that extra step to ultimate satisfaction; and when she did then nothing on earth would prevent her taking it.

Was she happy for Rob? Miriam Carson glanced at the photograph set in pride of place on the mantelpiece. He had been so pleased by his selection for the Royal

Navy. Looking again at the photograph showing a young man with a thick crop of chestnut brown hair she smiled, remembering his first letter home. '*I have only one regret so far as being in the Navy,*' he had written, '*they clip a man's hair closer than he shaves.*' But the Navy had done nothing to thin his smile – that still broke impishly across his face and his eyes laughed the same way.

May God grant they remain so.

Why had she thought that? Half-peeled potato forgotten in her hand, Miriam felt unease pull at her stomach. Why had that thought come again? There was no reason for it, yet push as she had that day he had wed, it had refused to release its hold and now it plagued again.

Rob had walked on air all during that two-week leave yet she could not banish the feeling that something was not right. Perhaps it was simply because everything had happened so quickly.

He had never written of Becky Turner, not one of his letters referred to her in any way nor had there been any courtship before his being called up, yet within that two weeks he had married her.

'*He be old enough to know what he be about.*'

Her father's response had ended her attempt to discuss the impending marriage. Could it be he felt as she did, that the bed of roses Rob had made for himself might contain thorns? Was it a hint of such a feeling had him murmur quietly as they walked together into the Register Office, '*Smile for 'im, Miriam wench, let 'im be happy while he can.*'

'... *while he can.*'

There had been such an ominous ring to her father's words and each time they returned to her they held a sense of dread. Fear of losing Rob to the war was a worry they all shared, that had to been the reason behind her father's words. Draining water from the vegetable peelings, Miriam carried them out to one of the communal bins placed at intervals along every street for the collecting of any scraps which would provide food for pigs. She glanced along the row of houses clutched together as if to close away a world filled with anxiety, the constant fear of all you know and love being torn apart, the torment of war. As her glance carried along the huddled row to the Turner home, the presentiment she did not want yet could not prevent pricked along every nerve.

Miriam walked into the living room.

She looked at the photograph on the mantelpiece, the happy laughing face of her brother.

'*Give that rogue of a nephew of mine a kiss, he thinks himself too grown up to let a man kiss him.*' Rob had laughed the request then, taking her into his arms to say goodbye before returning to his ship, he murmured against her ear, '*Watch out for Becky for me.*'

She had tried to do as he had asked, tried to draw Becky closer, to get her to feel truly a part of the Eldon family. But the girl who had once been so ready to spend minutes chatting was now quiet and withdrawn. Becky was no longer the girl she had known, but what had instituted the change? Was some secret behind the change in that girl?

Miriam felt her heart twist.

'Are you part of that secret, Rob?' She held the photograph against her breast. 'Is it one you know about or something waiting to break your heart?'

'It were a real surprise.' Alice Butler's trill paid no mind to shoppers hurrying to find a last onion, maybe cabbage and potatoes from O'Connel's market stall or, if heaven smiled, a sausage or two from Hollingsworth Butcher Shop. 'Mother heard tell of it while her were at the cemetery on Sunday. Becky an' me couldn't believe it, but then on Monday Nora Bates were full of it, talked of nothin' else but you and the boss gettin' married, was her favourite topic all week; Becky and me both said it couldn't be true, we said that somebody had got the wrong end of the stick, that it must be some other couple: But Nora weren't havin' any of that, her were positive there'd been no mistake, said Katrin Hawley and Arthur Whitman were the names had been called in that church.'

'And Nora would make it her business to find out!' Katrin's answer was tart.

Wrapped in a dull red scarf, Alice's head bobbed like an overripe cherry. 'Well, you knows Nosy Nora, her can get where castor oil couldn't, speakin' of which,' Alice's glance swept to both sides to assure herself no one was paying them attention, 'Becky took herself a big dose of castor oil day before yesterday.'

'Why did Becky do that, was she ill?'

'Not afore her took that stuff, but her were sick as a dog afterward. Seems her remembered once hearing

A Step Too Far

her mother and next door talkin' of a woman who'd drunk half a bottle while sittin' in a hot bath, said the babby the woman were carryin' were born within hours. Becky thought if her sat in hot water and swallowed castor oil then it would rid her of the one her be carryin'!'

Anger tingled live along Katrin's veins. Had Becky induced a miscarriage? To have the child removed would cheat her of a means of injuring Robert Eldon and also the despised Isaac.

'Did . . .' She paused, unswallowed anger blocking the words, 'did it work for Becky?'

'No!' Alice snorted. 'Bloody old wives' tale be all that were, but true to form Becky believed it!'

'But didn't Mrs Turner wonder why Becky drank castor oil?'

'Never found out. Becky chucked the bottle away afore gettin' into the bath and as for the sickness, her told her mother it were most likely the fish her'd eaten earlier, said it hadn't tasted as fresh as it might, anyway . . .' she left the subject of Becky behind, 'what about this weddin' then? You and old Whitman, how long has this been goin' on? When did he ask you? C'mon, I want to hear all about – Oh Lord!' She broke off, her glance going past Katrin's shoulder, 'Here comes me mother, tell me later at work.'

'When did he ask you?'

Katrin excused herself quickly, the words a sting in her mind. Arthur Whitman had not asked nor would he ever have. He was marrying her because he thought he must, it was his duty. He would discover his mistake in trusting her, just as Jim Slater had found trusting her word had proved a mistake.

A flush of elation had warmed through her when she had read the newspaper report of the findings of the Coroner's Court.

'*The deceased was found to have a considerable amount of alcohol in the blood. It is thought due to the effect of this he stumbled, striking his head and causing the bottle he carried to smash against the wall. Upon falling, he landed on the broken glass thus severing a carotid artery. The verdict being death due to accidental causes.*'

Accidental causes! It would be 'accidental causes' would result in her own 'miscarriage'. But unlike Becky's her 'child' would be well and truly lost, but she would still be Mrs Arthur Whitman.

33

Woden Place. The home of Arthur Whitman and her home for the past six months. Katrin glanced about the bedroom she shared with her husband. Elegantly furnished with a taste that of his former wife, she had made no effort to change it. That would come later – as would a change of residence. Though set at the prosperous end of town and facing the prettily laid out Brunswick Park, Woden Place was smart but not smart enough; marriage to a prominent businessman was only the first step.

She crossed the thick Axminster carpet and drew open the drawer of a beautiful marquetry and rosewood bureau, taking from it the box and scarf she had brought with her on her wedding day.

'What do you think of it, mother? Is Woden Place the home you dreamed you would one day live in?' Yes! She smiled mockingly, her eyes steel hard. 'But then, mother, your dreams were always small: Arthur Whitman for a son-in-law, this house to live in, that would have satisfied you, but not me mother, they do not satisfy me. There are steps yet to take, rungs on the ladder yet to climb and I intend to climb them all, right to the top.'

Love? A sneer replaced the smile dying on her lips. 'No, there is no love, mother, I did what you wanted, I married for wealth, for position, while Arthur married to give his name to a child which does not exist, love did not enter the equation, neither for him nor for me.'

He had tried pretending. In the time preceding his departure for Australia, Arthur Whitman had made love to her, but even in the short space of two months what she had known was no more than physical satisfaction had happened on fewer and fewer occasions until it had stopped altogether. Was that because his mind was caught up in the illusion of having seduced an innocent girl?

Innocent? She threw back the cream satin covered eiderdown. In the Biblical sense yes, but in the mind? Katrin Hawley had not been innocent of mind since that game of hopscotch in a junior school playground, nor would she let that asset slip from her now.

She had fretted that the deviousness would fail, that Arthur would not believe the lies she told that there was no one the Labour Exchange Office could recommend for the post of works manager. But each time she had reported the line engaged, or made any excuse which delayed the threat of herself being relegated to an inferior position within management, Fate had played on her side and created some problem with construction of the machinery designated for Australia.

Fortune had been her team mate. Slipping into bed, Katrin breathed contentment. Arthur had gone to Australia leaving Isaac Eldon and herself as they were.

'As they were' could become 'as they had once been'.

But for that to happen she had to find a way of getting Isaac Eldon gone from Prodor before her husband returned.

'*What about this weddin' then? You and Whitman?*'

Katrin could have answered the question, told Alice Butler how Arthur Whitman had allowed himself to be seduced then been fool enough to believe himself a father-to-be. She could tell the girl now, months after that short ceremony attended only by Jacob Hawley, a church deacon and an altar server, both of whom had been requested by the priest to act as witnesses. She could tell Alice of living here at Woden Place and of the husband who so soon had stopped making love to his wife. Becky would no doubt view that as tragedy, but it was no heartache for a woman interested not in the man but only in what he could provide. She intended Arthur Whitman to provide plenty.

She could tell but she would not, she would tell no one. It would continue to be thought she and her husband were deeply in love. She was the wife of the owner of Prodor and New Crown Forgings yet still of little influence should matters concerning dismissal of Isaac Eldon come to a head. He would be deemed of more value to the company than herself.

She must see what could be done to bring about a devaluation.

'I asked Mr Eldon could I 'ave a minute to come speak with you, I told him I hardly gets to see anythin' of you since you wed.'

'Things have become extra busy since Mr Whitman's departure, it has meant my being here a great deal more than before.'

Trying not to show her distaste for the oil-smudged overalls and smell of slurry, Katrin's glance was brief and without interest.

'Eh Kate!' Alice breathed admiration. 'This be a real turn up, don't it Kate? I mean you there in old Whitman's place, folk could take you to be really the boss 'cept you be a woman; but I bet you be boss along of Woden Place, that be a step up from Hollies Drive eh!' She shook her turbaned head. 'Who'd 'ave thought when we was kids together at school, who'd 'ave thought Kate Hawley would one day marry the owner of a factory and go to live in a house smarter even than your mother's! Her would 'ave been real proud, can't be no denyin' of that. Pity her ain't alive to see what you've made of yourself, Kate, her would 'ave been like the goose that laid the golden egg.'

She ought to have put an end to this familiarity months ago! Her position as wife of the factory owner rendered any such approach unacceptable. About to tell her so, the girl's next words had Katrin thankful she had not made that plain.

'I just had to tell you, Kate, I had to tell you, Becky's had her babby.'

'When?'

'Yesterday,' Alice replied. 'Don't know exactly what time, mother said the midwife were at the Turners night before last, and was still there when mother seen the little 'uns off to school.'

This was what she had waited for.

'Becky and the baby, they are both well? Has she had a boy or a girl?'

The face developed a puzzled frown. 'A lad, that much me mother were told when her called round to the Turners, but when her asked could her see Becky and the babby her were told there was to be no visitors for a while, Becky was tired out and the little 'un? Mother were told he be middlin'.'

Chagrin sped along Katrin's veins. If the child should not live, then the desire she had nurtured all these months would count for nothing.

Taking a moment to force all trace of frustration from her next question, she spoke with pretended concern. 'Has the doctor been called, has he said what is wrong with the baby?'

'Mother asked the same. Said Mary Turner seemed as though her didn't want to talk about it, in fact her almost showed mother the door. That don't be the Mary Turner we knowed, that woman couldn't never wear lipstick, her couldn't keep her mouth still long enough to put it on; so why the sudden change, Kate? Why the refusal to say anythin'?'

Why indeed? It was certainly not the way neighbours were usually treated and the Turners and the Butlers were long-standing friends. What Becky's mother had said, was it true or was it a lie? And if the latter what could it have been intended to hide? Was the child somehow deformed? Was that the problem Mary Turner was keeping from her friends, the 'sickness' Becky's child was suffering?

'I think Mrs Turner is simply being protective.' She smiled across the desk. 'Having a baby can't be the most pleasant of experiences and Becky hasn't had an entirely easy time, not with morning sickness lasting for most of the nine months. I wouldn't worry, Alice, give it a few days and Mrs Turner will be welcoming you in to see her grandchild.'

'You probably be right.'

'Alice.' Katrin called to the girl as she turned to leave. 'Will you let me know when Becky is recovered? I would like to visit.'

Katrin smiled at the closed door. A visit that would enable her to describe to Robert Eldon the child of an American airman.

'I called round to see Becky today. I wanted to offer some help p'raps with the cleaning or the washing; Becky's lying in will add a great deal to the chores, especially with nappies needing to be scrubbed and boiled every day.'

'How is the girl and the little lad?'

'I didn't get to see either of them.' Miriam looked up from a dish she was lining with slices of potato.

'Didn't get to see 'em?' Isaac Eldon slipped a packet of sandwiches into the pocket of his jacket. 'How be that then?'

'Her mother said Becky was tired and the child was not so well as it might be.'

Taking up the thick wool scarf his daughter had knitted against the cold of winter nights standing fire watch duties, Isaac tucked both ends inside his jacket before answering. 'There y' go then, that be the reason you didn't get to see the wench and her lad.'

Reason maybe, but the truth? Miriam added a shake of salt and pepper to the sliced potato. Mary Turner had behaved oddly, it had seemed she did not want her there in that house and on hearing the baby cry had virtually pushed her out.

'I spoke to a woman a couple of houses down the street who said that nobody had been allowed to see Becky or the child. I knew what giving birth be like, dad, I know it leaves you feeling worn out but that feeling is gone after a few hours of sleep.'

'You be frettin' over nothin'!'

'No.' Miriam's reply was sharp and quick with anxiety. 'You see the woman said something else, she said there had been no doctor call at the Turners, isn't that strange, seeing a newborn child is poorly?'

Cutting one thin slice of 'Shag' tobacco – all he allowed himself of the half ounce block – Isaac answered, 'You know what gossips be, some of 'em talk so much their tongue gets sunburn.'

'What about this one?' Miriam laughed sticking out her tongue.

'You 'as sense to keep it in the shade.' Isaac packed the sliver of tobacco into the bowl of a smoke-browned briar pipe.

'But what if it be true?'

Slipping matches and pipe together into another pocket, Isaac met the worried frown.

'And what if it be no more'n hearsay? Be sensible, Miriam wench, it stands to reason we, the child's father's family, would 'ave been told were aught amiss with that little 'un. Now,' he smiled, 'you just worry over that "poor man's goose" you be cooking, I be lookin' forward to a plate o' that when I come home.'

'Do you have to go back? You've been at that works from first light, surely someone else can manage for one night at least.'

'Ar wench, likely they could.' Isaac nodded buttoning his jacket. 'But it were Isaac Eldon give promise it would be him would oversee the settin' up of hydraulic feed to them machines bein' installed at New Crown Forgings, and I reckons a promise be a promise. For that reason if for no other I 'ave to see the project through to the finish.'

Miriam returned to her cooking. Slicing bullock's liver she had queued an hour to get into the dish, she covered it with another layer of potatoes, and then one of sliced onion before adding sage mixed with lard and finally two slices of bacon which was her own weekly ration. She could have eaten it when serving the rest with mash and Oxo gravy to Reuben and her father but using it to make 'poor man's goose' would see that ration go further.

Carrying the prepared dish to the fireside oven where it would bake slowly, she pondered her father's dedication and his pride in his work.

Pride and dedication! Firelight splintered by tears spread a thousand slender darts. Isaac Eldon had a wealth of both.

34

No visitors permitted into the Turner house.

Katrin mulled over the girl's latest communiqué. It had been a simple matter to check on the time Alice's shift ended and coincide her own leaving to match.

'*Isaac Eldon had said nothin'.*'

Watching water rush into the bath, Katrin heard again the bewildered tone in Alice's voice.

'*He ain't never spoke of Becky nor of that new grandchild of his. Nosy Nora says Mary Turner be like a bulldog, won't let nobody through the door, her told Nora to bugger off and mind her own business. That bit give we all a laugh; but the other, Mary's keepin' everybody away, I thinks that be strange, what d' you think Kate?*'

Turning off the taps, Katrin reached for a pretty glass flagon half filled with tiny pearlised grains. She held them in her hand a moment, their delicate perfume drifting like a scented cloud.

'*Madame understands they are offered only to our most privileged clients . . .*'

The assistant at the London dress shop Arthur had taken her to had fawned, producing the Helena Rubinstein Beauty Casket when it seemed she might lose her frightfully expensive sale.

Katrin had consented to a church ceremony, agreed to wear white, albeit the silk shantung suit she had finally purchased was a very pale shade of cream. But she had opted for a church wedding for the reason Jacob Hawley believed. Her mother had always dreamed of seeing her girl walk down the aisle in a bridal gown. Jacob had smiled, taking her hand in his the evening Arthur had come to ask permission to marry her. But she had not done what was asked because Violet would have wished it, she had done it for him, the man who had been a father to her, the one man she felt any love for. She had asked him to stay here in Wednesbury, to tell Arthur Whitman he must find someone else to go with him to Australia, to let that someone be Isaac Eldon. But for once in her life Jacob Hawley had turned a deaf ear to her request. But it was not a lifetime separation, he would return — and so would Arthur Whitman!

Dropping the grains into the bath, she watched them circle then melt into the water, blending with it like so many crystal tears. Tears she had so often shed after finding she was— But those days were over, she was no longer that hurt little girl, she was a woman, a woman who would avenge those tears a thousandfold.

Katrin's thoughts dwelt on the return of her husband and the problem she had not yet resolved: how and why Isaac Eldon had to go.

'*He ain't never spoke of Becky nor of that new grandchild. I thinks that be strange Kate . . .*'

Strange was an understatement. Was Isaac Eldon privy to whatever it was had Mary Turner bar everyone who attempted to visit Becky and the child?

'Mary Turner be like a bulldog, won't let nobody through the door.'

Would 'nobody' include the wife of Wednesbury's most important industrialist?

The answer could well be yes!

So the wife of that industrialist must call when the 'bulldog' was away from the kennel!

Jacob had been so thoughtful in the choice of special gifts he had hung on the 'Katrin tree'. He had always tried to give her something useful and the one he had placed there some years ago would certainly be that.

'*I be in half a mind to take the risk . . .*'

Alice's words had given her the idea. '*I be of a mind to go round there while the dragon be out. I could tell Isaac Eldon I 'ave to go to the chemist to get a bottle of summat for mother's women's troubles. He won't argue with that 'specially when I promises I'll be back at work afore dinnertime be over. Becky's mother don't be forty yet so her has to help with the war effort same as everybody else. Her works at the Civic Restaurant and though Becky be lying in it don't mean Mary can take time off; her must be at that restaurant from around ten in the mornin' to about three in the afternoon. In the meantime Becky be on her own, that don't be no hardship, after all givin' birth don't mean you be crippled, Becky can manage 'til her mother be back.*'

Becky would be alone, just her and the baby in the house! Katrin glanced at her watch. A few minutes to twelve. It would raise no eyebrows if she left the office now. Slipping into her coat, lifting her bag onto her shoulder she reached for the plain cardboard box. It had been a brilliant idea replacing the gas mask with the item she was taking to the Turner house; an everyday thing, a gas mask had to be carried wherever you went so would raise no eyebrows, unlike the gift it housed.

A gift? It could be called that.

Would Becky see it as Jacob Hawley had meant it to be seen? Would she see the contents of this box as 'something useful'?

She had not come to this street in so many years. Katrin glanced at the smoke-grimed houses hunched together as if each was trying to hide behind the other. Queen Street! Distaste became a sneer in her throat. Despite its grander name it was no different to Cross Street; both were dismal. Was it any wonder Violet had moved to Hollies Drive at the first opportunity?

Doors hereabout scarcely ever being locked had been another tit-bit revealed by Alice Butler; really, if this venture proved a success she should thank the girl.

If it proved a success. Katrin smiled as the door swung open. Everything so far seemed to say it would.

Calling quietly, she moved from the scullery into the living room. Table, chairs and a worn sofa jostled for space with a dresser boasting an assortment of crockery. Opposite a sleepy fire dozed beneath a large kettle, its bottom and sides blackened from years of being hung over burning coals.

A fire, a steaming kettle, but no Becky! Katrin hesitated. Hadn't Alice said something about 'lying in'? Did that mean Becky would be in bed? Guessing the only door in the room would be shielding the stairs, she crossed quickly to it trying to keep her footsteps as quiet as possible on steps which, though uncarpeted, were bleached almost white with constant scrubbing.

She called again softly on seeing Becky in the third bedroom. Why did she not answer? Katrin moved further into the room.

Becky had not answered because she was asleep, as was the infant in her arms.

Looking at the tiny bundle, a smile curved Katrin's lips. Each movement deft and silent, she opened the gas mask container and lifted out the Brownie box camera which had been that gift left for her on the 'Katrin tree'. Becky would be thrilled with a photo of her baby. She could probably get a shot of Becky before she woke. A photo of her asleep with the child across her breast would make a beautifully tender picture.

Focusing quickly, she played in on the sleeping pair. She had thought the click would waken Becky, but when it did not she poised the camera again. Several shots would be better than a single one, they would provide more chance of success. Not much could be seen of the baby, just the dark fuzz of hair peeping above the white knitted blanket. Reaching to the sleeping bundle she gently drew the cover from the tiny occupant, drawing a quick involuntary breath as, disturbed by the touch, the head turned and the eyes opened, so brown they could almost have been black. Katrin almost forgot her reason for drawing the blanket aside then, as the baby snuffled, she brought the camera close gaining several takes before the eyes closed. Perhaps one more of Becky with the face of her son showing clearly as her own. A memory to treasure.

Becky had still not woken. Delighted with the surprise the photographs would give her, Katrin hurriedly replaced the camera in the gas mask box, then noticed the envelope that had been dropped onto the bed.

A letter from Robert Eldon?

She stared at the envelope.

To send him a photograph, to congratulate him on the birth of the child, she would need his military address and to ask Becky would entail explanations which would ruin the planned surprise.

She had promised herself she would tell Robert Eldon the true parentage of Becky's child, a promise she would not suffer be broken now!

Katrin reached to the envelope.

Not a letter from Robert Eldon! A letter to Robert Eldon!

'Kate, did mother let you in?' Her voice thick and drowsy, blue eyes blinking rapidly as though sleep still had them prisoner, Becky glanced at the half open doorway, 'Did her say for you to come up?'

Katrin's smile lied easily as the one ready on her tongue. 'I looked for her in the Civic Restaurant but she was probably busy in the kitchens, but I knew she would have told me to come see you.'

'But her wouldn't!' Disturbed by the sharp cry, the infant whimpered and Becky drew the cover across the small head, a flash of alarm in the look she directed to Katrin. 'Her wouldn't have said to come, her don't let nobody come, and if her finds you've been to the house then all hell will break loose!'

Tears, anguish, fear! How brightly they shone in those blue, blue eyes . . . and how she delighted in seeing them. But it was not the moment to allow Katrin Whitman's emotions to show through, for now the charade must continue.

'Becky.' She adopted a pose of sympathy. 'What is so awful? Tell me what is wrong.'

Arms jerking the child held against her chest, Becky laughed despairingly. 'This be what's wrong. I don't want it, I never wanted it, I tried everythin' I could think of to get rid of it but nothin' worked. Oh Lord Kate, why did nothin' work?'

Masking a flush of pleasure Katrin said quietly, 'You are overtired from the birth, you will feel differently in a few days, especially when telling Rob the good news.'

'I can't tell Rob, he mustn't know! Oh help me Kate, help me please, tell me what to do.'

Firm where she had been sympathetic she said, 'First thing you must do is lay the baby back in his bed, you must not risk falling asleep with him in your arms. It has been known for infants to be smothered by a mother so worn out and weary she has dropped asleep with the baby still feeding at the breast then has rolled onto it; and you are very tired Becky, best let me lay him down for you then you can sleep yourself.'

'I 'ave to feed him first.'

* * *

'I 'ave to feed him first.'

Had that reply come a little too quickly?

Queen Street behind her, relieved she had met with no one going to or coming from that house, Katrin walked quickly, following Holyhead Road toward Prodor.

'... *it has been known* ... *you are very tired* ...'

She had sown the seeds, despondency and misery would water them, it remained only for the crop to sprout.

35

'Matters are progressing well in Australia.'

Her husband's letter had not specified what was meant by 'matters' but had he done so it would most certainly have been censored by government authorities. While not a military operation, the revolutionary technology behind the project must be protected to the same degree. He would be returning next month, returning to find his wife showing no sign of pregnancy.

Sitting on the tram from Wolverhampton, Katrin's stare was intense but oblivious. Broken buildings, blackened roofless houses went unobserved, her mind too caught up in the problem facing her: how to tell Arthur Whitman he was not to be a father. It had been too soon to fake a miscarriage before his leaving England, and since? She had pushed that aside. To write she had lost the baby would have been simple enough, but on returning home Arthur may speak with their doctor, who would be obliged to say he had not been consulted, that he was not aware of any miscarriage.

That could not be allowed to happen! She must think of something, but short of throwing herself downstairs, which she had no intention of doing, she had come up with no idea.

'Can't stay on the tram luv, don't be allowed.'

Katrin turned, a sharp tut of irritation expressing her displeasure at the disturbance.

The woman said, almost apologetically, 'It be a nuisance, Lord we all knows that! But like wi' so many other things we be called on to do while this war be goin' on, we 'ave to grin an' bear it.' Heaving a small girl from her knee, juggling with a large basket, she struggled from her seat and followed the child into the aisle. She cast a brief look back to where Katrin still sat. 'Stop you there if you will,' she called back, 'but think on, wench, stubbornness an' folly goes 'and in 'and wi' regret followin' on behind. You be slow gettin' off this tram an' could be you'll meet regret sooner than y' look to.'

What on earth was all the fuss about? Conducting rods connecting the tram to overhead electricity cables often became disconnected, it was inconvenient and always exasperating but hardly a reason for mass evacuation, a few minutes and the journey would resume. Let the rest of the passengers do what pleased them, it pleased her to remain seated.

'Hey!'

A man's voice, loud and peremptory, drew her glance to the window and Katrin saw the uniformed conductor, his arms gesticulating as he shouted again.

'Get off! Get off the tram! You 'ave to get off now!'

'Now!'

How could so small a man have such a powerful

voice? The sound grew less and less, drifting behind as Katrin floated down a long dark tunnel.

She had felt in her heart that marriage with Becky Turner was not right for Rob. It had been arranged so hurriedly, almost a hole in the corner affair. The war saw a lot of quick marriages, bridegrooms leaving after a few days to return to the Armed Forces and Rob was no different, he too had had only a few short days at home.

'But there be a difference Rob.'

She picked up the photograph from the mantelpiece feeling that to hold it might soothe the hurt instinct told her lay in store for her brother, that to hold him as she had when some childhood prank had landed him in trouble would help it go away.

'A lot of marriages happen quicker than maybe,' she whispered to the photograph, 'but they be between couples who have long been sweethearts, couples one in love as much as the other, but that weren't so with Becky Turner, was it Rob? Becky don't feel for you what you feel for her. Oh Rob, I . . .'

Whisper cut off in mid-sentence, Miriam returned the photograph to the mantelpiece as her father entered the room.

'Did you see her?'

Slumping heavily into the chair drawn close to the iron fireplace, Isaac stared into the glowing bed of the fire and shook his head in reply.

'No! What was the excuse this time?' Her retort sharper than intended, Miriam glanced toward the kitchen where Reuben was finishing off his school work, then lowering her voice went on, 'Mary Turner's saying Becky is not well, I think that is a lie; there's no doctor calling at the house and no midwife neither. Dad . . .' She paused, that same quick stab of instinct thrusting deep inside. 'Dad, could there be something wrong? Could that baby not be all we hoped?'

'Ar, wench, there be summat wrong.'

How did he know? She looked at him, sitting with his head sunk into his hands. What gossip had reached his ears? What nasty rumour said so loudly Isaac Eldon would have heard it? He was normally so disparaging of rumour and hearsay, so if it were gossip he had heard, why was it affecting him this way?

Rumour mongering or not, there was something Mary Turner was keeping to herself. Miriam glanced at the photograph of her smiling brother. Was it being kept from Rob also?

She voiced the questions leaping like March hares into her mind.

'Dad,' she asked quietly, 'do you think Becky will have written to Rob, will he have been told why her mother is being so secretive?' She broke off, her heart twisting at the misery etched deep on her father's face.

'Won't make no difference whether Becky writes or don't write, neither will Mary Turner's tight-lipped way.'

'But Rob has every right to know if something is wrong with his child.'

'He'll know soon enough, wench, your brother will know soon enough.'

'Dad, what is it you are not telling me?'

Isaac hesitated as if to hold the pain to himself, then took from his pocket an envelope heavily smudged with oil-stained fingerprints. 'This be what Mary Turner d'aint want seen!'

'Eh Kate, be you all right? We heard of your bein' caught up in a raid, bloody Gerries! It's getting so you don't be safe nowhere.'

Katrin pushed away thoughts of Isaac Eldon and graced Alice Butler with a smile. 'I just took a knock to the head, nothing serious.'

'That's more than can be said for Wolverhampton, that place took a right poundin', seems it be another Coventry, so much of it blasted to smithereens; but talk has it them bombers weren't after that town at all, folk be sayin' it were Bilston with all of them iron works they was after destroyin', and it were just this side of Bilston you was hit so maybe folk be right.'

'It is tragic for any town that is bombed, so many people dead or injured.'

'That 'itler!' Alice's grey eyes sparked loathing, 'I agree with what my dad says about that man, he should be in Hell with a blanket round 'im.'

Pointedly shuffling the papers she had been dealing with, Katrin's patience thinned. 'I think we all agree with your father Alice but . . .'

'Sorry Kate.' Alice recognised the none too subtle hint. 'But I just had to come ask if you'd heard about Becky?'

'Heard?'

'So Eldon said nothin' to you neither.' Alice was scornful. 'But there be no real surprise in that, same as when Becky's little 'un was born, he said nothin' to anybody about that and it his own grandchild! I tell you Kate, his tongue can be stiller'n that of a man dead a week!'

Katrin's attention crisped. What was it about his daughter-in-law Isaac Eldon was not eager to discuss?

'Is Becky and her baby well? Is she being allowed visitors yet? I really would like to see her.'

'I don't think you stand much chance, Kate.'

'Perhaps if I speak with Mrs Turner, ask her nicely.'

Lips trembling, tears glinting Alice murmured, 'Becky's little 'un it . . . it's dead.'

Dead! Was that death due to natural causes or had the seeds she had sown resulted in fruit? Catching her breath, brow drawn together in a display of emotion Katrin gasped. 'Oh Alice, how dreadful! Becky must be beside herself, I really must go ask her mother . . .'

'Don't have nothin' to do with her mother any more.' Alice sniffed back tears. 'Becky's in prison, the police arrested her two days back. They think Becky killed the babby.'

Katrin sealed the letter she had written and smiled at the address on the envelope.

2493161 Able Seaman Eldon, Portsmouth.

Becky had been charged with smothering her child. She was to be tried for suspected murder.

She had not written of that in the letter, had not enclosed a cutting of the report in the *Express and Star* newspaper. She had simply enclosed a photograph, an exact copy of the one she had arranged be delivered to Isaac Eldon. Except that this one bore one single line: 'Congratulations on the birth of your son.' She need not inform Robert Eldon of his not being the father of Becky's child; the photograph would do that very well.

'He's so 'andsome, tall and tanned.'

Becky had enthused over her American airman.

Affixing an air mail stamp to the envelope, Katrin laughed softly. Bronzed Earl Feldman might have been, but not by the Miami sun.

'Congratulations Robert on the birth of your black son.'

That had been the reason of allowing no one into the house, of letting no one see the child; Mary Turner had hoped the secret would remain a secret. Had she thought to put it into a home for unwanted children, hoped that way to hide the shame Becky had brought on the family?

Poor Becky, but then she could be forgiven for not recognising Earl Feldman came of West Indian extraction; neither would most people in Wednesbury, seeing the town was without coloured people among its population.

She had fretted the exposure might have been incorrect, that the finished photographs might not clearly show the child's dark complexion.

But in the event that had been a worry she need not have had, and now she need have none of Arthur Whitman discovering he had been duped into marriage.

Not everybody injured in an air raid counted that

lucky, but it had been lucky for her. A bomb falling close to the road had exploded, the blast tipping the tram onto its side and covering her in breaking glass and crumpled metal. Rescued by Civil Defence volunteers and taken to a First Aid Post, she had been found to have suffered no more than bruises, a minor cut to the head and the possibility of concussion, which had not transpired.

That same evening had witnessed the onset of her monthly period. These were always heavy but what was normally an irritation had proved the opposite. She had waited two days before visiting the doctor. Telling of the incident of the bomb she had asked through floods of tears, 'Is my baby all right?' The doctor had been sympathetic, . . . *perhaps had she called him in when the bleeding started . . . it was most probably due to the shock, she was young and healthy, no reason to believe there would not be other children.*

Miscarriage brought about by shock. Not an accurate diagnosis but one Arthur Whitman would have no reason to disbelieve.

Katrin walked upstairs, trailing a hand along the smooth elegant mahogany banister rail.

Freda Evans, five years imprisonment for dealing in black market goods.

Alice Butler, denied her longed-for entry into the Women's Auxiliary Forces.

Jim Slater, found dead of accidental causes.

Becky Turner, accused of killing her baby.

One by one they had paid. But not every account had been settled satisfactorily.

The laying of information against Isaac Eldon and Reuben Carson had not achieved what she had hoped, the man had not been found guilty of treason.

Entering her bedroom she stared toward the drawer holding the scarf and box which had belonged to Violet Hawley.

'I have destroyed his son's marriage, mother,' she whispered. 'I have broken the heart of Isaac Eldon's son, I have made that family the object of gossip in the town and very soon that gossip will become derision, the whole of Wednesbury will point the finger and sneer; but that is not revenge enough for me, mother, nor will I settle for it being punishment enough for Isaac Eldon, for the man who gave away his daughter.'

36

'WEDNESBURY WOMAN GUILTY'.

Katrin smiled at the headline in the local newspaper. The trial at Stafford Crown Court had not taken long. The judge summed up that while an accusation of murder could not be proven, neither could the death of the infant be proven purely accidental, therefore he must declare a verdict of 'Manslaughter due to neglect, the penalty for which is to serve for fifteen years in one of His Majesty's prisons.'

Freda five, Becky fifteen, what a pity Alice Butler's payment was not reckoned in years. It was to be regretted she could not have been dealt a harsher blow than non-admittance into the Women's Auxiliary Services but then a little revenge was better than none at all.

Vexation a sudden dart in her veins, she flung the newspaper aside. A little revenge was all she had got from sending one of those photographs to Isaac Eldon. He had said no word, shown no sign of its effect, no recognition of knowing its sender and that had somehow reduced the feeling of triumph; she had not got from it the satisfaction she had thought, the same as that attempt with his grandson's maps had brought none. Both had proved futile just as her trying to oust him from Prodor was proving futile.

But she *must* find a way! And it must be found within the fortnight, for that was when Arthur Whitman would return home.

Two weeks! If Eldon were not gone before Whitman's arrival then her chance of that ultimate revenge, of taking away the employment Eldon had known and loved almost his entire life, of breaking the last straw which would hold that life together would be lost, for Arthur would never dismiss the man he regarded more as a friend than an employee.

'Excuse me, Mrs Whitman.'

Turning to face the middle-aged woman who for years had cleaned three times weekly at Woden Place, Katrin's hiss conveyed displeasure at the interruption.

'I just wants to be sure,' the woman went on, ignoring Katrin's frown, 'the things you wanted I should tek along to the Welfare Depot, be it them that be on your bed?'

'Yes!' Katrin answered shortly, then forced a smile. 'Sorry Mrs Briggs, I was a million miles away. Yes, please, it's very good of you to take them.'

'Saves them folk comin' to collect 'em and it be no trouble to me seein' I lives but a street from that depot; so I'll just nip upstairs and fetch 'em, will I?'

Katrin followed the woman from the room, turning aside into the study as the telephone rang.

That telephone call of two weeks ago had left her trembling from shock. Her husband and her father were both dead. The merchant ship they were travelling home on had been torpedoed by a German submarine; both were killed in the initial blast.

'*The Minister wishes to convey his deepest sympathy.*'

That had been the prologue, but what followed after showed the real consideration of a phone call in place of a telegram.

'*The Minister of course understands the terrible shock this will be to you, the ordeal of losing both husband and father, therefore he thinks it will lift some of the worry from you should the Ministry take on the running of your husband's factories.*'

It had not quite sunk in at the time but later the tremble of shock had become the quake of anger.

Those people thought to appropriate the business, '*to see to the management of it until hostilities ended.*'

Slipping into the black suit she had bought with the last of the clothing coupons her father had given her as he joked he could likely buy a whole new wardrobe in Australia and that without a single coupon, Katrin felt that same anger.

'*Until hostilities ended.*' Nicely put! She stared at her reflection. But once the war ended, how much hostility then? How much wrangling with the government in order to get back what rightly belonged to his widow? Matters had been resolved by Isaac Eldon assuming full responsibility for the maintaining of the level of production combined with a monthly inspection by the Ministry. That official visit would be one of the two changes introduced into the running of Prodor. The other? The other would be the replacement of Isaac

Eldon, a replacement she would choose and one who would quickly learn it was Katrin Whitman ran Prodor. There were several suitable candidates in the list she had already obtained.

It had been like an answer to a prayer. One moment she had been searching for a way of solving the problem of Isaac Eldon and the next the answer had dropped into her lap.

One more gift from Fortune's bountiful cornucopia, and with this visit to the office of Arthur's lawyer that gift could begin to be enjoyed.

Her glance went to the drawer of the dressing table.

'I think perhaps you should come with me, Violet.'

She drew the delicate cloth from the drawer and watched it ripple over her fingers, hanging from their tips like soft lavender-hued tears.

'Yes Violet, you should be there.'

Eyes hard and cold as the feelings inside her, she looped the scarf about her neck, catching it up onto her shoulder with a silver brooch. Then, handbag and gas mask in place, she turned one more glance to the mirror.

'I would have preferred you were with me, you deserve to see your brother pay the price for what he did to a child. After all, you were a part of the deal, weren't you, Violet? The deal which robbed a baby of its true identity. Well, now Isaac Eldon is to feel the heel of that child grind him into the ground.'

This would not take long, a quick call at Prodor, satisfy herself all was running smoothly. Nodding to the gatekeeper who touched a finger to his grease-stained flat cap, Katrin had reached the door leading into the office block when the call halted her.

'Kate.' Alice Butler ran across the space between the buildings. 'Kate, I was hopin' to see you.'

Nose wrinkling at the odour of slurry oil, Katrin answered curtly, 'I'm sorry, Alice, I do not have time . . .'

'I knows you be busy,' Alice intervened quickly, 'but this wont' take no more than a moment, it be about Becky.'

Their voices made the gatekeeper glance to where the two women stood, Alice's grease-marked overall and turban a sharp contrast to the smartly tailored suit and chic veiled hat of her late employer's wife.

Aware of the man's interest, Katrin motioned toward the door.

'No.' Alice shook her head. 'Better not come up, Isaac Eldon thinks I be across to the toilet, he'll have summat to moan about if I'm away from that machine more than two minutes; thinks a woman can whip it out, pee, shake the drips off the end, button it up and that be all there is to it, he should be all fastened up with sanitary belt and pads once a month, that'd change his tune.'

'Alice,' Katrin hoisted the gas mask box higher on her shoulder, 'I really do have to hurry.'

'Sorry,' Alice laughed, 'I went to see Becky last visitin' and her said you had been to see her the day . . . well, you know what day.'

'Yes, Alice, I know what day. It was reported Becky had fallen asleep and thinking I was in that room is no more than a dream.'

'That were my reckonin' but Becky be firm.'

Becky had spoken of that visit at her trial; the prosecution claimed she had dreamed it and her mother had testified that no visitor had been allowed into the house.

Anxiety stretching to breaking point, Katrin snapped. 'Had Becky Turner been as firm in saying no to Earl Feldman, had she listened to me then as she listened—'

The look in Alice's eyes warned of the slip of her tongue, but Alice's grasp of her wrist prevented Katrin leaving.

'As her listened to you that day! Don't deny it, Kate, it be clear in your face, you *did* get into the Turner house, you talked to Becky just like her says you did. It were you told her of newborns sometimes bein' stifled to death by mothers too tired to stay awake and rollin' onto the child. You seen Becky were beside herself yet you told her that. For God's sake, why?'

'Why?' Katrin spat the reply, snatching her wrist from Alice's grasp. 'Do you remember four young girls playing hopscotch in a school yard? Of three of those girls turning their backs on the other telling her she was a cheat and liar? There is your reason.'

'But . . .' Alice frowned disbelief, trying to come to terms with what she had heard, 'We were just kids, it didn't mean anythin'.'

'It meant something to the girl you snubbed!'

'And you've carried that with you all these years? Just like a kid you wanted to get your own back so much you deliberately fed that idea to Becky? What of us other two, Freda and me, be we to answer to your spite same as Becky has?'

'Freda!' she hissed, 'she has found it did not pay to say what she did.'

'You shopped Freda!' Alice glared. 'You got her five years in jail simply 'cos of what were said all that time ago! First Freda and then Becky! That leaves me. What does that stink hole you call a mind have in store for me?'

'Quite right, I have not forgotten. You might ask Arthur Whitman who recommended he refuse to release you to the Women's Auxiliary Forces. But of course he is unfortunately no longer here to be asked.'

'That were your doin'? You be nothin' but a snake and like a snake you'll need find a hole to crawl into when folk learn what you be.'

'A word of warning!' Katrin's smile was pure venom. 'Freda Evans is serving five years, Becky is serving fifteen years, I don't know how many are called upon to be served for defamation of character but you will find out if you speak one word against me.'

'Christ!' Alice laughed derisively. 'No wonder that family gave you away, they had no idea the favour they were doin' themselves. Isaac Eldon should go down on his knees and thank his maker, and if there be any justice in heaven I hope it'll be visited on you, and may it be as terrible as the sufferin' you've brought to Becky and Freda.'

'Isaac Eldon should go down on his knees.'

And so he would! Shoes rapping a tattoo Katrin walked quickly along Walsall Street. But it would not be to thank heaven. He would go down on his knees to Katrin Whitman, to beg her not to sack him. Would she refuse with sadness? No. She would not answer at all, but simply turn away from him as he had turned away from a daughter.

'Ah Mrs Whitman, good afternoon, please take a seat.'

Katrin nodded at the small rotund figure of Thomas Jones, Arthur Whitman's lawyer.

'Mrs Briggs you know, of course.' The lawyer glanced at the seated figure then, as the door opened, added, 'And you are also familiar with Mr Eldon.'

Isaac Eldon! Katrin watched the man, awkward in Sunday suit, shake hands across a vast desk. Arthur must have named him the recipient of a small sum of money, as he no doubt had his cleaning woman. Well let him enjoy the moment, it would not last for long!

Katrin listened to the lawyer begin to read from a document taken from a large manila envelope.

It was over. In the bedroom she had shared with Arthur Whitman, Katrin stared at the clothes strewn across the bed.

'To Isaac Eldon I give and bequeath . . .'

In the silence of the house, Katrin's laugh rang out.

37

'*To Katrin Whitman . . .*'

Who had been the more surprised at what had followed, Isaac Eldon or that lawyer?

Taking the last dress from the wardrobe, Katrin held it against her, one hand lifting wide the filmy blue skirt. She had thought to wear it to her wedding, then it was to be worn the evening of Arthur's homecoming and now. . . ?

Katrin sank to the floor beside the bed, the drone of the lawyer's reading running in her mind.

'*I had my suspicions regarding Harriet Simpson's accident, these were further aroused when you said Isaac Eldon's arrest had to be because of those maps, maps which I knew nothing about; but when later Isaac referred to maps leading to trouble, I made it my business to find out what he meant . . .*'

'*No, not me.*' Isaac Eldon's words had halted the reading. '*I knew who had informed about those maps. Reuben pointed you out one day in the town, he said it was you helped pick his papers up after you bumped into each other but that I kept to myself.*'

It had to be a lie; there was no way Whitman could have known it was her unless Eldon had told him. The lawyer had continued reading her husband's words.

'*During my stay in London, I spoke to a man called Philip Conroy who would only reveal it had been a woman who had telephoned the Local Information Office, that woman had to be you. Then we come to the question of the child.*'

The lawyer had droned on. '*The child you claimed I had fathered on you, that too had to be a lie. Were you indeed carrying a child, then that child could not be mine for as medical records will show I was, and always have been, infertile.*'

He had known all along!

'*So why did I marry you? Greed and revenge, my dear, are two sides of the same sword, a sword which can cut the wielder as easily as it cuts the victim, a sword you yourself so often applied; now I apply that sword.*'

The lawyer had hesitated, professionalism keeping the look bland on his face.

'*So to Katrin Whitman, to the woman who lied her way into my life, who attempted to ruin the lives of others, I give and bequeath that which had I lived would have been my parting gift: the sum of one month's salary together with any personal effects.*'

A month's salary! Rage burned like acid in Katrin's throat. It had been Whitman's intent to dismiss her as he would any employee! One month's salary! But that had not proved all of his parting gift.

'*To Isaac Eldon, my long-term friend and colleague, I give and bequeath Woden Place, Prodor New Crown Works and all of my estate in its entirety. Should this bequest be refused, Woden Place is to be converted, at the expense of my estate, into a Rest and Care Home for the treatment of wounded returned from the battlefield and, with the cessation of hostilities, is to remain a Care Home for those people of Wednesbury who may need it. The said properties Prodor and New Crown Works will at the end of the war be sold, the proceeds of which sale to be used for the building and maintaining of a Care Home for the people of Darlaston; but to that same long-term friend I say, the sick and the elderly need care but the young and healthy need work. I ask that you, Isaac, give this Black Country that work, take the factories, carry them forward, make them grow into the worldwide name we both know they can become; build my dream for me.'*

Had Eldon expected her to weep? Had he expected her to cry on his shoulder when he had begun to offer help? On the floor beside the bed, Katrin laughed.

'Don't pretend concern for me, we both know that emotion has never lived in you!' Once outside of the lawyer's office, she had spat the fever of anger built inside her.

'Katrin—'

She had repeated as he had spoken her name, *'Even now it is Katrin, not Ellen, not the name my mother gave me, you allowed even that to be taken from me. It was easy for you, wasn't it? Your son was too precious to part with and you already had a daughter, what use was there in keeping another?'*

Eldon had robbed her of her true family, had taken what should have been hers from marriage with Arthur Whitman, but he would not deny her the hatred that had lived in her heart from finding that birth certificate; Isaac Eldon would not deprive her of showing him that loathing.

'That was it, wasn't it, father?'

She laughed at the distinct flinch, at the indisputable sadness darkening his eyes.

'The choice was obvious, the child was something you didn't want, so why keep it?'

'It wasn't what you think,' he had said quickly. *'I loved you, but at barely thirteen and Rob not yet twelve months, caring for another child would have been too much for Miriam.'*

'So it was give away Ellen!'

He had looked at her for a long moment, as if searching for something in her eyes, then had said quietly. *'I loved you, I have always loved you.'*

'Love!' she had snorted the rebuke. *'Oh I saw that love the day Arthur Whitman asked you be fetched to his office, I heard it when you said, "Is it Robert, is it my son?" There was no thought of "Is it Ellen, is it my daughter?" But then have you ever once thought of your daughter, the child you gave away?'*

Katrin did not hear the tap at the door but looked up to see the woman who had fared better from Arthur Whitman's will than she.

'Excuse me, Mrs Whitman – eh! Be you all right?' A look of concern crossed the cleaning woman's face as she saw the clothing strewn around the normally perfectly tidy room.

Katrin rose to her feet, saying sharply she would leave the house when *she* was ready.

'Ain't that I come about!' Huffed at the tartness of her reception the woman's reply was resentful. 'Be to tell you there be somebody downstairs a wantin' to speak wi' you.'

Clearly understanding the former mistress of Woden Place was no longer in a position to dismiss her for answering without the usual show of respect, the woman added, 'I'll tell 'im y' be comin' down.'

It must be Eldon! Catching sight of herself in the dressing mirror, Katrin touched the lavender scarf still looped about her shoulders. 'You know the saying, mother,' she said grimly, ' "where there is life," your brother will find I am not finished yet.'

'Do you recognise this, Mrs Whitman?'

Katrin stared at the object held in the hand of the Police Inspector who had once interviewed her at the house in Hollies Drive. It had been a surprise to find him to be the 'somebody' waiting to talk with her.

'I would have thought a young child could tell you that is a button!'

'Yes, a button. Perhaps I should have asked do you recognise the piece of cloth attached to that button?'

Drawing on strengths which had assisted so well in the past, Katrin answered calmly, 'No, I do not recognise either button or cloth, now I must ask you to leave.'

'All in good time, but first perhaps you might help with something else.'

Following his nod to the uniformed constable, the cleaning woman entered.

'Thank you, Mrs Briggs.' The Inspector nodded again to the constable, who took the folded bundle from the woman's arms holding it so its full length opened.

'Please look carefully, Mrs Whitman, do you recognise this garment?'

The coat! Katrin's brain screamed. The coat she had been wearing the night she had stabbed that bottle into Jim Slater's neck! She had intended to burn it when chance allowed but then had forgotten it until that day she had been sorting unwanted items to be given to the Welfare Centre. She had found the coat hanging at the very back of the wardrobe and put it aside to get rid of when she was alone. Briggs must have thought it part of the clothes put ready for donation and taken it with the rest.

'Do you recognise the garment, Mrs Whitman?'

He was watching her closely for any sign of recognition. Katrin steeled herself to answer mockingly. 'Once again, Inspector, a young child could tell you that is a coat.'

'Precisely Mrs Whitman, it is a coat. Did it belong to you?'

Katrin cast a seemingly unconcerned glance at the coat, then with a brief toss of the head replied. 'It may have done, but then it could have belonged to someone else. Coats are manufactured in large numbers – unless of course for the very wealthy and they, Inspector, would require a much better quality.'

'Mrs Briggs, is this the coat you took from this house?'

'Yes, sir.' The woman nodded vigorously.

'Is it the coat you wore when you called at my home to go with my wife to help sort clothing at Wednesbury Welfare Centre?'

'Yes but . . . well, Mrs Whitman weren't a wantin' of it an' it be a good coat 'cept for that little rip of the pocket so I kept it for m'self, I d'ain't mean to steal.'

'It was not stealing,' the Inspector assured the trembling figure. 'But tell us, Mrs Briggs, the coat you see the constable holding, the one you brought at my request to the police station, is it the one you brought from this house?'

Assuring the woman once more she was in no trouble, and waiting until she had left the room, the Inspector began again. 'Mrs Whitman, you say this coat, the coat taken from this house, did not belong to you, is that correct?'

Katrin snapped, 'How many times do I have to answer that question?'

'None. However there is one question you might care to answer; how, if this coat did not belong to you, do you explain this?'

He lifted the lining which had been freed of stitching, then folded back the fabric to which it had been attached. Katrin could not prevent a quick indrawn breath. The name tag! Violet always sewed a name tag where no one would expect it to be!

'As you can see,' the Inspector held the button with its remnant of cloth against the tear in the coat, 'the match is indisputable. This,' he glanced at the button, 'was discovered clutched in the hand of James Slater when his body was examined at the mortuary; I must also tell you we have a witness.'

A witness! Katrin's senses reeled. Someone had seen her kill Jim Slater!

Pausing while the constable helped her to a chair, the Inspector went on, 'Perhaps I can answer a question for you Mrs Whitman, why did the witness not come forward at the time? He was on active service. It was not until he was repatriated that he learned of Slater's death. The two had spent time together that same evening, and though Slater had taken some drink he was still far from drunk when they parted company at Spring Head, Slater saying he was to meet a woman he named as Kate Hawley. The man came to the station and there, before a lawyer as witness, he signed a sworn statement.'

Returning the button to his pocket, he went on firmly. 'Katrin Whitman, I arrest you on a charge of suspicion of murder.'

Rising to her feet, the constable's hand at her elbow, Katrin touched a finger to the lavender silk draped about her shoulders. A laugh bitter as aloes preceded her murmur, 'Where there is life . . .'